SEVENTEEN
MOMENTS OF SPRING

By the same author

Petrovka 38 (to be reissued in a new translation)
TASS is authorized to announce . . .
Intercontinental Knot (in preparation)
Reporter (in preparation)

SEVENTEEN MOMENTS OF SPRING

a novel by

Julian Semyonov

Translated by Katherine Judelson

JOHN CALDER · LONDON
RIVERRUN PRESS · NEW YORK

First published in this edition in Great Britain, 1988, by
John Calder (Publishers) Limited
18 Brewer Street, London W1R 4AS

and in the United States of America, 1988, by
Riverrun Press Inc
1170 Broadway, New York, NY 10001

Originally published in the USSR in 1973 under the title of *Semnadtsat' mgnovenii vesny*.

British Library Cataloguing in Publication Data

Semyonov, Julian, *1931—*
    Seventeen moments of Spring: a novel.
    I. Title   II. Semnadtsat' mgnovenii vesny. *English*
    891.73'44 [F]

    ISBN 0-7145-4140-0
    ISBN 0-7145-4150-8 Pbk

Library of Congress Cataloging in Publication Data

Semyonov, Julian, 1931—
    Seventeen moments of spring—.
    [Semnadtsat' mgnovenii vesny, English]
    Seventeen moments of spring/Julian Semyonov: translated from
the Russian by Katherine Judelson
    p. 312   cm. 21.6 x 13.8
    Translation of: Semnadtsat' mgovenii vesny.
    Earlier translation published as: The Himmler Ploy.
    ISBN 0-7145-4140-0
    1. World War, 1939-1945—Fiction.   I. Judelson, Katherine.
II. Title.   III. Title: 17 moments of spring.
PG3486.E45S413 1988
891.73'44—dc19

Typeset in 11 on 12 Baskerville by Maggie Spooner Typesetting, London.
Printed in Great Britain by Hartnolls Ltd, Bodmin, Cornwall.

To my father

The entire action of this novel takes place between the 12 February and the 18 March 1945.

1

At first Stirlitz could not believe it: a nightingale was singing in the park. The air was crisp, with a bluish tinge to it, and there was a definite touch of spring in the gentle light reminiscent of a water-colour, although the snow underfoot was still firm.

The massive trunks of the old trees now looked black and there was a smell of frozen fish in the park. As yet there was no strong scent from last year's pine needles which always heralds the spring, yet a nightingale was filling the air with song, a flood of trills and cadences—an empty helpless echo in the dark quiet park.

The sun had faded from sight and the black tree-trunks shed even, lilac-coloured shadows across the white snow.

'She'll freeze, the poor creature,' thought Stirlitz to himself and pulling his greatcoat around him went back into the house. 'And there's no helping her, the nightingale is the only bird that will never trust people.'

Stirlitz looked at his watch: it was dead on seven. 'He'll be here any minute,' he thought. 'He's very punctual. I asked him to come from the station through the wood so that he wouldn't meet anyone on the way. Never mind, I'll wait. This is a pleasant spot to wait in, it's really beautiful.'

Stirlitz always fixed his meetings with this particular agent in the same place, at a small private house on the lake shore. It made a most convenient secret rendezvous, being quiet and out-of-the-way in the heart of an oak wood. It had taken him three months to persuade SS Obergruppenführer Pohl to allocate him the necessary money to acquire the villa that had been previously used to accommodate children of bomb victims from among the dancers of the Opera House. The children had asked a tidy sum and Pohl, chief of the SS Economic and Administrative Main Office, had refused him outright. 'You must be mad,' he had said, 'You can perfectly well rent something more modest, why this craving for luxury? We can't just throw money about! That would be dishonest towards a nation with a war on its hands.'

Stirlitz eventually had to bring his chief to see for himself. Thirty-four-year-old SS Brigadenführer Walter Schellenberg, head of political intelligence in the security service, was a subtle intellectual and an aesthete, and he needed no persuading to realise that the spot was ideal for conversations with high-ranking agents. The purchase was made on his behalf by people picked for the purpose, entitling a certain Bolsen, chief engineer from Robert Ley's Chemical Plant to use the villa. He hired a watchman for a large sum and extra rations. Bolsen was in fact SS Standartenführer von Stirlitz.

After laying the table Stirlitz turned on the wireless. London was broadcasting some light music, Glen Miller's band playing a piece from *Sun Valley Serenade*. That particular film had appealed to Himmler, and a single copy had been purchased in Sweden. The film had been shown fairly often since then in the cellar at Prinz-Albrecht-Strasse, particularly during night raids when it was impossible to interrogate prisoners.

Stirlitz rang for the watchman and when he appeared he told him that he could go into town to see his family but must be sure to be back by six the next morning and make some extra-strong coffee for Stirlitz if he had not left by then . . .

'JUSTAS' to 'ALEX'   *Berlin*

Information concerning the strength of army groups on the Eastern front as of February:

1. *Army Group Kurland*	*20 divisions*
over-all strength	*232,000*
effectives	*110,000*
2. *Army Group North*	*28 divisions*
over-all strength	*384,000*
effectives	*141,000*
3. *Army Group Vistula*	*37 divisions*
over-all strength	*527,000*
effectives	*280,000*
4. *Army Group Centre*	*43 divisions*
over-all strength	*413,000*
effectives	*191,000*

5. *Army Group South*   *35 divisions*
    over-all strength   *449,000*
    effectives   *143,000*
Total Strength   *2,005,000*
Total Effectives   *865,000*

Source: lieutenant-colonel in the reserve.
'JUSTAS'

'SCHWARTZ' to 'ALEX'   *Vienna*

Strength of the reserve army as of 1.2.45

(a)	*reserve personnel, including convalescents*	*546,000*
(b)	*permanent personnel of training units*	*147,000*
(c)	*trainees from military schools and courses*	*113,000*
(d)	*men undergoing hospital treatment*	*650,000*
(e)	*territorial units*	*205,000*
(f)	*garrison units*	*18,500*
(g)	*other services and units*	*143,000*
(h)	*miscellaneous personnel unclassified*	*310,000*
	Total:	*2,132,500*

Source: stenographer at the Wehrmacht headquarters.
'SCHWARZ'

'GRETA' to 'ALEX'

Documents recently obtained make it possible to conclude that Germany's industrial output in January 1945 was as follows:

Ammunition	*— three times the 1941 total*
Armaments	*— twice the 1941 total*
Tanks	*— seven times the 1941 total*
Planes	*— three times the 1941 total*
Ships	*— one and a half times the 1941 total*

Source: secretary to Reichsminister Speer's planning advisor.
'GRETA'

'SIEGFRIED' to 'ALEX'   *Copenhagen*

Yesterday a yacht flying a Spanish flag took on board two high-ranking SD officers. The yacht **Blue Skies** *then sailed for Stockholm. The SD officers* *were supplied with papers of hydrological engineers. They were seen off by Schellenberg, Chief of Political Intelligence.*

Source: port quarantine officials.
'SIEGFRIED'

'ANGELA' to 'ALEX'   Munich

Cars belonging to top-ranking SS officers arrive at the local branch of the Reich Security Office, where they are supplied with other cars usually of French or American make and drive into Switzerland. Yesterday five such cars left for Switzerland.

Source: motor-mechanic from the border zone.
'ANGELA'

'THOMAS' to 'ALEX'   Leipzig

Large sums of money are made over from the Handelsbank to Spanish banks every day. It has not yet been possible to ascertain their exact names. Rank-and-file party members or their wives are depositing sums between a hundred thousand and four hundred thousand marks. According to available information, this money could not belong to them.

Source: bank cashier.
'THOMAS'

This data reached Alex, Chief of Soviet Intelligence, and had, wherever possible, been checked and rechecked most thoroughly to ensure its reliability. After that it was circulated among all members of the State Defence Committee.

The chief of intelligence assumed with good reason that in the immediate future he would be set a very complicated task, seeing that an interesting, fairly complex situation full of unanswered questions was taking shape.

'Just to be on the safe side,' he said, turning to his secretary, 'contact the radio department. Tell them to prepare a special transmission for 'Justas': nothing specific, just to tell him to expect a mission in the near future. Something makes me think that he's going to be the one called on to carry out this next

10

mission. I very much hope that he will cope with it and that this mission will be his last.'

After the Russians broke through into Cracow in January 1945 and the town that had been so carefully mined managed to survive intact, Kaltenbrunner gave orders for Krüger, Chief of the Gestapo Eastern Department, who had been responsible for carrying out that particular act of revenge, to be brought to him.

Kaltenbrunner was silent for a long time as he looked at the heavy, large face of the Obergruppenführer, and then he asked in a quiet voice: 'Well, have you any explanation to offer that will be sufficiently objective for the Führer to believe you?'

Krüger, a man with something of the blunt peasant about him, had been waiting for that question and his answer was prepared. But this confrontation involved a demonstration of a whole range of feelings: during his fifteen years in the SS and the party he had had plenty of time to learn how to act. He knew it would be fatal to come out with an answer at once, just as it would be fatal to dispute the fact that he was to blame at all.

'No,' answered Krüger, frowning and stifling a deep sigh. In a voice filled with emotion he went on: 'I have no adequate explanation . . . and could not have. I am a soldier, war is war and I do not expect any special favours.'

His performance was perfectly calculated. He knew that the sterner his self-criticism, the fewer weapons he would leave to Kaltenbrunner. Nothing puts hounds in such a frenzy as a running hare. Krüger, admittedly, did not know how the hounds would behave if the hare lay down with his legs in the air but he had a fairly accurate idea of attitudes in the SS and knew that the more he castigated himself and the less he stood up for himself, the more Kaltenbrunner or anyone else in his place would mellow.

'Don't behave like a woman,' replied Kaltenbrunner as he lit up a cigarette, and Krüger realised that his tactics had been just right: 'The failure must be investigated so as to avoid any repetitions.'

Krüger went on: 'Obergruppenführer, I realise that my guilt

11

is immeasurable. But I should like you to hear what Standarten-führer Stirlitz has to say. He was completely *au fait* with the details of our operation and can vouch that everything had been prepared most thoroughly and conscientiously.'

'What did Stirlitz have to do with the operation?' inquired Kaltenbrunner with a shrug of his shoulders. 'He's from Intelligence and was busy with other matters in Cracow.'

'I know that he was dealing with the lost V2 but I considered it my duty to inform him of all the details of our operation, having every reason to assume that on his return he would tell the Reichsführer or yourself about how we had organised the whole affair. I was expecting some further directions from you, however they weren't forthcoming.'

'Was Stirlitz among those who were to be acquainted with the details of that operation?'

'That I can't be sure about. I alone am to blame,' replied Krüger, realising that he had brought Stirlitz into the story too soon. 'I have no explanation and it is only with blood on the battlefield that I can wipe out my guilt.'

'And who's going to fight the enemy here?! Me?! Alone?! Any fool can die for the Fatherland and the Führer at the front! It's definitely harder to sit it out here with bombs dropping on all sides and go on wiping out the vermin!'

After Krüger had left, Kaltenbrunner sent for his secretary and gave him the following instructions: 'Look out all the papers on Stirlitz over the last couple of years, but be careful about it so that Schellenberg doesn't notice. There mustn't be any panic. Stirlitz is a valuable man and a brave one, and it would be foolish to cast an unnecessary slur on him. This is just to be a routine check-up . . . and have an order on Krüger drawn up: I'll make him second-in-command of the Prague Gestapo—that'll keep him on his toes.'

'What d'you think, Pastor, which is dominant in the human being—man or animal?'

'I think there is an equal balance.'

'That can't be.'

'This is the only way possible.'

'No!'

'Otherwise one or the other would have got the upper hand long ago.'

'You reproach us for appealing to base instincts and putting spiritual considerations second. But they really are secondary: and grow like fungus on leaven.'

'And what about the leaven?'

'That's ambition. That's what *you* call lust, but I call a healthy desire to sleep with a woman and make love to her. It is a healthy urge to come out on top in one's chosen field. Without these aspirations there would be an end to all human progress. The Church has spent no little effort in holding back mankind's progress. You realise what period of the Church's history I am referring to?'

'Yes, of course, I know which period. I know it very well, but there are other things I know too. I fail to see any difference between your attitude to man and that upheld by the Führer.'

'Really?'

'Yes, really. He sees man as an ambitious beast, a healthy, strong beast eager to win *lebensraum* for himself.'

'You have no idea how mistaken you are, for the Führer sees in every German not merely a beast, but a blond beast.'

'Whereas you see in every human being a beast, pure and simple.'

'I see in every human being what he descended from. Man descended from the ape, and an ape must needs be animal.'

'This is where our ideas diverge. You believe that man has come from the ape; however you have not seen the ape from which man is descended and it has not whispered anything into your ear on that subject. You have not touched that ape and you couldn't hope to. You believe in all that because that belief fits in with your view of things.'

'But did God tell you personally that he had created man?'

'Of course nobody has told me anything and I cannot prove the existence of God. It is not something you can prove, only believe in. You believe in the ape and I believe in God. You believe in the ape because that fits in with your spiritual make-

13

up, and I believe in God because that fits in with my views.'

'So, that means God is manifested in every man?'

'Of course.'

'Where d'you find him in the Führer? Or Himmler?'

'Here you're asking a difficult question. After all, we're talking about *human* nature. Of course, one can find traces of the fallen angel in each of those villains. However, their natures have become to such an extent the prisoners of cruelty, necessity, lies, baseness, violence, that there is virtually no room left for anything human.

'The whole time you manage very subtly to avoid answering the questions which are plaguing me. You're not giving me a clear 'yes' or 'no' and every person seeking after faith wants definite answers and only appreciates a straightforward 'yes' or 'no'. But with you it's always 'yes and no', 'I don't think so', 'more likely not' and other variations on the 'yes' theme. It is this that puts me off, not so much your method as your presentation of it in practice.'

'Your attitude to my practices is a hostile one, yet you came to me straight from the concentration camp. How can you reconcile the two?'

'This serves to demonstrate once again that, as you say, there is a divine and an apish element in every human being. If my nature had only contained the divine element then I would not have turned to you. I would not have escaped, I would have accepted my death at the hands of the SS executioners and turned the other cheek so as to arouse a humane response in them. Now, if you happened to fall into their hands, would you, I wonder, have turned the other cheek or tried to avoid the blow?'

'What d'you mean by 'turn the other cheek'? Again you're approaching the actual machine of the Nazi state with some sort of symbolic parable. Turning the other cheek in the parable is one thing. As I said to you before, that is a parable of the human conscience. But it is quite different to be caught up in a machine which is not going to ask you whether you are prepared to turn the other cheek or not, a machine which is basically, essentially, lacking all conscience.'

'Pastor, I feel rather awkward bringing this up, perhaps I'm

14

touching on something you'd rather keep secret, but Frau Eisenstadt told me . . . Perhaps she let it slip inadvertently, which makes it almost impossible for me to ask the question . . . is it true that at one time you were held by the Gestapo?'

'Well, and how should I answer that one? Yes, I was there . . .'

'I see. You don't want to go into it, it's something you'd rather not touch upon. But don't you think, Pastor, that after the war your flock's going to have little faith in you?'

'Well, hundreds of people have been imprisoned by the Gestapo.'

'But if someone whispers in their ears that their pastor was sent along as a *provocateur* to the cells of other prisoners who did not return and that those who did come back as you did— were one in a million, what then? The flock's not going to have much faith in you, is it? Who are you going to preach your truth to then?'

'Of course, if you use those methods you can ruin anyone's reputation. In that case it would be most unlikely that I should manage to improve my situation at all.'

'And what then?'

'Then? Deny it all, deny it with my last ounce of strength, until people started to listen to me. If they didn't start to listen, that would be spiritual death.'

'Spiritual death? So that would mean that you'd still remain a living creature of flesh and blood?'

'The Lord shall judge us. If I survive, I survive.'

'Is your religion against suicide?'

'That is why I would not do away with myself.'

'But what will you do now that you're deprived of the opportunity to preach?'

'I shall continue to believe without preaching.'

'And why do you not see doing a job of work like everyone else as another solution to your problem?'

'What do you imply by the word "work"?'

'Hewing stones to build temples of science, for want of a better example.'

'If a man who has graduated in theology is only of use to society as a hewer of stones in your eyes, then I have nothing

15

more to say to you. In that case it really would be a better idea for me to return to the concentration camp and go up in smoke in the crematorium.'

'All I'm doing is asking the question "if". I'm merely interested to hear you project your thoughts into the future.'

'So you consider that a man who turns to his flock with a spiritual message is nothing but an idler and charlatan? You don't consider that work then? For you work is hewing stone, but in my eyes spiritual labours are particularly important.'

'I myself am a journalist by profession and my articles were ostracised not only by the Nazis but by the church authorities as well.'

'They were condemned by the Church for the simple reason that your interpretation of man was incorrect.'

'From the outset you make a heretic out of me who was actually a searcher. Why do you maintain that you are outside the fray when in actual fact you too are caught up in it?'

'That is true: I am caught up in the fray, really caught up in this war, but it is war itself that I am fighting.'

'Your arguments have a very materialist ring about them.'

'I'm arguing with a materialist.'

'So you can fight me using my weapons?'

'I'm obliged to do so.'

'Listen . . . For the sake of your flock's welfare . . . it's important for me that you should get into contact with my friends. I'll give you their address. I'm trusting you with the address of my friends . . . Pastor, you wouldn't betray innocent people . . .'

'There you go again! I've been telling you . . .'

When he had finished listening to the recording of that conversation Stirlitz quickly rose to his feet and went over to the window so as to avoid the gaze of the man who the day before had asked the pastor for help and was now grinning as he listened to his own voice, drinking cognac and puffing away eagerly at a cigarette.

'Weren't the pastor's cigarettes up to much?'

He was standing by the enormous window that took up the

16

whole wall and watching the crows fight over pieces of bread out in the snow: the watchman received double rations and was a great bird-lover. The watchman did not know that Stirlitz was from the SD and was firmly convinced that the house belonged either to homosexuals or to big wigs from the business world. Not a single woman had come near the place, and when groups of men got together there, their conversations were always of a quiet confidential nature, while the food was recherché and the drink top quality, more often than not French or American.

'Yes, I nearly did my nut without cigarettes . . . The old fellow can talk the hindleg off a donkey and I was dying for a fag.'

The agent's name was Klaus and he had been recruited two years before. He had turned up of his own accord, a former proof-reader on the look-out for some extra kicks. He proved a true artist at his work, disarming his interlocutors with his frankness and outspoken views. He was allowed to say anything as long as his work brought in rapid results. The closer Stirlitz studied Klaus the more he was filled with a sense of fear that grew from one day to the next.

'But perhaps he's ill,' Stirlitz had thought to himself on one occasion. 'A craving to betray is also a kind of disease. Klaus refutes Lombroso* out of hand—he's more terrible than any criminal I've come across, yet so prepossessing and charming . . .'

Stirlitz went back to the table, sat down opposite Klaus and smiled at him, as he asked: 'Well, so you're convinced that the old man will fix that contract?'

'Yes, it's a cert. I like working with priests and intellectuals most of all. You know it's amazing to watch how people walk straight into traps. Sometimes I even feel like saying: "Stop! You half-wit! What on earth are you heading for?!"'

'Now, that would be going too far,' said Stirlitz, 'that would be unreasonable.'

'You haven't got any tinned fish, I suppose. I'm going crazy without fish. It's phosphorus I need, you know. For the nerve cells . . .'

'I'll get out some good tinned fish for you. What would you like?'

* *Lombroso Cesare* (1335-1909) Italian psychiatrist and criminologist who laid the foundations for the reactionary anthropological trend in bourgeois criminology. Now discredited.

'I like fish in oil.'

'That I realise, but the brand? Local or . . .'

'Or,' said Klaus with a laugh. 'That may not sound very patriotic, but I have a great weakness for both food and drink from America or France.'

'I'll get you real French sardines in olive oil, highly spiced and oozing phosphorus . . . You know, yesterday I had a look at your dossier.'

'I'd give anything to have a peep at it, even with half an eye.'

'It's not as interesting as you might think. When you talk, laugh or complain of pains in your liver, that can impress when one bears in mind that you've just completed a highly intricate mission. But your dossier presents a very dull picture: reports, and more reports, denunciations against you . . . No, none of that provides any interest. What is worth noticing is that as a result of your reports and your initiative ninety-seven people have been arrested; I totted them all up. Yet none of them has informed against you, not one, although the Gestapo really put them through the works.'

'Why are you telling me all this?'

'I don't know. I suppose I am trying to analyse . . . Did it ever upset you when people who'd given you shelter were later arrested?'

'What do you think?'

'I don't know what to think.'

'God knows. I suppose I felt a sense of power when I embarked on single combat with them. Those battles I found interesting. But as for what'll happen to them afterwards—I don't know. After all what will happen to us? To everyone else?'

'You've got a point there,' agreed Stirlitz.

'*Après nous le déluge*. And then when it comes to our people what d'you find but base cowardice, greed, denunciation. And that applies to every one of them, every man jack of them. One can't be free among slaves . . . there's no denying that, so isn't it best to be the freest among the slaves? I, for one, have enjoyed complete intellectual freedom all these years.'

Stirlitz then asked, 'Listen, who came to see the pastor the evening before last?'

18

'No one.'

'At about nine o'clock.'

'You're mistaken,' insisted Klaus, 'at any rate none of your men appeared on the scene. I was there on my own.'

'Perhaps it was just someone coming to see the pastor. My chaps couldn't make out the face:'

'Were you keeping a watch on the house?'

'Of course, all the time . . . So you're convinced that the old man will play the game.'

'He'll do that all right. In general I have a sense of vocation as champion of the opposition, a tribune or a popular leader. People submit to my pressure, to the logic of my ideas.'

'Fine, fine, you're a good lad, Klaus. But don't get swollen-headed. Now let's get down to business. You're to spend a few days in one of our flats, because after that you'll have some important work to do and, what's more, not in my province . . .'

Stirlitz was telling the truth: some colleagues from the Gestapo had asked him to lend them Klaus for a week. Two Russian 'pianists' had been arrested in Cologne, caught red-handed while transmitting a radio message. They had refused to say anything so far and someone worth his salt was needed on the job. Klaus was just the man and Stirlitz had promised to look him out.

'Take a piece of paper from the grey folder,' Stirlitz went on, 'and write the following: "Standartenführer, I am tired to the point of exhaustion, really at the end of my tether. I have been carrying out my work to the best of my ability, but I cannot go on at the same pace. I need a break . . ."'

'What's this for?' asked Klaus as he signed the letter.

'I don't think it would do you any harm to take a trip to Innsbruck for a week,' replied Stirlitz, handing him a wad of notes. 'The casinos are functioning there and the girls are skimming down the slopes as usual. Without that letter I wouldn't be able to wangle you a week on the spree.'

'Thank you,' said Klaus, 'but I've got plenty of money on me already.'

'A bit more won't hurt, will it? Or . . .?'

'No, I suppose not really,' agreed Klaus as he put the money away in his back trouser pocket. 'They say that it's fairly expensive to cure yourself of gonorrhoea nowadays,' he added with a laugh.

'Think about it once more: you're quite sure no one saw you at the pastor's house?'

'There's nothing to think about, there was no one there.'

'I mean our people as well.'

'I suppose your people could have seen me if they were keeping a watch on the old man's house. But even then it's highly unlikely. I didn't see anyone.'

Stirlitz recalled how a week before he had dressed Klaus up in a standard striped uniform before organising a sham march of prisoners through the village where Pastor Schlag now lived. He recalled Klaus's face of a week ago, his eyes shining with noble courage: he had been completely absorbed in the part that he was about to play. On that occasion Stirlitz had talked to him in a very different tone because next to him had been sitting a regular saint. How edifying the expression on his face had been, how tragic his voice had sounded and how well he had chosen his words.

'We'll post this letter on the way to your new flat,' Stirlitz explained, 'and at the same time post another to the pastor so as to avoid any suspicion. That you can try and write yourself. So as not to disturb you, I'll go and make some more coffee.'

When he came back, Klaus was holding another piece of paper in his hand.

'Honesty calls for action,' Klaus intoned with a chuckle. 'Faith is founded on struggle. Preaching honesty while remaining completely inactive would mean betraying both the flock and yourself. A man can forgive himself dishonesty, but posterity will never forgive him. That is why I can never forgive myself inactivity. Inactivity is worse than treachery. I am leaving. Try and justify yourself, may God come to your aid.—Well, how's that? Not bad, eh?'

'A work of art. Tell me, are you acting yourself?'

'Of course, I have a life-span of thousands of years, because regardless of the person I'm working with I play myself, not the man you see before you but quite a different one, quite unfamiliar even to me—brave, strong and handsome . . .'

'Did you ever turn your hand to writing?'

'No, If I had been able to write, would I ever have . . .' Klaus fell silent at that and stole a glance at Stirlitz out of the corner of his eye.

'Go on, you old crank . . . You and I don't have to go in for any pretences. You were about to say, if you'd been able to write you would never have come to work for us.'

'Something like that.'

'Not something like that,' Stirlitz corrected him, 'that was precisely what you were about to say, wasn't it?'

'Yes.'

'That's my man. What point is there in lying to me? None at all. Drink up your cognac and we'll be off. It's dark already and the planes will most likely soon be overhead.'

'Is the flat far?'

'About six miles through the wood. It's quiet there and you'll be able to sleep like a log tonight.'

After they had set off in the car Stirlitz asked if Pastor Schlag had said anything about ex-chancellor Brüning.*

'But I wrote about that in my report—he shut up like a clam as soon as the subject came up. I was afraid to push it.'

'Quite right too . . . And he didn't say anything about Switzerland either?'

'Not a word.'

'So far so good. We'll have to approach the matter from another angle. The important thing is that he agreed to help a communist. Good for you, Pastor!'

Stirlitz killed Klaus with a shot in the temple. He did not tell him why he was doing it and on whose behalf, as always happens in films. They were standing on the shore of a lake when the allied aircraft appeared overhead. They were in a prohibited zone but the nearest guard post—Stirlitz had checked this in advance—was over a mile away. With the enemy aircraft overhead the report of a pistol-shot would not be heard. He had also reckoned that Klaus would fall from the concrete landing-stage, from which people had once used to fish, straight into the water, leaving no traces of blood behind him. However, that was a minor detail: every night brought sleet showers so that

* *Henrich Brüning*—a reactionary German politician who held the post of Reichskanzler from 1930 to 1932.

21

blood on the concrete landing-stage inside the prohibited zone was not really dangerous, in fact not dangerous at all.

Klaus fell into the water without a sound, a dead weight. Stirlitz threw the pistol in after him at the spot where Klaus hit the water (the suicide theory on the grounds of nervous exhaustion fitted perfectly, after all the necessary letters had already been written by Klaus in person), took off his gloves and walked back to his car through the wood.

'CENTRE' to 'JUSTAS'

Are you aware of the contacts between Nazis and Western diplomats in Stockholm and if so to what extent? What can you tell us about Ribbentrop's associate Kleist?

'JUSTAS' to 'CENTRE'

I do not think that any major contacts between Nazis and the West are possible at the moment. On an order from Hitler Reichsführer Himmler announced that he would punish with death all traitors who ventured to establish contacts with the Allies. Doctor Kleist is the Gestapo informer in the Ministry of Foreign Affairs. We were able to ascertain that he had no important links with the West in the past. His mission in Stockholm was concerned with questions of protocol and, as far as I know, he had not been given any instructions to make contact with the Allies.

'JUSTAS'

Ernst Kaltenbrunner, Chief of the Reich Security Service spoke with a marked Viennese accent. He knew that this irritated the Führer and Himmler and that was why at one time he had taken lessons with a first-class phonetician in order to learn to speak genuine *hochdeutsch*. However nothing useful had come of it—he loved Vienna, it was the breath of life to him, and he could not bring himself even for an hour a day to speak *hochdeutsch* instead of his light-hearted, although somewhat coarser, Viennese dialect. This was why Kaltenbrunner had for some time given up pretending to be German and had been speaking to everybody in undisguised Viennese. With his staff he did not even speak Viennese, but the Innsbruck dialect. Up in the mountains the Austrians have a particular way of speaking and Kaltenbrunner occasionally derived pleasure from catching out the men on his staff: they were afraid to ask him to repeat words they had not understood and felt most bewildered and ill at ease.

'Not Siblitz but Stirlitz,' said Kaltenbrunner, chuckling down the receiver, 'as far as I know there is no one by the name of Siblitz on our permanent staff, and your agents do not interest me. Yes, and if you can, please hurry things up a bit. Thank you. I shall be waiting.'

He looked at Gestapo chief Obergruppenführer Müller and said: 'I do not wish to arouse your suspicion unnecessarily with regard to comrades in the party and our common struggle, but the facts indicate the following: firstly, Stirlitz, although indirectly, is party to the failure of the Cracow operation. He was there, yet the city owing to a series of strange coincidences was not harmed in the slightest, although it should have gone up in smoke. Secondly, he had been investigating the disappearance of the V2 but did not find it; it never came to light and I pray to God it sank in the swamps near the Vistula. Thirdly, at the moment he is also in charge of a number of questions concerning the retaliation weapon, and although no obvious fiascos can be attributed to him, we have noticed no spectacular successes or victories either. Nor does "being in charge" mean merely getting people whose ideas conflict with ours thrown into prison. It also means helping those who think along the right lines and with an eye to the future. Fourthly, a roving radio-transmitter, which to all appearances, carries out strategic intelligence work for the Bolsheviks, and which Stirlitz had been told to track down, is still active in the environs of Berlin. I should be glad, Müller, if you could dispel my suspicions at once without waiting for his file to be brought in. I like Stirlitz and I should be happy to receive from you some conclusive refutation of these suspicions which suddenly occurred to me recently.'

Müller had been working all the previous night and his head was going round in circles, so, without one of his customary coarse jokes, he replied: 'No one has ever put me on my guard against him. When it comes to mistakes and failures in our work no one is guaranteed against those.'

'Am I to infer you think I am wildly mistaken?'

There was a harsh ring to Kaltenbrunner's question and Müller, despite his tiredness, did not miss it.

'Why?' Müller replied. 'Your suspicions should be analysed in detail, after all what is my outfit for? Otherwise we would be nothing but idlers shirking service at the front. Have you any other facts to go on?' he asked.

Kaltenbrunner kept silent for a moment, taking a hasty bite at his cigarette. Some tobacco got into his throat and he had a long fit of coughing; his face went blue, the veins on his neck dilated and were soon crimson and swollen.

'How shall I put it,' he replied wiping away the tears the coughing had brought to his eyes. 'I don't even know what words to use . . . A few days ago I gave instructions for all his conversations with our men to be recorded. People whom I trust implicitly talk openly to each other of our tragic position, the short-sightedness of our military leaders, Ribbentrop's idiocy, call Göring a nincompoop and refer to the terrible fate that awaits us all if the Russians force their way into Berlin. Stirlitz, on the other hand, replies: "Nonsense, everything's all right, things are going satisfactorily . . ." Love for the fatherland and the Führer does not blind lying to friends at work. I asked myself: perhaps it's he that's the nincompoop. After all, we've got a lot of nincompoops on our staff who repeat Goebbels's eye-wash in mindless fashion. But he's no nincompoop. What is it then that makes him hide his feelings? Either he has no faith in anybody, or he's afraid of something or he's hatching something big and wants to keep his reputation spotless. But if that is the case, what can he be hatching? All the operations that Stirlitz is in charge of must give him a way out to one of the neutral countries. I went on to ask myself, will he come back? And if he does won't he make contact with opposition elements there or other people up to no good? I couldn't find a clear-cut answer to that question either way.'

All the arguments he had been confronted with failed to impress Müller in the slightest, but the last remark obliged him to acknowledge the Obergruppenführer's analytical mind. He

24

then inquired: 'Will you look at his dossier first or shall I take it straightaway?'

'You take it right away,' replied Kaltenbrunner, who had in fact managed to study all the material prior to their conversation. 'I've got to go and see the Führer now.'

Müller cast an enquiring look at Kaltenbrunner, waiting for him to come out with some of the latest news from the Bunker, but none was forthcoming. Kaltenbrunner brought out a bottle of Napoleon cognac, moved a glass over in Müller's direction and asked:

'Did you have a lot to drink last night?'

'I didn't touch a drop.'

'Why are your eyes so red then?'

'I didn't sleep, there was a lot of work in connection with Prague: our people are on the track of some underground groups. There will be some interesting developments there in the next few weeks.'

'Krüger will be a great help to you there. He's as painstaking as they come, although a bit short on imagination. Drink up your cognac, it'll cheer you up.'

'On the contrary, cognac makes me come over muzzy. I prefer vodka.'

'That won't make you feel muzzy,' said Kaltenbrunner with a smile, as he lifted his glass. '*Prosit!*'

He drank it down at a single gulp and his Adam's apple gave a quick upward jerk.

'He really knows how to throw it back,' thought Müller to himself, as he sipped his own cognac, 'now he's sure to pour himself a second glass.'

Kaltenbrunner lit up a 'Karo', one of the cheapest brands of strong cigarettes, and asked: 'Well, will you have another?'

'Thank you,' replied Müller, 'with pleasure. The cognac really is excellent.'

2

Verbatim report of a meeting called by the Führer and attended by Keitel, Jodl, Hewel from the Ministry of Foreign Affairs, Reichsleiter Bormann, SS Obergruppenführer Fegelein from the Reichsführer's staff, Reichsminister of Industry Speer and also Admiral Voss, Captain, 3rd grade, Lüdde-Neurath, Admiral von Puttkamer, ADCs and stenographers:

Bormann. Who keeps pacing up and down all the time? It's disturbing us! Would the military gentlemen also be so kind as to keep their voices down!

Puttkamer. I was asking Colonel von Below to give me information on the Luftwaffe in Italy.

Bormann. I'm not talking about him in particular. Every one is talking, which leads to constant irritating noise.

Hitler. It doesn't disturb me. Herr General, the latest changes in the situation in Kurland have not been marked in on the map.

Jodl. Mein Führer, you had not noticed, perhaps, but here are the changes made this morning.

Hitler. The writing on the map is very small. Thank you, now I see them.

Keitel. General Guderian is again pressing for withdrawal of our troops from Kurland.

Hitler. That is unreasonable. At the moment General Rendulic's troops, remaining deep in the Russian rear—three hundred miles from Leningrad, are tying down between forty and seventy Russian divisions. If we withdraw our troops from there the strength ratio on the approaches to Berlin will change immediately and not at all to our advantage, as Guderian would have us believe. If we were to withdraw those troops from Kurland there would be at least three Russian divisions to every German one in the Berlin area.

Bormann. One must be a sober politician, Herr Feldmarschall . . .

Keitel. I am a soldier, not a politician.

Bormann. Those two concepts are inseparable in an age of total war.

Hitler. It would take at least six months to evacuate the troops now in Kurland if the Libau operation is anything to go by. That would be ridiculous. Hours, precisely hours, are all that we have left to us to gain a victory, if we take into account real facts instead of illusions. Everyone who is able to use his eyes, analyse, draw conclusions, has to answer but one simple question for himself—is immediate victory possible? Nor am I asking that the answer should be blindly categorical. Blind faith is not what I need, substantiated faith is what I am looking for. Never has the world known such a paradoxical coalition marked by such deep contradictions as the present Alliance. Incompatible ideas and aspirations, elements and characters can only exist side by side at no loss to themselves when a situation is hopeless. I refer here to prisoners in concentration camps where, they say, papal nuncios, communist atheists, French radicals and British conservatives all get on like a house on fire. Hopelessness engenders an alliance. It is an alliance of despair, with no hope and no goals. While Russia, Britain and America pursue diametrically opposed goals, our goal stands clearly before us all. While they move spurred on by conflicting ideological aspirations, we are inspired by a common ideal towards which our lives are directed. While the contradictions between them are growing and will continue to grow, our unity now as never before has acquired that very monolithic quality which I was seeking to achieve during the long years of the trying yet great campaign. To facilitate the collapse of our enemies' coalition by diplomatic or other such means is an Utopian dream, if not something worse, such as a sign of panic or the abandonment of any hope for the future. Only by dealing them blows in the field and demonstrating our unflinching resolution and our inexhaustible might shall we bring nearer the end of that coalition which will fall apart at the thunder of our victorious guns. Nothing has such a strong impact on the Western democracies as a show of strength. Nothing brings Stalin down to earth so much as confusion among his Western allies on the one hand, and the blows we deal him on the other. Bear in mind that Stalin is now having to wage battle not in the

Bryansk forests or the plains of the Ukraine. His troops are now in Poland, Rumania and Hungary. The Russians, now that they have come up against the 'outside world', are looking weaker and to a certain extent demoralised. But it is not on the Russians or Americans that I am now focusing my attention. It is the Germans I turn my gaze to! It is only our nation which can and must emerge victorious! At the present time the whole country has come to resemble a military camp. When I say the whole country I mean Germany, Austria, Norway, part of Hungary and Italy, large territories in the Czech and Bohemian protectorates, Denmark and part of Holland. This is the heart of European civilisation, a concentration of material and spiritual might. The prerequisites for that victory are in our grasp. It is up to us, to the military, to ensure that these prerequisites be made use of rapidly to bring about that victory. Believe me, after the first crushing blows at the hand of our armies the Allies' coalition will fall apart. The selfish interests of each of the Allies will get the better of their common strategic plans. In order to hasten our victory I recommend the following: the Sixth SS Panzer Army will begin a counter-attack near Budapest, thus ensuring the reliable strength of National Socialism's southern bastion in Austria and Hungary on the one hand, and preparing to attack the Russians' flank on the other. Remember that is precisely down there in the south, that we have seventy thousand tons of oil. Oil is the life-blood throbbing through the arteries of war. I would rather surrender Berlin than lose that oil which makes Austria impregnable and links her up with Kesselring's million-strong grouping in Italy. Further, the Army Group Vistula, after mustering its reserves, should undertake a resolute counter-offensive against the Russian flanks, using Pomerania as a bridgehead. The Reichsführer's troops, after breaking through the Russian defences, should come out into their rear and seize the initiative. With the support of the Stettin grouping they will be able to cut through the Russian front. Bringing up reserves is Stalin's major problem: enormous distances are working against him. Yet those very same enormous distances play into our hands. The seven defence lines that protect Berlin, and to all practical purposes make the city impregnable, will allow us to go against the canons of

28

military art and transfer a large group of forces from the south and north to the west. We'll have enough time in hand: Stalin will need two or three months to regroup his reserves, while to transfer our armies all we need is five days. German distances allow us to do that, flying in the face of traditional strategy.

Jodl. Yet it would be desirable to link up this question with traditional strategy.

Hitler. What do you mean by that, Jodl?

Jodl. What you have said is full of wisdom and foresight, but I make so bold as to disagree on one point: on the decision not to make the details of this plan compatible with the traditions of military science.

Hitler. It is not details but the overall plan that I have in mind. When all is said and done individual details can always be worked out by groups of experts at headquarters. The military have more than four million people at their disposal, organised in a mighty tide of resistance. Our task is to organise that mighty tide of resistance so as to deal the crushing blow. We are now holding the borders we gained in August 1938. We are forged together as one—we, the German nation. Our war industry is producing four times as much as in 1939. Our army is now twice as large as it was then. Our hatred is formidable and our will to win knows no bounds. I ask you: is there any reason to doubt that we shall attain peace by means of war? Or that military success shall engender political success?

Keitel. As Reichsleiter Bormann pointed out, nowadays the soldier must also be a politician.

Bormann. Don't you agree?

Keitel. Very much so.

Hitler. Herr Feldmarschall, please elaborate details by tomorrow.

Keitel. Yes, *mein Führer*. We shall draw up a general outline and if that meets with your approval we shall start work on all the details.

SS Obergruppenführer Fegelein, Eva Braun's brother-in-law, went to Himmler's HQ to inform him of the recent meeting in the Bunker.

'Any political solution of the problem is rejected out of hand by the Führer,' he said.

'How did the military react to his plan?' asked Himmler.

'With ill-disguised irony. Strange though it may sound it is precisely the military who have now become firmly convinced that the outcome of the war cannot be settled except by political means.'

'Capitulation?' asked Himmler in a pensive tone. 'Are they tired of fighting?'

'Why necessarily capitulation? Negotiations . . .'

Stirlitz arrived home at seven o'clock just as it was starting to get dark. He loved that particular time of year when there was hardly any snow left, when the tops of the tall pine trees were lit up by the sun in the morning, and when it seemed as if summer had already come and one could go and spend the whole day at Müggelsee, fishing or sleeping in a deck-chair.

Stirlitz was now living alone in a little house out in Babelsberg, not far from Potsdam. His housekeeper had left for Thuringia a week before to join her niece in the mountains. The woman had not been able to put up with the endless bombing raids—her nerves had given way.

The cleaning was now being done by the daughter of the proprietor of the local inn, the 'Huntsman'. She was a young slip of a girl, bright and attractive. 'Most probably from Saxony,' thought Stirlitz, as he watched her coping with the large vacuum cleaner in the sitting-room, setting about cleaning the carpet; 'with that dark hair and those blue eyes. Admittedly, she has a Berlin accent but I still think she must be from Saxony.'

Stirlitz looked at his old-fashioned watch and thought: It's time I got a new one. If my Longines was either fast or slow all the time I would have adapted to it. But it's fast one minute and slow the next which is hopeless, no use at all.

'What time is it?' Stirlitz asked the girl.

'About seven.'

'Lucky creature . . . she can allow herself the luxury of an "about seven". The most fortunate people on earth are those who can be casual over time, without having to worry in the slightest about the consequences. But she speaks with a Berlin accent, there's no doubt about that. Even with a touch of Mecklenburg dialect.'

After the girl had left, Stirlitz drew the heavy blackout curtains and switched on the reading lamp. He bent down by the fireplace and only then noticed that the logs had been arranged exactly as he liked to have them, in a neat square, and some dried birch bark had even been put out ready on a blue earthenware saucer.

'I hadn't told her about that . . . or perhaps . . . yes, I did. In passing . . . The girl's got a good memory,' he thought to himself as he put a light to the birch bark, 'when we think about the young we always approach them like old teachers, and from their point of view it must seem very funny. Yet I suppose I've already got used to thinking of myself as an old man, after all I'm forty-nine . . .'

Stirlitz waited till the tongues of flame started hungrily to lick out at the dry birch logs and then walked over to the wireless and switched it on. He tuned in to Moscow, a programme of old Russian music. Stirlitz recalled how Göring had once said to his staff officers: 'It's not patriotic to listen to enemy broadcasts but at times I have an urge to listen to the trash they're putting out about us.' Stirlitz had realised then that Göring was an unintelligent coward; information to the effect that he listened to enemy wireless programmes was furnished by his servants and his chauffeur who had been recruited by Müller. If 'Nazi No. 2' was trying to provide himself with alibis in that fashion it all went to show what a coward he was and pointed to his complete lack of confidence in the future. On the contrary, mused Stirlitz, he shouldn't have concealed the fact that he listened to such programmes. It would have been better just to comment appropriately on enemy programmes, pouring harsh ridicule on them.

The music finished with a soft piano passage. The far-away voice of the Moscow announcer, who sounded like a German, started to list frequencies at which transmissions could be picked up on Fridays and Wednesdays. Stirlitz noted the numbers: it was a coded message specially intended for him, the one he had been waiting for for six days. He took down the

31

figures in a neat column. There were a good number of them and the announcer, as if to make sure people had time to write them all down, read them out a second time.

Then another magnificent Russian melody rang out over the air.

Stirlitz took out a volume of Montaigne from the bookcase and substituted words for the figures, matching up these words with the code hidden amongst the wise truths of the great serene French thinker.

After decoding the radio message he burnt the piece of paper with the figures and words on it, mixed the ashes with the cinders in the fireplace and drank some brandy.

'What do they take me for?' he thought to himself. 'A genius or the Almighty? It's unthinkable . . .'

Stirlitz had good reason to react that way because the mission which had been assigned to him over the wireless from Moscow was as follows:

'ALEX' to 'JUSTAS'

Acording to information on hand, high-ranking SD and SS officers have been appearing in Sweden and Switzerland and are trying to find a means of making contact with those in charge of Allied intelligence. In particular, SD people in Berne have been trying to establish contact with Allen Dulles's staff. It is essential that you should find out if these attempts to make contact are (1) deliberate misinformation (2) personal initiative on the part of high-ranking SD officers (3) a mission carried out under instructions from the central administration.

If these SD or SS people are carrying out directives coming from Berlin it is vital to find out who sent them there with that mission, in other words, which of the leaders of the Reich is seeking contact with the West.

'ALEX'

'Justas' was the code-name used by SS Standartenführer Stirlitz, known in Moscow as Colonel Maxim Maximovich Isaev only to the top three security chiefs . . .

Six days before that radio message reached Stirlitz, Stalin, on reading the latest reports sent in by Soviet intelligence agents, called the chief of intelligence to his country house outside Moscow where he had the following to say to him:

'Only political novices could believe that Germany's strength has been finally sapped and has ceased to present a real danger. Germany is like a tightly compressed spring which must and can be broken if equally powerful pressure is brought to bear on it from both sides. On the other hand, if pressure on one side turns into a prop the spring can leap up and strike out in the other direction. And it would be a strong blow in the first place because the Hitlerites' fanaticism knows no bounds and, secondly, because Germany's war potential has by no means been exhausted. For this reason all attempts on the Nazis' part to come to terms with anti-Soviet elements in the West must be regarded by you as a mission of the highest importance. Naturally, you must bear in mind that the main figures in any possible separate negotiations will most likely be Hitler's closest associates enjoying authority both in the party apparatus and among the people. These associates must be subjected to most thorough observation on your part. It is indisputable that the closest associates of a tyrant about to meet his fall will betray him so as to save their own lives. This applies to any political game. If you overlook these possible developments you will have only yourselves to blame.'

Somewhere a long way away the whine of the air-raid sirens started up and almost at once there followed the rattle of ack-ack. The lights at the power station went off and Stirlitz sat for a long time in front of the fireplace, watching flickers of blue flame coil round the burning logs that glowed black and red.

'If I shut the air-vent I'd be out in three hours,' thought Stirlitz drowsily to himself. 'That almost happened to me once with Granny in our Moscow flat in Yakimanka Street when she shut the stove too soon and there were still logs like these with a black-red glow and tongues of blue flame. The gas that nearly poisoned us was colourless and had no smell, I think . . .'

33

He waited till the smouldering logs were quite black and the flames had disappeared before shutting the air-vent over the fire and lighting a large candle fixed in the neck of a champagne bottle. He liked the strange patterns the tallow drips had made down the sides of the bottle. Stirlitz had used many candles, and there was hardly anything of the bottle to be seen: it was now just a strange vessel reminiscent of a Greek amphora apart from the fact that it was red and white.

Somewhere nearby two big explosions followed each other in quick succession. 'Explosive bombs,' he decided. 'Whopping great explosive bombs. Our chaps really know where to drop them. Hot stuff. It would be a damned shame if they were to knock me off when the end is in sight. There wouldn't be a single trace of me left by the time our troops got here. Anyway, to vanish into thin air like that is a horrible thought, Sashenka,' and at that thought Stirlitz suddenly saw his wife's face before him. 'Little Sashenka and my boy Sasha: now is not the time to die at all. Whatever happens I must try and pull through. It's easier to live alone because then it's not so terrible to die. But after seeing one's son the prospect is terrible. Those idiots of novelists write—"he died calmly in the bosom of his loving family". But there's nothing more terrible than to die sur- rounded by one's children, to see them for the last time, feel their nearness and realise that it's for ever, that all that's left is eternal darkness and their sorrow.'

Twenty-three years ago in Vladivostok he had seen Sashenka for the last time before setting off to carry out a mission, entrusted to him by Dzerzhinsky, among White Russian emigrés, first in Shanghai and then in Paris. Yet ever since that terrible, windy, far-off day her image had lived within him; she had become a part of him that could never be taken away.

He then recalled his meeting with his son in Cracow late at night. He remembered how 'Grishanchikov' had come to see him in his hotel and how they had whispered together after turning on the wireless and how excruciating it had been to leave his son. Stirlitz knew that he was now in Prague to save it from destruction just as his father, together with Major Whirlwind, had saved Cracow. He knew what a difficult task faced his son, but he also knew that any attempt on his part to see Sasha—although Berlin was a mere six hours away from Prague—could prove fatal.

Stirlitz rose to his feet, picked up the candle and walked over to the table. He fetched several sheets of paper and spread them out in front of him like cards for a game of patience. On one sheet he drew a tall fat man and wanted to write the name Göring underneath, but decided against it. On the second sheet he drew Goebbels's face, and on the third the strong face marked with a scar that was Bormann's. After pausing for a while he wrote the words 'SS Reichsführer' on the fourth sheet—that was the title of his chief, Heinrich Himmler.

Putting three sheets aside, Stirlitz took the one with Göring and added a series of circles and squares, comprehensible to him alone, joining them up with lines, either two thick ones or one thin one, and sometimes a barely visible line of dots.

An agent if he finds himself at the very centre of extremely important events has to be a highly emotional person, sensitive almost to the same degree as an actor; but his emotional intensity has to be held down under cold-blooded logic, rigorous in its precision.

When Stirlitz allowed himself to be Isaev, something that happened rarely and then only at night, he used to think along the following lines. What does being a real agent involve? Collecting information, analysing facts, data and transmitting them to Centre for the political conclusions to be drawn and the decisions to be taken? Or should the agent draw *his own* conclusions, make *his own* plans, put forward *his own* arguments? And, Maxim Isaev, if you hold that it is precisely you who can feel what the future holds, are you entitled to influence that future? The agent's bugbear, in Isaev's opinion, is that the exceptional abundance of fresh information blurs and conceals his picture of the future. If intelligence services were allowed to plan politics, then a situation might arise where there would be plenty of recommendations but little solid information. An agent ought to be objective; it was most regrettable when intelligence work was made subordinate to a political course that has been charted in advance. Hitler's undoing was believing that the Soviet Union was weak and paying too little attention to the more cautious opinions put forward by the

35

military leaders. Equally regrettable were situations in which intelligence services try to take charge of politics. Ideally, the intelligence agent should have his own view of the main developments and be able to suggest to the politicians a number of possible and, from his point of view, the most expedient solutions.

As he embarked on this latest analysis of the material that he had been able to amass over all those years, Stirlitz was obliged to weigh up all his 'pros' and 'cons': the lives of millions of people were at stake and he could not possibly afford to miscalculate in this analysis.

Stirlitz had started to make a really detailed study of Hitler's successor or 'Nazi No. 2', Göring, in April 1942 after the air raid by eight hundred Flying Fortresses on Kiel. The town had been virtually reduced to ashes. Göring informed the Führer that three hundred enemy planes had taken part in the raid. Groche, Gauleiter of the city whose hair had turned grey in the course of twenty-four hours, refuted Göring's report with well-documented evidence, informing Hitler that eight hundred Flying Fortresses had taken part in the raid and the Luftwaffe had been powerless to do anything to save the city.

Hitler had looked at Göring in silence and an expression of disgust had come over his face, his left hand had started to fidget, creating the impression that the Führer was itching like someone with scabies. Then he let fly.

'Not one enemy bomb shall fall on German cities?!' he started up in a tense pained voice without looking at Göring. 'Who told that to the nation? Who gave that assurance to the party?! I have read about card games played for money and am familiar with the term bluff! Germany is not green baize for gamblers' tricks!' At that Hitler threw an ominous gaze in Göring's direction and went on: 'You have been wallowing in prosperity and luxury, Göring! In these days of war you are living like a Roman emperor or Jewish plutocrat! You are shooting deer with bow and arrows, while my people are being shot at by guns of enemy planes! A leader's calling is to enhance the greatness of his nation! A leader's lot is modest living! A leader's profession consists in matching his promises with actions!'

Later it leaked out that Göring, after hearing those words, had gone home to bed with a temperature and a fit of hysterics. After that he would visit in person the towns that had been bombed, meet the local people, demand immediate assistance for the victims, reorganise the town's anti-aircraft defence and afterwards take to his bed with a high temperature, his blood pressure up and his forehead gripped in a vice of pain. Later when Himmler was trying to collect compromising material for his dossier on Göring, medical experts confirmed that Göring's blood pressure really did show a marked rise on such occasions.

It was in 1942 that Hitler's official successor was first subjected to such humiliating criticism and, what was more, in the presence of Hitler's staff. This incident was immediately included in Himmler's dossier on him, and the next day, without even asking Hitler's permission, the SS Reichsführer gave instructions for all telephone conversations made by the Führer's 'closest associate' to be tapped.

However, even after that dressing down, Hitler used to remark in his conversations with Bormann: 'No one else but Göring can be my successor. In the first place, he has never tried to dabble in independent politics, secondly, he is popular among the people, and thirdly, he is the chief subject for cartoons in the enemy press.'

The First World War pilot and hero of the Kaiser's Germany had fled to Sweden after the fiasco of the Nazis' false start. There he started work as a civil-aviation pilot and on one occasion, when he was carrying Baron Rosen in stormy weather, by some miracle he managed to land his plane in the grounds of Castle Rockelstadt. There he made the acquaintance of Karina von Kantzow, daughter of Colonel von Fock, persuaded her to leave her husband and left for Germany. On his arrival he met the Führer and took part in the abortive Nazi *putsch* in Munich on November 9, 1923, during which he was wounded. He escaped arrest by the skin of his teeth and emigrated to Innsbruck. The Görings were subsequently invited to Venice where they stayed until 1927, when an amnesty for Nazis was proclaimed in

Germany. Within less than six months Göring was elected to the Reichstag along with eleven other Nazis. Hitler was unable to stand for election being an Austrian.

In accordance with a decision of the Führer, Göring gave up party work, remaining a deputy to the Reichstag. He was to make contact with the powers-that-be, as a party intending to take power needed wide contacts. It was decided that he should rent a luxurious residence in Badenstrasse and it was there that Prinz Hohenzollern, Prinz Cobourg and rich magnates started to call on the Görings. Karina was the life and soul of these gatherings. She was a charming, aristocratic woman who enchanted everyone she met, the daughter of a Swedish dignitary married to a war hero in exile.

It was at this particular private residence, rented with party funds, that Hitler, Schacht and Thyssen met on January 5, 1931: it provided the luxurious setting for the deal between the financial and industrial tycoons and Hitler, leader of the National Socialists.

Then came Hitler's victory, soon after which Karina left for Sweden where she died of an epileptic fit. Her last wish was that Hermann should continue to serve the Führer with unswerving devotion.

After the Röhm *putsch*, when many Nazis of long standing came out against the Führer on the grounds that he had betrayed party principles by concluding an alliance with Big Business, criticisms were to be heard among rank-and-file party members.

When Göring built himself a castle outside Berlin, called Karinhalle, complaints were lodged with Hitler not just by the rank and file but by prominent figures, such as Ley and Sauckel. Goebbels maintained that the rot had set in when Göring had been given his original private residence in Badenstrasse. 'Luxury always has a corrupting effect,' he commented. 'Göring needs help, he means too much to us all.'

Hitler then went to visit Karinhalle and, after being taken over the castle, remarked: 'Leave Göring in peace. After all he is the only man who knows how to behave with Western diplomats. We'll let Karinhalle be used as a residence for foreign guests. Let things be! Hermann's deserved it! We'll consider that Karinhalle belongs to the people and that Göring is merely a tenant . . .'

A report intercepted on its way from the Czech Embassy revealed that Göring used to spend all his time re-reading Jules Verne and Karl May, his two favourite writers. In the grounds he used to hunt tame deer and in the evenings he spent a great deal of time in the private cinema: he was capable of watching as many as five adventure films at a single sitting. While they were being shown, he would assure his guests that the plot would turn out all right in the end . . .

Stirlitz pushed over to one side the paper with the sketch of Göring's fat bulk and started to study another sheet on which he had drawn Goebbels's profile. Goebbels had been nicknamed the 'Babelsberg Bull' because of his adventures in Babelsberg where the Reich film studios were situated and all the actresses used to live. The dossier on Goebbels contained a recording of a conversation between Frau Goebbels and Göring at the time when Goebbels had been infatuated with a Czech actress by the name of Lida Baarova.

'Women will be the death of him,' Göring remarked to Frau Goebbels. 'It's a disgrace! The man who is responsible for our ideology brings shame on himself with these casual affairs!'

Later the Führer recommended to Frau Goebbels that she seek a divorce. 'You can be sure of my support,' he told her, 'as for your husband, so long as he fails to learn how to behave himself as befits a National Socialist, who should be a man of high moral principles always acutely aware of his duty to his family, I shall refuse to have any direct contact with him.'

But this belonged to the past, because in January that year Hitler had appeared at Goebbels's house on a birthday. He had brought a bouquet of flowers for Frau Goebbels, which he presented to her with the words: 'I must ask you to forgive my late arrival but I had to tour the whole of Berlin before I could get hold of any flowers—the Gauleiter of Berlin, Parteigenosse Goebbels has had all flower shops closed, since total war has no need for flowers . . .'

When Hitler departed forty minutes later Magda Goebbels remarked: 'The Führer would never have paid a visit to the Görings.'

While Berlin lay in ruins and the front line was a mere eighty miles away from the capital of the thousand-year Reich, Magda Goebbels revelled in her success, radiant with triumph. Her husband was standing beside her, deeply moved by the Führer's visit to his home after an interval of six years.

None of that's of any consequence any more, Stirlitz thought to himself, a lot of empty nonsense now.

He went on to draw a large circle and slowly filled it in with clear, straight lines. He was recalling to himself all that he knew about Goebbels's diaries. He knew that Himmler had shown an interest in those diaries and had in the past tried hard to acquaint himself with their contents. Eventually, he had managed to see a photocopy of a few pages but no more. Stirlitz had a phenomenal memory and he had memorised the text almost mechanically without any effort as soon as he looked at it.

'December 9, 1943: In Britain there is a flu epidemic— Goebbels had noted—even the King is ill. It would be fine if the epidemic were to prove fatal for Britain but that would be too good to be true.'

'March 2, 1943: I shall not rest until all Jews have been cleared out of Berlin. After talking to Speer in Obersalzberg I went to see Göring. In his cellar there are 25,000 bottles of champagne and he calls himself a National Socialist! He was wearing a tunic the colour of which made me turn over inside. But what can you do, one just has to accept him for what he is.'

Stirlitz sniggered to himself: he remembered how Himmler had said exactly the same, word for word, about Goebbels. That had been back in 1942, when Goebbels had been living in the country, not with the family in the big house but in a small modest cottage built for 'work purposes'. The cottage stood near a lake and it was possible to get into the grounds by way of the reeds at the lake's edge and thus avoid the main entrance without having to cope with the railings that surrounded the building on three sides. The water at that spot was shallow, only ankle-deep, and the SS look-out post was strategically placed on the other side. Actresses used to visit Goebbels there, coming by the suburban tram and then making their way through the wood. Goebbels considered it an exorbitant luxury, quite beneath the dignity of a National Socialist, to have women brought to one's residence by car. He used to lead them through the reeds himself and then the next morning, while the guards were asleep, he would show them the way out again. Himmler, of course, learned about these goings-on and it was at that period that he had said of Goebbels: 'One just has to accept him for what he is.'

Stirlitz crumpled up the pieces of paper with sketches of Göring and Goebbels, held them to the candle-flame and after they had burnt right down, almost as far as his fingers, threw the remains into the fireplace. He stirred them round with an elegant cast-iron poker, then came back to the table and lit a cigarette.

This time he took up the two remaining sheets, those with sketches of Himmler and Bormann. 'Göring and Goebbels I rule out', he thought. 'Nobody would put their stake on them, either of them. Göring is probably capable of resorting to such negotiations, but at the moment he's in disgrace and doesn't trust anybody. And Goebbels? No, he wouldn't get tied up in anything like that. He's a fanatic, he'll go on to the bitter end: anyway, he could never be counted on because he'd start straightaway looking for an alliance. That leaves one of the other two: Himmler or Bormann. If only I could have a guarantee from one of them, so as to know I could work against all the rest, then I win. If I miscalculate, it'll mean the end for me, and straightaway too. But which one of them should I put my stake on? Himmler, I suppose. He could obviously never resort to negotiations—he knows the hatred that surrounds his name. Yes, Himmler's the one.'

At that particular moment Göring was on his way back from the Führer's Bunker to Karinhalle, looking pale, with sunken cheeks, and tortured by a splitting headache. That morning he had driven out to the front line, to the spot where the Russian tanks had made a break-through. From there he had rushed straight back to Hitler.

'There's no kind of organisation at the front,' he had explained, 'complete chaos. The eyes of the soldiers are quite

41

dazed, and I saw drunken officers. The Bolshevik offensive is striking fear into the army, animal fear . . . I consider . . .'

Hitler listened to what he was saying with his eyes half-closed, cupping his right hand under his left elbow to keep the constant twitching of his left arm under control.

'I consider . . .' Göring repeated, but Hitler did not allow him to continue.

Hitler rose heavily to his feet, his bloodshot eyes wide open and his moustache bristling in contempt. 'I forbid you to drive out to the front in future!' he declared in a strong voice, reminiscent of the old days, 'I forbid you to spread panic!'

'It's not panic, it's the truth!' remonstrated Göring, contradicting the Führer for the first time ever and at once he felt his toes and fingers turn icy cold. 'It's the truth, *mein Führer*, and it is my duty to inform you of this truth!'

'Be silent! You'd better stick to planes, Göring! Don't stick your nose around in places, where a cool head, foresight and strength are required. It appears they are beyond you. I forbid you to drive out to the front from now on and that's final.'

Göring felt crushed and humiliated; his back sensed how those nonentities, the Führer's ADCs Schmundt and Burgdorf, smiled after him as he made his exit.

Some men from Luftwaffe HQ were waiting for him when he reached Karinhalle: on leaving the Bunker, Göring had given instructions for his staff to assemble there. However, he had no chance to get the meeting under way for an ADC reported that SS Reichsführer Himmler had arrived.

Göring received the Reichsführer in his library. As always, Himmler was calm and full of smiles. He came in carrying a thick leather document case, sat down in an armchair, took off his glasses, gave the lenses a long clean with a piece of chamois leather and then announced without any preamble: 'The Führer can no longer be the leader of the nation.'

'Well, so what's to be done?' asked Göring mechanically before he even had time to take fright at the words pronounced by the SS leader.

'After all, there are SS men in the Bunker staff,' Himmler continued in the same quiet, even-toned voice as before, 'but, of course, that is not the most important thing. The Führer's lost his guts. He's not capable of taking decisions any more. We are obliged to turn to the people.'

Göring looked at the thick black document-case lying on Himmler's lap and remembered how the year before his wife had said during a telephone conversation to a woman-friend: 'It would be better if you'd come round here, it's risky to talk over the phone because the line's being tapped.' Göring remembered how he had rapped with his finger on the table and made a sign to his wife implying: 'Don't talk about that, you're mad.' And now he looked at the fat black document-case and thought that there might be a tape-recorder inside it and that their conversation might be played back to the Führer within a couple of hours, which would mean the end.

'He's capable of saying absolutely anything,' thought Göring as he looked at Himmler. 'The father of *provocateurs* cannot possibly be an honest man. He already knows about my disgrace with the Führer this morning and he's come here to put the finishing touches to his mission.'

Himmler, in his turn, realised what 'Nazi No. 2' was thinking and this made him decide to prompt Göring. He sighed and said: 'You are the successor, hence you are the President, which makes me Reich Chancellor.' He realised that the nation would not follow him, the leader of the SS. He needed a cover and Göring was the most suitable choice available.

Göring answered, again quite mechanically: 'That is impossible.' He hesitated for a moment and then added very quietly, reckoning a whisper would not be picked up by the tape-recorder if there was one hidden in the black document-case: 'That's impossible. One man will have to be both President and Chancellor.'

Himmler's face showed a hint of a smile, then, after remaining seated for a few minutes in silence, he sprang up like a jack-in-the-box, took his leave of Göring with the Nazi salute and left the library without a sound.

3

Stirlitz left his study to go down into the garage. The bombing was still going on but now it was somewhere in the Zossen area, or so it sounded to him at least. Stirlitz opened the gate, sat down in the driver's seat and switched on the ignition. The boosted engine of his Horch started up with an even, powerful roar.

Stirlitz enjoyed driving. When he had a mission to accomplish and did not know how to set about it, he would get into his Horch and drive for hours along the roads skirting Berlin. First of all, he would look straight ahead, putting his foot hard down on the accelerator: speed forced him to be on the alert, he needed to feel at one with the car, which meant that his head was freed of all trivial and unimportant thoughts. Speed could be relied on to sharpen his wits, and enabled him to forget everything. Only afterwards, when the dangerous hair-raising drive came to an end and he went to rest in some small café— cognac was never rationed even at the bleakest periods of the war—he would sit at a little table near a window, listen to the rustling trees in the nearby wood, imbibe a double Jacobi, calmly and deliberately thinking out the problem in hand. After driving at high speeds Stirlitz always had a particularly clear head. Flirting with danger facilitated cool thinking or, at least, so it was in Stirlitz's case.

His radio operators—Erwin and Käthe—lived in Köpenick on the bank of the Spree. They had already gone to bed, the two of them. They had made a habit of going to bed very early recently, since Käthe was expecting a baby.

'You look wonderful,' remarked Stirlitz. 'You belong to that rare category of women whom pregnancy makes quite irresistible.'

'Being pregnant makes any woman attractive,' relied Käthe. 'Simply you haven't had the chance to notice it.'

44

'No, I haven't,' Stirlitz agreed with a laugh, 'you're right there . . .' He gave Käthe a gentle pat on the cheek and asked: 'Will you play us something?'

Käthe sat down at the piano and picked out some Bach from among the pile of music. Stirlitz walked over to the window and beckoned Erwin to follow him.

'It's like this,' he said, wondering where to start. 'I've been given a new mission.' Again he gave a soft laugh, 'I'm to find out which of the big shots is planning to go in for separate talks with the West . . . They mean one of the top leaders, no less. Quite a job, eh? Real fun? It looks as if they've got it into their heads that since things have gone smoothly for the last twenty years, I must be all-powerful. It wouldn't be a bad idea for me to become Himmler's deputy or even perhaps aspire to the Führer's post! Heil Stirlitz, how does it sound? I'm getting to be quite an old grouser, have you noticed?'

'It suits you,' replied Erwin.

'How are you planning to have the baby, my girl?' asked Stirlitz, when Käthe stopped playing.

'As far as I know, no one's thought up an alternative method yet,' she answered.

'I was talking to a gynaecologist the other day . . . I don't want to frighten you . . .' He walked up to Käthe and asked: 'Play some more for us, my girl, please do. I don't want to frighten you, although I myself got a real fright. The old doctor told me that he can determine the nationality of any woman during confinement.'

'What d'you mean?' asked Erwin.

Käthe interrupted the piece she was playing.

'Go on playing, Käthe, please,' asked Stirlitz, 'don't get worked up. First listen to what I have to say and then we'll work out how best to get over this hurdle. You see, women cry out during confinement.'

'Thank you,' commented Käthe with a smile, 'I thought they sang songs.'

Stirlitz shook his head with a sigh. 'You see, my dear, the trouble is they cry out in their mother tongue, in the dialect of the place they were born in. So you'll start crying out "Mama" in your best Ryazan . . .'

Käthe went on playing, but Stirlitz noticed that all of a sudden her eyes had filled with tears.

'What shall we do?' asked Erwin.

'What if we packed you off to Sweden? I could most likely manage that.'

'And lose your last contact?' inquired Käthe.

'I should still be here,' said Erwin.

Stirlitz contradicted him with a firm shake of his head. 'They wouldn't let Käthe out alone, only if she went with you: Erwin, the war invalid needs treatment in a sanitorium and you have received an invitation from your German relatives in Stockholm . . . They'll never let you out on your lonesome, Käthe. After all it's *his* uncle who's one of the Swedish Nazis, not *yours* . . .'

'We shall stay here,' said Käthe. 'Never mind. I shall cry out in German.'

'You can always pop in a few Russian curses but make sure you pronounce them with a Berlin accent,' joked Stirlitz. 'That decision we can put off till tomorrow. We'll think the matter over thoroughly leaving all heroics out of it. Off we go, Erwin. We've got to send out a message.

'The answer I get tomorrow will decide the matter.'

Five minutes later they left the house. Erwin was holding a case which contained a wireless-set. They covered a distance of about ten miles to Rahnsdorf and, after driving deep into the woods, Stirlitz switched off the engine of his car. The bombing was still going on as before. Erwin looked at his watch and asked: 'Shall we begin?'

'Yes,' replied Stirlitz, 'Yes, off we go.'

'JUSTAS' to 'ALEX'

As before am convinced that not one major Western politician would negotiate with the SS or SD. However in so far as have been given this mission, will embark on it.

Believe it could be achieved if I conveyed part of the data you sent me to Himmler. Given his support could then in the future keep under direct observation those persons who in your opinion are reconnoitering channels

46

for possible negotiatons. My 'report' to Himmler—shall organise the details on the spot without previously consulting you—will help me to keep you informed about all news, which either confirms your hypothesis or refutes it. See no other way at the moment. If this meets with your approval please transmit a 'go-ahead' via Erwin.

'JUSTAS'

'He's about to walk into the noose,' commented the centre chief when Stirlitz's coded message reached him in Moscow. 'If he goes straight to Himmler, that'll be the end right away and nothing can save him. Even if we were to assume that Himmler will decide to play cat and mouse with him. That is hardly likely though. Stirlitz isn't the kind of person the Reichsführer goes in for when it comes to that kind of thing. Tomorrow morning a message must be sent out forbidding him categorically to do this.'

Isaev could not know what Centre already knew, because the information that had been collected over the last few months had given them the key to the human enigma with the name of Himmler.

He woke up suddenly, as if someone had given his shoulder a shake. He sat up in bed and gave a quick look round the room. It was very quiet and the luminous hands of the small alarm clock showed five o'clock.

'It's early,' thought Himmler to himself, 'I must get some more sleep, at least an hour.'

He yawned, flopped back on to his pillows and turned over to face the wall. The noises of the wood could be heard through the open fan-light. It had been snowing all night and Himmler could see in his mind's eye what a beautiful picture the quiet empty wood must make.

Himmler smiled as he thought back to the early days when he had been living with his wife and little daughter in an unheated room in Nuremberg and there had never been enough to eat. Good God, how long ago that all seemed now and and yet, at the same time, only the other day. It was a mere eighteen years ago. In those days he had been secretary to Gregor Strasser, the

47

Führer's 'brother'. He had to go all over Germany, sleeping in stations, living on bread and coffee, organising liaison between the various party organisations. Back in 1926 Strasser's plan to set up SS security detachments was a fruit of the incipient struggle against Röhm, the leader of the SA. At that time Himmler seriously believed that the creation of the SS was essential to protect the party leaders from the Reds. He believed that the Reds' main objective was to annihilate Adolf Hitler, the one and only friend of toiling Germans. He put an enormous portrait of Hitler over his desk. Later, when Hitler came to see Strasser and noticed the skinny freckled young man sitting under the enormous portrait of himself he inquired: 'Is it wise to raise up one of the party leaders so high above other National Socialists?'

To that Himmler replied: 'If you were just another leader I would not be in the party. I belong to the party that has not just a leader but a guiding star!'

After the 1933 triumph the Führer appointed Himmler chief of München's police force. Himmler was then visited by Gregor Strasser, the man who had originally admitted him to the party, who was the party's main theoretician and ideologist and had been the first to put forward the plan to set up SS detachments. By that time Strasser was already in opposition to Hitler, declaring outright to party veterans that Hitler had sold himself to the industrial magnates.

Himmler paid close attention to all that went on at the top of the ladder. He observed how victory had gone to people's heads and to a certain extent pushed practical work into the background. He felt, and not without good reason, that the party leaders in Berlin were spending all their time making speeches at rallies and frittering their nights away at diplomatic receptions, in short, reaping the sweet fruits of victory. Himmler considered all that was premature and he, for his part, managed to organise a model concentration camp in Dachau in a mere month.

'It is a fine school for fostering genuine German civic consciousness among those eight million who voted for the Communists. It would be ridiculous to put all eight million of them in concentration camps; first of all an atmosphere of terror must be created in one camp and then broken men must gradually be released from it. These former prisoners will be the best possible promoters of national socialism. They will instil into their friends and children devout obedience to our regime.'

At that stage Göring sent one of his personal representatives to visit Himmler. After spending a number of hours at the Dachau camp, he inquired: 'Don't you think this concentration camp will be seriously censured in Europe and America—at least in view of the fact that this step is unconstitutional?'

'Why do you consider the arrest of the enemies of the regime unconstitutional?'

'Because the majority of people you have arrested have not even seen the inside of a court-room. There has been no indictment, not even a hint of legality.'

Himmler promised to give the problem thought. After Göring's man left, Himmler wrote a private letter to Hitler containing a magnificent justification of the need for these arrests and incarceration in concentration camps without trial or inquest. He pointed out to the Führer: 'This is merely a humane means of protecting enemies of national socialism from the people's wrath. If we do not put the nation's enemies into concentration camps we shall not be able to answer for their lives: the people would take justice into their own hands.'

A month later, without being summoned to Berlin, he was appointed chief of the political police in Mecklenburg and Lübeck; after another month had passed, on December 20th, he was made chief of the political police in Baden, in Hessen on December 21st, in Bremen on December 24th, in Saxony and Thuringia on December 25th and in Hamburg on December 27th. In the course of a single week he had been put in charge of the police throughout Germany with the exception of the Prussian section which was still under Göring.

On June 20, 1934, Hitler summoned Himmler to come and discuss the forthcoming anti-Röhm campaign. Himmler had been expecting the summons. Although he was not yet aware of the form the Führer's action would take, he realised some kind of action was inevitable, since this was obvious from thousands of pages of agents' reports and recorded telephone conversations that he had been going through daily.

Himmler understood that Hitler's action against Röhm was merely a pretext for annihilating all those who had been with Hitler in the early days. For the veterans he had campaigned with in the early days, Hitler was just a man like any other, a brother in the party, whereas now the time had come for Adolf Hitler to become the guiding light and idol of the German people. The veterans in the party had become a millstone round his neck.

Himmler had grasped all this as he listened to the thunderous invective Hitler had been hurling at the utterly insignificant group of the veteran Nazis who had come under the influence of enemy propaganda. Hitler could not tell the whole truth to anyone, even his closest friends. Himmler had grasped that as well, and this is what led him to help the Führer by placing before him dossiers on four thousand veterans, virtually all those with whom Hitler had started out to build the National Socialist Party. This proved a subtle piece of foresight, for Hitler did not forget the service: no help is valued more than that which enables a villain to justify his own villainy.

But Himmler went further still: realising what the Führer was about to embark on he decided to make himself so indispensable to his leader that he might not merely rule out the possibility of being a victim of any future purge, but ensure that all subsequent purges should only take place under his supervision.

'I'm just another veteran like Strasser,' thought Himmler, 'but I shall make myself a permanent veteran if I can prove to the nation that Strasser was not a veteran but a careerist and bitter oppositionist.'

When Hitler invited Himmler to Göring's country house in Schorfheide, Himmler staged a special incident for the occasion. An agent dressed in the uniform of Röhm's SA was planted on the route along which the Führer was to pass and instructed to shoot at the Führer's open car. At the vital moment Himmler shielded his revered leader with his own body, crying out: '*Mein Führer*, how happy I am to be able to give my blood to save your life!'

That had been the first time anyone in the party had said '*Mein Führer*'. It was Himmler that coined the words which lent Hitler the aura of a God.

'From this moment you are my blood brother, Heinrich,' said Hitler, and those words had been audible to the people standing around at the time.

After Himmler had pulled off the operation designed to annihilate Röhm and after his teacher Strasser and four thousand other veteran Nazis had been shot, the pen-pushers immediately created a myth to the effect that it had been Himmler and none other who had stood at Hitler's side ever since the beginning of the movement.

After saying 'a' it was imperative to start seriously thinking about 'b'. Heydrich came up with an idea: the moment was ripe to set up SS divisions which would be the main prop of the state machine. Göring had the Luftwaffe, the General Staff had the army, while all Himmler had at that stage were detectives, intelligence agents and provocateurs. It was imperative that there should be military formations as well. The 'Germania' SS division in Hamburg and the 'Deutschland' division in Munich were to provide just such formations.

On October 7, 1935, the Führer sent Himmler the following telegram on his birthday: 'Dear Comrade Himmler. On the occasion of your birthday I send you my best wishes for your future work in safeguarding national socialism, Adolf Hitler.'

In 1936 after Himmler, prompted by Heydrich, had proposed to Hitler that Goebbels's propaganda machine should explain to the world that the occupation of the Saar Territory was in no way a challenge to Paris and London but merely an unavoidable measure in connection with preparations for armed opposition to Moscow, he was first admitted to the Führer's 'Round Table' meetings which were held in the evenings and attended only by Hitler's closest friends.

While exchanging friendly handshakes with Göring, Hess and Goebbels, Himmler never stopped for a moment compiling dossiers on his fellow fighters for the Nazi cause.

Stirlitz was driving slowly now, because contacting Centre had completely exhausted him—his nerves had been stretched to breaking point, and now extreme physical tiredness had come over him like a dead weight.

His route lay through a wood: by this time the wind had died down and the sky was clear and full of stars.

'Moscow is obviously right to consider the possibility of such negotiations, I suppose,' Stirlitz thought to himself as he weighed up the situation. 'Even if they have no concrete clues, this is possible in so far as there are ample grounds for this. In Moscow they know about the in-fighting that's going on here in the Chancellery round the Führer. All the squabbling used to be for a distinct purpose—to get on closer terms with the Führer. Now it's possible that the reverse process is getting under way. All of them: Göring, Bormann, Himmler and Ribbentrop are part and parcel of the Reich, the SS and the party. They have a vested interest in the Reich's survival. For each one of them—if anyone could achieve it—a separate peace would mean the chance to save his own skin. They give no thought to their unfortunate people and its sufferings: nor are they concerned about German statehood. Each one of them is thinking about himself, himself as an individual, while not pondering for a moment on the fate of Germany and the Germans. In this particular situation fifty million Germans are merely cards to be used in the game to save their own skins. While these men still have control of the army, the police and the SS, they could steer the Reich whichever way they choose, provided they were to receive a guarantee of personal immunity in return . . .'

A blinding beam of light suddenly cut across Stirlitz's line of vision. He blinked and automatically braked. Two motorcycles came out of the bushes, blocking the road, and one of the riders pointed a sub-machine gun at Stirlitz's car.

Himmler rose from his armchair and moved over to the window: the wood under its blanket of snow made a breath-taking sight. Silver branches glistened in the moonlight and white silence reigned in that wintry world, while bright, low stars sparkled in the violet canopy of the sky.

All of a sudden Himmler remembered how—contrary even to his own expectations—he had succeeded in carrying out an operation directed against the Führer's closest associate, Hess. Admittedly, for a moment Himmler himself had been on the

52

brink of disaster, for when all was said and done Hitler was a man of most unpredictable decisions. He thought back to the occasion when he had received from one of his men a piece of film showing Hess in the lavatory masturbating. He had taken it straight to Hitler and given him a run-through.

The Führer had been beside himself. Although it had been late at night, he had summoned Göring and Goebbels to come round and given instructions for Hess to be called to the waiting-room. Göring arrived first, looking extremely pale. Himmler knew why the Reichsmarschall was so scared: he was in the middle of a wild affair with a Viennese ballerina (Himmler had noticed that the Reichsmarschall had always been attracted by skinny ballerinas: he had seen eight reels of film immortalising Göring's primrose path and each of his infatuations was thinner than the one before). Hitler turned to his friends and invited them to take a look at 'that vermin Hess'. Göring burst into loud guffaws but Hitler cut him short, exclaiming: 'You must show compassion for other people!' He then called Hess into his study, ran up to him and shouted: 'You filthy, stinking scoundrel! You have sunk to masturbating!'

Himmler, Göring and Goebbels all realised that they were witnessing the crumbling of a giant—the party's No. 2 man.

'Yes,' answered Hess in a calm voice which took all those present aback. 'Yes, *mein Führer*! I shall not deny it! Why do I do this? Why do I not sleep with actresses?' Although Hess did not look over in Goebbels's direction, the latter cringed uneasily in his chair. 'Why do I not skip off to Vienna for the night to enjoy the ballet?! It is because I live for one thing and one thing only, for the party! And the party and you, *mein Führer*, are one and the same for me! I have no time for a private life! So I live alone!'

Hitler stopped in his tracks, walked up to Hess again, gave him an awkward hug and a pat on the head.

Hess had won the battle and Himmler held his breath, for he knew quite well that Hess was a past master of revenge. When Hess had left, Hitler said: 'Himmler, select a wife for him. I understand that splendid man so devoted to the movement. Bring me photographs of possible candidates and I'll decide on one: he'll accept my recommendation.'

Himmler realised that the all-important moment that could decide everything was at hand. After waiting for Göring and Goebbels to leave for home, he said: '*Mein Führer*, you have rescued a loyal soldier of national socialism for the movement. We all admire Hess's selfless devotion. No one else could have decided his fate so wisely. So allow me now, without delay, to lay before you some other material so that you shall be able to help the other soldiers of your cause just as you have helped Hess.'

With that he brought out a dossier on Ley, head of the German Labour Front. He was an alcoholic and his drunken brawls were a secret to nobody but Hitler. Himmler also brought out a dossier on the 'Babelsberg Bull' whose liaison with women of blood that was far from pure used to shock all true National Socialists. Material compromising Bormann was also put out on Hitler's table that night: Himmler had good reason for suspecting him of a homosexual relationship with Hess.

'No, no,' commented Hitler in Bormann's defence, 'he has nine children. Homosexuals are not able to have children. That's pure gossip.'

Himmler did not try to convince Hitler of the contrary but he took note of the intense interest with which the Führer leafed through the papers in front of him, reading the reports several times. Himmler realised that he finally had the upper hand.

Subsequent events were to prove him right: Hitler gave instructions for the tenth anniversary of Himmler's appointment as Chief of the SS to be celebrated throughout Germany like any red-letter day. From then on all Gauleiters—provincial party leaders—realised that the only person, apart from Hitler, enjoying absolute power was none other than Heinrich Himmler. This meant that all the provincial and local party bodies started sending their main reports to Himmler's departments rather than to Hess at party HQ. The most important material that was sent in to Himmler from his groups of special agents did not pass through anyone else's hands but went straight into his bullet-proof archives: this material consisted of compromising information on the party leaders. In 1942 Himmler first began collecting compromising material on the Führer himself: this was after a certain conversation Himmler had had with Schellenberg, his deputy from the political intelligence department. Schellenberg had flown out to visit the Reichsführer at his HQ outside Zhitomir in the Ukraine early one August morning in 1942 when the victorious advance on the Eastern Front was in progress and North Africa was reeling under the impact of Rommel's victories. Yet after a detailed report of recent successes Schellenberg remarked to Himmler: 'Now, Reichsführer, there is just one more thing to discuss, an idea.'

Himmler looked at him uneasily: 'About someone in particular? Has there been any trouble?'

'No, nothing like that. It's just that I keep thinking of Bismarck's warning: never embark on anything unless you have some alternative up your sleeve. May I ask, Reichsführer, up which sleeve you keep an alternative to this war?'

Himmler turned on the wireless—to make quite sure that no one, God forbid, should record their conversation—and replied: 'I'm giving you five weeks' leave. Your nerves are obviously in a bad way. You are not well, Schellenberg. D'you understand? Yes, and what's more—who has entitled you to talk like that to me?'

'We are so powerful at the moment,' Schellenberg went on, 'that we could dictate our peace terms. We are at the summit of our glory and Bismarck always sought peace when he was at the summit of *his* glory.'

After that—Himmler could remember even now the minutest details of that encounter—he had lain down on the divan and started to prod his stomach (he suffered from low acidity and was very much afraid of cancer). Then he remarked: 'As long as the Führer keeps turning to that idiot Ribbentrop for advice on foreign policy, peace is out of the question.'

'Ribbentrop and Göring are at loggerheads—we could help Göring and topple Ribbentrop. He could be made Gauleiter not merely of the Burgundian vineyards, but of Brabant and its cognac as well. Our drunk would be willing to accept such a transfer.'

Himmler reached over to a small table on which there was a Brockhaus atlas and, as he leafed through it, he started tapping

55

the pages with his finger: 'How d'you see all this in practical terms? What's to be done with Belgium? Holland? Or the Ukraine?'

'Each part of the problem must be approached separately,' replied Schellenberg. 'Russia is out of the game, which means that the problem of the Ukraine no longer exists. Belgium and Holland are subjects for discussion with the British and Americans. All that worries me is America and Bormann.'

Himmler responded with a barely perceptible smile. 'All well and good,' he said, 'And what about France?'

'We must make an alliance with her. Her colonies would give us real power.'

'Does that mean you want to sound out the Allies through Fritzchen?' asked Himmler in a question that was more like a recommendation. 'On your head be it, do not involve me in this game.'

Schellenberg then began to act. He did not hurry when it came to contacting Dulles's men in Berne. Nor did he use Fritzchen, in other words von Papen. First of all Ribbentrop had to be got out of the way. Schellenberg found someone in his department who was prepared to challenge Ribbentrop in public, namely State Secretary Luther. Spurred on by preliminary conversations with Schellenberg, Luther went up to Himmler at one of the government receptions and, in full view of the assembled company, started engaging him in a friendly conversation and then, on returning home, wrote three reports—to Bormann, Himmler and Göring—all denouncing Ribbentrop. However, since Ribbentrop was an Obergruppen-führer in the SS, Himmler did not make the most of the opportunity to open an inquest against him: that would have been a violation of party etiquette. There would have to be a party trial first and only then an SS trial before Ribbentrop could finally be relieved of his post.

Himmler hesitated to deal the final blow and meanwhile the police machine did its work: the Gestapo chief arrested Luther on the strength of documents supplied by Ribbentrop's agents. The man who had sought to compromise Ribbentrop was himself now compromised and, what was more, Müller, after making the most of Luther, sent a report to Bormann informing him that someone was planning to engage in separate negotiations with the West. Bormann, in his turn, passed the information on to the Führer, who gave instructions for a decree to be issued to the effect that negotiations with any enemy power constituted treachery for which the punishment was death.

It was then that Himmler realised for the first time that he had left things too late and lost out to Ribbentrop, and he lamented in a tired voice to Schellenberg: 'I'm fed up with fighting *for* the Führer. I shall start fighting against him, if that's what he wants.'

'Your papers,' said one of the motor-cyclists.

Stirlitz held out his pass and asked: 'What's up?'

The motor-cyclist checked his pass, saluted and replied: 'There was an alarm and we came out to look for wireless operators.'

'Well, and how goes the search?' Stirlitz asked, putting his pass back into his pocket. 'Found anything?'

'Your car has been the first.'

'D'you want to look in the boot?' offered Stirlitz with a smile.

The motor-cyclists started to laugh and warned: 'Mind how you go, Standartenführer, there are two bomb craters a bit further on.'

'Thank you,' Stirlitz said. 'I always keep a good lookout.'

He realised that this check was a result of Erwin's recent transmission and that a road-block to the south and east had been put up. He saw it as a rather naïve, although basically correct move, if they had been up against a dilettante with little experience of Germany.

Stirlitz skirted the craters, which were quite fresh, and sensed a faint smell of burning. 'To go back to where I left off,' he thought to himself. 'So, the trump card that I'll make sure of for myself is personal vested interest in a peace on the part of Ribbentrop, Göring, Bormann or Feldmarschall von Kluge; that's the main thing that's going to help me understand what Centre is getting worried about. But who is going to negotiate with them? Roosevelt? Of course not! What about British public

57

opinion? Never in your life! However, on the other hand, a German capitulation to the West alone could be advantageous for monopoly capital there, which is also represented by individuals. That means once I've worked out what's what in top circles in the Reich it would be as well to make a close study of what Speer's up to: the man running Germany's industry is not merely a talented engineer but more than likely a far-sighted politician as well. It is time I really got my teeth into that character who maintains close contacts with the leading lights of the Western business world.'

Stirlitz did not put his car away in the garage, for the frost that night was only a light one.

'I'm getting up early tomorrow morning anyway,' he decided, 'and the water in the radiator won't have time to freeze. Tomorrow is going to be some day! An officer of the SD trying to offer his services to Himmler. Yet, I suppose it's all part of the paradox of the imminent showdown. In the past I took the oath of allegiance to Hitler, but nowadays that is not enough—I must be loyal to the SS Reichsführer, who bears the name of Himmler.'

It was actually after 1942, when Heydrich was murdered in Prague, that Schellenberg became Himmler's most trusted associate. Himmler had no particular liking for Kaltenbrunner, Heydrich's successor, on account of his limited intelligence and blunt ways. He drank a great deal, smoked anything up to a hundred cigarettes a day and—what really annoyed Himmler— spoke with a frightful Austrian accent. Himmler was always hard put to it to understand what Kaltenbrunner was saying, not only because of the accent, but also because of the false teeth which made the last reason worse than the first.

'Go and see a dentist,' he once advised Kaltenbrunner, 'I can't understand a word you say, especially when you speak quickly.'

Kaltenbrunner took that very badly—Himmler noticed this and thought to himself: 'It's a good thing that he's so dim-witted —there'll always be someone to use as a buffer, but nevertheless I must give him a wide berth. Stupidity is catching.'

Bormann . . . Oh, how Himmler hated him . . .

It was Bormann who had said to the Führer: 'We have had ample opportunity to see that it is highly unreliable to pin our hopes on the army. It is extremely fortunate for the nation that we have the SS divisions—the hope of the party and national socialism. Only the leader of the SS, my friend Himmler, could take upon himself the command of the Eastern Front, the Army Group Vistula. Only under his leadership will the SS and the armies subordinate to it be able to throw back the Russians and rout them.'

Himmler turned up at the Führer's headquarters the next day still unaware of the appointment that had already been decided. That obviously accounted for the readiness with which Hitler endorsed the decree Himmler brought him, stating that all Gauleiters in Germany, who had formerly been responsible to Bormann, were now also to be responsible to him, the SS Reichsführer. Himmler had been preparing a crushing blow for Bormann. He was even somewhat surprised at the speady way in which the Führer endorsed the decree. However, a minute later everything was all too clear.

'I congratulate you, Himmler. You are appointed Commander-in-Chief of the Army Group Vistula. You are the only man who can rout the Bolshevik hordes. You and no one else can break Stalin and dictate my peace terms to him!'

That was the end. Himmler grasped at once what had happened. He had lost everything that could be lost. It was January 1945, and there was no possible hope of victory. To hell with all sentimental illusions! There was only one thing left to stake his chances on—an immediate peace with the West and then joint action against the Bolshevik hordes.

Himmler thanked the Führer for such a high honour and then went home. Later he went to see Göring but nothing came out of their talk.

. . . And now he had woken up at five o'clock in the morning, could not go to sleep again and was lying awake listening to the quiet of the pinewoods, afraid to telephone his daughter, because Bormann might find out about it, or to telephone his sons and their mother, whom he loved, because he was afraid of the consequences, for the Führer would not forgive what he used to refer to as 'moral laxity'. Damned syphilitic . . . a fine example of moral rectitude he was. Himmler fixed the telephone with a look of hate: the machine which he had spent eighteen years perfecting was now starting to work against him.

'This is it,' he said to himself. 'This is it. If I don't start fighting for myself now, at once, I'm done for.' In the light of his agents' reports Himmler had reason to believe that the C-in-C of the troops in Italy, Feldmarschall Kesselring, would not object to negotiating with the West. This was something known only to Schellenberg and Himmler himself. Two agents who had reported this had since been removed by a carefully arranged air crash when they were on their way back to Kesselring. A monopoly of secrets was the key to success. Italy bordered on Switzerland, and in Switzerland there was Allen Dulles, the head of the American intelligence service in Europe. That was already the real thing. That was a direct link with people that counted, especially as Kesselring's friend, the SS leader in Italy, Karl Wolff, Obergruppenführer and Colonel-General in the SS, was someone whose loyalty Himmler could rely on.

Himmler eventually picked up the telephone and issued the following instructions: 'Please summon Obergruppenführer Karl Wolff round to my house immediately.'

He had faith in SS veteran Wolff. He was the man to have embark on serious negotiations with the West in Himmler's name . . .

4

Stirlitz did not contemplate even trying on any intrigue in connection with Pastor Schlag when he was brought along to him for the first interrogation: he simply carried out Schellenberg's orders. After talking to him for three days he started to take an interest in the old man who was behaving with such striking dignity and almost childish naïveté. Stirlitz realised that if the pastor were to fall into the clutches of Müller's men, he would quickly be turned into something little better than an animal.

Stirlitz—whenever possible—tried to help people who had been arrested on insufficiently reliable evidence and in connection with insignificant matters. He, naturally, made sure that he did not endanger his chances of success in his main objectives, but he was not the kind of man who could remain indifferent to the human lives that passed through his hands. He thought up a special method for rescuing them: he used to 'recruit' such detainees, who had committed nothing but negligible offences, and secure their release either immediately or after only a short period in a concentration camp. After their release such people would be sent to work in whatever establishment happened to be important in connection with Schellenberg's intelligence purposes and, of course, the intelligence network which Stirlitz represented. He would ask his 'wards' to collect material on prominent members of the party calculated to compromise zealous Hitlerites, material relating to their profiteering, their rash outbursts and moral misdemeanours. This meant that Stirlitz was able to kill three birds with one stone: save people who in varying degrees opposed Nazism, obtain secret information from his agents from the places where they were sent to work and, finally, use their material to bring down loyal servants of the Nazi order.

After his conversations with the pastor and after studying his dossier, Stirlitz started trying to find out in what way the pastor might be useful to him in his future work. Once he was sure that the pastor not only condemned Nazism but was also prepared to help the underground movement—this he had realised from listening to the recording of the conversation between the pastor and the *agent provocateur* Klaus—Stirlitz had decided to set aside for Schlag a part in the work that lay ahead, although he had not decided how he could make the best use of his services.

Stirlitz never tried to guess how events would develop in future, although he always had before him a clear general outline in any forthcoming operation. He used to smile over detective stories in which far-sighted heroes knew from the very beginning how they would expose and catch the criminal. He often recalled an episode that he had read about in a train on his way across Europe to Ankara—an incident that had imprinted itself on his mind. Some long-forgotten literary historian had recorded how Pushkin, on being asked what was going to happen to the heroine of *Eugene Onegin* at the time when the work was coming out in instalments, had replied in an irritated tone: 'Ask Tatyana, I don't know.' Stirlitz had had occasion to converse with a good number of mathematicians and physicists, particularly after the Gestapo had arrested the atomic physicist Runge and he had been interested to learn to what extent research scientists 'planned' their discoveries in advance. 'It's impossible,' they used to answer. 'We merely determine the direction of our research and the rest is determined in the process of experimentation.'

The same applied to intelligence work. If an operation was thought out in too much detail in advance, failure was almost inevitable in so far as the collapse of even a single link in the predetermined chain could disrupt a whole mission. Concentration on the key objective and efforts to forestall various alternative developments, particularly when a man had to work alone, was the surest way of achieving success. At least that was Stirlitz's opinion.

'The pastor,' he said to himself, 'I must see about the pastor. I've let Schellenberg know that nothing came of the attempt to establish that the pastor had been in contact with ex-Chancellor Brüning, and he seems to have lost interest in the old man. My interest in him, on the other hand, is increasing in view of the latest instructions from Centre.'

In general Stirlitz's reasoning was right on the mark, with the exception of one particular point: Schellenberg had not forgotten the pastor. On the contrary, it was only now that he had started to take a real interest in him.

Müller had summoned Obersturmbannführer Eismann to his office very early in the morning: he had had a sleep after Kaltenbrunner's cognac and felt rested. 'That cognac really is something rather special,' he reflected, rubbing the back of his head with the thumb and index finger of his right hand. 'Ours gives you a splitting headache but this stuff really helps you along.'

Eismann looked at Müller out of blood-shot eyes and smiled his disarming childlike smile: 'I've got a splitting head,' he said, 'I dream of having seven hours' sleep at a stretch, that's all I want. I never thought that being robbed of one's sleep was the most terrible of all tortures.'

'Listen,' Müller started up, 'there's some wild-goose chase afoot. Today the boss called me to his office. They've all got their heads in the clouds, these bosses of ours . . . They have plenty of time for day-dreaming, because they have nothing concrete to get down to, and issuing directives is something even a chimpanzee at the circus can do. You see, he's got it in for Stirlitz now.'

'For whom?'

'Yes, yes, for Stirlitz, the only man working under Schellenberg whom I liked. He's no flunkey, he's calm and goes about his work without getting hysterical or overzealous. I haven't really got much faith in those people who are always hovering round the powers-that-be and holding forth at rallies for no apparent reason. Those are just mediocrities and idle chatterers . . . but not so Stirlitz, he is a silent type. I like silent types . . . If a friend is sparing with his words then he's a real friend. When it comes to enemies, well, silent enemies are real enemies, the kind I respect. They're the ones you can learn something from.'

'I have known Stirlitz for eight years,' said Eismann, 'I was with him at Smolensk and watched him during an air raid: he's a man of iron courage.'

Müller frowned: 'What's made you start indulging in heroic

63

phrases? Is it because you're tired? Leave epithets like that to the big wigs in the party. We detectives must think in nouns and verbs: "he met", "she said", "he delivered" . . . So, you don't think . . .'

'No,' replied Eismann, 'I cannot believe that Stirlitz is a dishonest man.'

'Nor can I.'

'We'll probably have to try and tactfully convince Kaltenbrunner of that.'

'Why?' asked Müller after a pause. 'And what if he wants Stirlitz to appear dishonest? Why dissuade him? After all, Stirlitz does not belong to our outfit. He's from the sixth department. Let it be Schellenberg's headache . . .'

'Schellenberg will want proof . . . And you know that he will have the support of the Reichsführer in this matter.'

'You think so?'

'I'm sure of it.'

'But why?'

'It's difficult for me to prove . . . Yet I am convinced of it, Obergruppenführer.'

Again Müller started to rub the back of his head with the thumb and index finger of the right hand.

'Well and what's to be done in that case?'

Eismann shrugged his shoulders and said: 'I personally consider that we should be completely honest with ourselves, that will help us determine the course of subsequent steps and actions.'

'Steps and actions are one and the same thing,' remarked Müller. 'How I envy the people who merely have to carry out orders and nothing else. How I long merely to have to carry out orders! "Be honest!" One might believe that all I think about is how to be dishonest. Go ahead, I shall give you the opportunity to be absolutely honest: take this,' Müller pushed over to Eismann a number of files containing type-written material, 'and draw your conclusions, genuinely honest ones. I shall make use of them when I report to the boss on the results of our inspection.'

'Why is it me who is called on to do this, Obergruppenführer?' asked Eismann.

Müller started to laugh: 'But where is your honesty, my friend? It's always easy to advise others to be honest. Yet when it comes to the point every individual worries about how to make his dishonesty look like honesty, how to justify himself and his actions. I am right, aren't I?'

'I am ready to write the report.'

'What kind?'

'I shall write in the report that I have known Stirlitz for many years and can vouch for him in all respects.'

Müller paused in silence, fidgeted a moment in his chair and then handed Eismann a sheet of paper.

'Write away,' he said. 'Carry on, do.'

Eismann brought out a pen, chewed over his first sentence and then wrote in his immaculate hand: 'To department head SS Obergruppenführer Müller. In view of the fact that I consider SS Standartenführer von Stirlitz a true Aryan, loyal to the ideals of the Führer and the NSDAP, I ask you to release me from participation in the inspection of his work.

SS Obersturmbannführer Eismann.'

Müller blotted what Eismann had written, read it through twice and said in a quiet voice: 'Well, good for you . . . I have always respected you and had complete trust in you. Now I have had the opportunity to witness a further example of your upright behaviour, Eismann.'

'Thank you, Obergruppenführer.'

'There is nothing to thank me for. It's for me to thank you. That will be all for now. Here are three files: use this material to draw up a favourable report on Stirlitz's work. There's no need for me to prompt you as to how that is done: the art of the intelligence agent, the subtle investigator, the courage of a true National Socialist . . . How much time will you need for that?'

Eismann leafed through the files and replied: 'To have everything neatly drawn up and substantiated with documentary evidence I would ask you for a week.'

'Five days and that's stretching it.'

'Very good.'

'And try to present Stirlitz's work on that pastor in a glowing impressive light.' Müller prodded one of the files with his finger.

'Kaltenbrunner maintains that someone is trying with the help of priests to make contact with the West, the Vatican and so forth . . .'

'Very good.'

'Well, good luck to you. Now go and get some sleep. I can't give you seven hours but five—that you can have. Sweet dreams.'

When Eismann had left, Müller put his letter away in a separate file and sat pondering at his desk for some time. Then he summoned another member of his staff, Obersturmbann-führer Holthoff.

'Listen,' he said without even asking the man to sit down— Holthoff was one of the younger men of his staff—'I am entrusting you with a highly important top-secret mission.'

'Yes, Obergruppenführer.'

'This chap'll move heaven and earth,' thought Müller to himself, 'he's champing at the bit already. He still likes our games, he's still wallowing in them. He'll come up with God knows what . . . So much the better . . . we'll have something to haggle over with Schellenberg.'

'It's like this,' Müller went on. 'You are to go through these files which cover the work carried out by Standartenführer Stirlitz over the past year. They deal with the weapons of retalia-tion, that is atomic weapons, and the physicist Runge. In general, it all looks somewhat fishy but try go through it with a fine-tooth comb. Come and see me if any questions crop up.'

When Holthoff turned to leave Müller's study feeling rather deflated but doing his best not to show it, his superior stopped him and added: 'Have a look through some of the earlier files on him while he was at the front and see if Stirlitz's and Eismann's paths have crossed at any time in the past.'

The Gestapo, the Kanaris service and Vichy counter-intelligence knew that in those hectic days of summer 1942 some mysterious American was to cross through France. French counter-intelligence, the Gestapo and Admiral Kanaris's department started hunting him down. Secret agents were sent to keep watch at railway stations and glass-walled airport buildings and started scrutinising anyone who might look like an American.

However they were unable to catch him. He managed to disappear in restaurants and appear out of the blue in aeroplanes. He was clever, cool-headed, calm and brave and succeeded in outwitting both the German security service and Vichy counter-intelligence: miraculously he got as far as neutral Switzerland by the end of 1942.

He was tall and his eyes hidden behind the gleaming lenses of a pince-nez looked out at the world indulgently with a gaze that was gentle and stern at the same time. He was never without a straight English pipe in his mouth; he was sparing with his words and generous with his smiles. He used to win over everyone he talked to, being an amiable and attentive listener and a lively wit and always willing to admit straight away when he was wrong and make no bones about it.

If the staff of Himmler's, Kanaris's and Petain's networks had known whom they were up against they would probably have multiplied their efforts tenfold to get their hands on the American while he was 'accessible' in that part of France which the German army had invaded in November 1942 thus putting an end to the 'sovereignty' of the southern zone with its capital in Vichy. The man who was outwitting them was none other than Allen Dulles, then working for the Strategic Services Office, who had been sent to Berne by General Donovan.

In Switzerland he soon came to be referred to as President Roosevelt's personal representative. Dulles published a denial of these rumours in the press, worded in a strange mystifying way, and Dulles well realised that the double 'advertisement' resulting from the rumours and their denial would be extremely useful in the given situation. He was soon proved right: in the early months of his stay in Berne all sorts of people from many countries started flocking to see him—bankers, sportsmen, diplomats, philologists, princes of the blood royal, actors, in a word, all the types from which intelligence networks recruit their agents.

Unfortunately, there is little information in *Who's Who* to shed light on the past of Allen Dulles. When Himmler's department succeeded in penetrating Dulles's house in Berne (the charming and efficient cook who used to work for Allen Dulles was on the staff of the sixth department of the Reich security service) Schellenberg, Himmler, Müller from the Gestapo and, consequently, Kaltenbrunner learnt much of interest and importance. The cook informed them that Allen Dulles's 'bible' and favourite reading matter was a book entitled *The Art of War* by Sun-tzu. In this book the Chinese theoretician expounded the fundamental principles of spying, principles that were adhered to in China in the fourth century B.C.

Sun-tzu divided agents into five different categories: indigenous, internal, double, expendable and live. Indigenous and internal agents (Dulles made a note of all this on small slips of paper which were later to find their way to Schellenberg's department) correspond, according to Dulles, to what we now call local agents. Double agents are enemy spies who have been taken prisoner and then recruited for the other side and sent back home but in the capacity of agents of the country where they were taken prisoner.

Allen Dulles underlined in red pencil the term 'expendable agent'. The subtlety of the Chinese term appealed to his imagination. Sun-tzu applied the term to those agents through whom false information was passed to the enemy. He called them expendable because the enemy, in all probability, would have them killed, once it came to light that the information they had supplied was false.

The agents termed 'live' by Sun-tzu were known in the current period as infiltration agents. They infiltrate enemy territory, carry out their work there and then return alive.

Sun-tzu maintained that the intelligence officer worth his salt needed all five types of agent working for him simultaneously. He wrote that the man who had five such agents in his employ possessed a 'divine spider's web', a fishing net consisting of a multitude of fine, invisible, yet extremely strong, threads fastened together by a single cord.

Schellenberg's agent also reported to her superior that during his free time Allen Dulles used to make a detailed study of the practices and methods of the leading espionage organisations in nineteenth-century Europe.

This and a great deal of other information on Allen Dulles piled up in the bullet-proof archives of Himmler's department.

Nevertheless the leaders of the Third Reich were unable to reconstruct a complete and precise biography of this cunning secret agent of the mid-twentieth century.

There had been nothing really out of the ordinary about Dulles's early life. After obtaining his Master's Degree in arts, at the age of twenty-three, he had worked as a missionary in India and China, and in May 1916 he had taken up his first diplomatic post in Vienna. He had later worked in Paris in the delegation headed by Woodrow Wilson. Then he was sent on a special mission to Switzerland and Austria designed to prop up the Austro–Hungarian Empire. It was there, in 1918, that he had engineered his first conspiracy, which might have proved really spectacular if Dulles had carried it through. However, the November Revolution in Germany led by the Communists prevented him from implementing his plans. The future Hapsburg monarchy, which was to have become a *cordon sanitaire*, a mighty armoured shield enabling the West to prevent Bolshevism from spreading through Europe, vanished into thin air.

A year later, in 1919, Dulles was appointed First Secretary at the US Embassy in Germany. It was while working at 7, Wilhelmplatz in Berlin that Dulles came face to face with the people whose main task was to stem the spread of Bolshevism in Europe. It was also there that he had the opportunity to bring together the US chargé d'affaires in Germany, a certain Mr Dressel, and General Hoffmann, who devised the first plan for the German attack on the Kremlin.

From Berlin Allen Dulles was sent to Constantinople for two years where he found himself in the capital of a country bordering directly on Soviet Russia, a country, which held the key to both the Black and Mediterranean Seas and was a stepping-stone on the way to the world's oil stocks.

After that Dulles at last returned to Washington where he was put in charge of the Middle East section of the State Department. At that time the Middle East was one of the most explosive areas of our planet. The Middle East meant oil, the life-blood of war. Industrial magnates in America, whose business was oil, were concerned about the colossal successes of their British rivals in the world market.

It was at that period that Bedford, Chairman of Standard Oil of New Jersey declared that it was 'vital for the United States now to pursue an aggressive policy'.

Dulles was not the man to let opportunities pass him by: he did not spare any effort, and it was under him that the first American victory over Great Britain in the oil market was achieved when in 1927 Rockefeller obtained twenty-five per cent of the shares in the Iraq Petroleum Company. That same year the Gulf Oil Corporation, that formed part of the Mellon Group, secured preferential rights to the oil concession in the Bahrein Islands.

After carrying out the groundwork for these victories Dulles decided to retire. A study of the intelligence service attached to the House of Rothschild brought him to the conclusion that his term in the State Department had been no more than the first step in his real career.

Allen Dulles obtained a post in the legal firm Sullivan and Cromwell, one of the largest of its kind on Wall Street. The firm maintained close links with the Rockefellers and Morgans. It was while working for Sullivan and Cromwell that Dulles carried through a large-scale operation enabling the United States to acquire major oil concessions in the Republic of Colombia.

Dulles's new employers had collaborated with the Panama government at the time of the canal's construction. When Dulles started working for them Sullivan and Cromwell was building up close contacts with Germany, the country into which American industrialists had been pumping enormous quantities of dollars ever since the conclusion of the Treaty of Versailles.

In particular, Allen and his brother John Foster Dulles were paving the way for close contacts with Thyssen's trust IG Farbenindustrie and the Robert Bosch concern. In fact, Allen and John Foster Dulles later became the American agents of those German corporations.

At the very beginning of the war Allen Dulles was on the brink of disaster. Robert Bosch had a branch in the United States known as the American Bosch Corporation. The firm was about to be black-listed, and to avoid this its owners quickly concluded an agreement with the Swedish bankers, Wallenberg Bros., who received nominal control over the American Bosch Corporation on condition that the firm would be restored to its original owners once the war was over.

Wallenberg Bros agreed, but they needed an American contractor to put through all the necessary formalities, and this job was assigned to the Dulles brothers. Allen Dulles succeeded in hoodwinking the American authorities, giving Nazi property a cloak of respectability with the help of the Swedish flag. After that he was not only made a partner in Sullivan and Cromwell but also a director of the Schröder Trust Company and the John Henry Schröder Banking Corporation.

This Schröder managed to be a German citizen in Germany, an American citizen in the United States and a British citizen in Great Britain. In the 1930s this particular concern was headed by Baron Kurt von Schröder. It was at his house in Cologne that Hitler had his meeting with von Papen on January 7, 1933. There he elaborated his plan for the Nazi seizure of power. Kurt von Schröder was later rewarded with the title of SS Gruppen-führer and was also made chairman of the secret organisation 'Freundenkreis' (Circle of Friends). This organisation collected funds for Heinrich Himmler's SS detachments from the industrial magnates of the Ruhr.

The British branch of the Schröder concern financed the Anglo–German Society in London, and was designed to disseminate the Führer's ideas in Great Britain. Little effort is required to imagine the nature of the J. Henry Schröder Banking Corporation's activities in the United States, and the director of that firm was none other than Allen Dulles.

This man with an expert knowledge of contemporary Europe, Germany, Nazism, big business and oil markets was put in charge of the US strategic services in Europe.

When Karl Wolff left Himmler's office, the Reichsführer sat for a long while in silence as if glued to the spot. It was not fear that gripped him, or so it appeared to him at least. It was just that for the first time in his life he found himself a renegade. He was used to renegades, he had even refrained from impeding them,

71

preferring to wait and see who actually came out on top in July 1944, but now he himself had actually committed an act of treason: there was only one punishment for negotiating with the enemy and that was death. He could explain conversations with Göring, if the worst came to the worst, by probing the moods of a man now outside active political life. If it were to come out that he had known about the conspiracy of the previous July . . . but even that he would have been able to refute on the grounds that all the conspirators had been arrested so quickly after the event: 'I had the game under control, I had them all where I wanted them, but Stauffenberg was an extremist and, after all, events have been known to take unexpected turns, and when all's said and done I was in the Bunker next to the Führer—surely that's a good enough alibi.'

But now Karl Wolff had already set off for Switzerland in order to make direct contact with Dulles: a top SS officer was on his way to meet the Allies' top secret agent.

As was his wont, Himmler took off his glasses—on that particular day he was wearing rimless glasses—and started slowly cleaning them with a piece of chamois-leather. He could feel that a change had come over him but did not grasp at first what it was. Then the penny dropped and he smiled to himself: 'I've started acting. The most awful thing of all is numbed bewilderment, it's like a nightmare.'

He sent for Schellenberg. The chief of political intelligence was with him in a matter of seconds, so that it seemed to Himmler he must have been sitting outside in the waiting-room instead of in his own office on the second floor.

'Wolff has flown off to make contact with Dulles,' began Himmler cracking his finger-joints.

'That's sensible . . .'

'It's crazy, Schellenberg, it's crazy, playing with fire.'

'You mean that the plan could end in fiasco?'

'I mean that anything might happen! It's your doing, it's all your work! You put me up to it!'

'If Wolff comes to a sticky end all the material will be handed in to us.'

'It might first land in the lap of that Viennese . . .'

Schellenberg gave Himmler a puzzled look who explained in

72

an irritated voice: 'Kaltenbrunner. And I don't know to whom the material would be sent after that—to Bormann or to me. And you know what Bormann would do as soon as he got hold of material of that kind. And you can imagine how the Führer would react on seeing all that and, what's more, as presented by Bormann.'

'I have thought over that possibility as well.'

Himmler frowned crossly; he was wishing he could get Wolff back, keep him on the spot and forget about the conversation that had taken place, banish it forever from his memory.

'I have thought over that possibility,' repeated Schellenberg. 'In the first place, Wolff is obliged to speak to Dulles not in his own name, still less in yours, but in the name of Feldmarschall Kesselring, to whom he is responsible. After all, as second-in-command in Italy, he is not directly subordinate to you . . .'

Himmler threw a quick glance in Schellenberg's direction. 'Bright chap,' he thought to himself. Feldmarschall Kesselring had in his day been Göring's right-hand man, in charge of the Lufftwaffe. Everyone thought of him as one of Göring's supporters.

'That's reassuring,' said Himmler. 'Did you think of that before or has the idea only just come to you?'

'It occurred to me as soon as I learnt of Wolff's trip,' replied Schellenberg. 'Do you mind if I smoke?'

'Please do,' answered Himmler.

Schellenberg lit up; ever since 1936 he had only smoked Camel cigarettes and would not acknowledge any others.

'I have thought over all possibilities,' he went on, 'even the most unpleasant.'

'That is . . .?' inquired Himmler with a wary note in his voice. He had calmed down by this time and was his usual self: the outlook for the future seemed straightforward now; indeed, what unpleasantness could there possibly be now that everything was falling into place so satisfactorily?

'What if Kesselring or, still worse, his patron Göring managed to come up with alibis?' inquired Schellenberg.

'We can rule out that possibility by taking care of them in advance.'

'Yes, we can,' agreed Schellenberg, 'but then it was with good reason that you kept Kaltenbrunner in the dark with regard to this particular operation of ours. He might *not* rule out that possibility. He and Müller, incidentally,'

'All right, all right,' said Himmler wearily, 'but what do you suggest?'

'I suggest that we should kill two birds with one stone,'

'Things never work out like that in real life,' commented Himmler in a voice that sounded still more tired and lifeless.

'The Führer maintains that the Allies are about to split up, doesn't he? Hence this split is one of the main things we should be working to promote, isn't it? How would Stalin react if he were to learn that separate negotiations were being carried on between SS General Wolff and the Western powers? I would not presume to hazard a guess as to the exact nature of his reaction, yet I do not doubt for one moment that this knowledge would spur him to action of some sort. So this means we can present Wolff's trip as a false lead specially set up for Stalin, to further the Führer's cause! So our line will be that these negotiations are a bluff laid on for Stalin! That is how we shall explain the operation to the Führer if it does not come off!'

Himmler got up from his chair—he did not like armchairs and always used an old upright chair—walked over to the window and took a long look at the ruins of Berlin. In some places the grass was starting to peep through and he could see a few children walking home from school, laughing as they went. Two women were ambling by, pushing prams. As he surveyed the peaceful scene, Himmler felt more at ease and suddenly thought to himself: 'How I'd enjoy a trip to the woods and a night by a camp fire. What a head Walter has on his shoulders, it's incredible . . .'

'I'll think about what you have have been saying,' said Himmler without bothering to turn around. He wanted to claim the victory for himself. Schellenberg would have been only too happy to relinquish it to the Reichsführer—he had always made a habit of relinquishing his victories to Himmler and Heydrich before him. That was what prompted him to go on and say: 'Will you want to decide on the minor details, or shall I go into those myself?'

'You go into them yourself,' replied Himmler, but when Schellenberg was about to open the door to leave, he turned round and inquired: 'Actually this business doesn't involve any minor details. What did you have specifically in mind?'

'In the first place a division operation ... In other words, there must be a decoy, someone from another department, not ours, investigating possibilities of negotiating with the West. Then we shall hand over material about that ... person to the Führer. If need be we can make that look like a feather in the cap of our intelligence service that managed to expose an enemy scheme—that's how Goebbels phrases it, I think ... Secondly, thousands of people will be hot on Wolff's trail in Switzerland and it may well be that among those thousands there will be some of our agents who will send reports on his movements immediately. The question is in whose hands will those reports land? Whose agent will get on to him first? Mine or Müller's? An intelligent person who will size up the situation with a cool head or a blind fanatic of the Kaltenbrunner mould? This is why I want to see to it that there will be five or six pairs of my 'eyes' keeping track of the thousands of pairs working for the Western Allies. Wolff will not be aware of the fact that our people are keeping track of him, for they will be told to pass on their information to me direct. This, on top of everything else, will give us a third alibi. If the operation fails, Wolff will have to go by the board, but the reports sent in by the men keeping track of his actions will still provide us with another alibi.'

'You,' Himmler corrected him, 'They will provide you with another alibi.'

'I've frightened him again,' thought Schellenberg to himself. 'These details are frightening him. He's afraid of plans that involve risks; in fact he's afraid of almost everything. With him I ought just to see that he agrees in principle and then do all the rest on my own.'

'Whom do you want to send down there?' Himmler inquired.

'I have some highly suitable candidates,' replied Schellenberg, 'but those are details that I can work out on my own without taking up your time when you could be seeing to more important things.'

75

The candidates Schellenberg had in mind for the first task in his plan were von Stirlitz and the pastor, whom the Standartenführer had taken under his wing.

5

The next morning, when Erwin was due to receive the reply from Centre, Stirlitz drove slowly along the familiar route to his house. On the back seat of his car was an enormous gramophone. For the sake of cover Erwin was the proprietor of a small gramophone firm, which gave him the opportunity to travel round the country, attending to the needs of his various clients.

The road leading to Erwin's house was chock-a-block with traffic, for the wall of a six-storey house had collapsed during the bombing the previous night, and the road clearance squads and the police were working all out to clear a passage for traffic as quickly as possible.

Stirlitz looked round and saw that behind his Horch there were already at least thirty other cars. A young lad driving a lorry called over to him: 'If they come over now there'll be real chaos and nowhere to take cover, what's more.'

'They won't come over now,' remarked Stirlitz, looking up at the sky. The clouds were low and, judging by their dark grey edges, were heavy with snow.

The policeman in front of him gave an abrupt flourish to wave the traffic on and shouted a gruff: 'Move along there!'

'Nowhere else in the world,' thought Stirlitz to himself, 'do policemen love throwing their weight about and brandishing their truncheons as much as ours do.' He caught himself thinking of the Germans and Germany as his own people and country all of a sudden. 'Yet probably that's as it should be. If I thought of myself as an outsider I would probably have come to grief long ago. It's all a crazy mix-up anyway, for I clearly am attached to this people and this country . . . After all, the Hitlers of this world come and go . . .'

There were no more obstructions, and Stirlitz put his foot hard down on the accelerator. He knew that taking his corners close 'ate away' the tyres and that they were very hard to come by but nevertheless he loved taking really sharp corners that made the tyres scream and the car lurch violently, like a ship in a storm.

In Köpenick where he had to turn off to reach Erwin and Käthe's house he found a police cordon.

'What's up?' Stirlitz inquired.

'The street's a shambles,' answered a pale young policeman, 'a real brute of a block-buster came down.'

Stirlitz felt his forehead break out in a cold sweat. 'No. 9 as well?' he asked.

'Yes, it was blown to smithereens.'

Stirlitz drew in to the pavement, got out of the car and walked down the narrow side-street to the right. The same haggard-looking policeman stopped him again: 'The whole place is out of bounds now, sir.'

Stirlitz brought out his SD pass, at which the policeman raised his hand in a salute and said: 'The sappers think there might be delayed-action bombs around that haven't gone off yet.'

'That means we'll go up together then,' answered Stirlitz in a tired voice and walked up to the ruins of No. 9. He felt a great weight of incredible tiredness come over him and wanted to walk very slowly, but he knew he had to walk with his usual springy step and his face had to retain its perennial hint of a wry smile, although before him he saw nothing but Käthe with her large round belly. 'It'll be a girl,' she had told him. 'When you jut out in front that means it'll be a boy, but I'm bound to have a girl.'

'Was everyone killed?' asked Stirlitz turning to the policeman who was still watching the firemen get on with their work.

'It's hard to say. It happened before it was really light and there were lots of ambulances toing and froing . . .'

'Were any of their things left intact?'

'Not a hope . . . Take a look at that mess . . .'

Stirlitz helped a crying woman carrying a small baby pull a pram away from the pavement that was knee-deep in rubble and then went to his car . . .

'*Mamochka!*' screamed Käthe. '*Gospodi! Mama-a-a-a! Pomogite kto-nibud!*'

She was lying in the labour room. She had been concussed when they had brought her to the maternity home with two head wounds. She had been screaming out pathetic disconnected words, Russian words.

The doctor who had assisted at the birth of her boy, a large lad with a lusty voice, commented to the midwife: 'A Pole and yet what a giant she's produced . . .'

'She's no Pole,' said the midwife.

'What then? A Russian? Or a Czech?'

'Her identity card says she's German,' answered the midwife. 'There was an identity card in her coat pocket saying she was Katherina Kien.'

'Perhaps it was someone else's coat?'

'Perhaps,' agreed the midwife. 'Just look what a strapping baby, he must weigh at least ten pounds. He's gorgeous . . . Will you contact the Gestapo or shall I?'

'You ring them,' replied the doctor, 'only it can wait for a bit . . . We've got a good deal of work to do yet . . .'

'That's that,' thought Stirlitz wearily, feeling in a strange sort of way detached from his immediate surroundings. 'Now I really am all on my own. Absolutely on my own . . .'

He sat for a long time in his office behind a locked door, without answering any of the telephone calls. He counted them automatically: there were nine altogether. Two people rang insistently as if there was something important he had to be told or it was some subordinate or other trying conscientiously to get through. The rest of the calls were short ones, the kind that bosses or friends make.

Then he took a piece of paper out of his desk and wrote the following letter:

TO SS Reichsführer Heinrich Himmler
Top-secret
Private
Dear Reichsführer,
The interests of the nation oblige me to address this letter to you. It has come to my knowledge from sources with close access to journalists from

neutral countries that behind the back of the SD and behind your back certain persons are establishing contact with the enemy, investigating the possibilities of making some kind of deal. I cannot back up this information with watertight documentary evidence but I would ask you to receive me and hear my suggestions in connection with this matter which I see as extremely important and something that brooks no delay. I would also ask your permission to make use of my contacts so as to keep you informed of further details and put before you my view of this hypothesis which unfortunately looks too much like the truth to be disregarded.

Heil Hitler!
SS Standartenführer von Stirlitz

Stirlitz knew to whom he would refer as his source in his conversation with Himmler, for three days before a newsreel cameraman from Portugal, Pueblos Wassermann, had been killed during an air-raid. Stirlitz knew that he had been in close contact with the Swedes which meant that that part of his story no one would be able to fault.

Apart from his masseur, there was probably only one person whom Himmler trusted one hundred per cent and that was Schellenberg. He had been keeping an eye on him ever since the beginning of the 1930s when Schellenberg had been no more than a student. He knew that the handsome youth had been educated at a Jesuit college and from there had gone on to graduate from the university with an arts degree at the age of twenty-three. He also knew that his favourite professor at the university had been a man of Jewish extraction. He knew that Schellenberg had at first poured ridicule on national socialist ideas and had come out with the occasional deprecatory remark with regard to the Führer.

Himmler had under him several thousand staunch, blindly obedient men, who, he knew, would remain loyal to him till their dying day. Yet he needed in addition at least five clever, astute assistants who, despite their scepticism, would serve him devotedly and help him to elaborate precise plans of action to reap the desired results.

That was why Schellenberg accepted Heydrich's offer of a

post in the intelligence service of the Third Reich after several talks with Heydrich himself and a single meeting with Himmler: at that time he had already become disillusioned with the attitudes adopted by German intellectuals who had shut themselves off from the outside world in their lake-side residences in the quiet of the pine woods around Berlin, and were merely shaking their heads sadly over Hitler's villainy and cautiously making fun of his hysterical outbursts.

His first introduction to SS work was Kitty's salon. Nebbe, then in charge of the criminal police, with the help of his card index picked out the most elegant prostitutes of Berlin, Münich and Hamburg for those sophisticated social gatherings. Later, in accordance with Heydrich's instructions, he collected together attractive young wives of diplomats and high-ranking officers, women who were condemned to lives of almost unrelieved solitude at that time, while their husbands spent whole days and nights conferring at meetings, travelling all over the country and abroad. Those grass widows were extremely bored and hungry for entertainment, which they found in abundance at Kitty's salon, a popular rallying-point for diplomats from Asia, America and Europe.

Experts from the SD technical department fixed up double walls in the house and installed hidden cameras and bugging devices. Schellenberg implemented Heydrich's plans, and it was he who ran the place, playing the role of a high-class pimp.

Schellenberg and Heydrich were then able to spend long evenings in a small private cinema watching highly interesting footage of their friends' wives passing the time with foreign diplomats.

Their subsequent recruiting work took two forms: they made compromised diplomats carry out intelligence work for them under Schellenberg's direct supervision, and the wives of high-ranking officers and party and government officials of the Third Reich were entered on the card index kept by Gestapo chief Müller.

Müller, however, was not required to participate in the work in the salon, for his peasant-like appearance and coarse jokes might well have put the guests on their guard. It was then that Müller was first made to feel he depended on a twenty-three-year-old novice. 'He thinks I'll start getting my hands on his green-faced tarts,' Müller said to his assistant. 'A great honour! I wouldn't have taken any of them to bed—not even if they paid me. Back in the our village women like that are called dung-beetles.'

When Frau Heydrich telephoned Schellenberg, while her husband was away on business, to lament how bored she was and he suggested that they go out into the country to a nearby lake, Müller learnt of this at once and decided that the moment had come to catch out the winsome youth. He was not one of the 'old hands' in the Gestapo who regarded Schellenberg as a light-minded person who took out Latin and Spanish books from libraries, dressed up to the nines, made no effort to hide his countless affairs, walked about on foot in Prinz-Albrecht-Strasse, refusing to use an official car—in short, as someone who could not be considered a serious intelligence agent, indulging as he did in idle chatter and drink . . . Müller's slow but shrewd, peasant wit told him that Schellenberg was the first of a new generation of intelligence agents, the new favourite would usher in others like him.

Schellenberg escorted Frau Heydrich to Plönersee. She was the only woman for whom Schellenberg entertained profound respect: with her he could converse about the noble tragedy of ancient Greece and the coarse sensuality of ancient Rome. The two of them wandered along the banks of the lake and talked spiritedly, interrupting each other in their eagerness to express their profusion of ideas. Meanwhile, two fat-faced stalwarts from Müller's department were swimming about in the cold water, keeping an eye on Object No. 2 and Object No. 75. Object No. 2 was Müller's way of referring to Frau Heydrich, in accordance with her husband's place in the hierarchy of the Reich Security Office. Schellenberg could not have even dreamt that the two idiots swimming in the icy water, and the only people foolish enough to be doing so, were Gestapo men. In his opinion, no agent had the right to attract attention to himself so blatantly. Müller's shrewd peasant cunning proved superior to Schellenberg's elegant logic on that occasion. The agents had been instructed to photograph the 'objects' if they should decide to 'lie down in the bushes', to use Müller's expression.

However the 'objects' did not lie down in the bushes: after a coffee on the open terrace of a café they went back into the city. Undeterred, Müller decided that blind jealousy is more formidable than the seeing variety and he laid before Heydrich a report to the effect that his wife and Schellenberg had gone for a walk *à deux* in a wood and spent the afternoon out at Plönersee. He did not bother to supply any commentary of his own, knowing that Heydrich was a man possessed of inordinate pride and known for his unpredictable decisions.

After reading the report Heydrich did not say anything to Müller but merely permitted him to leave the room with a curt nod. Müller had not been able to glean anything from the expression on Heydrich's stern, peaked face. He was put out by that and was in suspense the whole day. Later that evening after first telephoning Müller, Heydrich walked into Schellenberg's office, gave him a hearty pat on the shoulder and announced: 'Today I'm in a sour mood, we'll all go out for a drink.'

The three of them were up that night until four o'clock, rushing round small seedy taverns, drinking away at the same tables as hysterical prostitutes and black-marketeers, laughing and joking and singing folk songs for all they were worth. Then, when it was almost morning Heydrich, looking quite white by that time, leant across the table till his face was almost touching Schellenberg's and proposed they drop the formal *Sie*, switch to *Du* terms and drink on it. They both drained their glasses and then Heydrich put the palm of his hand over Schellenberg's glass and said:

'I poured poison into your wine, just think of that! If you do not tell me the whole truth about the way in which you spent your time with Frau Heydrich you shall die. If you tell the truth—however terrible it might be for me to have to listen to—I shall give you an antidote.'

Schellenberg at once put two and two together: he re-membered the two stalwarts swimming in the lake, noticed Müller's evasive eyes and forced smile and said: 'Why not? I can call witnesses, two at once even, who know how we spent the time. We went for a walk and talked about the greatness of Greece eventually undermined by informers, who betrayed her to Rome. Incidentally, it was not only that which brought about

83

her downfall. Yes, I was with Frau Heydrich, I idolise this woman, the wife of a man whom I regard as truly great. Where is the antidote?' he asked. 'Where is it?'

Heydrich laughed under his breath, poured a little Martini into an empty glass and handed it to Schellenberg.

Six months after that incident Schellenberg went to see Heydrich to ask his permission to marry, explaining that his future mother-in-law was Polish. This meant an investigation would have to be carried out by SS Reichsführer Himmler and his experts. Himmler personally perused the photgraphs of Schellenberg's future wife and mother-in-law. Specialists were called in from Rosenberg's department. The proportions of their skulls were measured with a microcompass and also the size of their foreheads and shape of their ears. Himmler gave his permission for Schellenberg to go ahead with the marriage.

One night, after the marriage had taken place, Heydrich, who had been drinking heavily, came up to Schellenberg, took him by the arm and led him over to the window to ask: 'D'you imagine, I was not aware that your wife's sister is married to a Jewish banker?'

Schellenberg felt his heart sink within him and his hands came over cold.

'To hell with it all,' went on Heydrich, and all of a sudden gave a deep sigh.

Schellenberg did not realise at the time why Heydrich had sighed. He only learnt what lay behind that sigh long afterwards: the grandfather of the chief of the Reich security service had been a Jew and played the violin at Viennese operetta performances.

6

Schellenberg noticed Stirlitz sitting in the waiting-room outside Himmler's office. Stirlitz had his name down on the waiting list: he was holding a grey–green, embossed document-case with gold edges. It contained a single sheet of paper, the letter he had written on his return from Köpenick.

'You're next,' the ADC reminded Stirlitz as he showed Obergruppenführer Pohl, Chief of the SS Economic and Administrative Main Bureau, into Himmler's office. 'I don't think he will be in there for long: he only has local questions to discuss.'

'Good morning, Stirlitz,' said Schellenberg. 'I've been hunting for you.'

'Good morning,' replied Stirlitz. 'Why are you looking so tired?'

'Is it very obvious?'

'Yes.'

'Come along to my office, I need to discuss something with you.'

'But I have an appointment with the Reichsführer.'

'What have you got to see him about?'

'A private matter.'

'You'll be finished in an hour and a half,' said Schellenberg. 'Arrange another appointment for later, the Reichsführer will be here till the end of the working day.'

'All right,' agreed Stirlitz reluctantly, 'Only I'm afraid he may find it inconvenient.'

'I'm making off with von Stirlitz,' Schellenberg informed the ADC, 'Please make another appointment for him in two hours' time.'

'Yes, Sir!'

Schellenberg took Stirlitz by the arm and as they walked out of the waiting-room he whispered gaily: 'What a voice that chap's got! He rattles it off like an actor at the operetta, with a voice from right down in his boots and so terribly anxious to please.'

'I always feel sorry for ADCs,' remarked Stirlitz. 'They have to put on such an important air all the time, otherwise everyone would realise how dispensable they are.'

'You're wrong there. Aides are very important. They're like hounds, and, incidentally, if their exterior is superb, then other huntsmen will covet them and feel jealous.'

As they approached the main staircase they bumped into Müller.

'Heil Hitler, my friends!' he said.

'Heil Hitler, pal!' Schellenberg replied.

'Heil,' echoed Stirlitz, without raising his arm in salute.

'Grand to see you. Young devils!' Müller went on, 'busy hatching up your next plot, I suppose?'

'Hatching away,' replied Schellenberg, 'and why not?'

'Our plots are not a patch on yours, though,' remarked Stirlitz, 'we're nothing but a pair of innocent lambs beside you.'

'Beside me?' repeated Müller in a tone of surprise. 'But to be honest, it's even pleasant to be regarded as a devil. You die and there's something to be remembered for. Even if it is only for your devilish ways.'

Müller gave both Schellenberg and Stirlitz a chummy pat on the shoulder and then went into the office of one of his colleagues: he enjoyed popping into their offices without warning, particularly while interrogations were in progress.

When during the last few months of the war Hitler kept repeating like some sacred vow that the collapse of the Anglo–American Alliance would only be a matter of weeks and went on assuring everybody that the Western nations would yet be turning to the Germans for help after their decisive defeat, many people saw all that merely as a manifestation of the Führer's character,—his ability to believe up until the bitter end in whatever his morbid imagination might dream up. However, in this particular case Hitler's assertions did have some factual basis: Bormann's intelligence network, which functioned independently of Himmler's and Ribbentrop's channels, let alone military intelligence, which had bungled itself out of the running as a result of Admiral Kanaris' unfortunate blunders, had obtained a top-secret document in London as far back as mid-1944 that contained the following lines: 'A terrible catastrophe would happen if Russian barbarism were to destroy the culture and independence of the ancient European states.' Hitler's phenomenal memory immediately linked that statement with 1936, when, at the National Socialist Party rally in Nuremburg, he had declared: 'If the Bolsheviks' methods prove successful, the European culture will be replaced by the most terrible barbarism that has ever existed.'

That sentence from the stolen document to which Hitler turned again and again came from the pen of Winston Churchill. It had appeared in a secret memorandum in October 1942 when the Russians were in Stalingrad, not Poland, outside Smolensk and not in Rumania, in Kharkov and not Yugoslavia.

Probably Hitler would not have issued orders that all attempts to negotiate with the Western powers were punishable by death if he had known about the fierce controversy that was going on in 1943 and 1944 between the British and the Americans as to the direction of the main strike of the Allied armies. Churchill pressed for a landing in the Balkans, in order to prevent communist infiltration and invasion of the area and reminded his allies of the advantages the Western democracies would gain, if *their* armies occupied Budapest and Vienna and liberated Prague and Warsaw.

Cool-headed Americans were aware that Churchill's attempts to bulldoze the Allies into directing their main strike against Hitler in the Balkans, instead of France, were highly selfish. They realised full well that if Churchill were to have his way it would mean Britain would dominate the Mediterranean and, hence, be able to lord it over Africa, the Middle East, Italy, Yugoslavia and Greece. In other words, the resulting balance of power would have definitely been weighed against the United States, and so, in the end it was agreed that Allied troops would be landed in France.

In the early months of 1945, Churchill's strategy was formulated for his closest associates. He emphasised that Soviet Russia had become a mortal danger to the 'free world' and therefore it was vital to open a new front as far east as possible to

87

counter her rapid advance. He also stressed that the main and true goal of the British and American armies was Berlin, that the liberation of Czechoslovakia and entry of American forces into Prague was also important, and that Vienna, or rather the whole of Austria, should be controlled by the Western powers.

Being a bold yet cautious politician, Churchill was well aware that it was impossible to make contact with any member of the Nazi party leadership—even if the Russians were to make a sudden thrust forward into Europe—for while he saw Russia as a mortal danger, to the people who had suffered under Nazi occupation Russia was a symbol of liberation. Churchill could not even contemplate seeking contacts with Berlin because he had no illusions as to the Hitlerite leadership's infinite capacity for breaking its word; he also realised that public opinion would never condone contacts between any Western democracy and the Nazis . . . Churchill—given specific critical circumstances— could have tried to make contact with those who opposed the Führer, so as to set up a united front capable of holding back any rapid Russian advance in the direction of the Atlantic coast, the thing he feared most of all. But, after Hitler had wiped out those who had taken part in the July 1944 conspiracy, no such opposition remained in Germany. Still, Churchill held that any cautious 'flirtation' with those members of the Hitlerite leadership who might be prepared to arrange a capitulation of the Wehrmacht in the West—although such a thing seemed highly improbable in view of Roosevelt's firm stand and the pro-Russian mood throughout the world—would nevertheless enable him to take a tougher line with Stalin, particularly as far as the Polish and Greek problems were concerned.

When military intelligence informed Churchill that the Germans were seeking to contact the Allies, he declared that, although Britain could be accused of dilly-dallying or flippancy, she could never be accused of treachery, and he prayed to God that that never would be and stressed the need to draw a fine distinction between diplomatic games aimed at consolidating the Commonwealth of Nations and the folly of downright perfidy.

Thus Churchill made it clear to his intelligence staff that contacts with the Germans were feasible in a specific situation,

on specific conditions and provided that an adequate loophole
was left open, allowing him to declare these contacts to be no
more than a game, a probe aimed at promoting the Allies'
common cause in their struggle against Nazi tyranny.

He went on to add that since his American colleagues were as
well, if not better, informed on the subject, they should be given
the chance to play first fiddle in this particular orchestra. At that
the Assistant Chief of Intelligence suggested that if the game
proved expedient then it might develop into something else, a
more important action. To that Churchill replied that games
were important, the most important thing in the world, on a par
with painting, and the two of them put together made
everything else look futile and trivial. Politics in the conventional
sense of the word was dead, for global politics had replaced the
local politics complete with its elegant operations; the whims of
individuals, the selfish aspirations of one or another group of
people had given way to a science as exact as mathematics and
as dangerous as experimental radiation in medicine; global
politics would over-ride painters and astronomers, lift-operators
and mathematicians, kings and geniuses. He amplified this
contention by adding that global politics would provide scope
for such unexpected alliances, such paradoxical twists of
strategy that his own message to Stalin of June 22, 1941, would
one day appear as the quintessence of logic and consistency.

'Good morning, Frau Kien,' began the visitor, bending down at
the head of her bed.

'Good morning,' answered Käthe in a voice that was scarcely
audible.

She was finding it hard to talk, her head was still buzzing and
the slightest movement brought on a feeling of nausea. Only
feeding the baby helped her to relax a little. The baby boy would
start dozing off and she would lose herself at the same time.
When she opened her eyes, before her head started going round
in circles again, and a new wave of nausea came over her, each
time she caught sight of her little son she experienced a new
feeling. It was a strange feeling that she could not really put into
words: an unfamiliar mixture of fear, a sense of flight, an

unexplicable, almost bumptious pride and an ennobling serenity she had never known before.

'I should like to ask you a few questions, Frau Kien,' the visitor said. 'Can you hear me?'

'Yes.'

'I shan't disturb you for very long.'

'Who are you?'

'I'm from the insurance company.'

'Does that mean my husband's dead?'

'Yes, I am afraid I have to bring you that sad news, Frau Kien. He was killed. We are trying to help all those who suffered during those barbarous air raids. What can we do to help you while you are here in hospital? You are most probably receiving the necessary food and we shall provide you with clothing when it is time for you to leave hospital: for the two of you, you and the child. What a fine little baby you have there . . . Is it a girl?'

'No. A boy.'

'Does he cry a lot?'

'No.' That question suddenly made her realise that she had never heard her baby cry. 'Should they cry a lot?' she asked in a worried voice. 'D'you know?'

'Mine used to howl like anything,' the man replied, 'their screams were enough to deafen you. But mine were all very thin when they were born and you've got a real champion there. Strapping babies are always quiet. Forgive me, Frau Kien, but if you are not too tired I should like to ask you how much your property was insured for.'

'I don't know: my husband used to deal with all that.'

'And what branch are you insured at—or you probably don't remember that either?'

'I think it's on the corner of Kudamm and Kantstrasse.'

'Ah, that'll be branch 27 . . . That'll make it much simpler to get things sorted out . . . But you don't remember the sum?'

'I think it must have been ten thousand marks.'

'A large sum . . .'

The man wrote all that down in his scruffy little notebook and then after another introductory cough leant over towards Käthe and said in a very quiet voice: 'Young mothers mustn't cry and get worked up, that'll never do . . . I know, I'm the father of

90

three . . . It'll affect the little one's tummy in no time and then you'll be hearing plenty of that bass . . . You no longer have the right to think only of yourself, that part of your life is over once and for all. Now you must put your bonny baby before anything else . . .'

'I shall,' whispered Käthe and stretched out icy fingers to shake his warm clammy hand. 'Thank you.'

'Where are your relatives? Our company can help them reach you. We can pay their travelling expenses and supply them with accommodation. Of course you realise that a good many hotels have been bombed and others requisitioned by the army, but we can find them a room to rent. Your relatives will be satisfied, of that you can be sure. What address should we write to?'

'My family stayed on in Königsberg,' Käthe replied. 'I don't know what's become of them.'

'And your husband's relatives? Whom should we inform of his death?'

'His relatives live in Sweden . . . But it would be better not to write to them: my husband's uncle is a true friend of Germany's and asked us not to write to him . . . We used to send letters by hand, whenever the possibility arose, or via the Embassy.'

'Do you remember the address?'

At that moment the baby started crying and Käthe asked the insurance agent to excuse her while she fed him: 'Forgive me, I'll give you the address afterwards.'

'I wouldn't dream of getting in the way,' the man replied and walked out of the ward.

Käthe watched him walk away and slowly struggled to swallow the hard lump in her throat. Her head was still full of dull ache as before but she was no longer plagued by nausea. She had no time to think over the questions she'd just been asked, because the boy had started sucking and all the worries and alarm of the outside world faded into the background. There was just the baby sucking eagerly and moving his little hands about; she unwrapped him and saw again how big and red he was, covered with tiny little wrinkles.

Then she suddenly remembered how two days before she had been in a large ward with numerous other women, and all the babies had been brought in to be fed at one and the same

91

time and the ward had rung with cries that she had heard as if through a mist. 'Why am I alone in here,' she wondered. 'Where am I?'

The man came back half an hour later. He looked admiringly at the sleeping boy for some time and then brought out some photographs from his briefcase, spread them out on his knees, picked one out and asked: 'While I write down your uncle's address, please could you look at these photographs and see if you can recognise any of your belongings. After the bombing some of the things from the house where you lived were recovered: you know, in your predicament even one suitcase of things can be a godsend. There might be something you could sell that would help buy the vitals for the baby . . . Of course, we'll try and get what we can by the time you leave hospital, but all the same . . .'

'The address is: Franz Paakenen, Gustav Georgplatz 25, Stockholm.'

'Thank you. I haven't exhausted you, I hope?'

'I do feel rather tired,' replied Käthe, for in the photographs among the tidy row of cases and boxes in the street near the ruins of their house stood a large suitcase which could not be confused with any of the others. It was the case Erwin had kept his wireless equipment in.'

'Take a last careful look and then I shall be on my way,' said the man as he held out the photograph again.

'No, I don't think so,' replied Käthe, 'there aren't any of our cases there.'

'Well, thank you, we can consider that question closed,' he said, putting the photograph carefully back into his briefcase. Then he rose to his feet and took his leave with a bow. 'In a couple of days I'll pop by again and tell you what headway I've been able to make. The commission I have to take—the times demand it, I'm afraid—will be very small, nothing that will put you out.'

'I shall be most grateful,' answered Käthe.

The investigator from the local department of the Gestapo who had visited Käthe sent the photograph to be tested for fingerprints at once: the photograph of the cases had been coated with a special chemical in advance. The fingerprints on

92

the wireless transmitter hidden in the suitcase had already been analysed. It had emerged that on the wireless-equipment there were fingerprints belonging to three different people . . . He also contacted the sixth department of the Reich Security Office asking to be supplied with all available information concerning the life and activities of a certain Swedish subject by the name of Franz Paakenen . . .

Eismann spent a long time pacing up and down his office. He was taking large strides and holding his hands folded behind his back, feeling all the time that something familiar and all-important was missing. This prevented him from concentrating and distracted his attention from the job in hand: he was unable to analyse the problem that was plaguing him—why had Stirlitz fallen into disrepute.

At last, when the oppressive drawn-out whine of the sirens started up, he realised what had been missing: it was an air raid that he needed to help him concentrate. War had become so much part of life that quiet seemed menacing and fraught with far more terror than the raids themselves.

'Thank God,' thought Eismann when the siren mournfully faded into silence. 'Now I can get down to work. Everyone'll leave the building and I can sit and think without people popping in and out with their stupid questions and idiotic suggestions.'

Eismann sat down at his desk and began to leaf through the file on the protestant pastor Fritz Schlag who had been arrested in the summer of 1944, suspected of activities detrimental to state interests. The decision to make the arrest had followed on two reports made by Barbara Krain and Robert Nitsche. They were both his parishioners and in their reports they had noted how Pastor Schlag in his sermons used to call for peace and brotherhood of all peoples, condemning the barbarism of war and the senselessness of bloodshed. Further checks had revealed that the pastor had met, on several occasions, ex-Chancellor Brüning, who had since emigrated and was now living in Switzerland. They had been on friendly terms, but no evidence of any political ties between the pastor and the ex-Chancellor had come to light despite thorough investigation both in Germany and in Switzerland.

This led Eismann to question why Pastor Schlag had ever been taken up by the intelligence authorities in the first place? Why had he not been sent to the Gestapo? Why had Schellenberg's people shown an interest in him? The answer to that question Eismann found in a short note that had been added to the file: in 1933 the pastor had made two visits abroad, one to Great Britain and the other to Switzerland, to take part in pacifist congresses. 'So they must have been interested in his contacts,' Eismann concluded, 'and wanted to know whom he had met there. That was why the intelligence service dealt with his case and handed him over to Stirlitz. But why Stirlitz? He was given the job and he did it . . .'

Eismann took another look at the file and noted that the interrogations had been short and to the point. For the sake of objectivity he wanted to take some notes from the report on the interrogations so as to substantiate his conclusions with documentary evidence, but there was nothing really suitable.

Then he telephoned a special card-index department. He had to wait a long time for an answer and thought at first that everyone must have left for the shelters. He was just about to put the receiver down when someone eventually answered.

'This is Eismann here from the fourth department. Good morning. Please, could you look and see if you have a recording of the interrogation of a Pastor Schlag conducted by Standarten-führer Stirlitz on September 29, 1944?'

'I wish to warn you that you have been arrested and that for those who find themselves in the hands of National Socialist justice, which is called upon to punish the guilty and protect the people from scum, a return from here to a normal way of life and activity is virtually impossible. The same applies to the lives of your relatives. With one reservation though: all that would be possible on condition that you, after confessing your own guilt, expose those members of the Church who are not loyal supporters of our state and that in future you help us in our work. Do you accept these conditions?'

94

'I must have time to think.'

'How much time do you need?'

'How much time does a man need who is preparing to meet his death?'

'I suggest that we return to my proposal once more. You say that in either case you are a condemned man, but surely you are a German patriot?'

'Yes, I am. But what am I to understand by "German patriot"?'

'A loyal adherent of our ideology!'

'Ideology does not make a country.'

'Yet you cannot deny that our country lives by the ideology of the Führer. Surely you see it as your duty, the duty of a spiritual shepherd, to stand with the people who profess our ideology.'

'If I were to argue with you on equal terms I should know what answer to give to that question.'

'I invite you to argue on such terms.'

'To stand with the people is one thing and to feel you are acting justly and in accordance with your faith is another. Sometimes the two are compatible and sometimes not. In this particular case you are proposing I take a way out that is incompatible with my convictions. You are preparing to use me, to make me sign some declaration or other. You present the proposal in such a way as if you regarded me as a human being. Why do you talk to me like that when you propose to use me not as a human being but as a mere lever? Put things bluntly: either we kill you or you sign the paper. Where the German nation is going and what language it talks is of little importance to me, seeing I am virtually a dead man already.'

'That is not correct. It is not correct for the following reasons: I am not asking you to sign any paper. Supposing I take my first question back, my first proposal is for you to make a public statement in the press and on the wireless in which you would censure your fellow priests who are opposing our regime. I would first ask you to accept the truth inherent in national socialism which I profess, and then, once you had accepted that truth, to help us in our work to a degree commensurable with your belief in our truth.'

'If that's how the question stands, try then to convince me

that national socialism gives man more than anything else can.'

'I am prepared to do that. Yet national socialism is our state, the state led by the great ideas of our Führer, and you men of religion have nothing to put forward as an alternative to that state. All you can offer is moral perfection.'

'Quite correct.'

'However man does not live by moral perfection alone, just as he does not live by bread alone. So this means we seek to enhance the welfare of our people. Let us consider that as the first step on the way to achieving the moral perfection you exhort the nation to aspire to.'

'All right, but in that case I should like to ask you one question: the concentration camps or interrogations like the one you're putting me through; me, a representative of the Church, are they the inevitable consequence of your kind of statecraft?'

'Undoubtedly, for we are protecting you from the wrath of our people, who, on learning that you oppose the Führer and our ideology, would subject you to physical annihilation.'

'But where is cause and where is effect? What gives rise to the wrath of the people and is that wrath an indispensable attribute of the kind of regime you advocate? If so, since when has wrath as such been a positive phenomenon? It is not wrath that is positive, but reaction to evil. If wrath is the basis, if wrath is cause and everything else is effect, in a word, if evil is elevated to the status of cause, then why do you want to convince me that evil is good?'

'No, "evil" was your word, I used the phrase "wrath of the people". I referred to the hatred of the people who for the first time after many years of humiliation, following the Treaty of Versailles, and after the domination of Jewish bankers and shopkeepers, were able to live in peace and quiet. The people rise up in wrath when anyone, even a cleric, calls into question the great gains which have been achieved thanks to our party led by the great Führer.'

'All well and good. To live in peace and quiet and fight—is that one and the same thing?'

'We are only fighting to secure *lebensraum*,'

'But to keep a quarter of the population shut up in concentration camps—is that for their good or is that the harmonious way of life that I must lay down my life for?'

'You are mistaken: in our concentration camps which, incidentally, are not instruments of extermination—you are clearly going by information gleaned from enemy sources—the total number of inmates is nowhere near a quarter of the population. On the gates of one of our concentration camps is written: "Work Makes Free". It is there that we reform those who have gone astray, yet, naturally, those who have not merely gone astray but are our enemies have to be exterminated.'

'So, it is you who decide who is guilty before you and who is not?'

'Of course.'

'Consequently, you know in advance what each person is after, where he is mistaken and where not?'

'I know what the people want.'

'The people! But who makes up the people?'

'Men and women.'

'How do you know what the people want, if you do not know what every individual man or woman wants? Or rather when you know in advance what he or she wants as you dictate and prescribe it all? It's nothing but a flight of fancy.'

'There you are wrong. People want to eat well . . .'

'And are prepared to go to war for it?'

'Wait a minute. Good food, good houses, cars, family happiness . . . and wars to achieve that happiness! Yes, wars!'

'And in addition to all that they want those whose ideas do not conform to the norm to be thrown into camps? If the one follows from the other that means there must be something wrong in your scheme for happiness, because, obtained by such methods, it can in my view no longer be real happiness. Perhaps I just have a different way of looking at things! Probably in your eyes the end justifies the means; the Jesuits maintained that as well.'

'You, as a pastor, do not appear to subject the evolution of Christianity to a critical analysis! Or do you allow yourself to pass a veil over certain periods in the evolution of Christian teaching? The Inquisition, for example?'

97

'I have an answer for you. The Inquisition is undeniably a part of the history of Christianity. Incidentally, as I see it, the decline of the Spanish people was directly bound up with the fact that they substituted the means for the end. The Inquisition, which was originally set up as a means of purifying faith, gradually degenerated into an end in itself. In other words, the purification as such, the *auto-da-fé* as such, the cruelty as such, the persecution of all those whose ideas differed from the official norm, that was first conceived of as purification through faith, all began gradually to turn evil into an end in itself.'

'All well and good, but tell me how often in the history of Christianity have dissenters been exterminated by the Church so that the rest of the flock might live better?'

'I see what you are getting at. As a rule, it was heretics who were exterminated, and all heresies in the history of Christianity were in fact revolts that can be traced to material motives. All heresies in the history of Christianity have preached the idea of inequality, while Christ himself preached equality. The vast majority of heresies were based on the assumption that the rich man was not the equal of the poor man and that the poor man should do away with the rich man or become rich himself and sit in the rich man's place, whereas Christ taught that there was no essential difference between one man and the next and that wealth was something transient, as was poverty. Christ tried to pacify people, while all heresies called for bloodshed. What is more, the very idea of evil is, as a rule, something to be found in heretics' teachings, and the Church resorted to violent means to suppress heresies, to prevent violence from, becoming in whole or in part the moral code of Christianity.'

'Correct. Yet when combatting heresies which presupposed violence the Church resorted to violence?'

'Resorted to it but did not make it an end in itself and did not justify it on principle.'

'Violence directed against heresies was practised, if I remember correctly, for eight or nine centuries, wasn't it? That would mean then, that for eight or nine centuries the Church resorted to violence so that it might root out violence. We came to power in 1933. What on earth are you asking of us? In these eleven years we have put an end to unemployment, supplied all the Germans with adequate food, while subjecting dissenters to violence! And you hinder us in our work with your words! But, surely, if you are such a convinced opponent of our regime you would surely do better to adopt a practical rather than a spiritual approach. For example why 'not try and organise some opposition group amongst your parishioners and work against us? Distribute leaflets, engage in sabotage, subversion, armed action against certain members of the leadership?'

'No, I would never have taken that path for the simple reason . . . don't think it was because I am afraid of anything . . . simply because that path seems to me essentially unacceptable, in so far as, if I start using your methods against you I shall involuntarily come to resemble you.'

'So if some young man from your flock were to come to you and say: "Father, I cannot accept the regime and wish to struggle against it . . ."'

'I would not stop him.'

'And if he says: "I wish to kill a Gauleiter"—and that Gauleiter has three children, three little girls aged two, five and nine, and a wife with paralysed legs—what would you do then?'

'I don't know.'

'And if I started asking you questions about that man, would you refuse to tell me anything? Would you refuse to save the lives of those three little girls and the sick woman? Or would you help me?'

'No, I would not tell you anything, for saving the life of one person can spell the death of others. When such an inhuman struggle is going on, every active step can only lead to new bloodshed. The only path open to a priest in such a situation is to dissociate himself from cruelty and refuse to stand on the side of the executioner. Unfortunately that is a passive path, but in such a situation any active path leads to increased bloodshed.'

'I am convinced that if we use third degree against you—which would be painful and unpleasant—you would eventually tell us the surname of the person concerned.'

'You mean that if you turn me into an animal crazed with pain I shall do what you require of me? Perhaps I would. But that would no longer be me. In that case why did you bother to go through the rigmarole of this conversation? Treat me as you please, use me as an animal or a machine . . .'

'And tell me, if you were asked by vicious enemies or lunatics to travel abroad to Britain, Russia, Sweden or Switzerland and be a go-between or hand over a letter, would you contemplate carrying out such a request?'

'Being a go-between is a function that is quite natural and familiar to me. The only conditions I would make would be that my mediation should lead to good and should involve only upright means.'

'Even if that mediation was detrimental to our State?'

'You oblige me to make generalised evaluations. You are well aware that if a state is founded on violence, I, as a minister of God, cannot approve of it in principle. Of course, I should like to see people living differently from the way they are living now. But if only I knew how to bring that about . . . In principle I should like to see the people who now make up a National Socialist state remain alive but constitute some other sort of unit. I should not like anyone to be killed.'

'To me treachery is something unspeakable, but still worse is indifference and passive observation of how treachery and murder are effected.'

'In that case there can only be one kind of participation or involvement: to strive towards the end of murder as such.'

'That is not something that you can decide.'

'No, indeed. But what do you call treachery?'

'Treachery is passivity.'

'No, passivity is not tantamount to treachery.'

'It is still more terrible . . .'

Eismann felt the building start to shake. 'The bombs must be coming down right nearby,' he thought to himself, 'or they must be dropping very large ones today . . . A strange conversation, very interesting and yet a strange ring about it.'

Eismann telephoned through to the man on duty in the card-index department and he soon appeared in a cold sweat and deathly pale.

Eismann asked him whether the recording had been an official or a control one.

'Just a minute and I'll go and check,' the man answered in a low voice.

'Is the bombing getting near?'

'The glass in our windows has been blasted.'

'Can't you get down into the shelter?'

'No,' the man answered. 'That's against the rules.'

Eismann wanted to listen to the rest of the conversation but the man came back only to inform him that Stirlitz had not recorded the interrogation. The recording had been made on the instructions of counter-intelligence in the interests of keeping a check on the staff of the central security organ . . .

7

'Those must be at least one ton bombs,' remarked Schellenberg.

'Sounds like it,' agreed Stirlitz.

At that moment he felt a violent urge to leave Schellenberg's office and immediately burn the peace of paper in his document case—the report on the negotiations between 'SD traitors' and the West. 'This cunning move of Schellenberg's isn't as simple as it might appear,' Stirlitz thought to himself. 'The pastor has obviously been of interest to him from the outset as a decoy for the future. The fact that he required him now was symptomatic. Nor would he have embarked on all this without Himmler knowing of it.' Yet Stirlitz realised that he must put out feelers at once and discuss all the details of the forthcoming operation with Schellenberg without seeming to be in a hurry. The more calmly and deliberately he talked now the greater would be his chance of success in the long run . . .

'I think they're moving off,' said Schellenberg, listening hard for the planes. 'Or perhaps not?'

'They're flying away, to load up again with new bombs.'

'No, that lot will now be able to relax back at base. They've got enough planes to keep up a never-ending flow . . . So you think the pastor is bound to return, if we take his sister and her children as hostages?'

'No doubt about it.'

'And that after he comes back he'll keep his mouth shut when Müller gets on to him about whether it was precisely you who asked him to go and look out contacts?'

'There I'm not sure,' replied Stirlitz. 'It will all depend on who interrogates him.'

'It would be as well if you were to keep on hand some tapes of your conversations with him. What if he died in a bombing raid?'

'I'll think about it . . .'

'D'you need much time to think out those details?'

'I would ask you to give me time to chew over this plan carefully . . .'

'How much time d'you need to "chew it over"?'

'I'll try to come up with something by this evening.'

'Fine,' said Schellenberg. 'The planes have gone after all. Would you like some coffee?'

'Very much, but only after I've completed everything.'

'Fine. It's good to see that you've got such a good grasp of the whole business, Stirlitz. This will be a good lesson for Müller. He's started sticking his neck out. Even vis-à-vis the Reichsführer. This time we'll do his work for him and take the wind out of his sails. This will be a major service we're doing the Reichsführer.

'Does the Reichsführer know about it?'

'No . . . Let's say—No-o-o-o . . . Got me? And, in general, I really enjoy working with you . . .'

'It's mutual.'

'Why are you looking so angry?'

'What makes you think I'm angry?' mumbled Stirlitz. 'I'm always a lot gloomier when I'm angry. At the moment I'm just concentrating.'

Schellenberg accompanied Standartenführer von Stirlitz to the door and, as he shook hands, said: 'If everything works out according to plan, you can have five days off in the mountains: the skiing's wonderful at the moment, the snow's perfect and you'd be sure to come back with a tan . . . Divine thought, isn't it? What a lot of things this war has made us forget even exist . . .'

'Above all we've had to forget that we ourselves exist,' replied Stirlitz. 'We've had to leave our real selves behind like coats in a cloakroom after a rare old booze-up . . .'

'Yes, too true,' agreed Schellenberg with a sigh, 'like a coat in a cloakroom . . . Is it long since you stopped writing poetry?'

'I never began, in the first place . . .'

Schellenberg wagged a finger at him and warned: 'It's white lies that pave the way to black mistrust, Stirlitz . . .'

'I swear,' Stirlitz assured him with a smile, 'that I have tried my hand at writing everything except verses: I have an absolute blind spot when it come to rhymes . . .'

After destroying the letter he had written to Himmler, Stirlitz left the building on Prinz-Albrecht-Strasse and walked slowly down the street to the Spree. The pavement had been swept clean although only the previous night there had been piles of broken bricks lying about: two, if not three, bombing raids a night were now a regular occurrence.

'I just stepped back from the brink in time,' thought Stirlitz to himself. 'When Schellenberg instructed me to take over the Pastor Schlag case he was merely concerned to find out more about ex-Chancellor Brüning who is now living in Switzerland. He wanted to know about the foreign contacts the pastor might have and that was why he agreed so readily to let him be released once I had told him that the old man was prepared to co-operate with us. He saw farther than I did and was counting on the pastor agreeing later to play decoy in a really serious gamble. But that's ridiculous: what part could the pastor play in the Wolff operation? What kind of operation is it and in whose interests? Why did Schellenberg turn the wireless on while he was telling me about Wolff's trip to Switzerland? If he's afraid to talk about it out loud, that means something really stupendous is afoot, and Obergruppenführer Karl Wolff is vested with full powers: his rank in the SS is the same as Ribbentrop's or Fegelein's. Schellenberg could not help telling me about Wolff, for otherwise I would have asked him how such an operation could be prepared while we were just groping in the dark? I very much doubt that the West is going to sit down at the conference table with Himmler. Although Himmler, of course, is a major force in his own right and they must realise that, and there was no point at all in negotiating with anyone who has no real power. The prospect of them sitting down at one and the same table doesn't bear thinking about . . . All right then—let the pastor be the bait, the decoy, the guinea-pig—that was clearly what they were planning. But they had probably not taken into account that Schlag already has reliable contacts there. That means I must work on the old fellow, so that he uses his influence against those who, through my mediation, will send him there. I had reckoned to use him as a reserve liaison channel, but it looks as if there is going to be a much more responsible role in store for him. It's not *he* who's going to prepare the ground for contacts in Switzerland. If I supply him with a new identity of my own making, not Schellenberg's, he'll be approached by men from the Vatican, not by the British and the Americans. So much is obvious. I must work out a story for him that is bound to arouse real interest, enough to counterbalance and outdo the interest aroused by the other Germans who have arrived in Switzerland or are about to arrive. We'll see who'll come out on top. In any case what's important now is first of all for me to work out a suitable identity for him and then decide on the names of those whom he shall represent, men who are opposing Hitler and Himmler.'

He was a man whom nobody knew anything about. He was rarely to be seen in newsreels and still less so in photographs of the Führer and his close associates. He was short and bullet-headed and had a scar on his cheek that looked like a classical memento of student duels. he always tried to hide behind the backs of those standing nearby when reporters started clicking their camera-shutters.

It was said that in 1924 he had spent fourteen months in prison for a political murder. After that he had either been amnestied or escaped and gone undergound—nobody was quite sure. Or rather nobody was quite sure till the day when Hess flew off to England. Himmler was given orders by the Führer to put that 'foul brothel' in order. Those were the words the Führer had actually used to refer to the party chancellery that had been run by Hess, the only member of the party who had been on Christian name and *Du* terms with the Führer. In the course of a single night Himmler's men made over seven hundred arrests; some of these people were later released, while others were sent to concentration camps for long terms. Hess's closest associates were arrested, save Martin Bormann, the right-hand man and first deputy of the head of the party chancellery who was left in peace. Moreover, it was he who to a certain extent guided Himmler as he went about his local purge: he made sure the men he needed were not arrested, and the ones he did not need were sent off to concentration camps.

No changes of any kind were to be observed in Bormann after he became Hess's successor: he remained equally taciturn, walked around with a notebook in his pocket where he noted down everything Hitler said, just as before. He continued to live extremely modestly and just as far removed from the public eye. He remained extremely deferential in his dealings with Göring, Himmler and Goebbels, but gradually, in the course of a year or two, he managed to make himself indispensable to the Führer to such an extent that Hitler, on some occasion, actually referred to Bormann in jest as his shadow. He had things so well organised that if Hitler expressed interest in some matter or other before he sat down to dinner, by the time he had got to his coffee Bormann had a full report ready. What added to the impressive efficiency was the quiet, inconspicuous way he went about things, avoiding all outward show. On one occasion, in Berchtesgaden, when a special welcome was laid on for the Führer and it turned into a spontaenous but nonetheless colossal rally, Bormann noticed Hitler had had to wave to the crowds from a place that offered no protection from the sun. The next day Hitler noticed an oak-tree at that particular spot: overnight Bormann had had an enormous tree uprooted and transferred to Hitler's garden, roots and all. Hitler reprimanded Bormann for the waste of time and effort but in his heart of hearts he had been most pleasantly surprised by the consideration shown him by his loyal assistant. It was Bormann who prepared all Hitler's correspondence for him and looked through all the papers that found their way to the Führer's desk. When Goebbels once sent Hitler a book of photographs extolling the courage of German pilots, Bormann returned it with a note that read: 'Is there much point in disturbing the Führer with such blatant propaganda lies?'

Bormann knew that Hitler never prepared his speeches in advance: the Führer always relied on the inspiration of the moment and his impromptu speeches were usually a success. Yet Bormann took the trouble particularly during visits of foreign statesmen or the celebrations in honour of the revolution of November 9th, to draft a number of theses which, in his view, the Führer would do well to use as a basis. This inconspicuous, yet highly important, ground-work Bormann carried out with the utmost tact and the thought never occurred to Hitler that his major policy declarations were written by someone else: he looked upon Bormann's work as that of a secretary, albeit an indispensable and punctual one. Later, when Bormann once happened to fall ill, by the second day of his absence Hitler felt how everything was at sixes and sevens and sent his own personal doctor to attend to his party chief.

Bormann always managed, politely and without pushing, to find out who went to see the Führer and what about, and he knew how to advise whom on how to behave during audiences with Hitler. He briefed the visitors in such a way that their opinions coincided with those of the Führer. Those who took upon themselves the liberty of disagreeing with the Führer and sticking to their own point of view, Bormann tried to keep away from the Führer afterwards.

He always stumbled over his words as he spoke, yet he was a master of official correspondence. He was intelligent but knew how to conceal his intelligence behind a coarse, blunt exterior. He was all-powerful, yet knew how to behave as if he was a perfectly ordinary mortal who needed to seek advice from others before taking any decision that involved even the slightest degree of responsibility . . .

It was to this man, Martin Bormann, that a letter marked 'Personal' was delivered by the SD secret post. It read as follows:

Dear Comrade Bormann,

Some men from the SD have found their way into your secretariat—I do not know their surnames as yet, but with your authorisation I should be able to ascertain them. I am not sure that this letter will reach you but if it does then I take this opportunity to turn to you in connection with a matter of national importance. Behind the Führer's back certain people known to me are starting to engage in some gamble with representatives of the degenerate Western democracies in Sweden and Switzerland. This is going on at a time of total war, at a moment when the world's future is being decided on the battlefields. I am in a position to inform you of all details concerning these treacherous negotiations. I need a guarantee of my safety since if this letter of mine were to fall into the hands of the SD I would be exterminated immediately. For precisely this reason I am not putting my signature to this letter. If this information appears important to you, I would ask you please to come to the hotel Neues Tor *opposite the Natural History Museum tomorrow at 13.00.*

'A member of the NSDAP devoted to the Führer.'

107

Bormann sat holding this letter and ruminating for a long time. Several times he was about to lift the telephone receiver to contact Gestapo chief Müller. He knew that Müller was indebted to him. Müller, who was a police spy of long standing, had twice raided the Bavarian organisation of the Nazi party in the early 1930s. Later he began to serve that very same party when it became Germany's ruling party. The Gestapo chief had not been a party member until 1939: his colleagues in the security service could not forgive him the zeal he had shown when working for the Weimar Republic. It was Bormann, and none other—as Müller knew well—who had helped him join the party, personally vouching for him to the Führer. However Bormann had always kept Müller at a distance. In his heart of hearts he did not really trust anyone in the SS very much, for they were all in some way working for Himmler. So far he had been watching Müller and weighing up his tactics: if he were to confide in him, then he would have to go the whole way initiating him even into the holy of holies. Otherwise the game would not be worth the candle.

'What is this?' wondered Bormann, reading through the letter for the tenth time. 'A provocation? Hardly. A letter from someone not in his right mind? Not that either—it resembles the truth too closely. But what if it comes from the Gestapo and Müller is also involved in the game? Rats always scurry from a sinking ship—anything's possible . . . In any case, this might turn out to be a new trump card to use against Himmler. Then without having to worry about that scoundrel I can calmly proceed to transfer all the party funds to banks of the neutral countries in the name of my men, not his . . .'

Bormann went on pondering over the letter for a long time but did not come to any definite decision.

Eismann switched on the tape-recorder again. He smoked a leisurely cigarette as he listened attentively to Stirlitz's slightly muffled voice: 'Why do you not start using violent action against us? Give me a really sincere answer. I assure you this conversation will go no further than these four walls.'

'Probably because I personally tried to refrain from violence.

However, there comes a time for every individual when patience runs out. If you threaten to do away with me, by doing so you goad me on to act accordingly. But even in that case, even if I were to do evil, I do not want to call it good. The difference between us lies in the fact that you perpetrate evil calling it good, while I, answering evil with evil, am always mindful that it is evil.'

'Tell me, were these last two months that you spent in prison a terrible experience for you?'

'These past eleven years, ever since you came to power, have been terrible for me.'

'That's pure demogogy. I'm asking whether the period when you were in a cell of this prison was terrible for you?'

'Of course.'

'Of course. You wouldn't like to find yourself there again, would you, if a miracle were to happen? If we were to release you?'

'No. I shouldn't like to have anything more to do with you at all.'

'Fine. But if I make a condition of your release that you remain on good terms with me in a strictly personal capacity?'

'Of course. Good relations with you on a man-to-man basis will be a natural manifestation of my attitude to my fellow-men in general. In so far as you approach me as an ordinary human being and not as a cog in the wheels of the National Socialist Party, you remain one of my fellow-men for me.'

'Yes, but I'll be coming to you as a man who has saved your life.'

'Of course.'

'Will you remember that?'

'Of course.'

'Naturally, you will not get your parish back. You will live in seclusion. Can you give me your word not to do any preaching?'

'What choice have I?'

'You must be grateful to me, if I manage to release you.'

'Are you helping me as an individual in response to some spontaneous inner urge or are you calculating to turn this move to your own advantage?'

'Your last conjecture is the more apt.'

'In that case I must be sure that the goal you are trying to attain is a good one; if not, it will be difficult for me to give you an affirmative answer.'

'You may consider that my goals are exceedingly honest.'

'What will you ask me to do?'

'I have some friends in the state network—scientists, party workers, army officers, journalists—in brief, a variety of people. It would be of great interest to me, provided that I manage to persuade the authorities to release you, of course, if you could converse with these people. I should not ask you to give me detailed reports of such conversations. Admittedly, I do not guarantee that there will not be microphones planted in adjacent rooms, but you can also take them into woods to talk to them. I should simply be interested to ask you your opinion afterwards as to the degree of good or evil it is possible to see in these people from your point of view. Would you be able to do me this service as one friend to another?'

'Yes . . . Yes, of course . . . However, I already have a large number of questions to ask you as to why you are making me such a proposition?'

'Ask away, please.'

'Either you are placing excessive confidence in me and asking my support for something you cannot ask anyone to support, or this is some kind of provocation. If the latter is true then this conversation is just going round in circles.'

'What are you trying to say?'

'That once again we shall not be able to find a common language. You will remain a functionary and I an individual trying to choose a path I can feasibly follow so as to avoid becoming a functionary.'

'What would convince you that this is not a provocation?'

'If I were to look you right in the eye . . .'

'Let's consider then that we have exchanged credentials?'

'Bring me a report on the pastor's behaviour in prison,' requested Eismann when he had finished listening to the recording. 'Everything relating to his manner, his contacts, his

110

conversations with other prisoners, his inclinations . . . In brief, all possible details.'

The information that was brought to him an hour later turned out to be most unexpected. It emerged that in January 1945 Pastor Schlag had been released from prison. From his file it was not possible to ascertain whether he had first agreed to work for the SD, or whether his release had been the result of some other inexplicable reason. All there was on record was a verbal order of Schellenberg's to release Schlag whom Stirlitz was still to keep an eye on. And that was all, nothing else whatever. Eismann rose and started to pace up and down his office; he felt uneasy and a strange sensation came over him, an awareness of his own insignificance and weakness.

Half an hour later he was handed the most recent document bearing on the Schlag case: after his release a special agent from the sixth department had been working on Schlag.

'Where is the material he sent in?'

'He was in direct contact with Standartenführer Stirlitz.'

'And no recordings were made?'

'No,' came the answer from the card-index section, 'in the interests of the operation no recordings were made.'

Kaltenbrunner telephoned Müller and asked him to send Gruppenführer Krüger, who was in charge of the Prague Gestapo, a draft of the Führer's secret order: 'Make sure he does not bungle things in Prague as he did in Cracow! Read the order yourself, it is a classic illustration of the Führer's courage and genius.' The Führer had issued the following order:

Concerning the destruction of objectives within German territory.

The struggle for survival our people are waging compels us even within German territory to use all means at our disposal that could weaken the fighting efficiency of the enemy and check his advance. It is vital to make full use of all opportunities directly or indirectly to inflict maximum losses on the enemy's military potential. It would be mistaken to assume that after the return of lost territories it will be possible for us to use once again means of transport and communication, industrial enterprises and municipal services that have not been destroyed during the enemy's retreat or that have

111

only been temporarily put out of action. The enemy in retreat will leave us nothing but scorched earth and will not pay attention to the needs of the local population.

Therefore I issue the following order:

1) All means of transport and communication, industrial enterprises, municipal services within German territory and also stocks of any kind of materials that could be of any use to the enemy are to be destroyed immediately or within a short period.

2) Responsibility for their destruction lies with: commands, as regards all military objectives (including road installations and means of communication; gauleiters and state defence commissioners as regards all industrial enterprises and municipal services and also all kinds of stocks. Troops must afford gauleiters and state defence commissioners the necessary assistance in carrying out the tasks set them.

3) This order is to be immediately brought to the attention of all commanders. All instructions running counter to this order cease to be valid.

HITLER

8

Stirlitz drove slowly to the place where he was due to meet Bormann—he was fairly confident the party chief would turn up, seeing the bait was a tempting one. He took a meandering route to make sure, just in case, that there was no one on his trail. That was a precaution he had taken automatically: over the last few days nothing had given him cause for alarm and he had not once woken up in the middle of the night, as had happened in the past, when with every hair on his head he had felt anxiety. It had always taken a long time for him to go back to sleep again and he had lain there in the dark, his eyes wide open, analysing every minute, every word that he might have addressed to anybody, even the milkman, even a chance fellow-passenger in the Underground, anything that could have been observed and put on record and could mean that he had inadvertently walked into a chance trap. It was precisely for this reason that Stirlitz preferred a car to other forms of transport, which helped him to avoid unnecessary chance contacts. Yet at the same time he considered that to cut himself off completely from the outside world was also foolish. There was no knowing what kind of assignment might come next, and an abrupt change of behaviour would be bound to put anyone trailing him on his guard: the fact that everyone in the Reich was under observation of one kind or another was no secret for Stirlitz.

He made a habit of visiting museums and galleries. In the first place, there were usually few visitors about, which meant that in the high-ceilinged rooms where footsteps echoed clearly it was easy to hear whether anyone was trailing you or not: secondly, the attendants in such places were as a rule informers for the local Gestapo and they could be relied on to confirm how long he spent there, when and with whom. Stirlitz used to make their task easier for them by visiting such places more often than not in his impressive uniform which was difficult not to notice.

He was thinking through all the details of the forthcoming

encounter—it was the details that usually proved the undoing of men in his profession.

Stirlitz made another mechanical check in his driving mirror and let out a low whistle of surprise: the Wanderer, that had entered the lane of traffic behind him in Friedrichstrasse at the Kurfürstendamm end, was keeping hard on his heels. He accelerated abruptly, and his Horch shot off at a tidy speed. Stirlitz tore along to Alexanderplatz, turned down Bergstrasse past the cemetery and then, after coming out into Veteranen-strasse, he looked behind him again and realised that he had thrown off his pursuer, if it had been a pursuer. Stirlitz retraced his tracks just to make sure and then stopped after driving past his favourite restaurant, a little place called *Gruss Gottlieb*, deciding to have a drink as there was still time left to kill.

'If they start trailing me again,' he thought, 'that means that something's up. But what can it be? I must sit down and have a glass of cognac and think out what on earth it might be . . .'

Stirlitz had a real soft spot for the tumble-down eating place. It was called *Gruss Gottlieb* because the proprietor welcomed his guests, regardless of their ranks or status, with the words: 'What have you trundled along for, you fat old hog? Complete with wench I see—there's no telling . . . Real back of a bus with hips like a battleship and as flat as a flounder on top!'

Stirlitz noticed that Gottlieb kept his spiciest terms of abuse for his most honoured patrons: it was probably a sign of particular respect . . .

Gottlieb greeted Stirlitz with an absent-minded 'How goes it, cretin? Come in for some grub? . . .'

Stirlitz shook his hand, pressing two marks into it as he did so and sat down at the end oak table behind a pillar on which were written curses typical of Mecklenburg fishermen, spicy and highly cynical. This décor appealed in particular to industrialists' wives who were no longer spring chickens.

'What can have happened?' he pondered again as he started sipping his cognac. 'I'm not expecting any new contact,—there can't have been a gaff of that sort. Perhaps my past work . . . But they've got no time to keep up with new developments as it is, sabotage is on the up-and-up, there's never been anything like it

114

in Germany before. Erwin . . . Wait a minute! What if they've found the transmitter?'

Stirlitz brought out his cigarettes but precisely because he felt desperate for a long draw he refrained from lighting up at all. He also had a violent urge to set off straight away for the ruins of Erwin and Käthe's house.

'That was a real blunder,' he realised now. 'I should have ransacked all the hospitals—what if they had been taken along with the other wounded? I shouldn't have made do with telephone calls. I must get down to that as soon as I've spoken to Bormann . . . He's bound to show up—when they're in tight corners they always put on less airs. They're inaccessible when everything's going smoothly, but if they sense things are looking bad, they turn yellow, become kind-hearted and men of the people. Now I must put everything else aside, even Erwin and Käthe. First of all I must have things out with that butcher of a Bormann. Perhaps I dreamt up all that about the Wanderer?'

He walked outside, got into his car and drove at a leisurely speed to the Natural History Museum in Invalidenstrasse. It was there near the hotel *Neues Tor* that he was to meet Bormann in an hour's time. He still had time enough to shake off anyone who might have been sent to trail him. He drove along very slowly and kept on looking in the mirror but there was no sign of the black Wanderer.

'Perhaps Schellenberg decided to see what I was up to before embarking on the operation with Schlag?' he wondered. 'That, incidentally, would also be a plausible explanation. Or perhaps my nerves are just getting frayed?'

'He took another look in the mirror—the street was quite deserted. Some children were making the most of the quiet, chasing each other on roller skates and laughing gaily. There were queues of people lining the flaking walls of battered-looking houses: obviously meat deliveries were expected.

Stirlitz left his car near the Charité Clinic and after walking through the wide hospital grounds came out near the museum in Invalidenstrasse. All was quiet and peaceful and there was not a soul to be seen. He had chosen that particular place because it gave him an excellent view of all the surrounding territory, as if it were laid out on the palm of his hand.

'Yet they might have planted some of their people in the hotel itself. If Bormann has informed Himmler, that's what'll have happened. But if not, then his people will just be wandering about out here by the entrance opposite the museum, pretending they're research workers, that's a cert.'

Stirlitz was dressed in civilian clothes; he was wearing glasses with wide horn frames and a beret, pulled down low over his forehead that made him hard to recognise. In the entrance hall of the museum there was an enormous piece of malachite from the Urals and a Brazilian amethyst. After looking at those, Stirlitz walked slowly through an enormous hall with blasted windows, which housed a model of a ferocious-looking dinosaur. From there he had a good view of the square in front of the museum and the hotel. No, everything was quiet and calm, or rather too calm. Stirlitz was alone in the museum and on this occasion that was unfortunate.

He stopped in front of an interesting exhibit, showing the thirteen stages of the evolution of the skull. Skull No. 10 belonged to the orang-outang. No. 11 to the gorilla, No. 12 to the chimpanzee and No. 13 to man.

'Why does Man have to be No. 13? Everything works against him, even numbers,' he thought wryly. 'If he could only have been 12 or 14. But no, 13 it has to be . . . Nothing but monkeys round here, he observed to himself as he stopped to take a look at the stuffed gorilla Bobby. 'Why should such good care be taken of them?'

The plaque read: 'Gorilla Bobby was brought to Berlin on March 29, 1928, aged three, and died on August 1, 1935. He was 1 metre 72 cm in height and weighed 266 kilogrammes.'

'You wouldn't think it to look at him,' thought Stirlitz as he contemplated the stuffed beast for the hundredth time, 'he's not really fat. I'm taller than he was, but weigh only 72.'

Then he backed away from the exhibit as if he was trying to get a better view from farther away but really so as to move nearer the large window through which he could see the pavement on the other side of Invalidenstrasse. Stirlitz looked at his watch and saw that there were twenty minutes to go.

It was 12:40—the time at which he was to have met the agent Klaus. He had sent Klaus a coded message that morning via the secretariat. Everyone knew that he used to arrange meetings with agents in museums, and that would provide an excuse for his presence should anybody show interest in his appearance in the museum. In summoning Klaus, Stirlitz had had two aims in mind: first of all he needed an alibi if Bormann had told Himmler about the letter and the Reichsführer had given orders for the whole district and all buildings to be combed, and then, this step would give him another alibi, allbeit indirect, with regard to Klaus's disappearance.

Stirlitz walked on into the next hall after noting that Invalidenstrasse was just as deserted as it had been before he came into the museum. Here he paused in front of an unusual exhibit that had been found in the forest of Wedenschloss in the eighteenth century. It was a piece of wood with the antlers and bare skull of a deer sticking through it: the strong beast must have erred during some spring mating battle, ramming not his rival but a tree-trunk.

Soon Stirlitz heard the noise of a large number of voices and footsteps. As the steps came nearer he thought for an awful moment: 'The game's up!' However he soon realised the voices belonged to children and he turned to find a school teacher shepherding a group of pupils who were clearly about to have a zoology lesson. The children were staring at the exhibits wide-eyed and almost silently which made their hasty whispers sound anxious.

Stirlitz surveyed the children with their ashen faces, pinched noses and eyes robbed of any winning spark of childish mischief. They were listening to their teacher with serious, very adult concentration. 'What curse is it that assails this wretched people?' mused Stirlitz. 'How could things reach such a pass that crazy ideas condemn children to a hungry existence like this and having the childish vitality sapped out of them? Why does the idiotic ideology of these Nazis use the frail bodies of these little kids like some kind of screen behind which they hide away in their bunkers complete with stocks of chocolate, sardines and cheese? And the most terrible thing of all, who could have fostered in these children the blind belief that the supreme purpose of life is to die for the Führer's ideals?'

He walked out of the emergency exit at five minutes past one.

117

There was no one down near the hotel. By way of back streets Stirlitz went down to the Spree, came back by another route to his office in the SD building. He did not notice anyone who might have been trailing him on his return journey either.

'Something must have happened,' he said to himself, 'something looks funny. I couldn't have failed to notice Bormann if he had been waiting there. Nor was there anyone on my tail. I just worked myself up . . .'

Bormann had been unable to leave the Bunker: the Führer had ben delivering a speech and there had been a large number of people present. He himself had been standing behind the Führer slightly to his left, and could not possibly have departed during the speech—it would have been unthinkable. He wanted to go, for he had resolved to meet the man who had written the letter. Yet it was already three o'clock when he at last left.

'How am I to find him?' Bormann wondered as he made his way back to the Chancellery. 'Meeting him would not have involved any risk for me, but my not turning up may well prove dangerous.'

D-8 to Müller:
Top Secret. Only copy.

A Horch with registration number WKR 821 gave its pursuers the slip in the vicinity of Veteranenstrasse. It appears that the driver must have noticed the car following him. In accordance with your instructions, we did not try to catch up, though the boosted engine would have made that possible. After informing Service N-2 of the direction in which WKR 821 was heading, we returned to base.

'D-8'

W-192 to Müller:
Top Secret. Only copy.

After taking over surveillance of the Horch with registration number WKR 821 my colleagues ascertained that the owner of this vehicle entered the

118

Natural History Museum at 12.27. Since you had warned us of the object's high degree of professionalism, I decided not to send one or two 'visitors' into the museum to keep track of him. My agent Ilse was instructed to lead a group of pupils through the halls of the museum for a lesson. The details noted by Ilse enabled us to inform you with the utmost confidence that the object did not make contact with anyone in the building. I enclose a copy of the plan of the exhibits which the object scrutinised in particular. The object left the building by way of the emergency exit for the museum staff at 13.04.

'W-192'

Müller put the reports in a file and lifted the telephone receiver.

'Müller speaking,' he replied.

'Comrade Schellenberg greets Comrade Müller,' joked the chief of political intelligence. 'Or do you prefer the English Mister?'

'I prefer to be addressed as Müller,' replied the head of the Gestapo. 'Straightforward, simple and to the point. I'm listening, friend!'

Schellenberg covered the mouthpiece with the palm of his hand and looked at Stirlitz who said: 'Yes, give it to him straight. Otherwise he'll wheedle his way out of things like a crafty old fox . . .'

'Friend,' Schellenberg went on, 'Stirlitz has come round to see me. You remember him perhaps . . . Yes? So much the better. He's bewildered: either some criminals are after him and this worries him, seeing he lives alone in the woods, or some of your chaps have started trailing him. Can you throw some light on the subject?'

'What make is his car?' asked Müller, taking the reports out of the file again.

'What make is your car?' inquired Schellenberg, covering the mouthpiece of the telephone with the palm of his hand again.

'Horch,' came back the answer for Müller.

'Don't keep covering up the phone with the palm of your hand,' said Müller, 'Let Stirlitz take the receiver.'

'Do your eyes grow on stalks?' asked Schellenberg.

'But of course.'

Stirlitz took the receiver and said: '*Heil* Hitler!'

'Good day,' answered Müller. 'The registration number of your car isn't by any chance WKR 821, is it?'

'Right on the mark, Obergruppenführer.'

'Where did they start trailing you? In the Kurfürstendamm?'

'No, in Friedrichstrasse.'

'Did you throw them off in Veteranenstrasse?'

'Yes, sir!'

Müller laughed: 'I'll wring their necks—and they have the cheek to call that work! No cause for alarm, Stirlitz, those weren't criminals on your tail. You needn't lose any sleep out there in your wood. It was our men. They are following a Horch like yours—it belongs to a South American. You can go on living in the same old way . . . but if you are mistaken for South Americans again for some unlikely reason and reports come in to me to the effect that you have been visiting the *Zigeunerkeller* on the Kudamm, I won't hush things up for you any more . . .'

The *Zigeunerkeller*, or Gypsy Cellar, was a small drinking place which the army and party members were forbidden to attend.

'And if I am obliged to go there in the interests of my work?' asked Stirlitz.

'It makes no difference,' sniggered Müller. 'If you want to meet up with your people in foul holes like that, you'd do better to go to the *Mexiko*.'

The *Mexiko* was a favourite spot for Müller's more subtle manoeuvres, and it was there that counter-intelligence used to do a good deal of work. Stirlitz knew about it from Schellenberg, who, of course, had no right to tell him this: a special circular had been issued prohibiting the army and party members to go there. As a result, naïve windbags believed themselves to be in complete safety there, never imagining that each table was bugged by the Gestapo.

'Then I must thank you,' replied Stirlitz. 'If you will be so kind as to give me your permission, I shall meet my men in future in the *Mexiko*. But if they get their claws into me then I shall turn to you for assistance.'

'You're welcome. I shall always be pleased to see you. *Heil Hitler!*'

Stirlitz went back to his own office with mixed feelings: in general he believed what Müller had said to him, because he used to make a habit of playing things straight. But wasn't he rather overdoing it this time? A sense of proportion was the key to success in any kind of work. Still more so when it came to intelligence work. At times exaggerated suspicion seemed less dangerous to Stirlitz than excessive frankness. In any case, when he had to go about an important piece of business that evening he sent for an official car.

Werner to Müller:
Top Secret. Only copy.

Today at 19.42 our object sent for an official car WKN 441. He asked the chauffeur to drive him to the S-bahn station Mittelplatz. There he got out of the car and attempts to find the object later at other S-bahn stations proved fruitless.

Werner

Müller put that report in the shabby file where he kept top priority or secret papers. Then he resumed his study of material on Stirlitz. He underlined in red pencil the place where it had been noted that the object made a habit of visiting museums. It was also noted in the report that he occasionally met his agents in such buildings.

'An interesting character,' thought Müller, 'intelligent and most interesting. I would never have expected such insight on the part of Kaltenbrunner. If he were to work in the apparatus for another five years he'd made at least another Fouché.'

9

SS Obergruppenführer Karl Wolff handed the letter to Himmler's personal pilot and remarked in his gentle voice: 'If your plane's brought down—in war there's no seeing ahead—you must burn this letter even before you undo your parachute straps.'

'I can't burn the letter before I undo my parachute straps,' answered the pilot pedantically, 'otherwise I'll be pulled along the ground. But as soon as I have undone the straps I'll burn your letter.'

'All right,' agreed Wolff with a smile, 'I'll accept that alternative. What is more, you are obliged to burn the letter even if you are brought down inside the borders of the Reich.'

Karl Wolff had good reason to take precautions: should the letter fall into the hands of anyone else but Himmler his fate would be sealed.

Seven hours later the letter was opened by Himmler, revealing the following:

Dear Reichsführer,

Immediately after my return to Italy I started to work out how to approach Dulles, as far as strategic considerations, rather than organisational details, were concerned. The data which I had at my disposal here enabled me to draw the following principal conclusion: the Allies, just like ourselves, are alarmed by the real prospect of the setting up of a Communist government in Northern Italy. Even if the establishment of such a government were to be purely symbolical it would nonetheless open a direct way to the English Channel for Moscow, via Tito's Communists, with the help of the Italian Communist leaders and Maurice Thorez. This means there exists a real threat of a possible 'Bolshevist Belt' from Belgrade to Cannes and Paris via Genoa.

For the operation I used Eugen Dollmann, whose mother, incidentally Italian, has extremely wide contacts among the top aristocracy who, though anti-Nazi, are still pro-German. However, for me the concepts Germany and national socialism are inseparable and, seeing that Frau Dollmann's germanohil sentiments seemed to dominate over all others, I considered it expedient to enlist Eugen, when working out the details of the operation, on the grounds that his mother's contacts might prove most useful to us when it came to conditioning the Allies.

I decided to inform Dulles that the purpose of possible negotiations was to enable the West to establish its control over the whole of Northern Italy before the Communists take over the area, and Dollmann took it upon himself to convey the information using Italian channels. We also were of the opinion that the initiative should not come from us: I thought it would be for the best if the Allies should 'learn' of these attitudes of mine through their own agents. For this reason I authorised Dollmann to carry out the following operation: according to Gestapo reports, Guido Zimmer, a junior officer from the SS tank forces, was observed on several occasions telling the Italians that the war was lost and the situation was quite hopeless. Later Dollmann turned up 'by chance' at an informal party and in the small hours, when everyone had had a good deal to drink, said to Zimmer that he was fed up with this cursed and futile war. Subsequent reports sent in by agents enabled me to ascertain that the very next day Zimmer, in a conversation with Baron Luigi Parilli, had remarked that if Dollmann was talking about 'this cursed war' that meant Karl Wolff thought along the same lines, and indeed, the fate of the whole of Northern Italy and all the German troops stationed there lay in Wolff's hands. In the past, Luigi Parilli had been a representative of an American company and his contacts with America were common knowledge here in Italy, although he had always supported the Duce's regime. What was more, his father-in-law, who was an influential banker in the Lebanon, had ties with both British and French capital. Zimmer's conversation with Parilli had given Dollmann sufficient grounds to invite Guido Zimmer to a cover address where he confronted him with all the compromising material that had been collected against him. 'That is enough to send you straight to the gallows,' Dollmann had said to Zimmer. 'There is only one thing that can save you and that is to fight conscientiously for Germany from now onwards. In this fight diplomatic battles behind the scenes are also extremely important.' To cut a long story short, Zimmer agreed to work for us.

The next day Zimmer, on meeting Baron Parilli, told him that only Wolff, the man in charge of the SS in Italy, could save Northern Italy from the communist threat which the partisans, who were now operating in the mountains and in cities all over the country, were creating there; however, if he were to collaborate with the Allies then, naturally, it might be possible to achieve this swiftly and decisively. Baron Parilli, who has large investments in Turin, Genoa and Milan, listened to what Zimmer had to say with keen interest and offered to help us to set up similar contacts with the Western Allies. Naturally, Zimmer wrote a report on that conversation in my name and so, from that moment on, the whole operation was made to look above-board, to resemble a game with the Allies the moves of which were being controlled by the SS in the interests of the Führer and the Reich.

On February 21 Baron Parilli left for Zurich where he was in touch with his acquaintance Max Husmann, who, in his turn, introduced the baron to Major Waibel, a regular officer in the Swiss intelligence. Waibel explained his readiness to help arrange contacts between the SS and the Americans, proceeding from the selfish interests of the Swiss citizen: namely, the fact that Genoa was the main port used by Swiss firms. If Italy were to fall under Communist rule, Swiss firms would also suffer. I was also able to learn that Major Waibel had in his time graduated from the university of Frankfurt.

In his conversation with Baron Parilli, Waibel had pointed out that maximum precautions should be taken, since arranging these contacts involved considerable risk for him personally. This meant an infringement of Swiss neutrality, and at the present moment the Russians' position was so strong that any infringement of secrecy would force his government to disown him and concentrate all their anger on him personally. Parilli assured Major Waibel that no one had any vested interests in the divulgence of that secret apart from the Russians or the Communists. 'And as so far among us there is, I trust, not a single Communist,' he went on, 'let alone a Russian, there is no need to fear any information leak.'

As I was informed by Waibel, the next day, after his talk with Parilli, he invited Allen Dulles and his assistant Gävernitz to lunch with him. He told them that he had two friends who were putting forward an interesting proposal and that if Dulles so wished he could introduce them to him. Dulles, however, replied that he would prefer to meet Waibel's friends at some later date, after his assistant Gävernitz had had a talk with them.

A meeting between Parilli and Gävernitz was duly arranged. As I informed you earlier, this Gävernitz is not the son of Egon Gävernitz but of Gerhardt von Schulze-Gävernitz, professor of economics at Berlin University. Gävernitz had left for America after receiving his doctorate in

124

Frankfurt (incidentally, it occurred to me that perhaps the original contact between Waibel and Gävernitz dates back to their days in Germany, seeing that they both graduated from the same university) and he started working in international banking concerns in New York, where Allen Dulles was active at the time.

During his conversation with Gävernitz Parilli had asked: 'Are you prepared to meet SS Standartenführer Dollmann for a more detailed discussion of this and some other problems?' Gävernitz had answered that he was ready to follow up the proposal, although, in Parilli's opinion, he viewed it with that obvious distrust and suspicion typical of intellectuals who join intelligence.

I gave my permission for Dollmann to travel to Switzerland. There he was met by Husmann and Parilli on the shore of Lake Chiaso. When they arrived in Lugano and reached the small restaurant Bianci, Dollman, as had been agreed in advance, declared to the others: 'We wish to negotiate with the Western Allies in order to thwart Moscow's plan to set up a Communist government in Northern Italy. This task obliges us to forget former differences and think of the future, cancelling out all the pain we have caused each other in the past.'

Husmann replied that the only possible negotiations in the circumstances were negotiations for an unconditional surrender.

'I shall not resort to treachery,' countered Dollmann, 'and nor will anyone in Germany.'

However Husmann insisted on the term 'unconditional surrender', yet he did not put an end to the conversation despite the firm negative stand adopted by Dollmann who adhered to the 'score' which he and I had drawn up prior to the meeting.

Then Dulles's assistant Paul Blum interrupted Husmann to join in the conversaton. It was Blum who had given Dollmann the names of the two leaders of the Italian Resistance—Parri and Usmiani. Those men are now in one of our prisons. They are not Communists and that led us to draw the conclusion that the Americans like ourselves are concerned about the Communist threat to Italy. They need Resistance heroes who are not Communists and who could at the vital moment head a government loyal to the ideals of the West.

'If these people were freed and brought to Switzerland,' Dulles's representative had explained, 'we could continue our meetings.'

When Dollmann came back to me I realised that the negotiations had begun, for that was the only possible explanation of the request for the *release of the two Italians. Dollmann expressed the assumption that Dulles was expecting my arrival in Switzerland. I went to see Feldmarschall Kesselring, and after a five-hour conversation with him I came to the conclusion that the Feldmarschall would agree to an honourable capitulation although Kesselring did not give me any direct assurances to that effect, probably because of the traditional reluctance to talk frankly with a representative of the security service.*

The next day Parilli visited me at a secret address near Lake Garda and invited me, on Dulles's behalf, to attend a meeting in Zurich. So I shall be leaving for Switzerland the day after tomorrow. If this turns out to be a trap, I shall put forward the official kidnapping story. If, on the other hand, it is the beginning of negotiaions, I shall inform you in my next letter which I shall dispatch to you immediately I return to my own headquarters.

Yours, Karl Wolff

The medical superintendent of the Koch hospital died of brain paralysis. His elder brother Professor Pleischner, formerly Vice-Chancellor of Kiel University, returned home after a period of preventive detention at Dachau a quiet, broken man, his lips curved in a permanent smile of meek obedience. His wife had left him soon after his arrest: her relatives had insisted on it in view of the fact that Hugo von Ens, Frau Pleischner's younger brother, had recently been appointed Neurath's adviser on economic affairs at the German Embassy in Spain. He was regarded as a young man with a promising future and was well thought of at local party headquarters, factors which led the 'family council' to put an ultimatum to Frau Pleischner: either she was to disown the enemy of the state her husband had proved to be, or, if she put her own selfish interests first, she would be ostracised by her whole family—brothers, sisters, sisters-in-law, uncles and aunts—and a public announcement of the complete break would be made in the press.

After Pleischner was released, he came straight to Berlin without visiting Kiel. His brother, who was on close terms with Stirlitz, helped him to obtain a post at the Pergamon Museum where he worked in the Ancient Greece section. It was in that particular spot that Stirlitz used to meet his agents and fairly frequently, after completing his business, he would go and see

Pleischner and they would spend a long time wandering about the enormous empty halls of the magnificent museum. Pleischner soon got to know that Stirlitz would be sure to pause to admire the sculpture *Boy Taking out a Splinter* and walk several times round the sculptural portrait of Caesar in black stone, his white eyes fashioned from some strange transparent mineral. The professor arranged their route in such a way as to allow Stirlitz to linger by the antique masks representing tragedy, laughter and reason. The professor could not, of course, have known that Stirlitz, returning home from these excursions, used to stand before the mirror in his bathroom for a long time, practising suitable facial expressions, as any actor might have done. Stirlitz believed that the intelligence agent should learn to have complete control over his face: the ancients had mastered that art to perfection.

After the Pergamon had been bombed by the British the professor did not evacuate with all the other museum research staff. He secured permission to remain behind in Berlin and help look after what was left of the building.

It was he whom Stirlitz next went to visit. He had no way of contacting Centre now and was desperately in need of some solution to his problem. In the given situation, Stirlitz thought, it would be unreasonable to re-establish the necessary contacts through someone working 'in the dark', as a blind 'letter-box', unaware of what he was actually doing, to what end and for whom.

Stirlitz was then working out how to establish contact with other Soviet citizens in Switzerland, provided, of course, that Schellenberg would send him there to organise on the spot the 'cover operation' involving Pastor Schlag. However it might turn out that Stirlitz, after preparing the whole operation, would have to stay behind in the Reich and other people would be called upon to 'steer' the pastor in Berne. It was quite on the cards. Stirlitz was still seeking some means of contacting Bormann in the knowledge that if he managed to secure Bormann's support there would then be no trouble at all about organising a trip to Switzerland so that he might 'personally keep an eye on the negotiations'. However any kind of contact with Soviet citizens in Berne, who were subjected to vigilant surveillance by all the other intelligence services, would inevitably mean risking the irrevocable and final collapse of the whole operation.

This is why Stirlitz needed a man in whom he could have complete faith. He did trust Pleischner in this way, although he had no faith in his ability to hold out—if everything went up in smoke—and to keep silent once the Gestapo started working on him.

Pleischner was very pleased to see Stirlitz and took him down to his basement office. While he was making coffee on his electric hot-plate, he remarked:

'I never thought I'd miss your visits so much. I don't know your profession, all I know is that you were a friend of my late brother, but I've always found talking to you very interesting, Herr von Stirlitz.'

'Thank you. For me talking to you has been more interesting still. But don't you freeze down here?'

'Sometimes I'm quite numb with cold. What can you do about it, though? Who isn't nowadays, I'd like to know?'

'The Führer's Bunker is very well heated . . .'

'That's understandable . . . Our leader should live in the warm. You can't possibly compare our problems with the cares and worries he has to cope with now, can you?'

Stirlitz took a careful look round the cellar: there was nowhere any bugging device could possibly have been installed. After reassuring himself he started: 'Come now, Professor . . . That frenzied maniac has brought down bombs on the heads of thousands of people, while he, the scoundrel, sits in cosy safety watching films with the rest of the filthy bunch . . .'

Pleischner's face turned as white as a sheet, and Stirlitz regretted that he had said so much and that he had come to bother the poor old man with his affairs at all. 'But why *my* affairs?' he mused to himself. First and foremost they're *their* affairs, affairs that concern them, the Germans, and, consequently him too. I am doing for them what they should be doing themselves.'

'Well,'Stirlitz queried. 'Come now, don't you agree with me?'

The Professor remained silent as before.

'It's like this—your brother and my friend was an anti-fascist, active in the underground. He used to help me. You never asked me what my profession was: I am an SS Standartenführer and work in the intelligence service.'

The professor gave a gasp of horror, his hands went up in despair as if to shield his face from the blow. 'No!' he groaned. 'No, I refuse to believe it! My brother has never been an *agent provocateur* and could never have done that. No!' he repeated louder still. 'No! I won't believe you!'

'He was not a *provocateur*,' agreed Stirlitz. 'But I really am working in intelligence. Soviet intelligence.'

He handed a letter to Pleischner which the doctor had written on his death-bed.

'My friend. Thank you for your friendship. I have learnt a great deal from you. I learnt how one should love and I learnt how in the name of that love one should hate those who enslave Germany. Pleischner.'

'He wrote like that to be on the safe side with the Gestapo,' explained Stirlitz as he put the letter back in his pocket. 'As you yourself are well aware, it is the Bolshevik hordes and the American armadas that are enslaving Germany, of course! Or perhaps it is Hitler who has brought this slavery on you? Hitler and the Nazis?'

Pleischner was silent for a long time, sitting slumped in an enormous armchair. 'I understand,' he said at last. 'You can rely on me one hundred per cent. But I must tell you from the start: once the whip comes down on my back I'm sure to blurt out everything.'

'I know,' said Stirlitz. 'Which would you prefer—instantaneous death from poison or Gestapo tortures?'

'If there were no other way out,' replied Pleischner with one of his rare bewildered smiles, 'naturally I would prefer poison.'

'What was your immediate reaction when I told you who I really was?'

'Relief,' replied Pleischner. 'Enormous relief. Before that I was about to burst with hate and a sense of helplessness.'

'Then we'll start cooking up a nice plot,' went on Stirlitz with a smile.

129

'What must I do?'

'Nothing as yet. Just keep alive. And be ready at any moment to do what proves necessary.'

'In whose name?'

'In the name of Germany.'

'What?!'

'Germany. I mean Germany, not the Reich. I am sure you will agree there is an enormous difference between the two, don't you?'

10

'Good evening, Pastor,' said Stirlitz quickly shutting the door behind him. 'Forgive me for turning up so late. Were you asleep?'

'Good evening. I was asleep, but don't let that worry you.'

'Please forgive me.'

'You may consider yourself forgiven. Please come in and I'll light some candles right away.'

'Fine.'

'Has something happened?'

'Yes.'

'Won't you sit down?'

'Thank you. Where should I sit?'

'Wherever you like. It's warmer by the stove . . . Over here perhaps?'

'But I'll catch cold if I go into the cold afterwards, it's better to try and stay in a constant temperature. Pastor, who has been living here for the last week?'

'Is this an interrogation?'

'No.'

'Then I don't have to answer?'

'You are obliged to answer.'

'And if I refuse?'

'You won't refuse.'

'Why?'

'After your answer, I'll explain why.'

'A man was living here.'

'Who was it?'

'I don't know.'

'Didn't he tell you who he was?'

'No.'

'But didn't you ask him?'

'No. He asked me to take him in, because he was in trouble and I could not refuse.'

'It's good that you're lying to me with such conviction. He

131

told you he was a Marxist. You argued with him as if he were a Communist. But he is not a Communist, Pastor. He has never been one. He is one of my agents, he is an *agent provocateur* from the Gestapo.'

'Oh, so that's it . . . I talked to him as a human being. It's not important who he was: a Communist or one of your agents . . . He asked for protection and I could not refuse him.'

'You could not refuse him,' repeated Stirlitz, 'and it's not important to you who he was: a Communist or an agent of the Gestapo? . . .'

Stirlitz's face grew angry and he went on in a louder voice: 'And if because you see people as "just human beings", as people in the abstract, other men go to the gallows—does that matter to you?'

'Yes, that does matter.'

'And if, to be more precise, your sister and her children end up like that—does that matter to you?!'

The pastor rose from his chair, stretched out his arms in front of him and strode towards Stirlitz:

'But that's an outrage!'

'To say it makes no difference to you who you are dealing with—a Communist or a Gestapo agent—is still more of an outrage,' countered Stirlitz, as he sat down. 'What's more, your outrage is dogmatic and therefore all the more terrible. Sit down. Now listen to me. Your conversation with that agent has been recorded. No, it was not me who did it, but he. I do not know what's become of him. He sent me a strange letter . . . And anyway without the recording, which I have destroyed, no one will believe him. They won't even start talking to him, because he's my agent. As for your sister, she is to be arrested as soon as you have crossed the Swiss border.'

'But I'm not planning to cross the Swiss border.'

'You will cross it, but I shall make sure that your sister is safe.'

'You're like a werewolf . . . How can I believe what you say when you have so many different faces?'

'There is nothing else you can do but believe me, Pastor. And you *will* go to Switzerland, if for no other reason than to save your relatives. Aren't I right?'

132

'Yes. I shall go. To save their lives.'

'Why don't you ask me what you have to do in Switzerland? You'd refuse to go there if I insisted you blew up a church, wouldn't you?'

'You are an intelligent man. You have most likely worked out exactly what I am capable of and what is beyond my power?'

'Correct. Are you sorry for Germany?'

'I am sorry for the Germans.'

'Fine. Do you think that peace—immediate peace—is the best way out for the Germans?'

'I am listening . . .'

'Could you find any of your former friends in Switzerland with whom you used to work in the pacifist movement?'

'A dictatorship has need of pacifists?'

'No, a dictatorship has no need of pacifists. Those who need them are the people who are able to assess the present situation soberly and understand that each new day of the war means new sacrifices and, what's more, senseless ones.'

'So Hitler's going to negotiate?'

'Hitler would never negotiate. This will be done by others. But we're getting ahead of ourselves. First of all, I must have a guarantee from you that you will contact people in Switzerland who possess real weight and authority. We need people who can help us embark on negotiations with representatives of the Western powers. Who could help you in this?'

The pastor shrugged his shoulders: 'Does the President of the Swiss republic suit you?'

'No. That's not what we're looking for. Those are official channels. I mean Church leaders of real weight.'

'All Church leaders have weight in this world,' said the pastor, but on seeing Stirlitz's face quiver in irritation again, he added quickly: 'I have many friends there. It would be naïve on my part to promise anything but I think that it should be possible for me to discuss these questions with people who count. Brüning, for example . . . He's respected in the West. However, I am going to be asked whom I represent.'

'The Germans,' came Stirlitz's abrupt answer. 'If you are asked who exactly intends to take part in negotiations, you are to

133

ask: and who exactly will represent the West in such negotiations? But all that will be done through a contact whom I shall supply you with.'

'Through a what?' asked the pastor in a bewildered voice.

Stirlitz smiled and went on: 'We shall go into all the details later. What's important so far is that you should agree on principle.'

'But what guarantee is there that my sister and her children will not end up on the gallows?'

'Did I secure your release from prison?'

'Yes.'

'Do you imagine that was simple?'

'No, I don't.'

'Do you think I would have been able to send you to the gas chamber armed as I was with a recording of your conversation with the agent, in which you criticise the Führer?'

'Undoubtedly.'

'There's your answer. Your sister will be safe. That is of course, as long as you continue to do the duty of a man lamenting the fate of the Germans, the helpless old people and babes in arms.'

'Are you threatening me?'

'I'm warning you. If you behave differently, I shall be unable to do anything to save you or your sister.'

'When is all this to take place?'

'As soon as the need arises.'

'When might that need arise?'

'Soon. Lastly, whoever asks you about our conversation . . .'

'I shan't say a word.'

'I should like to be able to trust you.'

'Which of us is risking most at the moment?'

'What do you think?'

'I think *you* are.'

'Correct.'

'Are you sincere in your wish to bring about peace for the Germans?'

'Yes.'

'Have you only just come round to the idea of bringing people peace?'

134

'How shall I put it,' replied Stirlitz, 'it would be difficult to give you a completely honest answer, Pastor. The more honest my answer, the greater liar I would seem to you.'

'I should like to have a more concrete idea of what my mission will involve. For I'm not the kind of person who is able to steal documents and pounce on people in the dark . . .'

'In the first place,' said Stirlitz with a smile, 'those things don't take long to learn. And, secondly, I shall not demand that you start pouncing. It's just that we may have need of your friends. Tell them that Himmler is putting a fast one over the West through some representative or other of his—I shall tell you his name later. You shall explain that he or any other of Himmler's men cannot really be seeking after peace and that the *agent provocateur* in question has no real weight and commands no real respect, even in the SS. Tell them that to engage in negotiations with someone like that is not only foolish, but ridiculous. Bring it home to them that it is preposterous to negotiate with the SS, and with Himmler. Tell them that negotiations should be conducted with other people and you will give them the names of influential, powerful and intelligent men . . . But we'll come to that later, we'll go into it all some other time . . .'

Before he left, Stirlitz asked the pastor: 'Is there anyone else in the house apart from your maid?'

'She isn't at home either, she's gone to visit her relatives in the country.'

'May I have a look round the house?'

'By all means . . .'

Stirlitz went upstairs and looked out at the street through a chink in the curtains. He had a good view of the main street of the small town from up there, the whole length of it. There was no one in sight.

Forty minutes later he arrived at the *Mexiko* Bar, where he had arranged to meet one of his agents who was working to ensure strict secrecy around the 'weapon of retaliation'. Stirlitz wished to give the Gestapo chief something to smile about, let him listen to the talk they'd have the next day. It would be a conversation between an intelligent Nazi agent and an intelligent Nazi scientist: after the atomic physicist Runge had been arrested by the Gestapo, Stirlitz made a point of taking precautions for his own reputation from time to time and in no casual manner, but most thoroughly and punctiliously.

'Good morning, Frau Kien . . . How are you getting on? How's the baby?'

'Thank you, Sir. Everything seems to be all right.'

'Thank Goodness! Poor little mites . . . Such hard times for babies to come into the world . . . this frightening world of ours . . . But I have some news for you.'

'Good news?'

'Nowadays all news is bad news, but as far as you're concerned I'd say the news is good rather than bad.'

'Thank you,' replied Käthe. 'I shall never forget your kindness.'

'Please tell me, how's your head now?'

'Much better. At least the dizziness has nearly gone and I no longer have that feeling of nausea.'

'Those are symptoms of concussion.'

'Yes. If it hadn't been for my mane . . . That was what caught the full impact of the steel girder.'

'Why use the word mane? You have gorgeous hair. I admired it when I first came to see you. Do you use any special shampoo?'

'Yes. My husband's uncle used to send us Persian henna and good American shampoo from Sweden.'

Käthe had realised how matters stood during the previous night. She had been thinking back over the questions which the 'man from the insurance company' had put to her. She had decided to start by exposing to his attack the most watertight part of her story. The uncle-in-Stockholm line was reliable and had already been put to the test. She had thought out various ways of explaining away the suitcase. She knew that that would be the hardest thing of all. She felt a splitting pain in her temples when she tried to make herself be honest about the question as to how convincing her stories about the suitcase would be. She decided that if it came up she would try to avoid that matter today by saying that she was really ill. Käthe had decided that

136

she would watch the 'insurance agent' going about his job. The Swedish uncle was the simplest aspect of her particular case. Let that be the test for them both. The main thing was to get a word in first . . .

'By the way, I wanted to ask you something in connection with your uncle . . . Is he on the telephone in Stockholm?'

'To be honest, I don't know. My husband never made calls there.'

She still did not believe that Erwin was no more. She simply could not bring herself to believe it. After her first hysterical outburst, when she was shaken by desperate sobs, an old ward-maid had said to her: 'Come now, dearie . . . It happened to me too with my son. They thought he'd been killed as well, but all the time he was lying in an army hospital. Now he has to hop around on one leg but he's at home and that's the main thing . . . It means he won't be roped into the army and will stay alive.'

Käthe had felt the urge to send a note to Stirlitz right away, to ask him to find out what had happened to Erwin, but she realised that she could not possibly do that. She also realised that at some time she would eventually have to get in touch with Stirlitz. That was why she forced herself not to assume the worst: instead, she made herself think about how she could contact Stirlitz.

'My firm,' the man went on, 'can help you make a telephone call to your husband's uncle, as soon as the doctors let you get up. Those Swedes, you know, are neutrals and they're rich; it's his duty to help you. You let him listen over the phone to your baby's cries and I'm sure his heart'll melt. And now for the next thing . . . I have fixed up with the people who run our branch to pay out your first premium in the next few days before the total extent of your insurance has been verified. But we must have the names of two people who would vouch for you.'

'What?'

'Two people who would guarantee . . . forgive me but I am after all a mere representative of the firm, do get me right—who would vouch for your honesty . . . Please don't get the wrong idea . . .'

'But who would give you such a guarantee?'

137

'Surely you have some friends?'

'That kind? No, I don't think so . . .'

'All right . . . but you must have some acquaintances, surely? Mere acquaintances who would confirm that they had known your husband . . .'

'Do know,' Käthe corrected him.

'Is he alive?'

'Yes.'

'Where is he? Has he been here?'

Käthe shook her head and said: 'No. He's in some hospital. I'm confident that he's alive.'

'I have looked for him.'

'In all the hospitals?'

'Yes.'

'In the military ones as well?'

'Why do you think your husband could have landed up in a military hospital?'

'He's a war casualty . . . A former officer . . . He was unconscious after the bombing. He could have been taken off to a military hospital . . .'

'Now I needn't worry about you nearly so much,' said the man with a smile. 'You've obviously got a head on your shoulders, and things really look as if they're taking a turn for the better. Soon you'll be able to get up and take your little boy out for walks. Fresh air is the best medicine nowadays, just as it always was. But for the moment, please give me the names of some of your husband's acquaintances and then I shall be able to get them to act as guarantors by tomorrow so that we can soon have everything settled.'

Käthe felt the familiar ringing noise in her temples start up again. Each new question from the 'insurance agent' was making it worse and worse. It wasn't so much a ringing noise as a dull metallic hammering, but she realised that to fail to come up with some answer now after she'd avoided all the other specific questions would mean she'd lost out from the start. She tried to recall the houses on their street, particularly those that had been destroyed in the raid. Then all of a sudden she had a brainwave. There was a retired general by the name of Nusch whose radiogram Erwin used to repair. He had come from

Rahnsdorf, of that she was quite sure, near the lake. Let the man ask him.

'You could try approaching a retired general by the name of Fritz Nusch who lives in Rahnsdorf near the lake. He has known my husband for years. I only hope to God that he will prove a good friend now as well.'

'Fritz Nusch,' the man repeated, taking down the name in his little notebook, 'in Rahnsdorf. D'you remember the name of the street?'

'No. I'm afraid not.'

'The local authorities may not give me the address of a general.'

'But he's very old . . . He's long since stopped fighting. He's over eighty.'

'He's still in his right mind, I hope?'

'What?'

'It's all right . . . It was just that I was worried he might have a rather poor memory . . . If I had my way I would round up everyone over seventy, make them give up working and send them to special centres for old people. It's old people who trigger off all the trouble in the world.'

'How can you say that, Sir . . . The General is so kind . . .'

'Fine. Now, who else?'

'Should I mention Frau Korn,' wondered Käthe. 'It would probably be risky. Although we were only paying her a social call, we still had the suitcase with us then and she might remember it if they showed her the photograph. She would have been just the person to pick what with a husband who's a Sturmbannführer in the SS . . .'

'You could try and contact Frau Eichelbrenner. She lives in Potsdam, in a house of her own in a street called An der Mühle.'

'Thank you. That's given me something to get on with at least. I shall try and persuade those people to vouch for you, Frau Kien. Oh, yes, and there was just one other thing . . . Your landlord recognised two of your suitcases among the pieces of luggage that remained intact after the raid. Tomorrow morning I'll come round with him and he and I with the doctor's help will open the cases for you: perhaps you could pick out the things you won't be needing right away and then I could exchange them for some clothes for your bonny boy.'

'That's obviously what he came round here for,' thought Käthe to herself. 'He hopes I'll try and make contact with my friends today.'

'Thank you very much,' she said at last. 'God will repay you for the kindness you have shown me. Good deeds never go forgotten.'

'Are you a Catholic?'

'No, my family always belonged to the Protestant church.'

'And I am a Catholic . . . Not that it's of any importance; what counts is that everyone should let God into his heart . . . Now, the very last formality . . . He held out a piece of paper to her. 'Please sign this application for immediate payment of part of your premium. Sign here please. Thank you. I hope you'll be completely recovered very soon and give your strapping baby an extra kiss from me.'

After leaving the ward the 'insurance agent' summoned the ward-maid to the doctor's office to give her the following instructions: 'As soon as she asks you to telephone anybody or hands you a note, telephone me immediately, at home or at work—it doesn't matter. Any time. Any time whatever,' he repeated. 'And if anyone comes to see her, ring this number,' he added, passing her a piece of paper. 'These people are only three minutes away. Make sure the visitor remains on the premises on any pretext. Any pretext whatever.'

 As he was coming out of his office, Stirlitz saw Erwin's suitcase being taken down the corridor. He would have recognised it among thousands: it was the case with the transmitter.

Feeling dazed, Stirlitz started walking slowly down the corridor after it: two men, talking animatedly to each other, carried it into the office of Sturmbannführer Rolff. When he had followed them that far, Stirlitz hesitated for a moment, wondering whether he should go into Rolff's office immediately or wait for a bit. He felt himself go tense and, before he had really thought out how he should act in the circumstances, found himself blindly following his instincts. He gave a short rap on the door with the knuckle of his index finger. Without waiting for an answer he walked straight in.

'Are you planning to evacuate then?' he asked with a laugh. He had not thought the question out in advance; it had taken shape of its own accord and in the given situation, was more suitable than anything else he could have chosen even if he had spent hours wracking his brains.

'No,' Rolff replied. 'It's a wireless-transmitter.'

'Oh . . . Are they your hobby? And where's the owner?'

'We've only got his wife here. The owner, as far as we know, has kicked the bucket. She's in an isolation ward of a hospital with a new-born baby.'

'A baby?'

'Yes. The bitch has had her head knocked about too.'

'What on earth do you plan to do with a sick woman. You can't get much out of her if she's in that state.'

'On the contrary, we can make the most of her present condition. There's no point in just twiddling our thumbs and wasting time. The worst of it is, that a blockhead from the department showed her a photograph of some suitcases, including this one. He went to ask her if she recognised any of her things in the picture! Thank God she can't make a getaway though: her kid's in the same hospital and no one is allowed into the children's ward. I don't think she'd leave without the child . . . Although you never know . . . I've decided to fetch her along here today.'

'That's a good idea,' agreed Stirlitz. 'Have you got someone keeping an eye on things? We must make sure she doesn't manage to contact anyone . . .'

'Yes, we've briefed one of the ward-maids there to report on anything suspicious and we've replaced the hospital porter with one of our men.'

'Is there much point in bringing her out then? You might spoil the whole game. After all she might try and look up some contact.'

'I myself am in a quandary. I'm worried lest she come to. You know those Russians—you need to get at them when they're still in a daze and shaky.'

'What made you decide she was Russian?'

141

'That was what started the whole business off. She screamed away in Russian when she was giving birth.'

'Which hospital is she in?'

'The Charité Clinic, so bringing her over would be a matter of a mere ten minutes.'

Stirlitz braced his shoulders and, already heading for the door, urged, 'Fetch her over and don't linger . . . although perhaps you might spoil the whole game . . . We might get onto something really hot if she starts looking up contacts. Don't you think their men will be looking round all the hospitals to find her?'

'That is something we have not gone into fully yet.'

'I make a present of it to you . . . Today's not too late to start. So long for now, I wish you every success.' As he reached the door, Stirlitz turned round. 'It's an interesting case, an extremely interesting one,' he said. 'The vital thing here is not to hurry unnecessarily. I would advise you not to mention all this to the bosses yet: they'll only make you rush it.'

When he had already opened the door, Stirlitz clutched his forehead and laughing said: 'My memory's going to the dogs . . . What I had really come to see you about was sleeping pills: everyone tells me you've got some good Swedish ones.'

That last sentence will stick, deduced Stirlitz to himself. How one opens a conversation is important, but still more artistry is required to round it off. 'Now,' thought Stirlitz, 'if anyone asks Rolff who came to see him and what about, he's sure to answer that Stirlitz came by to ask for Swedish sleeping pills.' Rolff used to supply half the department with them, being lucky enough to have a pharmacist for an uncle.

After his exchange with Rolff, Stirlitz's next step was to go and read the Riot Act in Schellenberg's office. He opened with: 'Brigadenführer, I think I have no choice but to ask for sick leave—I really have had enough—and ask for ten days in a santitorium—otherwise I'm a write-off . . .'

Indeed, Stirlitz was pale with anger, if not blue in the face, as he let off steam in front of the chief of political intelligence, and not only because Käthe's fate, and, hence his own, hung in the balance. He knew what was in store for her after some four hours of interrogation, a pistol would be put to the back of the baby's head and she would be told that the baby would be shot in front of her very eyes if she did not come forward with the necessary information. It was an old, familiar trick of Uncle Müller's: so far they had not had to shoot any of the babies . . . It was not because of any sense of pity. Indeed, Müller's men were capable of devising horrors a good deal worse; it was just that they realised that after seeing her baby shot a mother would go mad and no longer be of any use to them. However, that particular type of intimidation always proved effective.

Nor was Stirlitz blue in the face at the thought of the torture that awaited him too if Käthe should mention his name. It was all much simpler than that: his fury was a part he was playing, and his mind exerted such precise and complete control over his body that the end result was the perfect harmony which only the greatest actors attain. A secret agent worth his salt has much in common with an actor or writer: the only difference is that while unconvincing acting or contrived illogical writing spell nothing more terrible than rotten tomatoes or scathing reviews, for the secret agent a false note can spell death.

'What's up?' asked Schellenberg. 'What's got into you?'

'Brigadenführer, as far as I can see, Müller's making a fool of us. Yesterday there was that ridiculous business with his car trailing me on Friedrichstrasse and today he goes still further: they find a Russian woman with a wireless-transmitter, who appears to have been most active. I've been hunting for that transmitter for eight months, but for some reason the case lands up on Rolff's desk, although he understands as much about wireless messages as I do about lesbianism!'

Schellenberg at once stretched out his hand to pick up the telephone receiver.

'You'd better not,' said Stirlitz. 'It won't help. It'll just mean another of those tiffs between Intelligence and Counter-Intelligence. It's best to leave it well alone. Just give me the go-ahead to go round to the Russian girl now, bring her back here to our department and at least conduct the first interrogation. Perhaps I flatter myself, but that is something I do better than Rolff. Then, let him try his hand—after all, what's important to me is not my own prestige but the final outcome of the affair.'

'Off you go,' replied Schellenberg. 'But nevertheless I shall still ring the Reichsführer.'

'It would be better to go and see him,' remarked Stirlitz. 'I don't like the idea of a whole lot of fuss.'

'Off you go,' repeated Schellenberg, 'and get on with the job in hand. After that we'll have to discuss the pastor. We'll be needing him tomorrow or the day after.'

'I can't do two things at once . . .'

'Yes, you can. A secret agent either gives in right away or never. Apart from rare exceptions, they collapse after Müller's blood-letters start using their special methods. Everything becomes quite clear very early on. If that girl is not going to give, then hand her over to Müller, let them wrack their brains over it. But if she does give, then we can chalk that up to our credit and it'll be one in the eye for the Bavarian.'

That was how Schellenberg used to refer to Gestapo chief Müller, one of the men whom he hated beyond words, whenever he was annoyed.

'Stirlitz produced his pass in the casualty ward and was told which way to go to reach the ward where Käthe was. When she caught sight of him, her eyes opened wide in astonishment and tears welled up in them: she made an involuntary movement towards him but Stirlitz, fearing that the ward was bugged, came out with a curt command that did not let Käthe get a word in edgeways: 'Frau Kien, collect your things. The game is up, and intelligence agents should know how to make brave losers. I know that you will try to deny everything, but it would be ridiculous. Forty of your coded messages have been seized. Your clothes will now be brought in to you and then you will come along with me. I guarantee that you and your child will be safe if you agree to work for us. However, if you choose to be stubborn I make no such guarantees.'

Stirlitz waited for the ward-maid to bring in Käthe's suit, coat and shoes. Then Käthe, who had grasped the kind of part she was expected to play, asked: 'Perhaps you wouldn't mind leaving the room while I dress?'

'No, I shall remain here but turn my back to you while I continue to explain the situation and you think over your answers.'

144

'I shall not tell you anything,' said Käthe. 'I have nothing to tell you. I don't understand what has happened and I am still very weak. I think the misunderstanding will soon clear itself up. My husband is an officer, invalided out of the war . . .'

A strange sense of joyous relief had swept over Käthe. At last she saw a friend and she was confident that now, whatever hardships might lie ahead, the most terrible thing of all, complete isolation, was already past . . .'

'Don't talk nonsense,' Stirlitz retorted, interrupting her. 'Your radio-transmitter is now in our hands and we also have various wireless messages that have been decoded. Such evidence is quite incontestable. One thing, and one thing only is required of you: that you should agree to co-operate with us. And I advise you,' he said, turning round and making every effort to use his eyes and pale face to convey that what was coming was something most important, to which she should pay the utmost attention and try to understand, 'to agree to my proposal and in the first place tell us everything you know, even if you only know very little, and, in the second, to accept my proposal and start to work for us without delay in the next couple of days . . .'

Stirlitz realised that they would not be able to talk in the car: outside a car was trailing them; however hard Müller might maintain it was mere coincidence, any conversation on the way back to headquarters might go on record. That meant they would have to make the most of the hospital corridor on their way out and at least get the essentials said. However, after listening to what he had said to her in the ward, Käthe ought to be able to grasp the situation in the course of a brief exchange. They had only about two minutes at their disposal—that he had calculated on the way up to the ward.

The ward-maid brought in the baby and said: 'The child is ready. I'll carry him out to the car.'

'There's no need,' said Stirlitz, 'that will be all. Frau Kien will take the child herself. Make sure that there are no patients walking about in the corridor as we make our way out.'

The woman left, and Stirlitz stood back to let Käthe go out of the door in front of him. As they walked along, he put one hand under her elbow to help support the baby and then, as he noticed how her arms were shaking, he took the child himself.

145

'Listen, Käthe,' he said in a quiet voice, and keeping his cigarette in his mouth, 'They know everything.'

'Throw the cigarette away, you'll get smoke in the baby's eyes,' asked Käthe.

'I can't,' he replied, 'I've only got a minute. That's not the most terrible thing that can happen in the present situation. Listen carefuly. They'll give you some information to pass on to our people. Bargain with them, demand guarantees, demand that they let you keep the child with you . . . Only give way if they threaten the child: they may well record all our conversations, so you must act your part out in my office very carefully. You don't know the code and our wireless messages have not been decoded. Erwin was the cipher expert, you—merely the wireless-operator. I'll cope with the rest. Tell them that Erwin used to meet our chief in the neighbourhood of Kantstrasse and in Rahnsdorf. Who they were you don't know. Tell them that a man from the Foreign Ministry used to come and see Erwin. When we're in the car I'll show you his photo. That's the lot. Got it?'

The man from the Foreign Ministry was an advisor from the East-European section of the Ministry by the name of Heinz Korner, who had been killed in a car accident the week before. That would give them a false lead and make the Gestapo people waste ten days, if not a fortnight. As things stood, each day could decide a great deal . . .

Five hours later Rolff reported to Müller that the Russian radio-operator had disappeared from the Charité Clinic. Müller was beside himself at the news. Then, two hours later, he had a telephone call from Schellenberg: 'Good evening, my friend . . . Stirlitz has prepared us a fine surprise: he brought over the Russian radio-operator who has already agreed to work for us. The Reichsführer has already congratulated him on this success.'

Stirlitz knew that the code had not been broken. It would have been virtually impossible to do so since it was his own personal code and the Gestapo did not have the key to it. The code, that Centre had sent to Stirlitz, involved another key which the radio-operator could not have known: only the cipher expert needed to know it, and nothing could break his silence now that he lay buried beneath the ruins of his house.

While he sat in Schellenberg's office and listened to him chatting to Müller, Stirlitz asked himself for the hundredth time if he had done the right thing by bringing his comrade-in-arms Katya Kozlova, Käthe Kien, Inge, to their headquarters, to prison. He could, of course, have bundled her into the car and driven off to Babelsberg, to hide her and eventually supply her with new papers. That would have meant that while saving Käthe's life the whole operation would have come to nothing, an operation planned by Centre, which affected the lives of hundreds of thousands of Russian soldiers and was bound in one way or another to influence the future of Europe. His 'kidnapping' of Käthe from hospital would have had the whole Gestapo alerted and would be traced to him without fail. He too would have had to go underground, thereby ruining the whole operation. To stay in any ordinary, outwardly inconspicuous house would have been more dangerous for Käthe than agreeing to work for the Gestapo and receive accommodation at one of their cover addresses. The agents living in such flats, who had agreed to work for the other side against their former employers, were treated quite tolerably. Stirlitz knew he was staking everything, that the war was nearly over, which meant that Müller's butchers would at any minute run amuck and destroy all those who were within reach in their torture chambers. That was what had made him tell Käthe that she should say that nothing linked her with Russia any longer now that her husband was dead and insist from the very start that whatever happened, she must never fall into the hands of her former chief. That was the story to be kept in reserve, in case Käthe was handed over to the Gestapo after all. If Stirlitz could know for sure that she would remain in his charge, he would feel less worried and not keep asking himself if he had done the right thing or not? He would take her round to the 'wireless flat' under SS guard and then at an opportune moment arrange her disappearance with the child so that no one would find her. But despite the tragic situation at the front and the flood of refugees pouring into central Germany, the Gestapo still continued to work with well-oiled precision: every other person was informing on his next-door neighbour, who, in turn, was reporting on the informer. So only people who were naïve and ill-acquainted with the German secret police could imagine that it would be possible to make an unobstructed getaway in the midst of all that complex double-think.

Müller spent three hours going into the details of the Russian girl's first interrogation. He compared the recording which Stirlitz had supplied with the tape-recording made with the help of a device concealed in the plug near Stirlitz's desk. The answers given by the girl matched up completely, but the questions the Standartenführer had put to her as written down in his report differed from what he had actually said.

'He sure is a sharp worker, that Stirlitz,' commented Müller to Rolff, 'just listen to the way he prepared her, first-class stuff!'

After winding back the reel of tape Müller switched on Stirlitz's voice: 'I'm not going to bother to repeat the home-truth for you that in Moscow your arrest will be as good as a death sentence. A person who lands up with the Gestapo inevitably comes to a sticky end. Anyone who comes out of those four walls alive is looked on as a traitor and only as a traitor. Am I not correct? That's the first point I want to make. I shall not ask you for the names of the other agents still at liberty: that is not important, for in their efforts to find you they're bound to fall into my hands. That's the second thing. You must understand that as a human being and an officer of the Reich I cannot regard your position without some sympathy: I am aware of how much you will suffer if circumstances obliged us to put your child into a home. It will mean that the child will be deprived of a mother for good. Don't misunderstand me, I am not threatening you. It's simply that even if I had not wanted to do so, I have superiors, and it will always be much easier for people who have not seen you with your baby in your arms to give orders. And I have no choice but to carry out orders: I am a soldier, and my fatherland is at war with your country. A final, fourth point: in the past we obtained some of your Soviet films made in Alma-Ata by Moscow film-makers who presented the Germans as fools and our organisation as a mad-house. If that were really the case then how did we get as far as the outskirts of Moscow and the Volga, if we're that stupid . . .'

At that moment Stirlitz had winked at Käthe and she, catching on at once, had replied: 'Yes, but now Red Army units have reached the outskirts of Berlin.'

'Correct. When our troops were on the outskirts of Moscow, you believed that you would get to Berlin, just as we now are convinced that we shall soon be returning to the Kremlin. But more of such discussion another time. I had started to tell you that our cipher experts are no fools, that they have already gone a long way towards breaking your code and that one of our men could carry out your work, as the wireless-operator . . .'

Again Stirlitz winked at Käthe, and she said: 'Your wireless-operator would not know my touch, which is something they're very familiar with at Centre.'

'Correct. However, we have some of your reports recorded on tape and it would be no problem to teach your touch to one of our men. Then he could take over your work. That would compromise you once and for all back home and there could be no question of any mercy—you must know that as well as I do, if not better.'

Again Stirlitz gave a nod to Käthe, but she sat there in silence clasping to her breast the sleeping baby.

'If you behave reasonably,' he went on, 'I promise you a convincing alibi that will satisfy even your bosses.'

'That's impossible,' broke in Käthe, not needing a signal from Stirlitz that time.

'You are mistaken. It is possible. Your arrest will not be noted down anywhere in any of our records. You will be given accommodation in a flat where some good friends of mine live and where you'll be able to take care of your little girl properly.'

'It's a boy.'

'Forgive me . . . If you come across any of your people later, tell them that a man found you after the death of your husband who gave you the password . . .'

'I don't know any password . . .'

'Yes, you do,' insisted Stirlitz, 'you do know it, but I shall not ask you for it. These are all minor details. Well, to continue, the man who gave you the password took you to this flat and gave you some coded messages to be transmitted to Centre. That is your alibi. In plays and films about secret agents they are usually given time to think things over. This is something I, for one, am not going to do: I want a straight "Yes" or "No", now, at once.'

Silence.

Müller looked at Rolff and commented: 'Only one gaffe, he mixed up the child's sex. He referred to it as a girl, but otherwise real virtuoso stuff.'

'Yes,'answered Käthe in a quiet voice that was almost a whisper.

'Come again,' said Stirlitz.

'Yes,' Käthe repeated, 'Yes! Yes! Yes!'

'Now that's fine,' said Stirlitz. 'And there's no need to get hysterical. You knew what you were letting yourself in for when you agreed to work against us.'

'But I make one condition,' said Käthe.

'I'm listening.'

'I have lost all contact with my own country since my husband died and I was arrested. I shall work for you only if you guarantee that I shall never fall into the hands of my former bosses.'

All of a sudden Käthe went white and started to slide slowly down from her chair onto the floor. Stirlitz managed to rush up to her in time to catch the baby. Then he called to the ADC on duty outside the door and said: 'See the prisoner is put into the prison hospital. Make sure that she is treated very carefully . . . Her nerves are in a bad way, it'll pass though . . .'

'We musn't let her out of our sight,' Stirlitz insisted when discussing the case later with Schellenberg. 'It would be the height of careless stupidity, particularly now when we're starting on the game with the Bible-basher. It would be first-rate if you could enlist the Reichsführer's support.'

'I'll have a shot,' replied Schellenberg. 'But what motives to use?'

150

'There's no shortage of those,' remarked Stirlitz with a nonchalant shrug of his shoulders.

'A plan to get misinformation to the British by way of Portugal and get the desired messages across to Moscow: we'll have them really guessing . . .' said Schellenberg slowly as a new plan started taking shape in his mind.

'Too risky, but interesting nonetheless.'

'All right, we'll be thinking it over. I congratulate you on your success, Stirlitz. We've really taken the wind out of Müller's sails this time. Very nice too . . .'

Although Stirlitz considered his most important task was to ascertain the extent of the atomic research then being carried out, he was all too well aware that one man, however intelligent, was not in a position to cope with everything. He was worried about the lack of any means of contacting Centre. People who know little about the intelligence agent's work tend to believe that such a position is the result of lack of initiative or incapacity for independent thought or reluctance to take bold decisions. But concern of this kind testifies to a high degree of professionalism. An agent worth his salt realises that without directives from above he may well let himself in for un-necessary, time-wasting activity involving senseless risks, for it may well emerge that the task he sets himself when out of touch with his superiors may well have already been carried out in some other corner of the globe, by someone else and at a different time. When an agent is abroad and has lost touch with his central organisation, he is unable to judge—at least with sufficient reliability—how important and effective is the work he happens to be engaged in.

The long years he had spent abroad had taught Stirlitz to grasp even the slightest nuances in the coded messages which he received from Centre.

Now that his frontal attack against Bormann had failed for some inexplicable reason, Stirlitz was desperately in need of direct contact with Moscow. He needed to get hold of at least a couple of names, a couple of addresses of those who, even if they had no direct or indirect links with Bormann himself, had

151

some means of contacting the niece of the cousin married to the sister of his cook's brother-in-law ... Stirlitz laughed to himself—he found the relationship amusing.

'Delay is tantamount to death at the moment,' he thought to himself. 'I can't send the pastor to Switzerland until I've got Fleischner over the border. And there's no sense in sending Pleischner over until I find a means of approaching Bormann. To wait till Centre sends me another radio-operator means losing at least a month. At the moment I can't possibly wait that long—it looks very much as if things are going to be decided in a matter of days or at the very most a few weeks.'

Stirlitz considered the possible reasons for Bormann's failure to turn up at the appointed meeting-place. He might not have received the letter—one. As he analysed the content of the letter, Stirlitz realised he had made some major mistakes in its composition—two. He was often saved by an innate quality enabling him to re-analyse actions, conversations, letters and then, without getting upset by possible mistakes, to search for and find a way out of a situation that the mistakes might have engendered, instead of burying his head in the sand and just 'hoping for the best'. The letter he had dispatched did not hold out any risk for him personally: he had typed it on a typewriter in the dispatch office during an air raid. So there was no direct means of tracing the letter to him. It was just that for a man of Bormann's calibre there had been too many protestations of patriotic loyalty and too few facts or concrete proposals. The mind of a statesman differs considerably from the mentality of those on the lower rungs of the totalitarian ladder. The enormous responsibility incumbent upon a man, who is virtually accountable to no one other than himself for the decisions he takes, would make someone like Bormann feel bound to talk to a subordinate only when given facts not known to anyone else and of national significance. However, Stirlitz reckoned that on the other hand even the tiniest crumbs of information that might compromise Himmler would be of interest to Bormann. Stirlitz knew what had started the feud between Himmler and Bormann, but he could not find a satisfactory explanation for the fact that it still raged with ever-growing ferocity. Finally, Stirlitz also took into account the fact

152

that Bormann could simply have been busy and therefore unable to come to the appointed meeting-place.

The whine of the sirens started up again. Stirlitz looked at his watch and noted that it was 10.00 p.m. The sunset that evening had been blood-red running into purple, which meant that the night would be frosty.

Bombs came down very near the building and Stirlitz decided he would go down into the shelter. 'It sounds as if they're about to bring this place down. It would be stupid to die now.'

He went out of his office and walked along the empty corridor to the stairs which led down into the shelter. Near the door leading to the hot-line telephones, he paused. He did not realise why he did so at first and then it dawned on him: the key was sticking in the door.

Stirlitz frowned in surprise and took a quick look round: the corridor was empty, for everyone had gone down into the shelter. He pushed the door with his shoulder but it didn't open, and he had to unlock it. The lights were turned off, although the windows were hung with thick black-out curtains. Stirlitz groped for the switch and turned on the light. Two large white telephones stood out from among the rest: those were the hot-line telephones leading directly to the Führer's Bunker and Bormann's, Goebbels's and Keitel's offices.

Stirlitz looked out into the corridor and saw that it was deserted as before. The window-panes were shaking from the bombing that was going on close at hand.

He walked up to one of the telephones and dialled Bormann's number: 12 00 54.

'Bormann here,' came the reply in a low strong voice.

'Did you receive my letter,' asked Stirlitz, disguising his voice.

'Who's that?'

'You should have received a letter of mine—a private one from a devoted party member.'

'Yes. How do you do. Where are you? Oh, yes . . . I understand. The number of my car . . .'

'I know it,' Stirlitz interrupted. 'Who will be driving?'

'Does that matter?'

'Yes. One of your chauffeurs . . .'

'I know,' Bormann interrupted.

They had both understood what the other was getting at. Bormann understood that Stirlitz knew all his conversations were being tapped, which showed that the person who was talking to him was initiated into the top secrets of the Reich. Stirlitz, in his turn, had been able to conclude that Bormann had understood everything he had hinted at between the lines and thus felt sure his message had got across.

'You are expected at the place where we were to have met, at the time you indicated before, tomorrow.'

'Now,' said Stirlitz, 'subtract fourteen and a half hours from that time and switch it to today.'

'*Heil* Hitler!' said Bormann and put down the receiver.

11

Half an hour later Stirlitz saw an armoured Maybach drive up to the Natural History Museum. He walked past it and saw Bormann sitting on the back seat. Making sure there was no one trailing him, Stirlitz retraced his steps and, opening the back door, said:

'Parteigenosse Bormann, I am grateful to you for the trust you have shown in me . . .'

Bormann shook his hand without saying anything at first, just looking hard at Stirlitz's face. 'Head for Wannsee,' he told the chauffeur.

Then Bormann shut the glass partition separating the driver's compartment from the rest of the car. 'Where have I seen you before?' he asked, taking another careful look at Stirlitz. 'Go on, take off your camouflage . . .'

Stirlitz put his glasses on his lap and raised the brim of his hat.

'I'm quite sure I've seen you before,' he repeated.

'Quite correct,' replied Stirlitz. 'When I was awarded my Iron Cross you remarked that I had the face of a professor of mathematics, not a spy.'

'At the moment the opposite applies,' joked Bormann. 'But now what's been happening, out with it.'

The telephone-link between Bormann's office and the Reich's security office had not been used the whole night through. So when data collected from recorded conversations were laid on Himmler's desk the next morning, at first he went wild with rage and then, after calming down, took fright and sent for Müller. The latter was instructed to try and ascertain, treading most carefully while doing so, who had used one of the special hot-line telephones to talk to Party HQ the previous night.

In the course of the next twenty-four hours Müller was unable to come up with any concrete information. Late that afternoon he was supplied with the fingerprints left behind on

155

the telephone receiver by Bormann's as yet unidentified caller. The striking thing about them was that, according to data already on hand the Gestapo had come across identical fingerprints a few days before, on the radio-transmitter belonging to the Russian woman.

Bormann's chauffeur, who in the past, with Bormann's permission, had refused to become an informer for the SD, was arrested on his way home from work. For three hours he said nothing but merely demanded to be allowed to talk to Bormann. However, after tougher interrogation he admitted that a stranger had got into Bormann's car the previous evening. What he had talked to Bormann about the chauffeur was unable to relate, since their conversation had gone on in the passenger compartment of the car behind a thick partition of bullet-proof glass. He described the man who had got into the car, saying that he had been wearing a hat pulled down low over his forehead, horn-rimmed glasses, and that he had a grey moustache. The chauffeur was then asked to look at two hundred photographs, among which was one of Stirlitz, but a Stirlitz without glasses or a moustache, which were easy to stick on and just as easy to take off again in an emergency, and in addition, the photographs were all five years out of date, and five years of war are apt to change people's appearance considerably, sometimes beyond recogniton.

After Himmler had been informed by Müller as to the results of the investigation, he approved Müller's proposal to take the fingerprints of every member of the SD staff without their knowledge. Müller also suggested that Bormann's chauffeur should be removed, but in such a way that it should look as if he had been run over by accident near his house. At first Himmler was ready to agree to that step which appeared necessary, but then he stopped himself, for he had ceased to trust anybody, Müller included.

'*You* think that one out. Perhaps he ought to be let off completely?' queried Himmler in a casual aside, well aware of what Müller would say next.

'That's impossible, he's been given the whole works.'

That was exactly the answer the Reichsführer had expected.

'I don't know really,' Himmler went on with a troubled frown. 'That chauffeur is an honest fellow and we don't punish honest men . . . Think up something yourself.'

Müller left Himmler's office quite furious: he realised that the Reichsführer was afraid of Bormann and was using him, Müller, as a scapegoat. 'No,' he decided, 'I can play that game too. Let the chauffeur stay alive. He shall be *my* trump card.'

Soon afterwards Himmler summoned Otto Skorzeny to his office.

'I need Bormann's archives,' he announced. 'You realise, I suppose, Skorzeny, what it is I'm asking for?'

'Yes, I realise.'

'It's a far tougher job than abducting the Duce.'

'I should think so.'

'But is it possible?'

'I don't know.'

'Skorzeny, an answer of that kind is unsatisfactory. Any day now Bormann will start evacuating his archives—where to and with what security—you must find out. Schellenberg will help you on the quiet, just with some general advice.'

'I understand, Herr Reichsführer.'

After telling Schellenberg about his idea to get Pastor Schlag across the border, Stirlitz took the night express to the Swiss frontier, so as to 'prepare the window'. He, like Schellenberg, considered that if the pastor were to cross the border openly, too much attention might be attracted to the whole affair. The whole operation was planned without the Gestapo's knowledge. If the Gestapo had known that a man, who was already compromised himself and who had been illegally released on Schellenberg's personal instructions were to cross the border, there was no doubt that, although he would have been allowed to cross into Switzerland, from the very outset he would have been kept under surveillance which was very definitely not part of the plan for this 'cover operation'. Schlag's 'exposure' after he had carried out his task, would according to Schellenberg's plan be carried out by none other than Stirlitz.

Before leaving for the border, Stirlitz, with Schellenberg's approval, had been preparing 'candidates' for the pastor's fellow conspirators, who, it had been decided, must be men from the Foreign Ministry and Göring's Luftwaffe staff. It was in those establishments that men were picked out who were particularly ardent servants of Nazism and whom he knew to be Gestapo informers. What appealed to Schellenberg in particular was the fact that all of them had been recruited by the Gestapo.

'That's a first-class move,' he remarked, 'really promising.'

Stirlitz looked at him inquiringly.

'Insofar as it enables us to compromise all those in the West who try to put out peace feelers using any channels other than our own,' Schellenberg explained. 'Over there a sharp distinction is drawn between our department and the Gestapo.'

'I hadn't thought of that,' Stirlitz admitted to himself. 'He really knows his stuff, and he's always a couple of moves ahead. Thanks for the tip, Schellenberg.'

The night express on which Stirlitz headed south was one of the few that still maintained pre-war standards of comfort: the straps supporting the berths in the sleeping compartments were made of real leather. The gleaming brass ashtrays and lampstands made you think you were on board a ship and the attendants brought round strong coffee. It was a train used almost exclusively by diplomats travelling to Switzerland from Scandinavia.

Stirlitz had berth No. 74. Berth 56 in the adjoining carriage was occupied by a Swedish professor with a deathly pallour and a long awkward Scandinavian surname. They were the only passengers in the two international carriages, apart from a general returning to the Italian front after convalescence leave. The general looked into Stirlitz's compartment and asked: 'Are you German?'

'Alas,' replied Stirlitz.

In his case it was possible to make such jokes, for he did it with official sanction. He could use jokes for provocation purposes. In cases where one of two people taking part in a conversation informs on the other there is a safety-valve—official permission. If, on the other hand, the second person does not inform on you, then there is the prospect that he might work on your side later. At one time the question had been discussed in the Gestapo: should such disreputable conversations be broken off at once or allowed to develop. Some people in the SD considered that they should be broken off at once, for fear was a reliable deterrent. Another group, to which Stirlitz also belonged, maintained that it was vital to provoke people to voice their opinions on the most touchy subjects whenever possible.

'Why "alas"?' inquired the general.

'Because I haven't been brought a second cup of coffee. They only bring you real coffee when you first ask for it, if you have a foreign passport.'

'Is that so? But I was given a second cup. And I've got some cognac! Would you like a drink?'

'Thank you. But I also have some with me.'

'So you and I seem to be getting the same service,' remarked the general, watching what Stirlitz was taking out of his brief-case. 'What is your rank?'

'I'm a diplomat. An advisor in the third department of the Foreign Ministry.'

'So you're the people whom everyone's been cursing,' the general went on, sitting down in the chair at the side of the hand-basin fitment. 'It's precisely you who are to be blamed for everything.'

'Why?'

'Because it's you who determine foreign policy, because it's you who have let things slide so far that we've landed ourselves in a war on two fronts. *Prost!*'

'*Prosit!* Are you from Mecklenburg?'

'Yes. How did you guess?'

'By the way you said *Prost*. All Northerners tend to swallow their vowels.'

The general laughed: 'That's true,' he said. 'Listen, I couldn't have seen you at the Ministry of Aviation yesterday, could I?'

Stirlitz was taken aback most unpleasantly: the day before he had indeed taken Pastor Schlag to the Ministry of Aviation to 'make contact' with people in close touch with Göring's entourage. If the whole operation proved a success, then the Gestapo would be brought in—this time at Schellenberg's request for elucidation of details of the 'conspiracy'—and it was necessary that the pastor should have left a trail behind him, leading among other places to the Ministry of Aviation, the Luftwaffe, and the Ministry of Foreign Affairs. In the Ministry of Aviation, Schlag, after registering his passport, had asked for information concerning Walter Schmiedekopf, and in the Ministry of Foreign Affairs he delivered a letter to be handed to Dr Kleist, who had been the first person to explore opportunities for making contact with the Western powers in Stockholm.

'No,' thought Stirlitz to himself, as he poured out cognac. 'That general couldn't have seen me. No one walked past me when I was sitting in the car. It's very unlikely that Müller would have put a general on my trail—that's not his way of going about things.'

'No, I wasn't there,' he replied. 'Strange thing about this face of mine: everyone thinks they've seen it somewhere before.'

'It's not one to stand out in a crowd,' agreed the general. 'The kind of face you come across rather often.'

'Is that a good thing or a pity?'

'For a spy it's probably useful, but for a diplomat I shouldn't think it's much of an advantage. You need distinctive faces.'

'What about you army people?'

'What we need nowadays is a strong pair of legs.'

'And when it comes to heads?'

'Do they really matter? Other people do our thinking for us, we merely put their ideas into practice. It's our legs that are important, our legs, so that we can flee in time.'

'Aren't you afraid to talk to a stranger like that?'

'But you don't know who I am.'

'It would be easy enough to find out, for you have a most distinctive face.'

'Do I? Funny, I'd always thought I had the most ordinary of faces. Never mind, it'll take time for you to write your report on me and then for them to get hold of a second witness, and by then it'll all be over. It'll be the other lot who'll be putting us in the dock then, and not the present gang. And you diplomats will be the first to get it in the neck.'

160

'You've been doing the burning, the killing and wreaking the havoc, and, you think, we are the ones to be called to account for all this?'

'We carried out the orders. The SS did the burning. We were doing the fighting.'

'Does that mean that a new method of fighting has been devised which didn't involve any burning or any victims?'

'Wars of one kind or another are always going to be with us, but not such stupid ones as this though. The present war is nothing but a dilettante affair. He decided that you can run a war without having studied at any military academy, just relying on intuition. He decided that he was the only person who knew what was good for us all. He decided that he alone loves our great Germany and that the rest of us spend our time wondering how we can betray it . . .'

'It's frightening talking to you, General . . .'

'Don't lie. Nowadays the whole of Germany is talking this way . . . Or at least thinking along the same lines.'

'But what about the Hitlerjugend boys? Is that the way *they* think when they go out to face the Russian tanks? They die with the words *Heil* Hitler on their lips . . .'

'Fanaticism never leads to final victory. People grow tired of it, and then it disperses in the thoughts and ways of the defeated. Fanatics manage to win victories in the early stages, but the final victory is never theirs, because they grow tired of themselves. *Prost*!'

'*Prosit* . . . Then why don't you rise in revolt with your division . . .?'

'Corps . . .'

'All the more, then. Why don't you surrender to the enemy and let yourself be taken prisoner with the whole corps?'

'What about the family? And the fanatics at HQ? And the cowards who find it easier to fight believing in some mythical victory than to sit tight in the Allies' camp?'

'You can give orders.'

'You can order people to die, but there aren't any orders telling soldiers to stay alive by surrendering to the enemy. No one has learnt to write them yet . . . not in any of the world's armies.'

'But if you were to receive such an order?'

'From whom? From that maniac? He's dragging us all into the grave with him as it is; it's dreadful to die all on your lonesome, but in a whole crowd there's nothing to it, you can even make jokes on the way.'

'But if the order came from Keitel?'

'His head's never been screwed on properly. He's a penpusher, no soldier.'

'Well, be that as it may . . . but what about your Commander-in-Chief in Italy?'

'Kesselring? He'd never go in for anything like that.'

'Why?'

'He was reared in Göring's HQ and anyone who works under some big leader like that is bound to lose all initiative. He learns to be agile, develops an analytical outlook but loses all capacity for independent decision-making. Before taking any such step he'll always make a point of running to the Hog.'

'Who?'

'To the Hog,' the general repeated stubbornly. 'To Göring.'

'Are you convinced that it would be impossible to persuade Kesselring to undertake a step like that without Göring giving him the green light?'

'If I wasn't, I wouldn't have said so.'

'You don't believe in any future prospects?'

'Oh yes, I do . . . A future of imminent disaster . . . for us all, the whole bang lot of us . . . It's not so terrible, believe me, if we all go down together. And our disaster will be so shattering that the memory of it will tear at the hearts of many generations of unfortunate Germans still unborn . . .'

Suddenly tears came to the general's eyes. Not a muscle in his face moved, but tears started to roll down his cheeks. Despite the torrent, his voice remained firm as he finished what he had to say: 'I have tried to instil into my children that any kind of democracy is a curse on Germany. Any democracy in our country can lead to one thing and one thing only, a dictatorship of shopkeepers. The more freedoms we have, the more we're going to pine for an SS, a secret police, concentration camps and universal terror. Only under those conditions do we feel at peace. No attempt is needed to defend one's view with regard to

162

the fate of our country in honour of the man who takes all those cares on himself for you and shout "*Heil* Hitler". All at once everything will fall into place, there'll be nothing left to worry about . . .'

All that night the Swedish professor with the long, awkward Scandinavian name was writing away in his compartment, making sure that his pen didn't tear at the paper, for the train shook a good deal every time they went over a joint in the rails.

At the border station Stirlitz got out. The general lowered his gaze as he went past him and raised his hand in the Nazi salute.

'*Heil* Hitler!' he said in a loud voice.

'*Heil* Hitler,' replied Stirlitz. 'I wish you good luck in routing your enemies.'

The General threw a frightened glance at Stirlitz: he must clearly have been loaded with drink when he first came into Stirlitz's compartment the evening before.

'Thank you,' he replied in an equally loud voice, probably to be on the safe side, in case the attendant was listening. 'We'll show them where they get off.'

'I'm sure you will,' replied Stirlitz and walked slowly down the platform.

The only passenger still in the international carriages was the Swedish professor who was going abroad, heading for the peace and quiet of free neutral Switzerland. Stirlitz wandered up and down the platform till the passport and customs formalities had been completed. As the train pulled out, Stirlitz watched the Swedish professor, who was glued to the window, until he was out of sight.

The Swede was none other than Professor Pleischner. He was on his way to Berne with a report for Moscow about the work Stirlitz had carried out, about the mission Schellenberg had given Stirlitz, about the meeting with Bormann and about Käthe's arrest. In the report Stirlitz had asked to be a sent a contact and given details explaining when, where and how it would be possible for him to meet up with a new contact.

Stirlitz gave a sigh of relief when the train had drawn out of the station and walked over to the office of the border guard for a car that would take him to the out-of-the-way crossing-point in the mountains where the pastor would soon make his 'illegal' entry into Switzerland.

To Reichsführer of the SS,
Heinrich Himmler.
Top secret.
To be delivered personally.
Only copy.

Dear Reichsführer,
Last night I embarked on the practical implementation of 'Operation Truth' after preliminary study of the landscape, relief and roads of the locality in question. I considered that any detailed enquiries about the drivers who will transfer the archives belonging to Reichsleiter Bormann or about the scheduled route might attract too much attention on the part of the guards.

I had been planning to carry out this operation with as little fuss as possible, but events of yesterday night have made it impossible for me to follow such a course. After my men, dressed in civilian clothes, parked a lorry across the main road, the convoy transporting the Reichsleiter's archives, instead of halting, opened fire at the lorry and at three of my men. Without asking who the men were or checking their papers, the first vehicle of the convoy drove into our lorry and pushed it over into the ditch. That meant the road ahead was free. Five men from the first cover vehicle jumped into the lorry behind and the convoy moved on. I realised that in each of the lorries there were at least five or six men, all armed with sub-machine guns. As it was to emerge later, the men were neither soldiers nor officers but employees from the local party organisation mobilised the night before the archives were due to be evacuated. On Bormann's personal instructions they were to shoot at anyone who came within fifty feet of the lorries, regardless of their rank.

I saw that we had to change our tactics. Part of my men I told to keep on a level with the convoy by way of a parallel road until they came to a level-crossing: the guard on duty there was replaced by one of my fellows who was

164

to block the road by lowering the barrier. I, with the rest of my men, split the
column into two, which involved setting fire to one of the lorries, the
thirteenth from the front, and then stayed put. Unfortunately, we were
obliged to use our arms: each lorry did its best to fight us off while their
ammunition lasted, although we offered them the chance to parley. The
thirteen lorries at the head of the convoy reached the level-crossing at the
same time as our men, but ten tanks from the 24th Army Corps were
already there to meet them and provide protection for the Reichsleiter's
lorries. Our men were thus forced to retreat so as not to compromise
themselves if anyone were killed in the fray that would have followed. The
lorries that we had been able to overpower were burnt and all the sacks and
zinc cases we seized were loaded into armoured vehicles and taken to the
aerodrome. The drivers who conveyed the captured articles to the aerodrome
were subsequently removed by our shock group.

Heil Hitler!
Yours, Skorzeny

Schellenberg's agent working in Dulles's household reported that he had been visited by a priest whose surname she had been unable to ascertain, and that the two learned men had then had a conversation that she had been able to record almost verbatim.

'The world will curse Hitler,' commented Dulles as he filled his pipe, 'not so much for the ovens of Maidanek and Auschwitz, as for the unprecedented development in Russia which the German invasion of that country had spurred on, however paradoxical that may sound. That invasion brought to light the tremendous potential of the Soviet system. Never in her history, even in that magnificent age of democracy after the 1861 reform has Russia made such a leap forward as she has during these war years. They have brought into play the tremendous resources of the Urals and Siberia with the help of our machinery, our strategic materials and our technology. After getting hold of our machinery they rejected their own out-of-date models. Hitler threw Russia and America into each other's arms. The Russians will put the devastated Western provinces back on their feet again and with the help of German reparations—Stalin's reckoning on getting twenty billion dollars from Germany—they will thus double their country's industrial potential.'

'My friends in the Vatican,' remarked the priest, 'consider that the Russians have become much more flexible both in their actions and their thinking during the war years.'

'At the moment, you know,' went on Dulles, puffing away at his pipe, 'I am reading Russian writers like Pushkin, Saltykov and Dostoyevsky . . . I regret very much that I do not know their language, for Russian literature is, I think, the most remarkable of all—I mean their literature of the nineteenth century. It is very important to make a thorough study of that period because what they had to say then has a direct bearing not so much on their past as on their future . . . And I have come to the conclusion that looking back to ideals of the past is more in keeping with the Russian character than taking the risk of constructing models for the future.'

'An interesting thought,' commented the priest. 'But I am afraid that in this philosophising of yours you rather tend to look down on them from above than see yourself alongside them . . .'

'Is that an appeal for me to join the ranks of the Bolsheviks?' queried Dulles with a smile. 'They wouldn't have me.'

Himmler decided not to risk showing that report to the Führer on acount of the words Dulles had used in the first part of it. However, he did issue instructions for more intensive work among the Turkestan, Ukrainian and Baltic units. He also asked for a careful survey of the personnel in those units to be made, to facilitate picking out the most talented and educated for possible recruitment to the organs of the SD, both for the present and, what was more important, the future . . .

The next day Kaltenbrunner sent Gruppenführer Krüger, deputy chief of the Prague Gestapo, a coded message asking him to select men from the local SS and SD network to prepare the destruction of Prague and also to pick out suitable candidates for this work from among the collaborationists.

At the border crossing Stirlitz was able to make all the necessary arrangements in no time at all. The lieutenant in charge of the

166

mountain-infantry unit there turned out to be an obliging, good-natured fellow. At first his helpfulness even took Stirlitz aback somewhat, for border troops were known for their arrogance. But after thinking it over a little Stirlitz realised what accounted for it: inevitably, life up there in the mountains bordering on neutral Switzerland, in a separate world of moonlit snow so far away from the bombs, the devastation and the hunger compelled even the lieutenant in charge of a whole border zone and all local bosses to bend over backwards to please anyone from the centre who might appear on the scene. Everyone was much too keen to stay put to ask any questions about the details of the planned crossing, let alone the motives behind it. Naturally, Stirlitz would not have answered those questions even if they had been asked, yet even so the almost obsequious politeness shown him by the border guards and their obvious eagerness to help him enabled him to come to a most useful conclusion: namely, that the border had ceased to be an insuperable barrier. If he had needed to send not one pastor but a whole bunch across, he realised, it would not have involved any particular effort even if he had not been armed with permits from the leadership.

Things would have been perfect, he thought to himself, if he had been able simply to contact Schellenberg on the spot and ask him to give the necessary instructions to some reliable member of the intelligence staff for the pastor to be brought along to that crossing-point straight away. Yet he realised that any telephone call to Berlin would be recorded by Müller's staff, which would endanger the whole of Schellenberg's operation. From one point of view that would have been to Stirlitz's advantage, for he made it a general principle to encourage strife between the leading Nazis wherever possible. However, on the other hand, the failure of Schellenberg's plan and the mission entrusted to the pastor was to be Stirlitz's trump card when he went to report to Bormann, and, what was more, complete with carefully prepared evidence such as photographs, tape-recorded conversations, addresses, details of secret meeting-places and the pastor's report. Only if Stirlitz brought ample proof to Bormann, only then would he be able to undermine from within the real negotiations, not the fictitious ones, those that

167

Karl Wolff was to conduct in Switzerland.

After deciding on the actual spot where the pastor was to be taken across the border, a gully overgrown with young fir trees, Stirlitz checked once more on the name of the small hotel visible on the other side of the border. He discovered the name of the proprietor and how long it took for taxis to drive out there from the nearby town, then found out where the nearest hotel was down in the plain below. According to his story, the pastor was on a skiing holiday and had lost his way in the wooded gorges on the way up to the mountains from the plain beneath. He would ask the hotel proprietor to call a taxi for him so that he could go back to his base in the plain. From there he would be able to get a bus to Berne or Zurich where he had friends. He would need to look them up himself without warning them in advance. To his friends he could tell the whole truth though: how Stirlitz had arranged his release, sent an *agent provocateur* to test him and then organised his crossing into Switzerland. After that the pastor was to announce that the same man was waiting for a postcard from him with a view of Lake Geneva from Lausanne. That would signify that preliminary meetings had already taken place, the necessary contacts made and that others could now follow for the serious talks. At first Schellenberg had objected to that plan of Stirlitz's: 'It's too simple,' he had protested, 'too straightforward.'

'But he can't go about things any other way,' countered Stirlitz. 'The best lie for him to have to tell is the straight truth. Otherwise he'll get himself tied up in knots and the police will soon be on his tracks.'

After settling all the details for the crossing, Stirlitz warned the border guards of the punishment that awaited them if they divulged his secret, pointing out that they were only allowed to give answers to questions concerning the operation to the Reichsführer personally. He also informed the men that before the pastor left Berlin he would send a telegram addressed to the Lieutenant that read: 'Mother heart trouble—send necessary medicines if poss Hans.' That would be the signal for a car with no chauffeur to be left outside the station, complete with keys, and for Swiss skis, that had already seen some wear and were waxed with Swiss wax to be laid out at the spot Stirlitz

168

had picked out for the crossing, together with mittens of the kind knitted in the neighbourhood and some used ski-boots made in Berne.

When Stirlitz got back to his house in Babelsberg it was already eleven o'clock at night. He unlocked the door, put his hand out to switch the light on but stopped halfway on hearing a soft but very familiar voice say:

'You'd better not put the light on.'

'Holthoff,' said Stirlitz to himself at once. 'How on earth did he get here? Something's up and it looks very important, what's more.'

Professor Pleischner booked a room at a small hotel in Berne, had a bath and then went down to the restaurant where he sat for a long time staring at the menu in dazed bewilderment. His eyes moved across from the word 'cream' to the price, from the word 'lobster' to the price. He spent a long time studying that waxed blue-white card and then, to his own amazement, burst out laughing and cried out: 'Hitler's a scoundrel!'

He was alone in the restaurant, out in the kitchen the cook was jangling saucepans around, the room was filled with the smell of yogurt and freshly baked bread.

Then again he shouted, louder this time: 'Hitler's a cad!'

Someone must have heard him, for a young rosy-cheeked waiter came hurrying over to the professor with a broad beam of a smile and said: '*Bonjour, Monsieur . . .*'

'Hitler's a vulture!' yelled Pleischner. 'A vulture! A scoundrel! A vampire!'

He was incapable of stopping himself, he had lost all control. He did not even know whether he was laughing or crying, but just went on shouting: 'Swine! Scoundrels! Blood-suckers!'

At first the waiter made an attempt at a smile, assuming the gentleman in the grey suit was merely joking, but then, noticing the tears on his cheeks, he quickly ran out to the kitchen to fetch the cook. When he had had a look too, the waiter asked: 'Should we ring the hospital?'

169

'Have you gone out of your mind?' exclaimed the cook. 'What kind of ideas would enter people's heads if they see an ambulance drive up to our restaurant. That would be sure to start up rumours that one of our customers is a victim of food-poisoning.'

An hour later Pleischner cancelled his booking at the hotel and transferred to a private pension on the bank of the river. He realised that it would be highly foolish to stay on there after his hysterical outburst, particularly since he was travelling on a forged Swedish passport.

His fit of hysterics at first unnerved Pleischner completely. He walked about the streets, turning round all the time to make sure no one was following him. He was afraid that all of a sudden there would be a screech of brakes behind him and that silent toughs would then seize hold of him and carry him off to some basement room where he would be beaten up for daring to use the great Führer's name in vain. However, no one showed the slightest interest in him as he walked about the streets. He bought some French and English newspapers at a news-stand, sporting cartoons of Hitler and Göring on the front page. He laughed away to himself and then took fright again lest he should have another hysterical fit.

'My God,' he thought. 'Surely all that can't be over yet?'

He walked down the deserted street that led to the secret address Stirlitz had given him. After looking over his shoulder a couple of times, once again to his own amazement—later, when he looked back over that first day in Berne, he was to remember doing many strange things—he started spinning round in a wild waltz. He hummed an old tune under his breath, quite carried away with his new freedom, and twirled round and round, sliding his toes out in front of him and taking wild runs reminiscent of dancers in the variety theatre at the turn of the century.

The door was opened by a tall, thick-set man. 'Otto asked me to tell you that he had been expecting you to phone yesterday evening,' said the professor, reproducing the password he had learnt.

'Come in,' the man said, and Pleischner went into the flat, although he was supposed to have waited for the password

170

reply: 'That's funny, I was at home; he must have got the number wrong.'

The intoxicating air of his new-found freedom had played a truly cruel trick against Pleischner. The secret address used by the Soviet agent had been tracked down by Nazis, who had been sitting there, waiting for any 'visitors' who might come along. Pleischner had been the first of these. Stirlitz's new agent was no more.

'Well?' inquired the tall man, after they had gone into the flat. 'How's he getting on back home?'

'Here you are,' said Pleischner holding out a tiny ampule. 'It's all in there.'

That move saved Pleischner. The Germans did not know either the password or what kind of people the contacts might be. So it had been decided that if a contact refused to come in without the password answer he would have to be seized, doped and sent back to Germany on the quiet by car. If he came into contact, the Germans would keep track of all his movements in the hope that he would lead them to the key figure.

The tall man walked into an adjacent room where he unsealed the ampule and took out of it a minute sheet of tissue paper with a report consisting of a series of five-figure numbers. Similar five-figure numbers were already being investigated in the decoding centre in Berlin, for the code was identical to the one used in reports sent by the Russian wireless-operator who had agreed to work for the Germans.

The tall man handed the coded message to his assistant and said: 'Take that round to our embassy straight away. Tell them to tail that fellow. I'll tie him up here for a bit and try to get him talking: he's obviously new on the job, it shouldn't be any trouble to loosen him up a bit.'

12

Käthe was walking up and down the room, rocking her son to sleep. Since her last meeting with Stirlitz, just as he had said, she had been transferred to a special Gestapo flat equipped with a small but powerful radio-transmitter. Käthe looked at the face of her sleeping baby and thought to herself: 'Everything in life has to be learnt, how to make an omelette, how to look up books in catalogues, let alone maths, of course, which requires infinitely more effort. Yet being a mother is not something you have to learn—one doesn't have to learn how to sing lullabies or rock babies to and fro so that they fall asleep quietly and comfortably.'

Fräulein Barbara, Käthe's guard, tried to put herself over as a kind, thoughtful girl. She was indeed very young and liked chattering away before the two of them had their supper. Helmuth, the SS man who lived in the next-door room, was laying the table for three. The baby was already asleep, and Barbara, Käthe and Helmuth sat down at the table covered with a white tablecloth in honour of the nineteenth birthday of the loyal product of the Hitlerjugend. During that celebration supper, consisting of goulash and potatoes, Barbara remarked that once Germany had won the war, women would at last be able to quit the army and get down to their proper task, starting to raise large German families.

'Giving birth and feeding families is woman's vocation,' she went on. 'Everything else is unimportant. People must be healthy and strong. There is nothing purer than animal instincts. I am not afraid of talking openly of such things.'

'But what's that going to mean?' came the sullen reaction from Helmuth, who had just been sent home from the front line after severe sheli-shock. 'Today you belong to me, tomorrow you're another's and the day after someone else's.'

'There's no need to wallow in filth like that,' replied Barbara with a squeamish frown. 'The family is something sacred and inviolable. Why should I not find as much pleasure making love with my husband, the father of my children, as if he were three different men rolled into one? Modesty is something we must shake off—it is quite unnatural. If we women could feel free to abandon ourselves in love-making with our husbands as we pleased, then there would be no unfaithfulness. Women leave their husbands in search of greater strength or skill in the art of love . . . You, most likely, don't agree with me?' she inquired, turning to look at Käthe.

'No, I don't.'

'Why?'

'I just don't . . .'

'That's no answer.'

'Yes, it is.'

'The desire to make an impression is also a feminine wile, as old as time. Can't you see that good old Helmuth here would prefer me to you?' said Barbara with a laugh. 'For one thing, he's in awe of Slavs and then I'm younger.'

'I hate women,' remarked Helmuth in a hollow voice.

'Why?' asked Barbara, giving Käthe a mischievous wink. 'What have they done to make you hate them?'

'Women are worse than scoundrels. With scoundrels everything's straightforward from the start and you know where you are, at least. But with women, first comes a torrent of treacle, enough to put you off your food, and then they start twisting you round their little fingers just as they please, while all the time they're having it off with your best friend. Especially if you're not up to much.'

'Your wife's walked out on you!' Barbara exclaimed with a little clap of excitement.

Käthe noticed what attractive hands Barbara had: they were delicate and soft, with childish dimples at the wrists and well-shaped nails that needed no varnish to make them shine.

Helmuth looked hard at Barbara but did not say anything: he was her subordinate from the ranks, while she was an Unterscharführer.

'Excuse me,' said Käthe, getting up from the table, 'But may I go to my room?'

'What's the matter?' asked Barbara. 'They're not bombing tonight and you haven't started work yet, there's no reason why

173

you shouldn't sit up a bit later than usual.'

'I'm worried lest the baby might wake. We've been talking very loudly.'

'Why should he? Helmuth, how long was the baby out on the balcony today?'

'I had him out in the fresh air for an hour this morning and another hour in the afternoon. It started getting a bit chilly towards evening and I decided to keep him inside. In this kind of weather children can catch cold very easily.'

'Perhaps you'd let me sleep in his room?' asked Käthe. 'I feel sorry for the soldier,' she went on, giving a nod in Helmuth's direction, 'he's probably not getting enough sleep because of the baby.'

'He's a quiet little fellow,' said Helmuth, 'a very peaceful baby. He hardly cries at all.'

'That's not allowed,' said Barbara firmly. 'You and the child have to have separate rooms.'

'But I won't run away,' Käthe said with an attempt at a smile, 'there are such tough locks on the door.'

'It would be impossible to run away from here,' Barbara confirmed. 'There are the two of us here and the locks really are reliable. But I am sorry, these are orders from above. You could try and talk to the man in charge of your case.'

'And who's that?'

'Standartenführer Stirlitz. He's a kindly sort, and he might be ready to waive a rule or two, that is if you do your work properly. Some women are ready to do things for money, for others the incentive is a man, but your incentive to do good work is the most reliable of all, your baby. That's right, isn't it?'

'Yes,' replied Käthe. 'You're quite right.'

'Did you want to ask me something?' inquired Barbara as she cut a tiny piece of potato ready for her next mouthful.

Käthe noticed that she was eating as if she were at some diplomatic reception: her movements were infinitely graceful and she was pecking at the worm-eaten potato as if it was some delicious exotic fruit.

'Tell me . . . if you were in my position, would you have agreed to work for the other side in order to save your child?'

Barbara paused for a while before answering. After finishing her potato, she put down her silver fork and, covering her mouth with the palm of her hand, she set to work with a bone tooth-pick.

'How shall I put it? . . . But, by the way, you still haven't given your child a name.'

'I'm going to call him Vladimir.'

'After whom? Was that your father's name? Or your husband's? What was his name, by the way?'

'Whose?'

'Your husband's.'

'Erwin.'

'I know that's the name he used . . . But what was his real name, his Russian name?'

'I knew him as Erwin.'

'D'you mean to say he didn't even tell you his real name? So it was as Erwin that you married him.'

'We only married after we got here.'

'That's not true.'

'It all happened here,' explained Käthe with a smile. 'I was smuggled here together with Erwin. As far as I know, your secret agents also know each other by their pseudonyms, just like agents all over the world. My chief in Moscow knew that my name was Katya, not Käthe, and probably the people who were in contact with Erwin here knew it as well, that is his immediate superiors.'

'To go back to your question,' said Barbara, and then, after another pause, she went on: 'Vladimir was Lenin's name, wasn't it? If I had found myself in a situation like yours I would have called my son Adolf. How I would have behaved in other respects, I don't know . . . I don't think I would have behaved the way you did . . . but enough of all that. Yes, I see no reason why you shouldn't go to your room now. Tomorrow they want to take you to Rahnsdorf. That was your idea, as far as I remember—to drive over to the places that Erwin used to visit, so that your local chief shouldn't start worrying about how you were getting on, once you start working with us.'

'Yes,' replied Käthe. 'That was my idea. It might well give our people a chance to see me walking around at liberty and that would reassure them. I don't know for certain that our local chief hasn't got a second transmitter and he might let Moscow know that we had come adrift if he did not receive a signal to the effect that I had not been caught: if that happened your scheme would be a complete flop.'

'Your local chief has no second transmitter,' retorted Barbara. 'You can count yourself fortunate to have someone in charge of your case like Stirlitz: he is known for liberalism and logic. Incidentally, I think it's he, who's going to take you out into the town tomorrow morning. Did he say anything to you about it?'

'I don't know who'll be taking me,' Käthe replied. 'My interrogator didn't say anything about that to me. I merely pointed out that the step would be an expedient one and I was not told who would be accompanying me.'

Later that night, however, it was not Stirlitz who came to the flat but Rolff with two of his assistants. He was a little tipsy when he appeared, and after waking Käthe he started oozing gallantry and peppering all his remarks with French expressions. Müller had informed Rolff that Kaltenbrunner had agreed it would be he who should work on the Russian girl whenever Stirlitz was away.

'Schellenberg told me that he had asked Stirlitz to go off on some mission,' Kaltenbrunner pointed out, 'I think it's sensible to get Rolff on the job, and we'll see what effect the contrast produces: after a harsh interrogator detainees are always prone to oblige for the gentle ones. Our Stirlitz is a gentle one all right!' At that Kaltenbrunner offered Müller a cigarette.

Müller lit the cigarette and hesitated for a moment: should he tell Kaltenbrunner about the fingerprints on the hot-line telephone and that they matched up with those that had been found on the suitcase belonging to the Russian woman? Yet after weighing up the matter between two draws of his strong cigarette he decided not to mention either that matter or the fact that he was secretly collecting the fingerprints of all members of the SD staff. The point was that responsibility for special security in the Reich Security Office lay with him or, in other words, Müller was responsible for the reliability of SD and Gestapo personnel. He was afraid that Kaltenbrunner would start people running in circles and create a panic. It might also mean that Kaltenbrunner would lay blame for any new fiasco on Müller since it was he who had failed to spot the enemy under his own roof. It suited Müller's purposes that Himmler had heard about the conversation that had taken place between Bormann and one of the Reich Security Office staff, while Kaltenbrunner remained in the dark. That 'gap' meant that Müller had the chance to manoeuvre between the two forces. For this reason he also refrained from initiating Himmler into the essential details of Kaltenbrunner's suspicions with regard to Stirlitz. Kaltenbrunner, in his turn, knew nothing of the mysterious conversation with Party HQ which Himmler qualified as the work of a treacherous informer.

'Would you like me to keep an eye on the way Stirlitz works with the Russian radio-operator?' asked Müller.

'Why?' asked Kaltenbrunner in surprise. 'What for? I would have thought Stirlitz was fairly skilled when it came to questions of radio work.'

'Surely, he can't have forgotten what he said,' thought Müller in surprise. Or is he double-crossing me perhaps? Should I remind him of what he said or would it be better not to? Damn this establishment where you have to play people off against each other all the time! Instead of deceiving other people you have to make a fool of yourself all the time! It's all up the creek!'—'So you suggest I give Rolff a free hand in his work with the Russian pianist?'

Radio-operators were usually called 'pianists' and intelligence chiefs—'conductors', but of late, in the general chaos that had begun when Berlin was flooded with refugees and when premises had to be found for the security staff who had evacuated the East Prussia, Aachen, Paris and Bucharest archives and converged on the capital, these terms had got lost by the wayside somehow, and arrested agents were coming to be referred to according to their nationality rather than occupation.

'The pianist?' Kaltenbrunner repeated the word in a wry tone to jog his memory. 'No, let Rolff co-operate with Stirlitz. The goal should be one even if the means of attaining it are different. Have any messages come in from the Russians yet?'

177

'Not yet.'

'How's work on the decoding going?'

'They're half way there. It's proving a hard nut to crack though.'

'Give that pianist a proper shaking up: I don't believe she doesn't know the local chief's code.'

'Stirlitz is working on her with his usual methods.'

'He's away at the moment, so let Rolff have a round or two.'

'In *his* usual style?'

Kaltenbrunner was about to say something in reply, but at that moment a telephone call came through from the Führer's Bunker: it was a summons from Hitler to come to a meeting there.

Kaltenbrunner remembered his conversation about Stirlitz. But when he had met Bormann two evenings before that, they had had a long conversation about security measures in connection with the transfer of the party archives, and Bormann had said in passing: 'Let your people see to it that this action is kept strictly secret. Put your most reliable men on to the job, the people we can really trust—Müller, Scholz, Stirlitz.'

Kaltenbrunner knew the rules of the game well enough to realise that if Bormann asked no questions about someone, but made direct reference to him, that meant the man in question was a person Bormann would turn to if anything important cropped up.

'Incidentally, have your men found my chauffeur yet,' Bormann had inquired later on in the course of the same discussion. 'I gave instructions for him to be found. Let them have a proper look, not just for the fun of it, but so as to be sure to find him.'

Kaltenbrunner had said he knew nothing about the chauffeur but that he would definitely make inquiries and then inform Bormann of the results straightaway.

It was only later, when he was already on his way to Hitler's Bunker, that Kaltenbrunner remembered about the chauffeur, because he realised that the first person he would come across in the Bunker was bound to be Bormann.

Himmler's closest associates did not come up with any of the material that the Reichsführer had been so anxious to find in Bormann's captured archives, even after working flat out on their search for forty-eight hours. They had not come across a single document that shed any light on how party money had been transferred to foreign banks. The papers concerned had apparently either been evacuated on a previous occasion or Bormann was simply storing up in that phenomenal memory of his all the necessary account numbers and the names of his financial agents of whom he might have need as soon as the war was over, or—and that would be the most discouraging explanation—they must have been in one of the thirteen lorries at the head of the convoy that succeeded in breaking through Skorzeny's cordon and meeting up with the tanks.

Nevertheless, in the archives that Skorzeny's men had obtained, there were some highly interesting papers, especially Stirlitz's report, which, although it was not signed, still bore witness to the fact that treachery was spreading within the SD.

Himmler showed the paper concerned to Schellenberg and asked him to follow it up. Schellenberg promised to carry out the Reichsführer's instructions, well aware that the task he had been given was impossible. However the very existence of the document led him to conclude that in the Bormann archives there must be some more important material which would allow him to check up afresh on his staff by finding out whether or not they were working simultaneously for Bormann and, if they were, how long they had been doing so, in what sphere and against whom in particular. The prospect of learning that some of his men were working for two masters did not worry Schellenberg. They might well have been recruited by Bormann's men appealing to their patriotic sentiments. The most important thing was to find out what Bormann actually knew about his holiest of holies, his peace feelers.

Schellenberg put several men on to the job and every day asked if there was any news, but the answer always came back: 'Nothing of interest so far.'

'How's your chief at the moment?' the tall man inquired.
'Well?'

'Yes,' replied Pleischner with a smile. 'Everything's all right.'

'Would you like some coffee?'

'Thank you. That would be very nice.'

The man walked off into the kitchen and from out there inquired: 'Have you found yourself a comfortable room?'

'Yes, a very nice one.'

'Is your roof reliable?'

'But my room's only on the first floor,' replied Pleischner, being unfamiliar with the jargon.

The Gestapo man laughed to himself as he ground the coffee: he had been right, it was a complete dilettante that had been sent along, a volunteer helper, who did not even know that the word 'roof' meant 'cover' to agents all over the world. 'But, all the same, I mustn't hurry things,' he thought to himself. 'The old man's in the bag right from the start. He'll blurt out everything, I must just play it carefully.'

'You won't find coffee like that anywhere in Germany,' he said, passing Pleischner a cupful. 'Back there the scum make their people drink nothing but dish-water, but here we get the real stuff from Brazil.'

'I'd forgotten what it tastes like,' agreed Pleischner after taking a little sip. 'I can't have drunk coffee like that for a good ten years.'

'In Greece I was taught to follow strong coffee with cold water. Do you want to try it?'

Pleischner was in a cheerful mood now; he no longer walked, thought and breathed like an old man. With a bright smile he replied: 'I've never done that before.'

'It's an interesting experiment: the contrast in temperature and taste has a special feel all of its own and also it makes the coffee less of a strain on your heart.'

'Yes, it does make an interesting change,' commented Pleischner taking a sip of cold water.

'What verbal message did he ask you to pass on?'

'There wasn't any, just the ampule.'

'Strange.'

180

'Why?'

'I thought he would have told me when to expect him.'

'He didn't say anything about that.'

'By the way, forgive me for not asking before: you're hungry perhaps?'

'No, thank you, I had a first-class breakfast.'

'How are you·off for money?'

'I've got enough to tide me over for the time being.'

'If you find you need any, just come round. I can't let you have very much of course, but I'll always be able to rustle up enough for you to keep body and soul together. Incidentally, have you been making sure that no one's tailing you?'

'Tailing? You mean following me?'

'Yes.'

'You know, I must confess I haven't really been paying attention.'

'Now that's very careless of you. Didn't he give you instructions on that score?'

'Oh yes, of course, but here for the first time in many years I feel free, particularly after spending several months in a concentration camp, and it has all just gone to my head. Thank you for reminding me.'

'You must never forget about that. So much for that . . . the police are very cunning here . . . very cunning, indeed. You didn't have anything else for me?'

'No, nothing.'

'Can I have your passport?'

'He told me I must always keep it on me.'

'But he also told you, I expect, that you should take instructions from me once you got here, didn't he?'

'No.'

'Oh yes, you're right, of course . . . that was mentioned in the coded message. We'll think how best to work that one out later. And your immediate plans?'

'I shall return to the hotel, go to bed and catch up on all the sleep I've missed.'

'No . . . but I mean what about your work?'

'First of all I must get some sleep,' Pleischner insisted. 'I dream of sleeping for a whole day, if not two or three, and then I

181

shall start thinking about work. All my manuscripts I left behind in Berlin. Yet I can remember almost everything I have ever written by heart.'

The man picked up Pleischner's Swedish passport and put it down casually on the desk. Then he said: 'Come round for it at two o'clock the day after tomorrow and meanwhile we'll get it stamped for you at the Swedish consulate. Or, to be more exact, we'll try and get them to stamp it: the Swedes are behaving abominably, the longer it goes on the worse it gets.'

'Who?' asked Pleischner, right out of his depth by this time.

The Gestapo man hummed and hawed somewhat. He'd almost forgotten the part he was meant to be playing. To cover up his mistake, he lit a cigarette and took several long draws to give himself time to think.

'The Swedes tend to see a Nazi agent in everyone who travels through Germany. For them it makes no difference what kind of German you are, a member of the resistance fighting against Hitler or a Gestapo informer. That's why you have to be very much on your guard where they're concerned.'

'But he didn't tell me I had to register at the consulate.'

'That was all said in the coded message.'

'The man who sent him is in Berlin,' thought the Gestapo man, 'that's obvious, for he said that he'd left his manuscripts there. That means we'll be able to get on to one of their Berlin staff. But I mustn't hurry', he repeated to himself, 'on no account must I hurry.'

'Well, I am most grateful to you,' said Pleischner as he got up to go. 'The coffee was delicious, especially with the cold water.'

'Have you let him know that you've arrived safely and settled in here or would you like me to do that?'

'Can you?'

'Yes, of course. But you, for your part, must also get a message through and don't put it off a moment longer than necessary.'

'I wanted to do it today but I couldn't find the kind of stamp he said I was to stick on the postcard.'

'If it's to be had, I'll get hold of the kind of stamp you need by the time you come round the day after tomorrow. What must it have on it?'

'The conquest of Mont Blanc . . . on a blue ground. It must be blue.'

'Fine. Do you have the postcard with you?'

'No, it's at the hotel.'

'That's unfortunate. You shouldn't leave anything like that around in the hotel. You're a foreigner and they might clean you out while you're not around. How could you be so careless?'

'No, there's nothing to worry about this time,' Pleischner reassured him with a smile, 'it's just an ordinary card, I bought a whole set of them in Berlin. The text I learned off by heart, so nothing has been left to chance.'

When he shook hands with Pleischner in the entrance hall, the tall man reminded him: 'Be careful, mind you, comrade. You must bear in mind that the peace and quiet here is only illusory.'

'Yes, I know. He warned me.'

'You had better give me your address here, just in case.'

'I'm staying at the 'Virginia', Pension Virginia.'

'Are there any Americans staying there?'

'Why?' asked Pleischner in surprise.

'Because it has an English name. As a rule, they like to stay in hotels with names that have a familiar ring to them.'

'No, I don' think there are any other foreigners there.'

'We'll check up on that. If you see me in your hotel please don't come up to greet me—we must appear strangers.'

'Just as you say.'

'And now . . . if anything untoward happens, ring me at this number. Can you memorise it?' At that he repeated a six-figure number twice.'

'Yes,' replied Pleischner, 'I have a good memory. Latin trains the memory better than any kind of mental gymnastics.'

After coming out into the street, Pleischner crossed over to the opposite pavement where an old man in a fur jacket was closing the shutters outside his pet-shop. In the windows there were cages with birds hopping about in them. Pleischner lingered by the window, watching them.

'Do you want to buy anything?' the old man asked.

'No, thank you. I'm admiring your birds.'

'The finest ones are inside the shop. I don't do things like most shopkeepers,' said the old man, obviously glad to have someone to talk to. 'Everybody else puts their best wares in the window, but for me birds are no ordinary wares. Birds are birds and that's all there is to it. Many writers come here to listen to my birds sing. One of them said to me once: "Before I descend into the hell of a new work, like Orpheus I have to have my fill of the greatest music of all, the music of the birds. Otherwise I cannot sing to the world the song that will find its Eurydice."'

Pleischner wiped away the tears that had suddenly come into his eyes, and all he could do was just murmur 'Thank you . . .' before he walked away from the shop.

'What, what?' queried the old man in the fur jacket, unable to understand what the matter was, but Pleischner, without answering him, walked quickly away down the road that led to the 'Virginia'. He was overcome with a violent desire to sit down and start working.

'Why can't we turn on the light? Who are you so scared of?' asked Stirlitz.

'Not you.' replied Holthoff.

'All right, let's grope our way along then.'

'I know my way about your house by now. It's cosy and quiet here.'

'Especially when there's bombing going on,' mocked Stirlitz. 'The small of my back's aching like mad. I must go to the bathroom and get some aspirins. Have a seat. Give me your hand and I'll lead you to the armchair.'

'Thank you. I've got that far.'

Stirlitz went to the bathroom and opened the medicine chest. 'I'll find myself taking a laxative instead of aspirins, if I'm not careful,' he said. 'The curtains here are very thick, let's draw them and put the fire on: if you're afraid you'll be photographed you'd better go and sit over there in the corner, where nobody'll see you.'

'I tried to draw the curtains but I didn't know the catch.'

'Nothing to it, it's just that the rings stick on the wooden rail sometimes. I'll see to it. What's wrong then? Who are you so afraid of?'

184

'Müller.'

'Your own chief?'

'Precisely.'

'What's been happening during the two days I have been away? Has the world turned upside down or has Kaltenbrunner married a Jewess?'

'Almost,' replied Holthoff.

Stirlitz drew the curtains and went to turn on the light. When Holthoff heard the switch click, he said: 'I've disconnected the electricity. It's more than likely that this place is bugged.'

'By whom?'

'Our outfit.'

'What for?'

'That's what I've come to see you about. Have you taken your aspirin?'

'Yes.'

'Please light the fire and sit down. We haven't got much time and there's a good deal of important stuff to discuss.'

Stirlitz put a match to the dry logs and a crackling noise started up in the fireplace.

'Well?' he began, sitting down in an armchair by the fire. 'What's up with you, my friend?'

'Nothing, nothing's happened to me. The question now is what you're going to do next?'

'In general?'

'That as well . . .'

'In general, I was planning to have a bath and hit the hay. I'm frozen and dog tired.'

'I have come to you as a friend.'

'Come on now, get on with it,' insisted Stirlitz, frowning impatiently. 'Why are you beating about the bush like some stupid little boy? Do you want a drink?'

'Yes, please.'

Stirlitz brought out some cognac and poured out a glass for Holthoff and himself. They drank in silence.

'It's good cognac.'

'Have another,' offered Stirlitz.

'Don't mind if I do.'

'They had another glass and then, snapping his finger-joints,

185

Holthoff began: 'Stirlitz, for the whole of the last week I've been going over your case.'

'What do you mean?'

'Müller instructed me to make a secret check of your work on the physicist's case.'

'Look here, Holthoff, enough of this talking riddles. I give you my word I'm not with you. Either explain what you're getting at in more detail and what the arrested physicist has to do with me or tell me why you've been giving my cases a secret check and why Müller is looking for evidence to use against me.'

'I can't explain it to you. I don't know what they're all getting at myself, for God's sake. All I know is that they're closing in on you.'

'Me?' exclaimed Stirlitz in amazement. 'But that's farcical! Have our chiefs simply lost their heads in all this confusion?'

'Stirlitz, it was you who taught me how important it was always to keep calm.'

'You have the nerve to appeal to me to be calm after what you've just told me! I admit, I am not calm. I'm stunned and indignant and I intend to go and see Müller here and now.'

'He's asleep and I wouldn't hurry to do that if I were you. Listen to what I have to say first. I want to tell you what I've managed to find out in connection with the physicist's case. I haven't told Müller about it yet, I was waiting until you got back.'

Stirlitz needed a moment to collect his wits and check back over his recent movements: had there been any compromising data, even of the most trifling variety, in the wording of the questions he had put to Runge, in his recording of the answers, or had he appeared too interested in details?'

'I'm sorry,' he said, 'I've got the collywobbles.'

'What?' queried Holthoff, not realising for the moment what Stirlitz was getting at.

'The runs,' Stirlitz went on, getting up from his chair. 'If you know what they are!' With that he walked off to the lavatory, locked the door and soon heard Holthoff tiptoeing up to eavesdrop.

'The little fool!' Stirlitz thought to himself, 'has he no brains? He needs to be taught a lesson.'

186

'Holthoff!' he shouted and heard him rushing back to his armchair on tiptoe so as to answer from there.

'Ye-es?'

'You could have answered me at once without running round the room . . . Tell me, who's got it in for me—Müller or the bosses in my own department?'

'Come out and then we can discuss all possibilities.'

'Just coming.'

'What's he trying on?' wondered Stirlitz. 'To come to tell me that the Gestapo is secretly checking up on me could mean the firing squad for him. He's a convinced Nazi, so what can have happened to him? Or, perhaps, he's been sent to give me the once-over by Müller? Hardly likely. There aren't any of his men out here and they must realise that after a conversation like this much the best thing for me to do would be to make a quick getaway. It's not like 1943, the front's within easy reach now. Did he come of his own accord? Hm-mm . . . What's he after? He's not intelligent enough to embark on any serious games, although he's quite a crafty lad. I never quite know where I am with his kind of naïve cunning, but it's precisely that kind that sometimes manages to get the better of logic and common sense. And if I make a false move now, that'll be my lot. It'll send the main operation up in smoke, and I'm afraid there won't be anyone else to take over for me.'

'What are you doing all this time in there, Stirlitz?'

'I'm getting the noose ready. I want to hang myself . . .'

Stirlitz came out of the bathroom, sat down in his armchair again and, after turning over the glowing logs, he said: 'Get on with it.'

'It's a very serious business.'

'What isn't in this world of ours?'

'I sent for three experts from Schumann's department.'

Schumann was the Wehrmacht's adviser on matters concerning the new weapon. His staff were working on problems connected with the splitting of the atom.

'I also sent for experts from that department after you arrested Runge,' Stirlitz reminded Holthoff.

'Yes, it was we who arrested Runge, but why did your people in Intelligence take such an interest in him?'

187

'Do you mean to say you don't understand that?'

'Yes. I see no reason for that.'

'Runge studied in France and in the States. Surely, it's not difficult to see that his contacts there are more important than his actual presence here? A lack of bold initiative in our long-term approach to any problem is always our undoing. We're afraid to use our imagination, every step we take is charted out for us in advance and we never dare move even an inch away from the charted path. That's where we all go wrong.'

'That's true,' agreed Holthoff. 'You're right there. When it comes to initiative I won't contradict you . . . But I beg to differ when it comes to the details. Runge maintained that it was important to go on studying the possibilities of obtaining plutonium from highly radio-active substances, and that was precisely what his scientific opponents held against him. And it was they who wrote the report against him, I made them confess to that.'

'I've never doubted it.'

'Why?'

'Because what I wanted to sort out was whether Runge was having us on about that work or not, and if he was, I wanted to know in whose interests he was doing so? Ours or the enemy's?'

'So you came to the conclusion that his proposals were in the interests of the enemy?'

'You've read the case. Haven't you?'

'But now our people in London have informed us that Runge was right all the time. The Americans and the British have been working along the same lines, while he had been thrown into prison by our Gestapo!'

'By *your* Gestapo,' Stirlitz corrected him. 'By your men, Holthoff. It wasn't us who arrested him, but you. We did not start up the case: it was you who did so, Müller and Kaltenbrunner. And it's not me, you or Schumann who has a Jewish grandmother, but Runge and he was hushing it up . . .'

'His grandfather can be a Jew three times over as well, for all I care!' Holthoff burst out. 'Who his grandfather was makes no difference, because he was working for us and fanatically so, into the bargain! And you went and took rogues at their word!'

'Rogues! Veteran members of the movement? Tested Aryans? Physicists on whom the Führer in person had conferred awards?'

'All right, all right . . . Calm down. I don't deny all that . . . Have it your own way. Give us another cognac.'

'You didn't throw out the fuses, I hope?'

'No, they're over there in the drawer of the table near the mirror.' Holthoff drained his glass at one go, jerking his head back sharply. 'I've started drinking heavily,' he remarked.

'Who doesn't nowadays, I'd like to know?'

'People who can't afford to,' joked Holthoff. 'Poor miserable wretches . . .'

'That's ridiculous.'

'It's sad,' countered Holthoff. 'But to get back to the point—what do you think Kaltenbrunner would decide to do, Stirlitz, if I hand him the results of my investigation?'

'Before you do that you're obliged to report on the results of your investigation to Müller. It was he who issued the warrant for Runge's arrest.'

'But you conducted the investigation for that very same case.'

'Yes, that's quite right, but in accordance with instructions from my superiors; I was carrying out orders.'

'But if you had let him go we could have been heaven knows how much nearer to producing the "retalition weapon" and six months ago at that, whereas we're still marking time.'

'Can you prove that?'

'I've already done so.'

'And do all the physicists back you up?'

'Most of them. Most of those whom I sent for to discuss the case. So what's in store for you is . . .'

'Nothing,' interrupted Stirlitz. 'Nothing, do you hear? The results of scientific research are always confirmed by practical experience. Have you any such confirmation?'

'Yes, here in my pocket.'

'Who'd have thought it?'

'Yes, I've got it here with me. Some interesting stuff has come in from London. Up-to-the-minute news, which means a death sentence for you.'

189

'What are you after, Holthoff? You're aiming at something, but quite what beats me?'

'I'm prepared to spell it out for you once more: it may have been deliberate or not, but in either case it turns out that you, precisely you, have been undermining the work on the "retaliation weapon". Deliberately or not, as the case may be, you, instead of consulting some hundred physicists, confined yourself to a mere ten, and on the basis of their evidence—and they all stood to gain from Runge's detention—brought things to such a pass that Runge's line of research was written off as misleading and far from promising!'

'In other words, you are calling on me to refuse to believe true soldiers of the Führer, people in whom Keitel and Göring place their trust, and start defending a man who has advocated an American approach to the study of the atom! So that's what you want me to do, is it? You want me to believe Runge, a prisoner of the Gestapo, and the Gestapo never arrests people for nothing, and not trust those who helped expose him?'

'That sounds all very logical, Stirlitz. I've always envied your ability to make everything fit into foolproof logical patterns. You're getting at Müller for ordering Runge's arrest, at me for defending a third-generation Jew, so that you yourself can tower like a monument of good faith on our crushed bones. Be that as it may. All very neat, Stirlitz. But that's not what I've come to see you about. Although Runge is in a concentration camp—it was far-sighted of you to get that organised—he is living in separate quarters within the SS compound and is able to pursue his theoretical physics. The thing is, Stirlitz, that I'm caught up in a frightful tangle . . . If I report my findings to Müller, he'll realise that you—never mind the fact that the noose is tightening on you and that not just I, but a whole group of people are investigating your work—possess a weapon you can turn against him. Yes, you are right, it was Müller who issued the warrant for Runge's arrest. If I tell him that the findings I have come up with are not in your favour, indirectly that will put him too in a difficult position. As for me, I'll be under fire from two sides, from both Müller and yourself. He'll be on at me because my findings will have to be checked and rechecked, and as for you, well . . . But you've already told me more or less how you plan

190

to deal with me. What can I, as a Gestapo officer, do in this situation? I'd like you, the Intelligence officer, to answer that one for me . . .'

'So that's what he's getting at,' mused Stirlitz, putting two and two together at last. 'Is it mere provocation or something more? If it is, then it's obvious how I should act. But if he should be leading up to something more serious? They'll soon all be abandoning the sinking ship, like so many rats. That distinction he drew between the Gestapo and the Intelligence Service was more than a chance remark. In that case it's still early to come out with any straight answers.'—'What difference does it make whether we're working for the Gestapo or the Intelligence Service?' inquired Stirlitz with a shrug of the shoulders? 'After all, despite all these differences, we're working to one and the same end.'

'Yes, one and the same end,' agreed Holthoff, 'except that we're notorious as butchers and thugs, while you are the master craftsmen, you lot in political intelligence. You'll be needed in any social order or state, while we are strictly a product of the Reich, and it's hand in hand with the Reich that we'll sink or swim . . .'

'You're asking me then how you should act?'

'Yes.'

'What d'you suggest?'

'First of all, I want to hear what you have to say.'

'Judging by the fact that you've disconnected the electricity and asked me to draw the curtains . . .'

'It was you who suggested the curtains should be drawn.'

'Really? Funny, I could have sworn it was your idea . . . To hell with it, that's only a minor detail . . . So you want to quit the game?'

'Would you have behaved the same way if you had been in my position?'

'Now I can't answer that question, Holthoff, until I hear your "yes" or "no".'

'And if—let's assume the impossible—I were to answer "yes"?'

'If we start assuming the impossible, you've come to the wrong person. Go and consult an astrologer, not me.'

191

'Have you got an arrangement at the border in case of emergency?'

'Well, suppose I have?'

'What if the three of us tried getting out to a neutral country?'

'The three of us?'

'Yes, *three* of us: Runge, you and myself. We'd be doing mankind a real service, rescuing a great physicist like that. I could do the rescue work here, and you could organise the escape. Well, how do you like it? Remember, it's not me they're out to trap now, but *you*. You know what that means when you're up against Müller. Well? I'm waiting for an answer.'

'D'you want some more cognac?'

'Pour away.'

Stirlitz rose, took the cork out of the bottle and walked slowly over to Holthoff, who stretched out his glass, but at that moment Stilitz swung the heavy bottle at Holthoff's head for all he was worth. The bottle smashed and the dark liquid cascaded over Holthoff's face mingling with his blood.

'I've done the right thing,' Stirlitz reassured himself, as he started up the engine of his Horch. 'I couldn't have acted differently. Even if he came to see me of his own accord and was being quite sincere, I still chose the right path. In this particular case the scale of priorities prompted me as to what action to take. I lost one round but the game as a whole is mine, for I shall come out of it with something more important, I shall now win Müller's unswerving trust.'

Holthoff lay sprawled over the passenger seat next to the driver's and was still unconscious. His wrists had been handcuffed.

Holthoff had been wrong when he had said that Müller was asleep. Müller was awake: he had only just been informed from the decoding section about recent events in the secret flat at Berne. The code used in the Russian woman's radio messages corresponded exactly to the one found in the message delivered in Berne. That led Müller to conclude that the chief of Soviet intelligence in Germany was looking for a new contact. Either he

192

had decided that his wireless-operators must have been killed in an air raid or that something else must have happened to them. At the same time, Müller tried continually to abstract himself for a moment from those ill-fated fingerprints on the Russian radio-transmitter and the receiver of the hot-line telephone connected to Bormann's office. But the more he tried to forget about them, the more the wretched fingerprints prevented him from thinking clearly. During his twenty years in the police force Müller had developed a specific routine: first he heeded hunches or his own intuitive guesses and only then did he put them to the test by analysing in detail the particular situation or individual he happened to be working on. Müller's hunches rarely led him astray; and this was true when he had been working for the Weimar Republic breaking up Nazi demonstrations and after he went over to Hitler's side later on and started sending the leaders of the Weimar Republic to concentration camps, then again in the days when he had carried out all Himmler's instructions and now when he was starting to turn his footsteps in Kaltenbrunner's direction. He realised that it was most unlikely that Kaltenbrunner should have forgotten the instructions he had given him with regard to the investigation of Stirlitz's work, and that led Müller to conclude that something had happened and evidently somewhere high up. However, what had happened and when Müller did not know. The hidden causes of the event that had clearly taken place were so far quite beyond his grasp. That was why he had sent Holthoff to Stirlitz to lay on that play-acting: if Stirlitz came to him the next day to report on Holthoff's action he could confidently put his dossier away in the safe and consider the affair closed. If, on the other hand, Stirlitz accepted Holthoff's proposal, then he could go straight to Kaltenbrunner and put his cards on the table, since by then he would be armed with concrete evidence supplied by his assistant. Holthoff's evidence would not have been any of that physical formulae nonsense—with that stuff you never know whether you were standing on your head or your heels—it would be solid, irrefutable fact.

'Well, that's that,' he thought. 'All I can do is wait for Holthoff and then I'll know what to do next. Now for the Russian pianist.

Seeing that her chief has started to look for a contact via Switzerland, I should say we could start using our methods on the girl, instead of those soul-searching conversations of Stirlitz's. It's out of the question that she's merely a tool in the hands of her bosses. She must know something. When it came to the point, she evaded virtually all the questions she was asked. There isn't a moment to lose. She may very well know the key to the code that was sent to Berne. If we were able to compare the contents of the message she received from the chief here and the other he sent to Berne, we'd really be on to something. We could start playing off the West against the Russians, and it's important, vitally so, to get down to that at once. It's our last chance now.'

Before he had time to think out his next move, the door burst open and in came Stirlitz. With one arm he was supporting a very battered Holthoff whose hands were secured behind his back with small chromium-plated handcuffs. Müller also noticed the bewildered face of his assistant Scholz in the background. 'You must be out of your mind, Stirlitz,' he said.

'There's nothing the matter with me,' replied Stirlitz, discarding Holthoff into the nearest armchair like some unwelcome bundle. 'As for him though, he's either out of his mind or he's turned traitor.'

At that moment Holthoff's lips started to move, and in a scarcely audible whisper he brought out the word 'Water'.

'Give him some water,' demanded Müller. 'What's happened? I want the full story.'

'He's got some explaining to do first, let him get on with it,' countered Stirlitz. 'I think I'd rather give you a detailed report in writing.' He then gave Holthoff some water and put the glass back on the tray next to the decanter.

'Go to your office then and write down all the details you consider important,' consented Müller. 'When can you get that done?'

'I can give you a brief outline in ten minutes and all the details I can have ready by tomorrow.'

'Why only tomorrow?'

'Because today I have some urgent business that I must get

194

finished. As it is he won't have come round till then anyway. Is it all right for me to go now?'

'Yes, do,' replied Müller.

As soon as Stirlitz left the room, Müller proceeded to unfasten Holthoff's handcuffs. He ran his fingers over the man's blood-stained cheek and walked over to the table on which Stirlitz had put down the glass. He picked the glass up carefully between his thumb and index finger and held it carefully to the light. Stirlitz's fingerprints stood out clearly. Prompted by force of habit and not because he suspected Stirlitz in particular, Müller decided to have the prints checked, seeing that Stirlitz was one of the few people on the SD staff whose fingerprints had not yet been checked, and Müller was a man who never abandoned an undertaking till he carried it out to the end. He called Scholz to his office and said: 'Have the fingerprints on this glass checked. When you've had it done, there's no need to wake me if I'm asleep. I don't think there'll be anything urgent.'

After Stirlitz had handed Scholz a short report for Müller he rushed off to see the pastor: it was vital that he should take him to Switzerland without delay that very same day. Everything had been prepared. He had no doubts with regard to Pleischner— he was bound to have carried out all his instructions to the letter. The pastor would serve as guinea-pig. Willy-nilly he would help disrupt Himmler's deal with those people in the West who saw the Russian liberation of Europe as no more than wild Asians threatening the future of civilised mankind . . .

Müller was woken: Scholz did it himself. The fingerprints which Stirlitz had left on the glass matched up with those found on the hot-line telephone and, what was still more ominous, with those on the Russian wireless-transmitter.

Strictly personal
Reichsführer Heinrich Himmler
Only copy.

Dear Reichsführer,
I am now back at my own headquarters after my visit to Switzerland. I wish not only to give you an immediate account of everything that happened but also to attempt to provide you with an objective analysis of what the immediate future holds: our prospects, I must say, show a marked change for the better in the light of my negotiations with Dulles.

Yesterday Dolmann and I left for Switzerland, taking with us the Italian rebel nationalists Parri and Usmiani. We were assisted in our illegal crossing of the Swiss border by an assistant Major Waibel in the Swiss intelligence service. Preparations for the operation were most thorough and we arrived in perfect time for the train that took us to Zurich, where Parri and Usmiani were given accommodation at the Girslandenklinik, a fashionable hospital on the outskirts of the city. Dulles went there immediately after their arrival, as I was to learn later. It appears that he and Parri are old friends: evidently the Americans are preparing a future Italian cabinet that will promote their interests, while being assured of its popularity thanks to the inclusion of partisan heroes—of the monarchist, rather than communist variety though—fanatic nationalists who have only recently split away from the Duce, when our troops were obliged to enter Italy.

Husmann came to fetch us and took us to see Dulles at a secret address. He was waiting for us when we arrived. He was on the reticent side, but cordial. We shook hands and started our talks at once. Dulles sat by the window against the light and listened to what was said in silence. The first person to begin talking was Gävernitz.

He asked me: 'Wasn't it you who helped to secure the release of the Italian Romano Guardini at the request of Mathilde Hedewils?'

I gave a vague answer, for the name was not one that stuck out in my memory. I thought to myself that the question might merely have been some kind of a feeler on their part.

'A truly prominent Catholic philosopher,' Gävernitz went on, 'he is held most dear by every thinking European.'

I replied by way of an enigmatic smile, remembering the lessons of our prize actor Schellenberg.

Husmann then asked: 'General, are you aware that Germany has lost the war?'

I realised that these men would give me the whole works and the ordeal would most probably turn out to be a humiliating one for me personally. I had adopted similar tactics back in the past when I had tried to win over to our side various politicians opposed to our regime, so as to be able subsequently to trust them with responsible posts in the administration: such testing through personal humiliation provides sufficient guarantee of loyalty in future.

'*Yes,*' *I replied.*

'*Do you realise that there can only be one realistic basis for negotiations: unconditional surrender.*'

'*Yes,*' *I replied, knowing that the fact that the negotiations were taking place was more important than their actual content. In the given situation the actual opening of the negotiations took top priority, regardless of what they might cost me personally as an Obergruppenführer in the SS and a member of the Nazi Party.*

'*If you nevertheless still wish to start discussions in the name of Reichsführer Himmler, then I am afraid that's as far as they'll get: Mr Dulles will be obliged to take his leave.*'

I looked over towards Dulles. I could not catch sight of his face for the light was in my eyes but I noticed him give a nod of confirmation after that remark, although he remained silent as before and did not utter a single word. I realised that this was above all a question of form, for they were quite well aware in whose name a high-ranking SS officer could and would be addressing them. They had put themselves in a ridiculous and humiliating position by asking that question. I could, of course, have said that I was only prepared to talk to Mr Dulles and to him alone, and that if I were to learn that he represented Jewish monopoly capital then I would at once break off all communication. I knew that they were waiting for my reply and this is what I came out with finally. 'I consider it a crime against the great German people and the great German state, which is a bastion of European civilisation, to continue fighting now, particularly when we could sit down together to negotiate. I am ready to put the whole of my organisation, and it is at present the most powerful organisation in Italy, namely the SS and the police force, at the disposal of the Allies to bring about the end of the war and to prevent the setting up of a Communist government.'

'*Does that mean,*' *asked Dulles, breaking his silence at last, '*that your SS units would be prepared to fight against Kesselring's Wehrmacht?*'

From this I realised that this man wanted to know exactly where he stood and that augured well for realistic talks about the future.

'I need guarantees from your side,' I replied, 'before I can start talking to Feldmarschall Kesselring in specified and conclusive terms.'

'Clear,' agreed Dulles.

Then I went on: 'You must understand that as soon as Kesselring gives orders for a capitulation here in Italy, where he has over one and a half million men under him, that step will trigger off a chain reaction on the other fronts as well, I mean the Western front and Norway and Denmark.'

I also came to realise that in this all-important conversation it was vital for me to come out with my trump card.

'If I receive a guarantee from you to the effect that you are prepared to continue negotiations, I shall take it upon myself to prevent the destruction of Italy as planned by the Führer. We have already been given orders to destroy all art galleries and historic buildings, in a word, to raze to the ground all that is a part of mankind's historic heritage. Despite considerable personal risk, I have already rescued and hidden in my own hideouts pictures from the Uffizi and Pitti galleries and Victor Emanuel's collection of coins.'

Then I put down on the table a list of the pictures I had hidden away. It included names such as Titian, Botticelli, El Greco. The Americans interrupted our discussion to study the list.

'How much might those pictures be worth in dollars?' they asked me.

'They are priceless masterpieces,' I answered, but went on to add: 'I should think something over a hundred million dollars.'

After that, for ten minutes or so, Gävernitz talked about Renaissance art and the influence of that era on the technical and philosophical advance of Europe. Then Dulles chipped into the conversation and without saying anything by way of an introduction came straight out with: 'I'm ready to have dealings with you, General Wolff. But you must give me a guarantee that you will not seek any other contacts with the Allies. That is my first condition. I hope you understand that the very fact that we have met here to negotiate must not go farther than those now present.'

'That means we would not be able to conclude any peace,' I commented, 'for you are not the President and I am not the Chancellor.'

My remark was followed by a silent exchange of smiles and I realised that Dulles's presence was a signal for me to inform you of the negotiations and ask for your next instructions. I am sending this letter to you via an

198

ADC of Feldmarschall Kesselring, who will be accompanying the Feld-
marschall when he flies to Berlin. I have put the man's reliability to a
most thorough test: not so much as my agent but rather as a person who is
loyal to us and thinks along the same lines as we do. You will no doubt
remember him, since it was you who approved his canditature when he was
sent to Kesselring to inform us about the Feldmarschall's contacts with
Reichsmarschall Göring.

It would be most expedient at this stage to invite Kesselring to come to
discuss the situation with you. Our second meeting with the Americans is to
take place in the next few days.

Heil Hitler!
Yours, Karl Wolff

One thing Wolf had omitted was the long confidential talk he
had had with Husmann and Waibel in a compartment of the
train they took back to Italy. They had discussed the future
German cabinet. It had been agreed that Kesselring would be
Chancellor, von Neurath, the former Governor of Bohemia and
Moravia, would be given the Foreign Ministry, and Hjalmar
Schacht, honorary member of the NSDAP, the Ministry of
Finance, while SS Obergruppenführer Karl Wolff would take
over the Ministry of the Interior. No portfolio in the new cabinet
was set aside for Himmler.

13

Meanwhile Stirlitz was driving his Horch at full throttle to get to the Swiss border as soon as possible. Next to him sat the pastor, pale and subdued. The wireless was tuned in to a programme of French songs performed by the popular young star Edith Piaf. Her voice was low and carried well, and the words of her songs were simple and ingenious.

'Moral standards are sinking daily,' commented the pastor. 'I'm not criticising her, no, I'm just listening to her and remembering Handel and Bach. It must just be that in the past artists set themselves higher standards: their art was inspired by faith and they were always reaching after a supreme ideal. They were like beacons pointing the way . . . As for that, well, people use that kind of language in the marketplace.'

'That girl's art will outlive her,' contradicted Stirlitz. 'Believe me, she'll be remembered long after she's dead and gone.'

'Your better nature's running away with you . . .'

'More likely my love of Paris! That's enough for now though, Pastor . . . We can talk about things like that after the war's over. Now you'd better run through everything you have to do in Berne once more.'

The pastor began to repeat all the instructions he had been given in the course of the previous three hours. As he listened to the pastor, Stirlitz thought to himself: 'Yes, Käthe is in their hands. But if I took her away now, they would turn their attention to the pastor, for it's obvious someone in the Gestapo is checking up on him as well. Then the whole operation would be doomed to failure, there's no doubt about that, and Himmler might start hobnobbing with those other people in Berne. Käthe—if something unforeseen should happen, a possibility, although unlikely—is certain to give me away if they start threatening her baby's life. But the pastor will soon be at work and Pleischner should carry out my instructions all right. Not one of them is aware of the part he is playing in my operation. Apart from the precautions I've already taken, our fellows should be keeping an eye on the pastor now that they've received my message via Pleischner. So everything should work out. I'm not going to let Himmler contact Berne. Müller knows nothing of my loop-hole at the border and the border guards won't give anything away to his men, because I am acting on instructions from the Reichsführer. So the pastor will make Switzerland today. By tomorrow my operation should be under way or, to be more precise, our operation.'

'No,' said Stirlitz, switching his thoughts back to what the pastor was saying. 'You must arrange the meeting not in the blue lounge at the hotel but in the pink one: you see run-throughs never do anyone any harm.'

'And I thought you weren't paying any attention to what I was saying.'

'I'm listening very carefully. Please go on . . .' 'If the pastor gets across the border all right, then I must get Käthe out. I can stake my all then. I can get across the border taking her with me, once I sense that the game is almost up. If it proves possible to continue the game—so far they have no evidence against me that's for sure—then I'll have to shoot my way out with her, after arranging some kind of alibi with Schellenberg's help. I should have to go and report to him at his home or in Hohenlichen— he's always hanging around Himmler out there—work out my timing very carefully, remove the guards at the flat, smash the wireless-transmitter and carry off Käthe. The timing of the whole plan is going to be of decisive importance. Let them search us out. Their time is running out too. Judging by Müller's horror at the sight of Holthoff with his head bashed in, he must have put the idiot up to that childish piece of provocation. Yet at the same time, Holthoff couldn't have acted so convincingly if he hadn't been voicing real fears, if the part he had to churn out had not contained his own thoughts. Nor is there any certainty as to how he would have reacted if I had agreed to make a getaway with him and Runge. Perhaps he would have gone the whole hog, more than likely in fact, if the way he looked at me and spoke, while I was interrogating that astronomer, is anything to go by. I could cover up my sudden departure with Schellenberg's help on the one hand and Bormann's on the other. The most vital thing now is to rescue

201

Käthe. Tomorrow I shan't go home, I shall go straight to her. Although I had better not, perhaps. In this game blind moves are the first thing to avoid. They have to be paid for afterwards, and not in money—it is the cause and human lives that are at stake.'

'Yes, that's quite correct,' said Stirlitz, turning to the pastor. 'That's a good point to have made, that you should take a second taxi, letting the first pass you by and that you should never accept lifts from passing cars. In general, though, I reckon that your friends from the monastery, whose names I gave you, should be able to keep you out of harm's way. But I want to make it quite clear once more that anything can happen, absolutely anything. If you make even the slightest slip, before you know where you are you'll find yourself back here in one of Müller's prisons. Should things reach such a pass, remember that if you mention my name even once, in delirium or under torture, it will mean not only my death but also that of your sister and her boys. That is the condition insisted on by the people who made it possible for me to get you out. Nothing can save your relatives if you mention my name. That is not a threat, don't get me wrong, it is how things actually stand at the moment and it is something you must bear in mind and never forget.'

'I understand.'

'So much the better. I shouldn't like to think that on that particular score you had misunderstood me in any way.'

Stirlitz parked his car some hundred yards from the station. The border guards had left the car for the next lap in the appointed place. The key was in the ignition and the windows had been specially splashed with mud to make it impossible to see the faces of any passengers inside. Later they found skis sticking out of the snow at the gorge up in the mountains, as arranged, and next to the skis, a pair of ski-boots also lay ready.

'Get changed now,' Stirlitz instructed the pastor.

'Yes, yes,' answered the pastor in a whisper, 'my hands are shaking and I must pull myself together a bit.'

'You can talk in an ordinary voice, nobody can hear us now.'

202

In the light of the full moon the snow in the valley had a silvery sheen and showed black in the gorges. The snow piled high on the branches of the pine trees looked like some beast of prey crouched to jump on its next victim. Somewhere in the distance the whirr of a power station could be heard at irregular intervals, when the wind blew in the right direction.

'Well,' said Stirlitz. 'Good luck to you, Pastor.'

'God be with you,' replied the pastor and, launched on his skis, he started making his way in a series of awkward fits and starts in the direction he had been told to follow by Stirlitz. He fell over twice, exactly on the frontier line. Stirlitz waited for a few minutes by the car until the pastor shouted twice in the wood on the other side of the gorge. Now it was only a stone's throw to the hotel, and things were all right so far. Käthe's rescue was now his first priority.

'Stirlitz drove back to the station, switched cars and, after he had driven about fifteen miles, he felt that he was quite incapable of keeping awake. He looked at his watch which showed that he had been on the go for almost forty-eight hours without a wink of sleep.

'I'll doze for half an hour,' he decided. 'Otherwise I simply won't get back to Berlin in one piece.'

He slept for a mere twenty minutes, then got out of his car, rubbed his face in the snow, took a swig of brandy from the hip-flask and, slumped across the wheel, drove all out for Berlin. The hotted-up engine of his Horch gave out a strong, even purr. The speedometer was registering almost 120 kph. The road was quite deserted and the dawn was making a timid attempt to break through the mist. To keep himself awake Stirlitz sang catchy French tunes to himself one after the other without stopping.

Rolff arrived at the flat where Käthe was living at eight o'clock in the morning while it was still dark.

'*Heil* Hitler!' Barbara greeted him, rising to her feet as he entered.

Before she had time to say anything else, Rolff said: 'Leave the two of us to talk alone.'

Barbara's face, which had been all smiles at once assumed a hard, official gaze, and she went out into the other room. When she opened the door Käthe heard her son crying—he must have woken up because he was hungry.

'Please, would you let me feed my son,' asked Käthe, 'or he won't let us discuss things in peace.'

'The boy can wait.'

'But that's impossible . . . He has to be fed according to schedule.'

'All right. You shall feed him after you have answered my question . . .' There was a knock at the door.

'We're busy!' shouted Rolff.

The door opened to reveal Helmuth standing on the threshold carrying the baby. 'It's time for him to be fed,' he announced. 'He's demanding his food very loudly.'

'He'll wait!' shouted Rolff. 'Shut the door!'

'But, you . . .' Helmuth began only to be stopped by Rolff walking quickly over to the door and slamming it in his face.

'To proceed . . . I want to know one thing. We have learnt that you know your local intelligence chief.'

'But I've already explained . . .'

'I know. I've read your answers and listened to recordings of them. They satisfied me until this morning. Since this morning those explanations have ceased to be satisfactory.'

'What happened this morning?'

'Something big. We have been waiting for it to happen, since we had long had our suspicions, but we needed proof. Now we've got it. After all we can't arrest someone if we have no proof of his guilt: we need concrete evidence or facts or at least the testimony of two witnesses. We've got conclusive evidence now.'

'But, if I remember rightly, from the very beginning I agreed to . . .'

'That's enough of your playing about now . . . It's not you I'm talking about! You know very well who I'm talking about.'

'I don't know who you're talking about and I beg you to let me feed the baby.'

'First of all you'll tell me where and when you used to meet your chief and after that you'll go and deal with the baby.'

204

'I've already explained to the man who arrested me that I do not know either the chief's name or his address, and that I have never met him.'

'Listen,' said Rolff angrily, 'stop fooling about. All the cards are on the table, the ace has been trumped.'

He was very tired because he, like all Müller's other close associates, had not slept since three that morning; they had been busy looking for Stirlitz's car all over the city. His house was being watched and people were also lying in wait for him near Käthe's flat, but Stirlitz seemed to have vanished into thin air. What was more Müller had given explicit instructions forbidding anyone to inform Kaltenbrunner, let alone Schellenberg, that Stirlitz was being hunted down. Müller had decided to organise the whole chase himself, realising that he had embarked on a very complex game which could end only in a major coup or a crushing defeat. He knew that it was Bormann who had control of enormous sums of money that were now safely deposited in various banks in Sweden, Switzerland, Brazil and—thanks to the work of various go-betweens—even in the United States. Bormann never forgot services rendered but neither did he forget wrongs anyone did him. He used to make notes on everything in any way connected with Hitler, using even his handkerchief for this purpose when there was nothing else at hand. But when something concerned himself, he never took notes—such matters he always remembered. That was why the Gestapo chief was organising this hunt for Stirlitz, who had telephoned Bormann and had a secret meeting with him, independently, and completely on his own. It was his own game in which he could not afford to make any mistakes. The whole case would have been simple and straightforward if it had not been for Stirlitz's telephone call to Bormann and their subsequent meeting. The rest made a clear chain: Stirlitz, the coded message in Berne and the Russian radio-operator. But that whole chain rested on a mighty pillar—Bormann. It meant that Müller either unseated Bormann and thereby gained access directly to Hitler—that too he saw as one of the possible prizes in this game—or, if the rules of the game would allow, he could become indispensable to Bormann as the man who exposed the conspiracy devised by Stirlitz who was connected with the

205

Russian radio-operators. Whichever path Müller chose could just as easily mean the final triumph or the final disaster. That was why neither he nor his close associates had had any sleep that night and had used all their strength to spread the net for their prey, as they made ready for the decisive duel.

'I shall not say anything else,' insisted Käthe. 'I shall remain silent until you allow me to feed the baby.'

The logic of a mother has little in common with the logic of the butcher. If Käthe had not said anything about the child, she herself would have been put through excruciating tortures. Yet her words, prompted by maternal instinct, put a new idea into Rolff's head that had not occurred to him before he entered the flat. He was familiar with the reputation Russian agents had for endurance, and he knew that they preferred to die rather than betray anyone, and that even when they were persuaded to 'co-operate', they somehow managed to continue to carry out their former work, having recourse to more subtle and cunning methods.

Rolff had an unexpected brainwave. 'Look here, we're not going to waste time for nothing. I know what you are trying to hide. Soon we shall be bringing you face to face with your chief: realising the game is up, he decided to slip abroad, but he did not make it. He was counting on his car,' Rolff went on in a sarcastic tone, his eyes boring right through Käthe's pale face, 'he had a fine little machine, didn't he? But he miscalculated this time, our cars are better than his, not worse. In all this mess it's not you who interests us, but him. And you're going to tell us everything you know about him. Everything,' he repeated. 'Every detail.'

'I have nothing to say.'

Then Rolff got up, walked over to the window, opened it as wide as it would go, cringed at the sudden cold and said: 'Frost again—will the spring never come? We're all so tired of this everlasting winter.'

He closed the window, walked over to Käthe and demanded: 'Your hands please.'

Käthe stretched out her hands which he promptly handcuffed.

206

'Now your legs please,' Rolff proceeded.

'What are you trying to do?' asked Käthe. 'What have you thought up this time?'

After snapping other shackles round her ankles Rolff called: 'Helmuth! Barbara! Bring in the baby!'

Helmuth went to fetch the baby, while Rolff moved over to a small table by the window. Then he pushed open the window and said: 'It was not for nothing that I mentioned frost to you just now. If I expose your child, stripped naked, to the cold here on this table for three or four minutes, that would be the end of him. It's up to you to decide.'

'You wouldn't do it!' Käthe screamed, struggling to get to her feet. 'You wouldn't do it! Kill me! Kill me! Not the baby! You can't do it!'

'Yes, it will be a dreadful thing for me to have to do,' replied Rolff. 'Believe it or not, I too am a human being, not an animal, born of a mother's flesh! Yet it is in the name of all our German mothers that I shall be doing it! In the name of the Reich's children, who are being killed by bombs!'

Käthe fell off her chair, dragged herself over to Rolff across the floor and kissed his boots, begging with desperate sobs: 'But you must have a heart! You can't really be going to do it. I don't believe you!'

'Where's the child?' shouted Rolff. 'Bring him in here and hurry up about it for God's sake!'

'You are a mother!' insisted Barbara. 'You must be reasonable . . .'

Helmuth came in with the baby in his arms. Rolff took the boy from him, laid him on the table and started to take off his clothes. Käthe started to howl like a helpless animal.

'Well I'm damned!' bawled Rolff. 'You're no mother! You're nothing but a thick-skinned murderess! Good God!'

The little boy started to cry in his hoarse little voice, his tiny mouth stretched in an indignant shriek: it was long past feeding time and everyone seemed to have forgotten about him.

207

Monseigneur Cadicelli,
The Vatican.

Dear friend,

I understand and appreciate the attention the Vatican authorities, which showed such courage at the time of the anti-Nazi resistance, are now devoting to a study of all possible ways of promoting mankind's attempts to secure peace so vital to all of us on this earth . . . I was aware of the reasons why the Vatican showed such readiness to take upon itself the organisation of contacts between Müller, representing the unfortunate Admiral Kanaris and other heroic generals who gave their lives in the struggle against Hitler's vandalism on the one hand, and official representatives of the British cabinet on the other.

Those people who were behind Doctor of Philosophy Müller, possessed sufficient positive qualities to allow you to exert your influence on the British cabinet in the search for a reasonable and honourable peace. However, after the tragic death of the true patriots last summer an ominous pause in the search for peace set in.

I am equally well aware of the motives leading you to regard with such scepticism the cautious proposals which General Karl Wolff submitted for your consideration. I know you have lived through the Nazi occupation, and seen with your own eyes the flagrant lawlessness perpetrated by SS men, directly responsible to a person who is now seeking peace—General Wolff. This led me to evaluate your stand as distinctly negative rather than a wait-and-see attitude: you cannot possibly trust a man who does evil with one hand and works good with the other. Half-measures and duplicity while understandable in ordinary children of God, can in no way be justified when it comes to those who determine policies of state or are vested with military or political power.

However, after his overtures had been repulsed at the Vatican, General Wolff succeeded in his present task, since here in Berne he managed to meet Mr Dulles, who is representing the venerable President Roosevelt. The information which we have received here allows us to conclude that the negotiations between Wolff and Mr Dulles are progressing most successfully.

My position here is thus most delicate: if I once again warn Mr Dulles against any further contact with General Wolff, our American friends may misconstrue the motives behind our actions: men who shape policies of state are by no means always able to understand the policies of God's servants.

It would seem to be of little purpose to tell Mr Dulles of General Wolff's perfidious actions and the atrocities perpetrated by the Nazis on his orders throughout our fair Italy; in the first place, he who has eyes to see will have noticed these things for himself, and secondly, it would not be fitting for us servants of God to put our own sufferings to the fore. We knew what would lie ahead of us when we chose our path.

The situation appeared to me to be grim and indeed hopeless until Pastor Schlag arrived here in Berne. You do, I am sure, remember that noble man who has always championed peace and who visited Switzerland, the Vatican and Great Britain on several occasions up until 1933 when leaving Germany did not yet involve those police complications which began once Hitler assumed power.

Pastor Schlag came here—to use his own words—to investigate the possibilities of concluding a swift and just peace. He says he was sent here by people concerned about the recent narrowing of the gap between the stands adopted by such diametrically opposed figures as Wolff and Dulles, with regard to the future peace.

He sees his task to lie in the prevention of further negotiations between Wolff and Dulles, since he is firmly convinced that Wolff is not seeking peace but merely exploring the prospects for preserving intact the Nazi regime in exchange for certain concessions on the part of the SS, which now constitutes the only real power in Germany.

He also considers himself called upon to help those people who risked their lives to get him out of Germany, to establish contact with representatives of the Allies. The people whom he says he represents, see it as their indisputable duty to demand the liquidation of everyone connected with the SS or NSDAP or that might be connected with them in the future.

I would ask your permission to engage in more frank conversations with Pastor Schlag. It would probably be worth our while to give him more extensive information on what is now going on in Berne.

Unless I am able to give Pastor Schlag tangible demonstration of our good faith in these matters, we cannot expect him to be more forthcoming or to give us detailed information with regard to his associates waiting for news from him in Germany.

I assume that his associates in Germany are by no means as powerful as we would wish. Pastor Schlag has never been a politician, merely an honest shepherd of his flock. However, assessing the situation with an eye to the future, I hold that it would be greatly to our advantage if the pastor, he and no other, a servant of God, were to be the honourable and high-principled person ready to risk his life to bring about peace without ever resorting to any compromises with the Nazis.

This inspiring example of civil courage on the part of a servant of God would clearly help us in our efforts to save the Germans from Bolshevism when the hard-pressed people of that country will have to decide its future. Pastor Schlag, or his hallowed memory, will help us servants of God to carry our light to those places where the darkness of Nazism once reigned supreme.

Impatient to receive a reply as soon as possible,

Yours, Norelli

Dulles received instructions from Donovan, Director of the Office of Strategic Services, to refer in future to his negotiations with Wolff by the code-name 'Operation Crossword'. In order to speed up the negotiations two generals had also been sent along to take part: the deputy Chief of Staff of the Allied Forces in Italy, General Airey, on behalf of Great Britain, and General Lemnitzer, representing the Americans.

The generals, disguised as Irish businessmen, were brought to the Swiss border from Naples. They were to cross the Swiss border with forged papers passing them off as neutrals travelling through Europe in search of their relatives.

General Lemnitzer answered the numerous questions put to him by the Swiss customs officials on the subject of Ireland. General Airey, from Britain, who had never visited the republic, found himself tied up in knots, and 'Operation Crossword' soon became a mere hair's breadth from fiasco. Major Waibel, who was hovering in the vicinity, instructed his subordinates working among the border-guards to let Airey through, regardless of the kind of answers he might give the customs officials.

When Airey's ordeal was over and he had wiped his sweating forehead with a cold, shaking hand, Waibel, dressed in civilian clothes, came up to him and handed over two train tickets for the generals' journey to Berne. At the other end a car was waiting for them that took Waibel and the two generals to a flat in a quiet street which had been rented by stand-ins, and it was there that Allen Dulles was waiting for them. In the same flat

210

they held discussions for two days, deciding on the common stand to be adopted during the negotiations with SS Obergruppenführer Karl Wolff.

'We have little time,' Dulles reminded them. 'Yet there is a great deal to be done. The Allies' position must be precise and well thought out, as far as main principles and details are concerned.'

'The position of the Anglo–American Allies,' echoed Airey in a tone which could have either implied a question or mere confirmation.

'Whether Anglo–American or American–English Allies is a purely formal distinction in this case, which does not affect the essential nature of the matter under discussion,' specified Dulles.

For the first time since America entered the war, the concept Allies was being used without including one word—'Soviet'. In Berne, the concept 'Anglo–Soviet–American Allies' had been replaced by a new term—'Anglo–American Allies'.

Eismann came to report to Müller without changing or cleaning himself up: his boots were caked in mud and his jacket was wet through. He had spent a long time trailing round Neustadt, looking for the flat where Pastor Schlag's sister lived. She was no longer to be found at the address given in the file. Eismann had then sought help at the local Gestapo office only to learn that they too knew nothing of the whereabouts of Schlag's next of kin.

The neighbours, however, were able to tell him that a few days before they had heard the noise of a car engine outside the house. But no one had any clear idea of who had come or in what kind of car they had arrived, and what had subsequently become of Frau Anna and her children.

She had disappeared just as mysteriously as the pastor. For the last two days on Eismann's instructions, police had been searching for both the pastor and his sister and nephews, but so far no traces of them had been found.

Müller greeted Eismann with an ironic smile. After listening to the Obersturmbannführer's report he did not say anything at

211

first but merely brought a document-case out of his safe and took a piece of paper out of it.

'So, what shall I do with this now?' he asked, handing the sheet of paper to Eismann.

It was Eismann's report containing a signed statement to the effect that he placed complete confidence in Standartenführer Stirlitz.

After a long pause Eismann gave a deep sigh and then snarled: 'The devil take the lot of us!'

'That's more like it,' agreed Müller, putting the piece of paper back into the document-case. 'Let that be a real lesson to you, my friend.'

'Well, what do you want me to do now, hand in a new report to you?'

'Why? There's no need for that . . .'

'But I consider it my duty to revise my previous assessment of his character.'

'Is that wise?' Müller asked. 'Taking back one's own opinions always smells somewhat fishy.'

'But what else should I do in the circumstances then?'

'Trust that I won't play on this precious report of yours. That's all. And just get on with your work. You should also bear in mind that you will soon have to go to Prague and after that you may possibly return to both the pastor and your loyal friend, with whom you took shelter from the bombing in Smolensk. But that's enough for now and there's no need to be upset. People working in counter-intelligence should know better than anyone that one should trust no one in times such as these, even oneself sometimes.

To SS Obergruppenführer
Kaltenbrunner,
Chief of the Reich security Office.
Printed in two copies.

Prague

Dear Obergruppenführer,
 After receiving the Führer's order to turn every town and every house into an impregnable fortress I made a further investigation of the situation in

Prague which, like Vienna and the Alpine Redoubt, is to be the centre of a decisive battle against Bolshevism or, if the outcome of this particular battle proves tragic, it will be razed to the ground.

In response to your instructions for me to select men ready to destroy Prague, not merely from among the Aryans but also from among those members of the local population who have proved their worth by co-operating with us for several years in a common struggle against Bolshevism, I have drawn up a list of likely candidates. I do not plan to include all their names in this letter and thereby take up too much of your valuable time when you have so much extremely important work on your hands and so many vital decisions to make. I shall be sending to your secretariat a list of 421 names, which include representatives of a wide variety of nationalities.

I have enlisted for this work Colonel Berg from military intelligence, who, as I learnt in Cracow, is personally known to you as a result of the work you carried out in connection with the case against enemy of the nation, Kanaris. He has been of substantial assistance to me; this was due, in part, to the fact that he works in conjunction with the Russian Grishanchikov, recruited to our outfit. Incidentally, this Grishanchikov was highly recommended by Standartenführer Stirlitz during the latter's visit to Cracow, as a first-class barber and masseur. He has indeed proved a rather competent counter-intelligence man and has helped me pick out candidates from among the Russians now serving in General Vlasov's army.

Since all persons who are to take part in the preparations for the destruction of the main centres of Slavonic culture must be subjected to detailed vetting by the Gestapo, I would ask you to give instructions to Obergruppenführer Müller to organise additional checks when it comes to Colonel Berg and, if possible, the Russian Grishanchikov as well. I make so bold as to ask you occasionally to keep me informed about everything connected with my work here, while appreciating that my tasks cannot be compared with your gigantic work in preparing our final victory.

Heil Hitler!
Yours, Krüger

Kaltenbrunner looked through the letter and then wrote the following note: 'Müller. I know of no Berg, let alone Grishanchikov. Check up on them, but do not take up my time with details of this sort again, Kaltenbrunner.'

Now that Müller needed to lay his hands on Stirlitz's contact in Berne as quickly as possible, he decided to disrupt the scheme now being implemented by the men who were still lying in wait at the Russian secret address in the town. Trailing the intelligence chief's contacts was not what he needed at the moment, he needed concrete evidence and right away. An operation designed to uncover the whole network was an idea of Schellenberg's; let him organise a new scheme now, that was his affair. Judging by the information he had received so far, the contact who had turned up in Berne, was a dilettante, an intellectual who could be made to 'talk' with no trouble at all; he would tell who had given him the coded message; he would not be a hard nut to crack. Then Müller would have the irrefutable evidence he needed and the game would be his.

He sent the following instructions to Berne: 'Stop trailing the contact. Have him seized and sent back over the border in the boot of an embassy car to be delivered personally to Obergruppenführer Müller.'

As he set off to go to the cover address at the appointed time, Pleischner was in as buoyant a mood as he had been the day before. His work was going extremely well, and he only left his room for meals. He was filled with joyous hope at the prospect of Hitler's imminent downfall. He was buying newspapers by the dozen and, being an experienced investigator of historical fact, he did not find it difficult to realise what the future held. Back in Berlin he had been afraid to listen to British information bulletins on the wireless and had merely tried to glean the truth by reading between the lines of Goebbels's all-persuasive propaganda. In general, he had indeed mastered the art. He used to read the communiqué and articles of the *Völkischer Beobachter*, scanned the mythical victory reports and then, after probing deeper, started moving little flags across the map, in his mind of course. There were red flags, stars and stripes and brown ones. A map, the names of the towns and a ruler—these three basic pieces of equipment were all Pleischner needed to grasp the basic truth. In Switzerland he was able to appreciate the aptness of the conclusions he had drawn back home in

Berlin. He had always held that the victory of fascism would mean the end of civilisation and would, in the final analysis, lead to the degeneration of the German people. Whenever the world began to be divided up into masters and slaves, the master nations would fall prey to corruption. Ancient Rome collapsed precisely because it had sought to rule the world and, instead, it fell at the hands of Barbarians. Indeed, Pleischner reflected, every ancient state that had decided it would rule the world found itself condemned to ultimate destruction at the height of its illusory might. He realised that Hitler had conceived a diabolical experiment, calculating that the Reich's victory over the rest of the world would ensure material prosperity for *every* German, regardless of his status in German society. He had planned to make the Germans the rulers of the world, and the rest of the world's inhabitants—their subjects. In other words, he had intended to rule out the possibility that any 'leaven of civilisation' might appear at all, or at least in the foreseeable future. If Hitler were to emerge victorious the German nation would become militarised on a total scale. Hitler would disarm all other peoples depriving them of their state institutions, and then any attempt at revolt on the part of the conquered would be doomed to failure.

Pleischner looked at his watch—there was still time to kill before his appointment. In front of him was a small café: through the window, down which raindrops were sliding, he could see children sitting at the tables eating ice-cream. Their form mistress must have brought them in for a treat.

'I'm thinking in Reich clichés,' thought Pleischner in horror, noticing a young man sitting at the head of the table who was laughing away with the rest of the group. 'It's only in our country that all the teachers are women, because all the men fit for active service are away at the front. But it's really men who should be staffing the schools, as it was in Sparta. A woman's role is to comfort and console, not educate. It should be men who prepare children for the future that lies ahead of them: children would then not be fed with unnecessary illusions, and there is nothing more terrible than the collision of childish illusions with adult reality.

Pleischner went into the café, sat down at a corner table and ordered strawberry ice-cream. He listened to the children laughing at the jokes their teacher was making. He was talking to them like equals, not adjusting down to their level in the slightest; unobtrusively and tactfully he was introducing them to his world.

'But if Hitler were to overrun this place, the children would be sitting silently at the table, obediently swallowing every word that left their mentor's lips—that mentor would more than likely be a schoolmistress rather than a master—and they would walk down the streets in neat files, instead of gay little clusters and greet each other with idiotic shouts of *"Heil* Hitler!"'. Perhaps it is terrible to wish defeat on one's own country, yet I can't help wishing a speedy finish . . .'

Pleischner ate his ice-cream slowly as he listened to the children's voices, a contented smile on his face.

At last the teacher said: 'Let's thank the owner of this cosy little café who let us have warm shelter and cold ice-cream. Shall we sing him our song?'

'Yes!' came the eager reply from all the children.

'Let's put it to the vote! Who's against it?'

'I am,' said a little red-haired girl with freckles and enormous blue eyes. 'I'm against it.'

'Why?'

At that moment the door of the café opened and, knocking raindrops off his mackintosh as he entered, the tall blue-eyed giant from the cover address appeared on the scene. He was accompanied by a tough, wiry little fellow with an olive complexion and an expressive face with prominent cheek-bones. Pleischner was on the point of jumping to his feet when he remembered the instructions the tall man had given him: 'I will do the recognising,' so he merely buried himself in his newspaper and went back to listening to the children's conversation.

'Tell us why are you against us singing?' the schoolmaster asked the little girl. 'You must learn to back up your opinions. Perhaps you're right and we're wrong . . . Help us decide.'

'Mummy says that you shouldn't sing after eating ice-cream,' the little girl replied, 'because it can be bad for your throat.'

'Your Mummy's right about lots of things. Of course, if we

216

sang loudly or shouted at the tops of our voices outside in the cold then we could get sore throats. But in here . . . I don't think anything terrible will happen. Anyway, you needn't join in if you don't want to: we shan't hold it against you.'

The schoolmaster gave them the opening note and the children started to sing a cheerful Swiss song. The proprietor of the café came out from behind the bar to applaud them. They then walked out of the café talking loudly and Pleischner watched them leave as he struggled to remember where he had seen the dark-haired companion of the blue-eyed giant before. 'Faces like that one remembers, however ordinary they may seem at first glance. Perhaps he was at the concentration camp that I was in? No . . . I didn't see him there. But the face *is* familiar, I remember it very clearly.'

Pleischner must have been taking too close a look at the man with the olive complexion, because when the latter noticed he gave a quick smile and that smile jolted Pleischner's memory like a still from a long-forgotten film. It even brought back the ring of his voice for Pleischner. He remembered him shouting: 'Let him sign the pledge to support the Führer in everything! In *everything*! We're not going to give him the chance to wag his head at us and say : "They were the guilty ones and I was not involved." Nowadays it is impossible for anyone to say they are not involved! Loyalty or death—that is the choice for any German when he comes out of a concentration camp!' That had been during the second year of the war, when he had been called to the Gestapo for the annual interview that usually took place in the spring. The small olive-skinned man came into the room for a brief period, listened to Pleischner's conversation with the Gestapo officer in uniform, who usually conducted these conversations with Pleischner, and then shouted those angry hysterical words that had imprinted themselves on Pleischner's memory. After that scene Pleischner had gone to see his brother Hugo. At that time he was still working as medical superintendent at one of Berlin's hospitals and no one thought then that within a year he would be dead. 'That's their way of going about things,' Hugo had commented.

'They want to rope you in along with themselves.'

Pleischner's hands began to tremble and he felt completely at a loss. He could not decide what to do next: should he go up to the tall man and take him on one side to warn him, or should he go out into the street and have a look to see if they walked off together or separated. But perhaps it would be better to get up first and make his way as quickly as possible to the flat to warn the other man—on that first occasion he had heard a second voice—so that he should fix up an alarm signal in the window.

'Wait a moment,' said Pleischner to himself, as all of a sudden another thought flashed through his mind. 'What was there in the window when I went round to the flat the day before yesterday? The pot-plant was standing in the window as Stirlitz had said it might be. Or was it? No, it can't have been, otherwise how has that fellow turned up here . . . No, I'm losing control of myself, stop panicking. Get a grip on yourself. Wait a minute . . .'

The tall man left the café with his small olive-skinned companion without even looking at Pleischner. Pleischner asked the proprietor for his bill and handed him a note, his last. The café-owner did not have enough change and ran across to a shop on the opposite side of the street. When he had given Pleischner his change and seen him to the door, the street was already empty: neither the blue-eyed giant, nor the small dark man were to be seen.

'But perhaps it's another case, like Stirlitz's,' thought Pleischner to himself. 'Perhaps he too is playing his part by fighting against the Nazis inside their own set-up?'

That thought reassured him somewhat, and although Pleischner found it difficult to banish the face of the olive-complexioned man from his mind, his repulsive manner of speaking and the sudden flashes of his malicious smiles, he nevertheless tried to convince himself that his panic had just been the result of his nervousness.

Pleischner walked up to the house where the flat was and, looking up at the window, he saw the tall man and the black-haired one, standing talking about something on each side of the large pot-plant—the signal that the game was up. The Russian agent had managed to put out the signal after he had sensed that he was being tailed, and the Gestapo men had not

218

managed to find out whether the pot-plant signified 'all clear' or that the cover address had been blown. Yet being convinced that the Russian had not known he was being followed, the Nazis had left everything as they had found it, and the fact that Pleischner in his absent-mindedness had turned up two days earlier without paying any attention to the pot-plant had convinced them that it meant 'all clear'.

The men at the window caught sight of Pleischner and the tall one smiled at him and nodded in greeting. It was the second time Pleischner had seen him smile and that smile helped him to grasp the true situation at last. He smiled back and started to cross the street, deciding that on the opposite side of the street they would not be able to see him from above and then he could give them the slip. However, when he looked round, he noticed two men following him at a distance of a hundred yards, window-shopping as they went.

Pleischner felt himself go weak at the knees. 'Shall I shout or call for help? They'd be the first to reach me though. I know just what they'd do to me: Stirlitz told me how they can dope you or pass you off as insane.'

At moments of extreme danger, if only a man can keep his wits about him, his perception becomes extra sharp and his brain works more intensively than ever. Pleischner caught sight of a patch of overcast snow-laden sky through the arch he had passed two days before when he had visited the fatal flat. He realised there must be a way out into the courtyard from which he could escape.

He walked into the porch on legs that were shaking at the knees and would hardly bend. The first door was open, for upstairs the men were expecting him to come up and had pressed the button to open it. Pleischner shut that first door behind him and rushed to the opposite one that led into the courtyard and had a small fan window at the top of it. He pushed it with his hand only to find it was locked. He pushed with his whole weight against it, but the door did not give an inch.

Before entering the Reich Security Office, Stirlitz drew up his car at the curb, got out and sat down on a bench that was badly in need of a new coat of paint and had been warped by frost and rain. Children were rushing by on roller-skates, skilfully winding their way in and out of the craters. They spoke little to one another and their faces wore concentrated expressions. Stirlitz noticed that they were wet with sweat, a sure sign that they were desperately under-nourished.

'Rushing about like that is bad for those poor strained little hearts of theirs,' he thought to himself. 'Bombing at night, roller-skating in the daytime and the constant ache for food: bread, sausages, potatoes, . . . and enough of them all to fill you up. The most awful thing about the war is the crippled bodies and minds of the children left in its wake.'

Stirlitz shut his eyes and saw Sashenka's face clearly outlined before him. Men remember the faces of the women they love particularly clearly as they see them at moments of parting or reunion. So many years had passed, so many people had lost their lives, whole new states had come into being, policies had switched, friends appeared and disappeared and yet Stirlitz still saw Sashenka's face before him, pale and frightened, whenever his thoughts turned to her—all he had to do was shut his eyes. The face would take shape out of a mauve-green echoing void; it was always the face he had gazed at during those last moments of parting. 'Women's emotions are stronger than those experienced by men. With them it is not reason that takes the upper hand, as it is with us, but something vague, that cannot be defined,' mused Stirlitz. 'I told her then I'd see her in a year's time, but she shook her head and, with her eyes closed, passed her fingers over my face like a blind woman eager to take in every tiny detail. Sashenka,' thought Stirlitz with a sigh. 'Oh God, Sashenka . . . How tough things must have been for her alone with our son. There were no whirring roller-skates back home in those days and a bicycle seemed miraculous. But Sasha, our little Sasha, didn't have a father, roller-skates or a bicycle—just my Sashenka and books . . .'

Stirlitz savoured those memories for a while, for there was little time left for him to think about Sashenka and their son— not more than a few minutes because after that he would have to go into the building behind him, make his way down to the basement, and then, once he had knocked at the door of the waiting-room outside Müller's office, there would be no time to think about everything he held most dear in that life of his which had been put wholly to the service of the cause. Down there he would have to fight and any fighter is bound to be defeated if he is unable to shut out of his mind everything which is not directly concerned with the imminent battle.

'Don't worry, Katyusha,' he thought as he got up from the bench, 'we'll get a chance to take up the fight again. I'll get you out: everything will be all right, and you'll be able to bring up your little son in safety.'

Stirlitz went over to his car at a leisurely pace, smiling at the sweating children chasing each other about on roller-skates. 'But I musn't deceive myself,' he thought as he got into the driver's seat, 'I've been counting too much on managing to get Käthe out of this mess. If you don't believe you'll win you're bound to lose, but fooling yourself is a still surer way of getting it in the neck.'

He turned on the ignition, the engine started up with its familiar hum and Stirlitz jollied his Horch along with the phrase he always used: 'Off we go, my beauty.' But this time he added: 'Let's drive through these streets just once more to look at the faces of the people going by, to breathe the fresh air that already has a hint of spring about it and then off I go to see Müller . . .'

14

When Müller was informed that Stirlitz was walking down the
corridor of the Reich Security Office he lost his bearings for a
moment. He had been quite sure that Stirlitz would have been
found somewhere else. He could not explain why, but his
confidence that success was within reach had never deserted
him. He did know where he had gone wrong: he remembered
how he had reacted on seeing an unconscious Holthoff carried
into his office. Stirlitz had obviously realised that Müller had
known about Holthoff's visit. That was why, as Müller thought,
Stirlitz had taken to his heels. But the news that he'd now
appeared in the Reich Security Office and was walking leisurely
down the corridor, greeting all he knew as he went, had taken
Müller completely unawares and he no longer felt so sure of
himself.

Stirlitz's tactics were straightforward: taking the enemy
unawares was half way towards winning any battle. He was
convinced that the duel with Müller that lay ahead of him would
be a tough one, for Holthoff had kept circling round the weakest
points in his handling of the physicists's case. Yet Holthoff's
unpreparedness and lack of respect for intellectual niceties in
general had prevented him from arriving at a clearly formulated
accusation, and every point that he actually made—thanks to
intuition rather than a thorough analysis of the facts—could
either be refuted or was at least open to a variety of
interpretations. Stirlitz had taken great pains to make the most
of the Runge case. He had known perfectly well that the
physicist would have been treated like any other prisoner if he
had fallen into the Gestapo's hands: none of those investigators
could have found a common language with a physicist
fanatically obsessed by his idea and therefore hysterical and
irrational when it came to affairs of everyday life. That had led
Stirlitz cautiously to bring one of his conversations with
Schellenberg round to the subject of the nuclear threat from the
United States. Schellenberg, as Stirlitz had expected, started

222

lamenting the fact that Germany was lagging behind in that field and put forward the idea that he would not put it past those scoundrels the other side of the Atlantic to be hatching yet another plot aimed at preventing the Reich from reaching a rapid solution to the problem of the 'retaliation weapon'. Although Schellenberg had not mentioned the prisoner Runge by name, Stirlitz expressed his opinion to the effect that it would only be possible to uncover a conspiracy of that ilk with the co-operation of the physicists themselves and that all the men Müller had working under him were thugs quite unsuitable for the purpose. Schellenberg then inquired to what extent the Standartenführer was acquainted with the latest trends in physics. Stirlitz replied in his usual, slightly sombre manner that made it difficult to tell whether he was joking or being serious.

'What interests me most of all is whether with the help of physical chemistry it is possible to put a stop to the stupefication of the masses ... It's becoming harder and harder to get anything done nowadays, there are so many idiots around spouting what's expected of them.'

'You'll finish up in a concentration camp,' commented Schellenberg with a smile. 'Müller, though, would never lock you up, because you know too much: people like you are given a funeral with full honours after coming to a sticky end in a road accident.'

'Thank you for those few kind words,' replied Stirlitz. 'Only I'd like to lay a wreath on his grave first.'

'Müller is immortal ... he'll go on for ever just as the art of the detective will, for the main thing that keeps people on the go is the desire to search. Those who are capable of following this urge in its highest form seek to break new ground in physics, but nonentities like ourselves sit and hunt for things in counter-intelligence work.'

'Müller won't forgive those words.'

'Why should he,' remarked Schellenberg with a shrug of his shoulders. 'They're his. If that Bavarian had only had some education—ah, there would be no knowing where he might be installed by now: here in our outfit or perhaps somewhere else, nearer the Brandenburg Gate.'

'What makes him hate you so much?'

'There are two reasons,' Schellenberg answered. He didn't even pause to think before coming out with the answer—he had obviously given the matter a good deal of thought in his time. 'In the first place, I'm half his age . . .'

'Not quite,' came a muttered correction from Stirlitz.

'In this case a few years one way or the other don't make any difference. In fact, he'd probably be glad to be able to maintain that he was three times my age. As for the second reason, well, anyone who has had to give up studying to earn his living by the sweat of his brow will have a grudge against the lucky fellow who has walked straight into a ready-made post after graduating from the university and then made a career for himself within a mere three years. In Müller's case it's meant a lifetime of hard work. I suppose, really, there's a third reason as well that's only just occurred to me. You know life has a strange way of ordering things so that some people come up with all the ideas, while others implement them. Müller is clearly highly envious of the fact that I very seldom have to implement ideas, most of the time I'm thinking them up, while he has to do the implementing: executing, rounding-up, the strong stuff. That's bound to be bad for a man's self-respect. I've been along to see him several times, you know, to have things out and make it up, so to speak . . . but no. He's jealous of me like some snivelling Bavarian peasant girl, jealous of my standing with the Reichsführer, with Heydrich that was, with . . .'

'That's plain enough,' commented Stirlitz, 'there's no need to go any further.'

'For you everything's plain,' remarked Schellenberg, echoing Stirlitz's slightly ironic tone, 'But enough of all that, God shall be his judge. After all we're engaged in the same work, and we are obliged to tolerate those things that none of us would ever want to tolerate . . . And, on the other hand, who else would be prepared to run that insanitary brigade—the Gestapo? I ask you, what self-respecting individual would do it?'

That conversation had taken place six weeks earlier: Stirlitz never hurried things—he regarded patience as the surest pledge of speed. Proportion was the decisive factor, whether it was a question of art, espionage, love or politics.

224

Stirlitz brought up the Runge case a second time in the course of a gala evening held in honour of the Führer's birthday. A concert had followed Himmler's speech and then everyone had proceeded into a large hall where drinks and refreshments were awaiting them. The Reichsführer remained true to his usual custom of drinking nothing but mineral water, while his subordinates started knocking back the cognac. That was the setting Stirlitz had chosen to bring to Schellenberg's attention the fact that Müller's men had adopted a quite unreasonable approach in their work with the physicist who had been arrested a whole three months before. 'For what it's worth I did graduate in physics and maths,' Stirlitz added, 'something I don't like to bring up more often than necessary since it almost reduced me to impotency, but it's a fact, nevertheless. Then we mustn't forget he's got contacts abroad, he has studied and worked in America. It would be more to our advantage if we were to take over the case.'

After putting that idea into Schellenberg's head Stirlitz began telling jokes that made his superior laugh heartily. They then went over to a nearby window and started discussing an operation which Schellenberg had entrusted to a group of his staff that included Stirlitz. It involved a major piece of false information designed to drive a wedge between the Allies. Even then Stirlitz had noticed that Schellenberg was already putting out cautious, gentle feelers, making quite sure not to overstep the mark as to the possibilities of causing a split between the Western Allies and Russia. Moreover, in that game he directed his main offensive against the Kremlin as a rule. One of his efforts to this end had been to equip the German units stationed on the Atlantic coast with British sub-machine guns. These had been purchased by the Germans through neutral intermediaries and transported through France without the usual precautionary measures being taken. After communist partisans had captured some of these British arms from German depots, orders were circulated threatening all those guilty of negligence in the guarding of munition depots with the firing squad. Numerous copies of these instructions were printed, and Schellenberg's agents, engaged in rounding up partisans, found an opportunity to 'supply' some of the communists working under Thorez in the Maquis with one. Those secret data could well have led people to draw the conclusion that the Western Allies did not plan to make a landing in France or Holland: otherwise why would they sell their arms to the enemy? Schellenberg was pleased with Stirlitz's handling of the affair; it was none other than he who had been in charge of the organisational side and who had prepared the highly interesting proposals for co-ordinating the operation with the work of the departments headed by Goebbels and Ribbentrop. Schellenberg at the time hardly left his office, waiting any moment for an outburst from the Kremlin or for a collapse of the Stalin–Churchill–Roosevelt coalition. Stirlitz worked from dawn till dark, and the proposals he put forward met with Schellenberg's complete approval. Yet nothing happened. In the Reich Security Office people were racking their brains and asking what could have gone wrong. Stirlitz put forward a number of possible explanations, each of which was bold and interesting. Naturally, these did not include the only true one: Stirlitz had informed Moscow of all that he knew about the operation from the very beginning and he had told Centre that the British had never sold arms to the Nazis, and that the whole affair was a sham from start to finish, a subtle piece of misinformation that could have had far-reaching consequences.

When talking to Schellenberg at the celebrations of the Führer's birthday, Stirlitz had deliberately changed the subject from the Runge case to a discussion of the failure of the recent gamble directed against the Kremlin. He knew that Schellenberg, being an intelligent organiser and born secret agent, while allowing himself occasionally to forget certain details for a while, never lost sight of the main points of any conversation, even if his interlocutor had only been his gardener. His professionalism had left its mark on his perception patterns. Stirlitz was well aware that in Schellenberg he had met his match, and when it came to questions of strategy it was very difficult, or rather impossible, to outwit him. Yet as he made a closer study of the man, he noticed an interesting detail: initially Schellenberg behaved as if he hardly took note of interesting suggestions made by members of his staff and would soon change the subject of conversation. Days, weeks or even months would pass before he would bring up the same ideas once again but already coloured by his particular understanding of the given situation—having most probably in the meantime put out feelers higher up—and not as someone else's but his own ideas that he had hatched, and taken great pains to elaborate. Yet he always managed to add such lustre to any casually mentioned suggestion and tie it in with the overall set of problems facing the Reich that no one ever thought of suspecting him of straightforward plagiarism.

Stirlitz's calculations proved accurate to the letter and two weeks later Schellenberg asked him to stay behind after an urgent meeting in his office. 'Stirlitz,' Schellenberg began, 'it seems more than likely that the question of technical superiority will be the issue which will decide the course of world history, especially once scientists have penetrated the secret of the atomic nucleus. I think that scientists in both East and West have realised this, but that the politicians have failed to keep up with them. You and I shall witness the degradation of the political profession, as people have known it for the past nineteen centuries of our history. Science will dictate the course of politics in future. You will have to take over the physicist now under arrest. I have forgotten his name for the moment . . .'

Stirlitz knew that was a test for him. Schellenberg wanted to see whether the expert Stirlitz had recognised the source of his monologue and who had put him on to the idea originally. Stirlitz said nothing but merely stared with a melancholy air at his fingers. He paused for just the right length of time and then fixed the Brigadenführer with a bewildered gaze. That was how he had landed the Runge case. That was how he had been able to undo the Germans' very real chances of almost getting as far as actually making an atom bomb as far back as 1944—if Runge's line had won through. However, after spending many days alone with Runge, Stirlitz came round to the opinion that Fate herself had stopped Germany from laying her hands on the new weapon, for after the battle of Stalingrad Hilter had refused to finance further scientific research in the military sphere unless scientists promised him tangible practical results within three or, at the most, six months. On the other hand, though, after news of the countless quarrels and feuds between the various groups of nuclear scientists working in the laboratories affiliated to the munitions board, the Kaiser Wilhelm Institute, the Medical Institute and the Postal Ministry reached Himmler's ears, he started to take an interest in the question of atomic weapons and set up a 'Combined Fund for Military Scientific Research'. However, Göring, who was responsible for scientific research throughout the Reich, demanded that Himmler's creation be transferred to his department. So the petty squabbles began, each of the main characters considering his ambitions to have been slighted. This meant that the leadership lost sight, as it were, of the real value of the brilliant German physicists, which was hardly surprising, considering that not one of the country's leaders had had a university education apart from Speer and Schacht. All these details Stirlitz passed on to Moscow, and, what was more, he also did his bit to aggravate the enmity between Runge's supporters and opponents.

Now the time had come for Stirlitz to win the next round of the fight: he would have to prove he had handled the case correctly. He thought out all the details of his defence, knowing that his position was a strong one. He had to get the better of Müller and get the better of him he would . . .

Stirlitz did not go into his own office but walked straight into the waiting-room outside Müller's where he said to his assistant Scholz: 'Convey my apologies to your chief: I promised I'd be back by nine and I'm twelve minutes late. What are his next instructions? Will he see me straight away or can I get half an hour's sleep in first?'

'I'll find out,' replied Scholz and disappeared behind the door for a couple of minutes. 'It's up to you,' he said when he came back. 'The Chief is ready to see you now or put off the conversation till this evening.'

'The latter would only complicate things,' Stirlitz said to himself, realising that Müller wanted to see where he would head in the interim. 'I'd better not put this business off. Everything will be decided in an hour or two at the most, even if they have to call in experts.'

'Just as you say,' Stirlitz said to Scholz. 'I'm afraid that in the evening he'll have some top-level meeting and I shall have to wait till tomorrow morning in that case. Sensible?'

'Quite,' agreed Scholz.

'So it'd better be now then, hadn't it?'

Scholz opened wide the door and said: 'Please come in, Standartenführer.'

It was dingy in Müller's office: The Obergruppenführer was sitting in an armchair near a small table, listening to Lord Haw-Haw's broadcast from Germany to Britain. He had a document-case lying open on his lap and was looking through the papers in it with painstaking thoroughness, every now and then tuning the wireless to get back onto the original wavelength. Müller was looking tired, the collar of his black jacket was unbuttoned, and layers of grey cigarette smoke hung in the air like a cloud in a cave.

'Good morning,' said Müller. 'To be honest, I hadn't expected you so early.'

'And I was afraid that I would be given a flea in the ear for being late.'

'All you lot are worried about getting fleas in your ears from old Müller. Just tell me when I've ever given anybody one. I'm really just a kind-hearted old man about whom people spread evil rumours. Your film-star of a chief is a thousand times tougher than I am. It's just that at those universities of his he learnt to lay on the smiles and talk French, whereas I still don't know whether you should cut apples into pieces or eat them whole as we always used to at home.' He got up, fastened the collar of his jacket and said: 'Off we go.'

Noticing Stirlitz's bewildered gaze, Müller gave a little laugh and said, 'We've prepared a little surprise for you.'

They left the room and on their way out Müller said to Scholz: 'We should be back soon.'

'But I haven't called for a car yet.'

'We're not going outside.'

Müller made heavy weather of the steep steps leading down to the basement where a few special cells had been set aside for particularly important prisoners. Two SS men were standing at the entrance to the basement. They were enormously tall and the Lügers in their belts looked ridiculous. What on earth should giants like that need Lügers for, was the obvious question: one blow from their fists would have been

229

enough to bring a horse to the ground, let alone a man.

Müller took his Walter out of his its holster and handed it to one of the guards. Stirlitz gave Müller an inquiring look, which was answered with a slight nod. He then handed over his parabellum, and the other guard put it on to the table. Müller picked up an apple that had been lying on the guards' table and said: 'It would be awkward to turn up without a present. Even if the two of us are proponents of free love—with no strings attached—nevertheless, one should always visit old friends with some little gesture.'

Stirlitz forced himself to laugh, because he knew why Müller had said that. Once his staff had tried to recruit a South American diplomat. They had shown him a number of photographs depicting him in bed with a fair-haired girl sent along for the purpose by Müller's men. They warned him: 'Either you help us, or we shall send these pictures to your wife.' After studying them for some time, the diplomat asked: 'Couldn't we have another session? You see, my wife and I are mad on pornography.' When told about the incident with the Peruvian, Stirlitz had merely raised his eyebrows and said: 'In my opinion, the Peruvian outplayed you: he must have been dead scared of his wife but didn't lose his presence of mind and played his part irreproachably so that your men believed him. Wouldn't you have been afraid of your wife's reactions in such a situation? Of course you would! But you can't catch me out like that—I have only myself to be afraid of, for I am under no obligations to anyone. The only unfortunate aspect of my situation is that there won't be anyone to bring me food parcels in prison.'

Müller stopped outside Cell No. 7. He looked through the judas for sometime, made a sign to one of the guards who then opened the heavy door. Müller went in first, followed by Stirlitz, while the guard remained outside. The cell was empty.

'Well?' shouted Rolff in the same pitch as before. 'Miracles only happen in the cinema, and it's only there that people count up to three to give you time to think! I am not going to count to three. I shall simply open the window and take the blanket off

230

your baby. Is that clear? You can do your duty by your people and I shall do mine!'

Suddenly Käthe felt a strange feeling of lightness come over her, there was a ringing noise in her ears, and she sank to the floor unconscious.

Rolff leant against the edge of the table and said: 'Helmuth, take the boy.'

The soldier picked up the child and headed for the door, but Rolff stopped him in his tracks: 'Don't go yet. She'll come round in a minute and I shall carry on where I left off.'

At that moment the telephone rang and Rolff picked up the receiver. 'Rolff here. Who's that? Yes, I'm listening.'

The baby was crying lustily at the top of his voice, his cries filling the whole flat. His face turned almost purple with the strain, his eyelids looked swollen and his lips had gone white.

'Get out!' shouted Rolff, waving them out of the room, and Helmuth disappeared. But the cries of the boy could still be heard from the next room. 'Yes,' Rolff said down the telephone. 'No, not yet. Do you think it's such a simple job? Oh, so you do, do you? Let's change jobs then, perhaps. When did he start questioning him? He's not giving? Oh, they talk away all right, like long-lost friends . . . Let them come and talk with this little girl-friend here, while I sit back and watch.'

Käthe came to when Helmuth carried the baby out of the room: even when she had been unconscious she had sensed rather than heard that her son was close by, in the same terrible room. The boy was crying somewhere not very far away, but the room was still warm so that they could not have opened the window yet. What was Rolff talking about on the phone? Who was being questioned and who was refusing to talk? 'He' was refusing to talk. 'They' were talking like long-lost friends. Had they really arrested Stirlitz? If she told them what they were forcing her to come out with, then they would start to break Stirlitz and beat him up, and she would be the person who had betrayed him. That was impossible. Yet it was still more impossible to think of the baby lying naked on the table over there by the window with his little red hands and tiny frog-like legs—and then the cold would pour in and he would be quite

231

helpless—all he would do would be cry, cry, cry till he suffocated.

'It would be better for me to die instead,' thought Käthe, her heart overwhelmed with pity. 'That would be the best solution for everyone. For the baby, for Justas and for me. That would be a perfect way out for me . . . Oh, my heart, why d'you have to be so strong? If only you'd burst, or just stop pumping! It can't go on like this . . .'

Rolff put down the receiver and said: 'I think she's come round.' Barbara knelt down on the floor in front of Käthe and opened her eyes with two fingers. Käthe looked at Barbara and one of her eyelids quivered.

''Yes,' said Barbara, 'she's with us again.'

'Give her some water.'

Käthe tried to pretend that she was still unconscious but her face gave her away: life had reasserted itself, refusing to submit to her will, because the baby boy was there, in the adjacent room, crying.

'That's enough, my girl,' warned Rolff. 'Now you're just trying on stupid womanish tricks. It won't work. You've got yourself caught up in men's work, and fancy business won't cut any ice this time. Barbara, help her to sit up. Come on now, open your eyes!'

Käthe did not move nor did she open her eyes. 'What did I have to come round for?' she thought. 'Why have I to go through these horrors?'

'All right for the moment,' said Rolff. 'Leave her alone, Barbara. I can see that she's listening to me. I am now going to tell Helmuth to open the window and then she'll open her eyes, but it will be too late.'

Käthe could not keep it up any longer, and she started crying.

'Well?' asked Rolff. 'Have you come to your senses at last?' He picked her up himself and put her down on the chair. 'Will you talk after all?'

'I don't know what to answer . . . Surely, you don't want me to lie to you?'

'No, I don't. I want you to tell me the truth.'

'I've told you everything I know.'

232

'I'll help you,' Rolff went on, 'so that you needn't feel you're letting your side down.'

With that he brought out a photograph of Stirlitz and showed it to Käthe, making sure that Barbara did not see it.

'You see? Is it clear now? What's the point of refusing to talk? Are you going to change your mind?'

Käthe said nothing.

'So we're not going to change our mind!' yelled Rolff and brought his fist crashing down on the table by the window. 'Well, we'll see about that! Helmuth!'

Helmuth came in with the baby and Käthe stretched out her arms, but Rolff opened the window, seized the baby from Helmuth and tore the blanket from him. Käthe instinctively lunged out in Rolff's direction but fell over because of the shackles on her ankles. Then she started to drag herself across the floor. She let out a scream of despair to which Rolff shouted something back in reply. Then the noise was cut short by two pistol shots.

'That's logical,' said Müller, after listening to what Stirlitz had to say. 'Your position with regard to Runge is perfectly tenable. You can consider me your supporter on that count.'

'He needed to look at his watch. He's waiting for something,' Stirlitz noted. 'He wouldn't have started on this show-down if he hadn't had some trump card up his sleeve. But who is it? The pastor? Käthe? Pleischner?—'I'd advise you to try Yoga breathing-exercises.'

'I don't believe in it. But show me just the same. I've been shown once, but I still don't hold with it.'

'Put your left hand on the back of your head. No, no, just the fingers. Your right hand must be flat against your forehead. That's right. Now begin massaging your head with both hands at once. But don't forget to keep your eyes closed.'

'If I shut my eyes, you'll bash my head in like Holthoff's.'

'If you're suggesting I betray the Fatherland, I shall do so . . . Obergruppenführer, you glanced at your watch: it's seven minutes slow, and we have been sitting here for over an hour already. I prefer games with all the cards on the table, at least

233

when it comes to games with my own side.'

Müller gave a wry laugh and said: 'I have always regretted that you did not work in my outfit. I would have made you my Number Two long since.'

'I should have turned down the offer.'

'Which one?'

'The post of your deputy.'

'Why?'

'Because of your jealous nature . . . like that of a passionately devoted wife. It's the most terrible form of jealousy . . . how shall I put it? The tyrannical sort.'

'Taken all in all, you've got me right. Perhaps you could have used a different name for the tyrannical jealousy, something like concern for colleagues, but that's only a technical nicety, not a matter of principle.'

Then Müller looked at his watch again, this time without bothering to disguise his action. 'He's a professional of the top class,' noted Müller for the nth time. 'Gestures and moods are enough for him to weigh up a situation. You can't help admiring him. If he has been working against us, I'd hate to start even guessing at the extent of the damage he's caused to the Reich. An artist of that calibre is worth a thousand of our wretched soldiers.'—'All right, I'll put my cards on the table then. Just a moment, my friend . . .'

He rose and with a gentle push opened the heavy cell door. The massive slab of bullet-proof steel responded to the slightest touch in spite of its great weight. He called for one of the guards who was casually cleaning his nails with a matchstick.'

'Ring through to Scholz and ask what news has come in?'

Müller reckoned that Rolff would manage to make the Russian woman talk within a matter of two or three hours. Then she'd be brought round to headquarters and they'd confront her with Stirlitz. Yes or no, and no nonsense about it. That would leave him room to manoeuvre in later on, for it was the counter-intelligence agent's first duty to check and double check facts. He had made careful preparations before questioning Stirlitz: as soon as Rolff had made the Russian woman talk, Müller would bring out his trump cards, watch Stirlitz's reactions and then bring him face to face with the pianist.

'It won't be long,' said Müller turning round to face Stirlitz again. 'I'm waiting for a report to come in.'

Stirlitz shrugged his shoulders and queried: 'Why did that necessitate bringing me down here? Couldn't we have discussed things in your office?'.

'It's quieter down here. If everything turns out as I'm hoping it will, we'll go back to my office together and then let everyone think that you and I were discussing a case with me in my department.'

'Will my chief know about that too?'

'Whose jealousy do you fear most—his or mine?'

'Well, which do you think?'

'I like the straightforward way you go about things.'

'I have no alternative, but then I always prefer clarity.'

'Clarity is merely one type of fog . . . I know you, you cunning fellow.'

The guard came in and said: 'Scholz asked me to tell you that there is no reply.'

Müller bit his lips in surprise but, after thinking for a moment, he concluded that Rolff must have left the flat without telephoning headquarters. 'Perhaps my line was engaged and he decided to leave without reporting first, so as to save time. All the better. That means he'll be bringing her along within ten or fifteen minutes.'

'All right then,' Müller resumed. 'As it says in the Bible: there is a time to gather stones and a time to throw them away.'

'The religious knowledge at your school obviously wasn't up to much,' commented Stirlitz. 'In the book of Ecclesiastes it is written: there is a time to cast away stones, and a time to gather stones together; a time to embrace, and a time to refrain from embracing.'

At that Müller asked: 'Was it with your protégé Pastor Schlag that you made such a careful study of the Bible?'

'I often reread the bible. In order to get the better of the enemy one needs to know his ideology, doesn't one? To learn that only in the heat of the battle is to condemn oneself to certain defeat.'

'Surely they can't have caught the pastor on the border?' Stirlitz asked himself. 'Or perhaps they have. Although, on the other hand, on my way back to the station I didn't come across a single other car. But perhaps they got there ahead of me and were lying in wait for us at the border itself. That would mean that they were now approaching Berlin—that would make sense time-wise. Well then . . . in that case I shall ask to see my boss immediately. I must keep on the offensive all the time. If I switch to defensive tactics I shall be done for. And what if Müller starts asking me where that agent Klaus is? Back home there's that letter I made him write, lying in the drawer. It's too obvious an alibi, but who could have thought that they would have seen the light in connection with the pastor of all people? The Klaus business they still have to prove though. And time will be on my side.'

Müller brought a light-blue envelope out of his breast pocket with a slow, deliberate gesture, looking at Stirlitz in the eye as he did so.

'If it comes to the worst, I have completed my mission after all,' Stirlitz thought to himself. 'That fool thinks that by dragging things out he'll hypnotise me into losing my nerve. God help him, he needs it! His playing about and hypnosis tactics give me an extra twenty seconds to think things over. The pastor may talk but that's not so dreadful. The main thing is that Pleischner by now will have let our people know about Käthe's arrest and the fact that Wolff has started negotiations in Switzerland, or is about to do so. It's up to our side to organise the next move now if I disappear from the scene—at least they know where to concentrate their activity. Müller will never break my code, for no one knows it except me and the chief. They won't get it out of me—of that I'm sure.'

'Well,' proceeded Müller, after taking three fingerprint cards out of the blue envelope. 'Look what a fascinating little puzzle I have here. These prints we found on the glass you filled with water and handed to the unfortunate, stupid and so trusting Holthoff.' He pushed the first card over to Stirlitz. 'Now where d'you think we found these?' he asked, throwing the second card down on the table as if to out-trump the one that already lay there. 'Well?'

'You could find my finger popping up in Holland,' Stirlitz replied, 'or, for that case, in Madrid, Tokyo, Ankara . . .'

'And where else?'

'I could give you a list, but that would take me at least half a day, and we'd have to go without lunch and supper . . .'

'Never mind. I'm prepared to go without food for a bit. Well, have you remembered?'

'This conversation isn't getting us anywhere. If I am under arrest, then you will be kind enough to inform me officially of that fact and I shall start answering your questions in the appropriate manner, but if I am not, then I don't intend to do so.'

'I don't intend to,' repeated Müller, lending the words exactly the same intonation as Stirlitz had used. 'I don't intend to.'

Again Müller looked at his watch: if Rolff had appeared by then he would have gone on to the wireless-transmitter but as he had still not turned up, Müller followed the other course open to him. 'Please try and reproduce blow by blow, preferably minute by minute, what you did after making a telephone call from the special hot-line room to which everyone is categorically denied access,' he demanded.

'After I went in there—the communications staff should be called to court for their negligence and cowardice, for running off to the shelters like so many scared rabbits in that way and leaving the key in the door—I went to meet Parteigenosse Bormann and spent over two hours with him. What the two of us talked about I, of course, am not prepared to tell you.'

'You could have avoided doing so if it wasn't for . . .'

'There are no "ifs" on that count.'

'Don't forget yourself, Stirlitz. Slowly does it. I *am* your senior, when all's said and done, both where rank and age are concerned.'

'He gave me that kind of answer to make it clear to me that I have not been arrested,' noted Stirlitz. 'In that case, they can't have the concrete evidence they need, but they're waiting for it, and from me too. So that means I still have a chance.'

'I must apologise, Obergruppenführer.'

'That's more like it. Well, what did you talk to Bormann about? To Parteigenosse Bormann . . .'

'I can only answer that question in his presence—please, don't misunderstand me.'

'If you could bring yourself to answer that question without him that might save you the trouble of having to answer my third question.'

As he said that, Müller looked at his watch once more and calculated that Rolff should be on his way to the basement by then: he had always prided himself on his keen sense of time.

'I am ready to answer your third question if it concerns me personally, but not if it touches on the interests of the Reich and the Führer.'

'It concerns you personally. These last fingerprints members of my staff found on the suitcase belonging to the Russian radio-operator. This question you're going to find hardest of all to answer.'

'What makes you think so? In fact, the opposite is the case. I had a look at the operator's suitcase in Rolff's office. If you send for him, he can confirm it.'

'He already has.'

'What's the trouble then?'

'The point is that these fingerprints were taken in the district Gestapo office before the suitcase was brought along to headquarters.'

'Is the possibility of a mistake ruled out?'

'Absolutely.'

'And what about a coincidence?'

'It is possible. But it would have to be a very convincing one. Why should your fingerprints have turned up on the one particular suitcase, in which the Russian radio-operator had hidden all her equipment, from among the twenty odd million that there happen to be in Berlin?'

'Hmm . . . hmm. Yes, that really will be difficult if not impossible, to explain. If I were in your position, I would not have believed a word of any explanation I happened to come out with . . . I understand what you must be feeling, Obergruppenführer . . . Oh yes, I understand you . . .'

'I would very much like to hear a satisfactory explanation from you, Stirlitz, I really mean that, for I can't help liking you.'

'I believe that.'

238

'Rolff is about to bring the Russian pianist down here and she will—I am sure of that—help you to remember when and where you could have left your "signature" on the suitcase in which the transmitter was kept.'

'You mean the Russian woman?' asked Stirlitz with an incredulous shrug of his shoulders. 'The one I went to fetch from the hospital? I have an absolutely photographic memory and I know I would have remembered her face if I had met her somewhere before. No, she won't be of any help to us.'

'Oh yes, she will,' contradicted Müller. 'And so will this,' he added, starting to fish in his breast pocket again. This time he showed Stirlitz the coded message that he had sent with Pleischner to Berne.

'Now that really does mean the end,' realised Stirlitz. 'That's the last straw. It means none of our people are going to be in the picture, and I've turned out to be a little better than a foolish amateur. Pleischner is either a coward, a scatter-brain or an *agent provocateur*.'

Prinz-Albrecht-Strasse, Berlin.
To Prague.

Dear Krüger,
On instructions from SS Obergruppenführer Kaltenbrunner my men have been making enquiries concerning Colonel Berg. It appears likely that you were misinformed with regard to him being known to the Chief of the Reich Security Office. At General Neubuth's request, we too had already started investigating Berg's background but had found no direct evidence giving us any grounds for accusing him of contacts with Kanaris. Yet at the same time there were no grounds to justify his selection for such responsible work as that which you entrusted to him. In so far as he has already embarked on the work, in my eyes it would be ill-advised to exclude him from the operation at this stage. On the contrary, while entrusting him with tasks of the more complex variety, although of purely local significance, and on no account key missions, I would ask you to keep an extremely tight check on Berg. As you know, Kanaris is at the moment in the concentration camp at Flossenburg, and the tiniest crumbs of information regarding his treacherous activity are most important to us. Therefore, if Berg could come forward either as a prosecution witness or even as a defence witness, I am

sure that the leadership would be most grateful to you for such an achievement. To be quite frank, after the Cracow fiasco when the town fell into the hands of the Russians completely intact, I am in no doubt that if you got that far with Berg, it would be marked up to your credit and restore your reputation completely. I realise that your present post as deputy chief of the Prague Gestapo is not in any way compatible with your experience and your capabilities.

As for Herr Grishanchikov in counter-intelligence, whom SS Standarten-führer Stirlitz singled out for such high praise as a massage expert, my men will also investigate his record. I would ask you not to misunderstand my motives: this does not in the least imply any lack of confidence in you.

The situation here in Berlin obliges me to take this decision. I hope that you will afford every assistance to Eismann whom I am sending to you with this letter. You know him already. He is a most loyal subject of the Führer's and a real asset to counter-intelligence, an intelligent and charming man. I am sure that the two of you will enjoy working together.

With best wishes,

Yours, Müller

Pleischner pushed against the door again, but it was well locked, and it was no use even trying to climb through the small window above the door, the same window through which he had glimpsed the patch of open sky.

'Anyway, this isn't like the cinema,' Pleischner thought, as a sudden wave of indifference and exhaustion came over him. 'An old man in spectacles like myself would only get stuck if he tried to climb through. Then they would just pull me down by my legs.'

He walked up one flight of stairs only to discover that the window he might have jumped through was a good ten feet above the ground and it looked out on a quiet deserted street along which the same two behatted men were walking. They were no longer window-shopping, or pretending they had nothing to do with each other. He went up another flight, but this time the window looking out on to the courtyard was boarded up with plywood: either the glass had been broken or repairs were soon due—indeed, the staircase as a whole looked rather the worse for wear and the paint was peeling.

240

'The most awful part of it all is when they strip you, inspect your mouth—then you really feel no better than some insect. I know I won't hold out under torture, that's clear from the start. The first time I had nothing to hide and even then I didn't hold out and said what they wanted me to say and wrote down everything they told me to do. I was younger then too. But this time, when they start to torture me, I know I won't hold out and will betray my brother's memory. To betray his memory is tantamount to death. So it would be better to disappear before I have time to betray anyone.'

He paused in front of a door. The brass plate read 'Franz Ulm, Doctor of Law'. 'Now I'll ring at this Ulm's bell,' thought Pleischner with a sudden brainwave. 'I'll tell him that I'm having a heart attack and get him to call the doctor. Let them shoot at me in front of other people. Then at least I'll have a chance to shout out something.'

Pleischner pressed the bell. He heard the echo of its long ring. 'But what shall I say if the doctor asks me where I live?' he wondered. 'Oh, well. Nothing terrible about falling into the clutches of their police. Hitler's days are already numbered and soon I will be able to tell them who I really am and where I'm really from.'

He pressed the bell again but there was no answer. 'This Ulm character must be sitting in a café now, eating ice-cream. Delicious ice-cream with strawberries and wafers,' Pleischner thought, drifting away into some distant world of day-dreams. 'He's probably reading the paper quite happily and I'm the last person he's worrying about.'

Then Pleischner turned to the next door and pressed a second bell which made quite a different sound. A peal of little bells rang out and a child's voice asked: 'Who's there?'

Pleischner for some reason knelt down and whispered through the key-hole: 'Open the door, my child.'

'Who's there?' the child's voice inquired again.

'Please open the door,' repeated Pleischner just a little louder, but even so in a voice that seemed thunderous to his frightened ears and audible up and down the stairway.

'But who are you? Mummy told me that Father Christmas wouldn't come again for a whole year.'

241

'I'm not Father Christmas, I'm his brother, and I've brought you some little presents from him.'

'What have you brought?'

'Open the door,' begged Pleischner, getting up from his knees and putting his face right up against the door. 'I've brought you a clockwork motorbike.'

'It's my brother who plays with clockwork motorbikes . . . I play with dolls, I'm a *girl*.'

'I've got a doll too, a big one that talks and has eyes that open and shut.'

'Has she got fair hair?'

'Yes.'

'I've got one like that. I want one with dark hair.'

'I've got one with dark hair too,' Pleischner assured her and implored once more: 'Please open the door, quickly!'

He heard the door at street level open, which meant that the two men must have come in from the street. He heard their steps coming up the stairs and then the little girl's voice announced: 'Mummy locked the door so I can't open it, but she's just coming.'

She went on to say something else, but Pleischner didn't catch anything else because he had already started to run up the stairs. He leapt up half a flight at a time, hoping to have time to ring at the door opposite the flat where the men were waiting for him. But at that moment the fatal door opened and the tall blond man came out onto the landing and said: 'You've got the wrong number, I'm afraid, my friend. The only people living on this staircase are ourselves and the people in the flat you've just been trying to enter. All the others are away. So you've got nothing to worry about.'

'To think that my manuscript's just lying there on the table back at the hotel. I had broken off in the middle of a page, and it was going so well. If I'd never come here but stayed in Berlin, then, when it was all over, I would have collected up all my material and had a book ready for the publishers. And now, who's going to rescue my papers? No one will even be able to make out my handwriting.'

He opened the window next to the top flight of stairs and jumped out, feet first. He had meant to shout out to attract

242

people's attention but he did not manage to, because his heart gave out as soon as he sensed the void beneath him.

15

Müller was sitting on the chair next to the door so as to be able to keep an eye on the detectives at their work and the photographer as he clicked away, and still see Rolff and Barbara sprawled grotesquely over the floor.

'There's nothing here,' said one of the detectives, 'not the slightest trace.'

Müller had rushed to the scene of Rolff's murder taking with him his top detectives, the veterans, who had helped him track down gangsters, Hitler's National Socialists and Thälmann's Communists back in the twenties. He took them with him only on extremely rare occasions. He had not had them transferred to the Gestapo, lest they should become too full of themselves: in his present outfit every criminal investigator relied on the help of expert criminologists, secret agents and tape-recorders. Müller, on the other hand, was an admirer of the Czech writer Karel Čapek, whose detectives always made do with their heads and their experience.

'A priest could never introduce reforms into his own religion,' Müller had once remarked. 'Reformers always come from outside. That's why I keep my veterans in hand, to make sure I am not unseated by future reformers. Those men and their experience enable me to do some reorganising from time to time on my own.'—'Absolutely nothing?' Müller echoed. 'Nothing? Not the slightest clue?'

'Not a thing,' replied a grey-haired old man with a sallow face. Müller had forgotten what his name was, but that did not alter the fact that he had been on *Du* terms with him since 1926. 'It reminds me of the murder you unravelled in Munich.'

'But where do we go from here?'

'Get your chaps to examine the bullets that finished off this pretty pair.'

'Don't worry, they'll examine them all right,' Müller assured him. 'They'll make a point of doing that, that much you can count on.'

A second elderly man walked in and drew up a chair to sit down next to Müller.

'Old devil,' thought Müller to himself, 'I do believe he dyes his hair. Yes, it's quite definitely dyed.'—'Well?' he asked. 'What have you come up with, Günther?'

'A little something at least. An old granny in the opposite house saw a woman and a soldier come out of this house about an hour ago. The woman was carrying a child and they were obviously in a great hurry.'

'What was the soldier wearing?'

'What a stupid question! Uniform of course.'

'I appreciate that he wasn't in his underwear. What kind of uniform though, black?'

'Ur . . . Of course it would have been black, you never put the regulars on guard duty.'

'What kind of car did they get into?'

'They took a bus.'

Müller half rose from his chair in astonishment: 'What do you mean, a bus!'

'What I say. Number 17.'

'In what direction did they head?'

'Over there,' Günther pointed, 'towards the West.'

Müller leapt up from his chair, grabbed at the telephone, hastily dialled a number and shouted down the line: 'Scholz! Quick! Have people posted down the 17 bus route. The pianist and the guard are on it. What? How on earth do you think I know what his name is! Find out and quickly! Second, get hold of his file immediately—find out who he is, where he's from, where his relatives live. I want the whole service record round here immediately. If you find out that he has ever been in any of those places Stirlitz frequented let me know at once. What? No, it doesn't matter where—at the front line, in a brothel or on the beach!'

Soon after the Gestapo experts and the photographer left Müller went back to his chair near the door. He stayed behind with the two old-timers and they talked about the past, interrupting each other as they shared reminiscences. Müller listened to them chattering on and at moments felt nostalgic: the men were recalling the years of their youth when everything had been straightforward and simple and when no one had had to hunt down their friends, when no one had needed sleeping-pills to get to sleep or pick-me-ups before having it off.

'Hello,' said Müller picking up the receiver again after dialling a second number. 'Send a group of men to lay an ambush around Stirlitz's house! How long for? Let them sit there for as long as necessary . . . they can say Stirlitz will be back in half an hour, if asked.'

'I've lost,' Müller admitted to himself in a calmer mood. 'But I've still got the Berne business in reserve. Of course, things are more complicated down there, what with the foreign police and foreign border patrols to contend with. As for these two, they were seen running for a bus, which means that the move can't have been planned. If it had, some sort of car would have been waiting for them without fail. It's ridiculous even to think in terms of a planned operation here. The Russians always take good care of their people, but it's highly unlikely that even they would send several men to their death in order to attempt to rescue the pianist with no guarantee of any success. Although, on the other hand, they realised that the child was her vulnerable spot. Perhaps that was what made them take such a tremendous risk? What am I babbling on about, though? There was no planned risk here—they just took a bus, no one would ever *plan* that kind of risk . . . It was just an idiotic blunder, there are no two ways about it . . .'

Müller picked up the receiver and dialled a third number to give further instructions. 'Müller here. Warn the police stationed at all U-bahn and S-bahn stations to keep a lookout for a woman carrying a baby. Give them a description of her and tell the police that she's a thief and murderess and must be arrested on sight. If they make mistakes and arrest innocent people, I'll forgive them . . . The one thing they musn't do is to let the one I'm waiting for get away.'

Stirlitz took another look at his watch and saw that Müller had been gone for over two hours. He concluded that either Käthe was refusing to talk or that they had confronted her with Pleischner. That thought did not alarm him for they knew nothing about each other. On the other hand, he could not understand what had happened to Pleischner. 'Something's up and I've got to make use of this breathing space to get my bearings,' he thought.

Stirlitz paced up and down his cell, taking slow, deliberate steps, as he considered all the possibilities. He tried to recall everything he could remember in connection with the ill-fated suitcase. Yes, sure enough, he had picked it up out in the woods when Erwin had slipped and almost fallen over. That had been the night before the air raid. That had been the only occasion.

'Wait a moment, though!' Stirlitz stopped all of a sudden. 'That's it . . . I picked up the suitcase the night before the air raid, and it was after the bombing that I drove over to see Erwin in the car. There was a whole cluster of cars there, a hold-up, because the firemen were at work. But why was I there? I was there because my usual route to the Kudamm was blocked with rubble. I'll ask them to summon the policemen who cordoned off the road that morning. So I can say I was diverted there by the police. There was a photograph of suitcases still intact after the raid in the file. I talked to the policeman on duty there, I can remember his face and he ought to remember my SS pass. I helped move that suitcase among others. He won't deny that, I'll demand a confrontation with him. I can say that I helped a crying woman lift a pram out of the rubble: she'll confirm that as well, because it really happened, for in a situation like that you don't forget such details.'

Stirlitz started drumming on the door of the cell with his fists and someone came and opened it: it had not been locked, but the two guards were standing outside. A third guard was leading a man, carrying a latrine pail, past the cell and then on down the corridor. The man's face was disfigured, but Stirlitz only needed a second to recognise that the travesty of a face belonged to Bormann's personal chauffeur. He was not a Gestapo agent, he was the man who had been driving the car in which Stirlitz had had that all-important conversation with the man in charge of the party chancellery.

Stirlitz felt his whole body go stiff, and he realised that every second counted now. 'Listen, fellow, ring Obergruppenführer

247

Müller at once. Tell him, I've remembered! I've remembered everything! Ask him to come down and see me immediately!'

Stirlitz's mind was now working on over-drive. 'Pleischner hasn't been brought in yet, A. Their plans for Käthe have not worked out, B. One thing and one thing only can decide whether I manage to wriggle out of this mess and that's time. Time and Bormann. If I don't hurry, Müller will win.'

'All right,' said the guard. 'Ill tell him straight away, Standartenführer.'

A tall soldier was standing by a hatch glistening with a fresh coat of enamel in the hallway of the infants' home. He was chewing at a cigarette he had forgotten to light and was evidently in a hurry, because he kept on looking at his watch. When someone came to the hatch, he peered inside timidly and said: 'Excuse me, I wanted to ask if I could . . .'

'We can't carry out any requests at the moment,' replied the woman with hair drawn back under a white cap. 'The children are being fed, and everyone's busy.'

'Yes, but I've been given half a day's leave from the front, and I've got to leave soon.'

'I'm very sorry, Sir, but at the moment all the children . . .'

'Perhaps I could talk to someone in charge . . .'

'None of those people are around either: they're away at the front or else dealing with the children. I'm sorry, I can't help you.' And with that the woman slammed the hatch shut in front of the soldier's nose.

'But when do they finish feeding the children?'

Without bothering to open the window, the woman answered: 'In half an hour. You're welcome to come back in half an hour and then we can help you.'

The soldier walked out of the building, crossed the street and then made his way down into the cellar of a ruined house. There, amongst the broken boxes, Käthe was sitting feeding her baby.

'Well?' she asked.

'Nothing for the moment,' replied Helmuth. 'We've got to wait half an hour.'

'Well, we'll just have to wait then,' said Käthe in a soothing voice. 'We'll wait. Nothing can happen to us now. How can they know where we are?'

'I suppose you're right, really, but the sooner we get out of town the better. Otherwise they're bound to find us. I know what past masters they are when it comes to looking for people. Perhaps you'd rather go on without me? And then—if things work out—I'll catch you up? Well, what about it?'

'No,' said Käthe, shaking her head, 'there's no need for that. I'll wait. After all, I have nowhere to go in this town.'

Scholz rang through to Müller at the flat. 'Stirlitz has asked us to tell you that he has remembered everything,' he said.

'Has he?' exclaimed Müller, jerked back to the present again by the unexpected news. He made a sign to the two detectives with him to be quiet and then asked: 'When?'

'This minute.'

'Fine. Tell him I'm on my way. No other news?'

'Nothing important.'

'Has anything on that soldier been found?'

'Nothing useful.'

'What precisely do you mean by that?' asked Müller, as he pulled his coat off the empty chair next to him.

'Just some details about his wife, children and relatives.'

'Nothing useful, my foot!' Müller shouted back down the phone. 'It may be just what we need on a job like this, my friend! I'm coming over right away and we'll have a look at your "useless" findings. Has anyone been sent round to his wife?'

'She left him two months ago.'

'What? I can't hear you!'

'He was in hospital recovering from shell-shock when she walked out on him. She went off with some dealer from Munich.'

'What about children?'

'Just a minute,' replied Scholz, leafing through the file, 'I'll have a look . . . Oh, yes . . . here it is.'

'Less blabber, Scholz, and a bit more action.'

'He has one child born four months ago. She was handed into an infants' home.'

249

'The Russian woman's got a small baby as well!' remembered Müller. 'So that's it. He needs a wet-nurse! And Rolff must have overdone things with the kid!' — 'What's the name of the home?' he asked.

'There's no name down here. It's in Pankow and the address is 7 Schillerstrasse. That's all on the kid . . . then there's his mother . . .'

Müller did not wait to hear the details on the mother. He hurled down the receiver and all traces of his lethargy vanished. He threw on his coat and warned the two men: 'There may be a bit of shooting now, chaps, so have your "bulldogs" ready. Do either of you know the infants' home in Pankow?'

'Schillerstrasse No. 8, isn't it?' asked the one with grey hair.

'You're muddling up your numbers again,' replied Müller as they moved out of the flat. 'You always mix up odd and even numbers. It's Number 7.'

'It's a very ordinary street,' the grey-haired man went on. 'Nothing special about it. It'll make a good setting, it's very quiet and no one will get in our way. But you're right, I always get my numbers muddled up. Have done ever since I was a kid. I was off school, sick, when we did our odd and even numbers.' He laughed at the thought and the other two followed suit: they were hunters closing in on a deer.

No, Helmuth Kalder had not been in league with Stirlitz. Their paths had never crossed. Kalder had been fighting since 1940. He had believed that he was fighting to defend the Fatherland, the lives of his mother, his three brothers and his sister. He had believed that he was upholding the future of Germany against the inferior Slavs, who had seized vast lands that they did not know how to cultivate, against the British and the French who had sold out to American plutocracy, against the Jews who were oppressing the common people and capitalising on its misfortunes. He held that the genius of the Führer, who had taken upon himself the heavy burden of securing happiness for the German people, would shine forth brightly over the centuries to come.

Such were his beliefs until the autumn of 1941 when German soldiers had marched through the world with songs on their lips, heady with victory, and Helmuth and his comrades in the SS panzer units had still been light-hearted and at times reckless revellers. But after the battle for Moscow, when they started fighting the Russian partisans and received orders to kill hostages, he began to have his doubts. Helmuth was a peasant, and there was no other being he honoured as much as his mother. She had brought him up along with his brothers and his sister. She had worked from morning till night after their father died, and she had not allowed Helmuth to leave school until illness made her unfit for work.

When Helmuth's platoon was ordered for the first time to shoot forty hostages near Smolensk, after partisans had derailed a train, he started to drink: before them stood women and children and old men. The women were clasping their children to them, making sure their eyes were closed and begging the soldiers to kill them quickly.

Later on Helmuth noticed that in Russia the mothers, just like German ones, would give their last scrap of potato to their children and be near to tears as they watched their children's delight over any war-time treat.

After that first massacre near Smolensk Helmuth was a broken man. He was not the only one to take to drink in the platoon: many of his fellow soldiers would gulp back vodka in morose silence, and no one told funny stories or played the accordion any more. But then they were sent into battle again, and the ferocity of the fighting against the Russians left them no time for thinking back to that nightmare.

When Helmuth came home on leave his mother invited in her neighbour with her daughter. The daughter's name was Luise; she was a model of tidiness and very pretty. Helmuth used to dream about her every night. He took her out to the cinema, and they went for endless moonlight walks. He was ten years older than she was and felt tenderly protective towards her. He dreamt of the wife and mother she would make. Helmuth had always longed for a house with lots of pairs of tiny shoes in the hall, for he loved children. Surely he did—after all it was for their happiness and their future that he was fighting!

During his next leave Luise became Helmuth's wife. After he had gone back to the front Luise pined for him for two months. After realising she was pregnant she started to feel frightened and disgruntled about her new way of life. She left home for the city lights, and her very first night in the city, after finding it impossible to get a hotel room and learning that the house where Helmuth's friends lived had been bombed, she spent with an officer from the Luftwaffe.

After the child was born Luise handed it into the infants' home. Helmuth at the time was in hospital, recovering from severe shell-shock. When he was discharged he was told that Luise had gone off with somebody else. That news made him recall a Russian woman: once a friend of his had persuaded a thirty-year-old schoolteacher to sleep with him for the price of five tins of meat, at a time when she had nothing to give her little girl. The next morning the Russian woman had hanged herself, after leaving the girl at a neighbour's house with a photograph of the baby's father and the five tins wrapped up in a spare nappy. Luise though, a member of the Hitlerjugend and a true Aryan into the bargain, not just some primitive Slav, had abandoned their daughter in a home like any common tart.

Helmuth used to go home once a week and sometimes he was allowed to take the baby girl out for some fresh air. He used to play with her, sing her songs, and his love for her, mingled as it was with pity, soon became something quite hysterical. As he watched Käthe rocking her baby to sleep, he had come to ask himself for the first time: 'What havoc we've been making! What devils we've been. They're people just like us and they love their children just the same and ¬re just as ready to die for them.'

When he had seen what Rolff was doing with Käthe's baby, it had been emotion not reason that had prompted him to act. In Rolff and Barbara, who had just stood by to watch a two-week-old baby being murdered, he had seen Luise, who for him had come to symbolise treachery.

Helmuth went back to the infants' home half an hour later when he had been told he could come to take the little girl outside for a little while. As he stood near the hatch glistening with fresh

252

white enamel, the terrible, unfamiliar tension that had taken hold of him when he had seen Rolff pick up the pink body of the Russian baby, started to die down. He could feel something in him giving way, cold shivers gripped him, and the whole of his left, shell-shocked side was turning numb with cold.

'Good afternoon,' he said to the woman who looked out through the hatch. 'I've come for Ursula Kalder . . . my daughter . . . They said I could . . .'

'Yes. I know. But she's got to have her sleep now.'

'I'm about to leave Berlin, to go back to the front. I'll take her outside for a bit and she can sleep in my arms. When she needs to have her nappy changed I'll bring her back to you . . .'

'I'm afraid the doctor won't allow it, Sir.'

'I'm leaving for the front,' Helmuth repeated in an urgent voice, 'you can't refuse me this last chance to see the child.'

'All right, I understand . . . I'll try. Wait a moment, please.'

The moment turned into ten minutes, and all that time Helmuth's shivers became worse and worse and he could hardly stop his teeth chattering.

At last the hatch opened and a white bundle of baby was passed out to him. Amidst the folds of blanket the little girl's face peeped out, ringed about with dazzling white linen.

'Do you want to take her outside?'

'What?' asked Helmuth, not taking in what she had said. Words were already drifting faintly towards him as if they came from some distant world or through a closed door. Since the shell-shock that usually happened to him when he got agitated. A number of times he had lost consciousness out in the street: it used to happen whenever he saw hospitals or children's homes in ruins after air-raids.

'If you want to take the baby outside, then we can give you a pram.'

'Why?'

'So that you needn't hold her all the time.'

'No, thank you, I enjoy being able to hold her.'

'It would be best for you to walk through into our garden; it's quiet out there, and if a raid begins the shelter will be near at hand.'

'Fine. I'll just have a look to see if the bus has come for me and then I'll pop into the house . . .'

'What house?'

'The garden . . . I'm sorry, I meant the garden . . .'

'Are you sure you're feeling all right?'

'Yes. Why?'

'You're very pale . . .'

'I'm feeling fine,' said Helmuth and with that walked out of the building. As he stepped off the pavement he heard brakes screech just behind him. An army driver had managed to stop only a couple of steps away from Helmuth: he poked his head out of the window and shouted: 'You, blind idiot! Use your eyes!'

Helmuth pressed his precious bundle tight to him and, muttering something, trotted over to the entrance that led down to the cellar. Käthe was waiting for him, standing by the door, and the baby was lying on an upturned box wriggling a little in his sleep.

'Here,' said Helmuth, handing his daughter to Käthe, 'Take her and I'll run over to the bus stop. From there I can see when the bus comes round the corner, and I'll have time to run back for all of you.'

He noticed how carefully Käthe had taken hold of his daughter and again tears came to his eyes as he ran back to the street.

'We'd better go together,' said Käthe, 'really!'

'Don't worry, I'll be back any minute now,' Helmuth replied, turning round once more before he disappeared from sight. 'You never know, they may have photographs of you, but I looked quite different before the shell-shock. You wait for me now.'

He walked as fast as he could to the bus stop. This time the street was quite empty. 'If they evacuate the home, I'll lose all track of the little girl. How on earth would I find her after that? And if the bombs are going to get us anyway, I'd rather we were together. And the Russian woman'll be able to feed her—after all people do manage to feed twins. And God'll forgive me for everything after what I did for her . . . or at least for that day outside Smolensk.'

254

As he waited for the bus, it started to shower. The rain was cold and clammy, but, thought Helmuth, rain in early spring is always a sign of warm weather round the corner. 'If only the maids from the home don't see us getting into the bus. We must go as far as Zoo Station and there we can get a train. Or we can join up with the refugees. It's easy enough to get lost in a crowd nowadays. She'll feed the girl till we get to Munich and once we're there Mutti will help. We'll be able to find a wet-nurse. Although they'll be on the lookout for me . . . No, we can't go to Mutti's place. Never mind, the main thing is to get out of this town. As soon as we get into the country and can use the cover of the woods things will be quite different. Or perhaps we should go North to the sea? We could go to Hans's home: after all who would ever imagine I'd go off to the home of a front-line comrade?'

Helmuth pulled his cap further down over his ears. He'd almost stopped shivering now, and his left side was gradually getting warmer. 'It's good that the rain came,' he pondered, 'at least something's happening. When you're just waiting and everything around you is dead quiet, it's eerie and your nerves get on edge. But if snow or rain start coming down then you don't feel so stranded somehow.'

The rain went on pouring steadily down, but all of a sudden a gap appeared in the clouds and high up in the sky a distant patch of blue and a glimpse of pale sun came into view. 'Spring is on its way after all,' thought Helmuth. 'The grass will be coming up any day now.'

And then he saw the blunt snout of the bus come round the corner. He was about to turn back to run over to the ruined house where Käthe was waiting, but then, out from behind the bus, loomed two evil monsters of black cars that careered up to the home, paying no regard whatever to any rules of the road. Again Helmuth felt himself go weak at the knees and his left hand grew numb, for they were Gestapo cars. His first impulse was to run back to Käthe, but he remembered in time that he would only attract attention to himself by running and then they would catch Käthe with his daughter and take them back to headquarters. He must stay put, and after they had left make a getaway by cutting through the back alleys. 'They'll tell the men

255

that I've only just taken the little girl out and then they'll start searching round here and be sure to find the Russian girl in the cellar.'

He had no clear idea of what would happen to his little daughter after that. He worried lest he should have another attack and the Gestapo men pick him up while he was unconscious. 'Then they'll find the little girl, they'll undress her and take her to an open window, and spring is only just beginning and there's no saying when it will start to get really warm. But if I shoot, the Russian girl will hear the noise and understand what's happened. I know she'll be grateful and she'll never abandon . . .'

Helmuth walked out into the road, drew his parabellum and fired several shots at the windscreen of the front car. The last thought that came to him after he had heard the rattle of sub-machine gun fire and before he sensed the last pain that ever came his way was: 'But I never told her what name I'd given . . .'

That thought plagued Helmuth for a fleeting moment before he lost consciousness for the last time.

'No, Sir,' replied the nurse who had handed Helmuth his baby daughter, 'it can't have been more than ten minutes ago.'

'But where's the baby then?' asked the grey-haired detective, trying not to look at the corpse of his friend with the dyed hair. He was lying on the floor near the door and there was no mistaking his age now: he had obviously not dyed his hair for some time, because it was dappled at the roots and chestnut on top.

'I think they left in a car,' said a second woman, 'because a car drew up right next to him.'

'What, the little girl got into the car by herself?'

'No,' continued the woman in all seriousness, 'she couldn't have got into the car all by herself. She's still a babe in arms.'

Müller told the other man to have a careful look round the immediate neighbourhood, for he had to get back to his office: 'A car will be coming for me any minute, it's already left. But

256

how could the little girl be in the car?' he asked, turning round again when he had already reached the door. 'What kind of car was it anyway?'

'A large one.'

'A lorry?'

'No, just an ordinary car, a green one.'

'You didn't, I presume, notice the registration number?'

'I didn't pay attention to it, I'm afraid.'

'Something doesn't match up here,' said Müller and opened the door. 'Have a look round the nearby houses. I smell a rat.'

'There is nothing but ruins.'

'Have a look in those as well,' Müller added. 'In general, the whole thing's so stupid and unprofessional that it's almost impossible to get on with the job. We're incapable of understanding the logic of an amateur.'

'And what if he is a cunning professional after all?'

'No professional would ever have come straight round to the infants' home,' replied Müller and with that he left the building. He had just learnt from Scholz over the phone that the flat in Berne had been raided and seized by the Swiss police after the Russian contact, who had delivered the coded message had committed suicide.

After posting a card with a view of Lausanne to Stirlitz in Berlin, as agreed, Pastor Schlag returned home: he was now living in quarters attached to the Saint Laurent Church. It was one of the places Stirlitz had listed when telling him where he might find shelter out of reach of the Gestapo. The room he was using was small, with a high vaulted ceiling. The ceiling was dazzling white and the only thing about the room that reminded the visitor that he was in a monastery. The furniture, on the other hand, was soft and upholstered with unexpectedly bright crimson plush.

Schlag had been told that this particular room was set aside for foreigners who for any reason were unable to find hotel accommodation or reluctant to avail themselves of it. It was pointed out to the pastor that these foreigners were people who

257

visited Berne with peace missions aiming to save Europeans from exterminating each other.

Schlag sat down by the window and spent a long time looking down at the town beneath him: here there was no black-out, the shop windows and cinemas were sparkling with different coloured lights. Schlag felt he would never tire of watching the people go by: for many years now he had not seen so many young faces all at once. In fact back in Germany he had begun to think that the world was growing older.

There was a knock at the door.

'Please come in.'

'Would you like some coffee?' asked an old servant.

'No, thank you.'

'If you decide you would like some later on, or some tea, or water, just ring for me.'

'Thank you.'

'Then I'll be going. Good night, Pastor.'

'Good night. Yes, I wanted to ask you, have you by any chance some luminal or bromide? I just can't get off to sleep.'

'I'll ask and I'll be back right away.'

After his conversation earlier that day with ex-Chancellor Brüning, whom the pastor had known well back in the twenties, he was sure he would not be able to fall asleep without some kind of sedative. He found it impossible to sit down at the table and record his impressions of the encounter when he first returned to his room. His impressions had been so unexpected and depressing that the pastor had to pull himself together first and then make a real effort to weigh up carefully everything Brüning had told him and only then commit it all to paper.

'At the beginning of our conversation,' he began slowly, pausing after each word, 'ex-Chancellor Brüning asked me questions about how various of our mutual acquaintances were faring, expressed admiration for the courage of the man who helped me get away, without making any conditions, despite the risk he was running; he asked me about the prisoners whom I had come across while under arrest and in the concentration camp. When I changed the subject to the problems of interest to us, Brüning said: "Absentees are always in the wrong. I have ceased to interest the people at the White House, because those politicians are of the realist mould and wield great power, while I am a has-been, a politician with no real influence. We talk a different language and there is no doubt that I appear a mere dilettante to them. No one ceases to be a professional as quickly as a politician bereft of power." When I asked him whom in that case one could regard as a serious politician in Germany after Himmler had removed the finest representatives of the opposition, Brüning answered: "Himmler". When I began to refute that, calling his attention to the fact that that statement could reflect to a certain extent his wounded ambition, his tiredness, his scepticism and the fact that he was cut off from his country, Brüning suggested I acquaint myself with a certain document. What was more, he allowed me to take notes from it. At first I was stunned by the contents of the document but then suggested that it could be a falsification put out by the Nazis. Brüning replied that he would have been only too happy to confirm my suggestion if he had not been convinced that the document was genuine. I then inquired to what extent he thought the German representatives at the negotiations had official backing, and Brüning replied that any categorical answer in the circumstances would be misleading, since, given the nature of the Nazi dictatorship, only the Führer could take decisions or one of his closest associates if he resolved to overthrow Hitler and take all power into his own hands. Brüning considers that either Reichsmarschall Göring or Bormann would best fit the bill in the second case. He said he did not believe that Himmler could come out on top. "Certain circles in the West would prefer to deal with him, but probably public opinion will never stomach democratic nations sitting down at the same table with Himmler, who personifies the horrors of National Socialism. Although it is Himmler who is now the most powerful figure in Germany, it is difficult to imagine negotiations with him actually taking place." I asked how serious the Allies' intentions of seeking peace with Germany actually were. To this Brüning replied that these negotiations—between whom and where they were being conducted, he could not tell me—had either just come to a head or were about to do so. I asked him how reliable his sources of information were. Brüning gave me to understand that a politician in exile usually makes use of reliable rumours. When I told him that my friends back in Germany had charged me with exploring the prospects for serious negotiations with the Allies, so as to put an end to the senseless bloodshed and give men at last the peace and rest they had waited for so long, Brüning inquired who they were. After receiving only a vague answer to his question, he suggested that I should make a further study of the record of the conversation between the American and the German, so as to be prepared for possibly divergent viewpoints in my further efforts to bring peace nearer. Enclosed is a copy of the conversation reproduced word for word . . .'

Early in the morning, one of the men working through the documents captured from Bormann's archives telephoned Schellenberg.

'We've come across something,' he told him, 'we'll have several papers put out ready for you, Brigadenführer, if you could be so kind as to come over.'

'I'll be with you at once,' came Schellenberg's brief reply.

When he appeared he came over to the table at once, without bothering to take off his coat, and picked up several sheets of paper that had been put to one side for him. After scanning them rapidly, he raised his eyebrows in astonishment, then slowly doffed his coat and slung it over the back of a chair, before sitting down with his left leg tucked underneath him. The papers were indeed *most* interesting. The first of them read as follows:

'On Day-X Kaltenbrunner, Pohl, Schellenberg and Müller are to be 'isolated'. Müller's name had been crossed out with red pencil, and Schellenberg made a note of that fact, complete with a large question-mark, on one of the small glossy cards that he always carried around with him. Further down the same sheet, that bore no signature and was not addressed to anyone in particular, he came across the following passage: 'It is to be assumed that the isolation of the above-mentioned Gestapo and SD leaders will provide a diversion. Searching for these isolated leaders, each with his specific responsibilities will preoccupy the minds of all those in whose interests it is to find them.'

Further on Schellenberg came to a list of 176 names classified as follows: 'These Gestapo and SD officers can, in varying degrees, shed light on key aspects of Reich foreign policy, not via its main premises but the secondary details. There is no doubt that each one of them, although unaware of the fact himself, is part of a mosaic, of no significance on his own but priceless in conjunction with all the other pieces. Therefore, these people could prove of service to the enemies of the Reich who seek to compromise the ideals of national socialism by referring to the malpractices of its implementation. From this point of view the work of each of the officers listed above, linked together with that of all the others, could create a situation that would be most unpleasant for the Reich. Unfortunately, in this case it is impossible to draw a rigid distinction between the aims of the party and the practical activity of the SS, in so far as all these officers are veterans of the movement who joined the ranks of the NSDAP between 1927 and 1935. In the light of these considerations, the isolation of these men would appear expedient and necessary.'

'Well, so there we are,' mused Schellenberg. 'He's soft-pedalling, he is, our party leader. We could use the word "exterminate" whereas he calls it "isolation". So I am to be isolated while Müller is to be left alone. When it comes to the point, it's what I expected; really, it would be foolish to count on anything else. What is interesting though is that Kaltenbrunner remained on the list. That too is not really difficult to understand, however: Müller has always remained in the background, and only the professionals know all about him, but Kaltenbrunner has been edging into the limelight, and he's already become known far beyond our frontiers. Ambition will be his downfall, I've always thought so. My undoing has been the fact that I wanted to be useful to the Reich. And I have been useful, revealing secrets both here and abroad. But that's where the paradox of our State lies—the more you strive to serve it, the more you risk, for men like me are not granted the right to carry with us to the grave the state secrets which have come to concern us personally. There is a tiny gap between life and a natural death when I could share those secrets with someone else. People like myself have to be removed from the scene suddenly,

261

without warning . . . like Heydrich.'

Schellenberg took another careful look at the names in the list of those singled out for 'isolation'. There were a large number of his staff among them: No. 142 was SS Standartenführer Stirlitz.

The fact that Müller had been crossed off Bormann's list and Stirlitz had not, testified to the tremendous haste and chaos that had reigned at the time the party archives were evacuated. Bormann's instructions for amendments in the lists came a mere two days before evacuation, but in the general rush Stirlitz's name had evidently been left as it was: probably only the first pages of such papers had been looked through, those bearing the names of the best-known figures. That oversight saved Stirlitz, not from 'isolation' in the future at the hands of Bormann's trusted henchmen, but from 'extermination' at the hands of Schellenberg's men. They were quicker and more competent at this job . . . after all 'extermination' was their profession.

'Has something happened?' asked Stirlitz when Müller came back to Cell No. 7 in the basement. 'I was getting worried.'

'You had good reason,' commented Müller. 'I was getting worried too.'

'I've remembered,' announced Stirlitz.

'What have you remembered?'

'How the Russian woman's suitcase would have my finger-prints on it . . . Where is she, by the way? I thought you were going to bring us together, face to face, so to speak.'

'She's in hospital. She'll be brought over soon.'

'What's happened to her?'

'Nothing's happened to her. It's just that to make her talk Rolff carried things too far with the baby.'

'He's lying,' Stirlitz thought to himself with relief. 'He wouldn't have shut me up down here if Käthe had talked. He's skirting the truth, but he's lying all the same.'— 'Never mind, there's no hurry for the time being . . .'

'Why "for the time being"? There's no hurry and that's it.'

'For the time being,' repeated Stirlitz. 'If you're really interested in this muddle over the suitcase. I've realised what it must be all about. It cost me a few more grey hairs, but truth always wins through in the end—I'm quite convinced of that.'

'Happy to note our convictions coincide. Out with the facts now.'

'To back up those you must call in all the policemen who cordoned off the Bayreutherstrasse where I had to stop and was not allowed to drive on, even after I had produced my SD pass. After that I made a detour by way of Köpenickstrasse where I was stopped again and found myself in another traffic jam. I got out to go and see what was happening and the police—a young but obviously seriously sick chap, suffering from TB I'd say, and his mate, whom I can't remember very well, for his face was all covered with soot—wouldn't let me go through to get to the nearest telephone booth to ring Schellenberg. Then I showed them my pass and went to use the telephone. There was a woman with children standing nearby and I helped her drag a pram out of the ruins. Then I helped carry some suitcases farther away from the blaze. First have a look at the photograph of the suitcase taken after the air-raid, then compare the place where it was found with the address at which the pianist had been living. After that summon the policemen who cordoned off the area and who saw me helping the victims lift their cases out of the ruins. If any single one of these facts proves to be a lie, just give me a pistol with one bullet in it and I'll do the job for you. I have no other way and I can't give you any other alibi.'

'Hmm. Well, we'll see,' replied Müller with a short laugh. 'We'll give it a try. It all seems very logical. First of all, we'll see what the German witnesses have to say and then we'll have a talk with your Russian girl.'

'With our Russian girl,' Stirlitz corrected him, 'or do you simply take me for a Russian agent?' he asked with a smile.

'All right, all right,' said Müller, 'don't put the words into my mouth.'

Müller left the room to make a telephone call, while Stirlitz continued to analyse the situation: 'Even if they've broken down

Käthe's resistance, they wouldn't have taken her back to hospital, they would have brought her here, if things had gone the way they'd planned . . . If they'd got Pleischner here, they wouldn't be keeping me hanging around either—in cases like that there's no point in dragging things out—you only lose the initiative then.'

'Have they given you anything to eat?' asked Müller when he came back. 'Shall we have a bite to eat?'

'About time by now,' agreed Stirlitz.

'I've asked for something to be brought down here.'

'Thank you. Have you sent for those policemen?'

'Yes.'

'You look a bit off colour.'

'It's nothing,' said Müller with a shrug of his shoulders, 'I ought to be thankful to be alive at all. But what were you implying when you said "for the time being"? "While there is still time"? Come on, out with it . . . keeping things up your sleeve won't get you very far at this stage . . .'

'I'll tell immediately after my confrontation,' replied Stirlitz. 'There's no point in mentioning it otherwise. If my alibis don't hold water there's no sense in saying things like "for the time being".'

The door opened and one of the guards brought in a tray covered with a white starched napkin. On it stood a plate of boiled meat, bread, butter and two boiled eggs in blue egg-cups.

'I wouldn't have minded having a couple of days' shut-eye in a prison of this class, in a nice quiet basement into the bargain. You can't even hear the bombing down here.'

'You'll have time to get some sleep in . . .'

'Thank you for that comforting thought,' said Stirlitz with a laugh.

'Why do you laugh,' said Müller with a wry smile. 'I meant it seriously. I like the way you face the music. I've brought some of my own chaps down here for a talk in the past and they've soon had their tails between their legs. Do you want a drink?'

'No, thank you.'

'Don't you touch the stuff at all?'

'I expect you even know the name of my favourite brand of cognac.'

'Don't you go thinking you're as important as all that! Okay then, if you don't want any, don't have any, but I feel like a drink. As a matter of fact, I'm not feeling my usual self.'

After hearing the shots Käthe realised something terrible had happened. She ran over to the cellar entrance, peeped out and saw the two black cars and Helmuth writhing in the middle of the pavement. She rushed back the way she had come: her baby was lying in the box, fidgeting restlessly. The little girl, whom she was carrying in her arms, was calmer, just smacking her lips contentedly in her sleep. Käthe put her down next to her son. Her movements had become jerky, her hands were shaking and she chided herself: 'I must be quiet.' Then, as she moved back farther down the cellar, she realised she had been talking nonsense to herself because she had not said anything out loud.

She moved forward with her hands stretched out in front of her, tripping over stones and beams in the pitch darkness. When she stopped and looked round she could no longer see the box on which she had put the children. Ahead was nothing but a wall of impenetrable darkness. Käthe was afraid lest she lose her bearings and be unable to find her way back to the babies: they were alone and her son would start crying at any minute, because by this time he was most likely wet through, and then he would wake the little girl, and with the two of them crying, their voices would carry through to the street. Käthe in her helplessness started crying herself. She turned and went back, keeping close to the wall. She started to go a little faster but her foot caught on a pipe and she lost her balance. Stretching out her hands in front of her and screwing up her eyes in pain she fell to the ground. For a moment she saw stars and then the sharp pain in her head made her lose consciousness.

Käthe had no idea how long she had been lying there when she came to, whether it was a minute or an hour. When she opened her eyes, a strange noise reached her ears. She was lying with the left side of her face pressed against some icy-cold ribbed iron that was emitting the noise. At first Käthe decided that the heavy blow on her head was its cause. But when she

265

lifted her face it stopped, or rather changed. Käthe was about to get to her feet when she suddenly realised that she had fallen on to the cover of a man-hole leading down to the sewer network. She patted all round the ribbed iron to find that she was right and tried to lift it up but it refused to budge. Then she started groping round the outside of the man-hole and eventually found an iron bar. She put it under the cover and managed to shift it over to one side. The sound that the metal cover had stifled now burst forth from the unknown depths below.

The grey-haired detective switched on a torch and a bright beam of light pierced the darkness.

'Listen, was the SS chap mowed down with one pistol or were there two people firing?' he asked the others.

Someone answered: 'I rang through to the Gestapo laboratory but the data aren't ready yet.'

'And they say the Gestapo has everything done before you can say knife. All a lot of hot air. Well, let someone have a look in there—my eyes are getting past it nowadays: are those footprints or not?'

'There's not much dust about: now if it were summer . . .'

'If it was summer, if we had a dog, if the dog had a glove from the woman who's given the SS the slip and if it had found the scent immediately . . . Wait a minute, what's that cigarette butt doing?'

'It's an old one. You can see that easily, it might almost be made of stone.'

'Seeing is one thing: you go ahead and feel it, you must always go by feel in a job like ours . . . Thank God Günther was a widower, I dread to think how you lot would have found the guts to tell my Maria that I was lying cold and clammy on the mortuary floor.'

Another detective came up to him, after looking round the whole cellar to see if there were any other exits.

'Well?' asked the grey-haired veteran.

'There were two exits but they're both blocked now.'

'What with?'

'Bricks.'

'Is there much dust on them?'

'No, no more than there is here. What dust would you expect to find on rubble?'

'So you found no footprints?'

'What traces could anyone hope to find on rubble?'

'Go and have just one more look round, just in case. They're cunning those devils.'

They walked on together talking in quiet voices and every now and then picking out distant corners of the cellar or broken bricks and beams with the light of their torches. Then the grey-haired man stopped and brought out a packet of cigarettes.

'Just a moment,' he said, 'while I light a cigarette.'

As he said it, he was standing on the man-hole cover.

Käthe heard the policemen stop when they were immediately overhead and she could hear them talking. She could not make out the actual words because deep down below, directly beneath her, the water was thundering along. She was supporting herself on two metal brackets, holding the babies in her arms in mortal terror of losing her balance and hurtling down with the two of them into the dirty roaring water. When she heard the voices above her she decided that if they opened the man-hole she would drop down into the void below, it would be the best way out for them all. She sensed that the boy was about to start whimpering, as he always did just before he cried. Rocking him up and down was out of the question—she would have no hope of keeping her balance then.

'Oh hell,' said the old detective, 'My matches are all damp.'

'I've got a lighter.'

'Thanks . . . the flint in mine fell to bits and a piece got jammed in the works and I just can't hook it out—my eyes are giving out on me.'

'You should take it to be repaired.'

'I've hunted for a place,' the old detective answered as he handed back the lighter to his companion. 'There's not one repairer to be found in the whole of Berlin. I suppose everyone's gone off to the front.'

'Let me try and mend it for you.'

'Thank you, mate . . . you'd be doing me a really good turn.'

'Shall we go on?'

'Yes, we must. We must have a look round everywhere, otherwise the old consciences start nagging away.'

On they went at last.

The baby boy began to cry. He started up with a faint little moan that was hardly audible, but to Käthe it seemed that he was crying so loudly that everyone for miles would be bound to hear. She leaned over towards him a fraction, but not enough to risk losing her balance, and started singing a lullaby to him as softly as she possibly could, doing little more than mouthing the words. But her son was crying louder and louder.

'Hush, little one,' whispered Käthe, 'please try and be quiet.' She realised he was hungry and that he would go on and on crying till she fed him, which she could not possibly do until she had climbed back up out of the man-hole. Fortunately, the little girl went on sleeping as before. And all the time in the darkness below the water continued its relentless roar.

'Are they ever going to leave?' Käthe wondered to herself. 'Oh God, help me.'

16

Müller, Scholz and Stirlitz were sitting in the office that had belonged to investigater Holthoff, on chairs drawn up against the wall. Obersturmbannführer Eismann opened the door and led in a policeman in uniform.

'*Heil* Hitler!' cried the policeman, on catching sight of Müller's general's uniform.

Müller did not make any reply and barely concealed his amusement: for the purposes of the identification parade it was out of the question to call in other Gestapo staff so as not to cast any shadow of suspicion on Stirlitz prematurely. That was why he had used just the three men who were *au fait* with the details of this particular case.

'Do you know any of these three men?' Eismann asked the policeman.

'No,' answered the policeman looking warily at the Iron Cross and rows of medals on Müller's jacket.

'Have you ever seen any of these men?'

'As far as I can remember, I've never seen any of them.'

'Perhaps you've come across one of them in passing, during an air raid when you were cordoning off ruined buildings.'

'There were always plenty of people in uniform about,' the policeman replied, 'they used to come and look at the ruins. So I don't remember anyone in particular.'

'Well, thank you, that'll be all,' said Eismann. 'Ask the next man to come in on your way out.'

When the policeman had left the room Stirlitz said: 'At this rate the only person they'll be capable of recognising will be the Reichsführer. Your uniform is putting them off.'

'Never mind, they'll recover,' Müller assured him. 'What do you want me to do—sit here naked?'

'Then at least remind them of the actual place,' requested Stirlitz. 'Otherwise they'll have a devil of a job to remember anything. After all they're standing out in the streets ten hours a day and that's enough to make everyone look the same.'

'All right,' Müller agreed. 'Help them along. Was that one of them?'

'No. I haven't seen that one before. I remember the ones I've seen.'

The second policeman did not recognise any of the three men either. It was not until the seventh time round that the sickly traffic policeman came in, the one who looked as if he was suffering from TB.

'If it were to Müller's advantage to finish me off or if he had some definite proof, first-hand—from Käthe or Pleischner, he would be treating me differently. He's in a quandary, looking for a foothold. He has no set plan of action and that's playing into my hands. It gives me a chance.'

'Have you seen any of these men before?' asked Eismann.

'No. I don't think so. No.'

'Did you help cordon off Köpenickstrasse after an air raid there?'

'Oh yes, yes,' said the young man, his eyes lighting up as he remembered. 'That officer there showed me his pass. I let him through to the smouldering ruins.'

'Did he ask you to let him through?'

'No . . . He just showed me his pass: he was in a car and I wasn't letting anyone through . . . Yet he went through . . . But what of it?' asked the policeman, worried lest he had done something he ought not to. 'If he hadn't been allowed to . . . But I know the rules, we were ordered to let anyone from the SD or Gestapo through, wherever they might want to go.'

'He had the right to do so,' said Müller, getting up from his chair. 'He's on our side, don't get the wrong idea. We're all working together . . . Now tell me, was he looking for the woman who was about to give birth in one of the houses that were bombed?'

'No . . . She was taken away the night before and he turned up in the morning.'

'He was looking for the belongings of that poor woman . . . Did you help him?'

'No,' answered the policeman with a frown, 'I can remember him helping a woman carry a pram out of the ruins . . . a child's pram. No, I didn't help him. I was just standing nearby.'

270

'Was she standing near some suitcases?'

'Now that I can't remember, I'm afraid. I think there were some cases lying about there, but I don't remember anything in particular about any cases. I do remember the pram though, because it was falling apart and the officer here screwed it together again and carried it over to the opposite pavement.'

'Why?' asked Müller.

'Because it was better out of harm's way there and the firemen were working on our side of the street. The firemen were using big hoses and they might well have crushed the pram to bits: then the baby would have had nothing to sleep in. But, as it turned out, the woman was later able to take the pram down into the air raid shelter and the child slept in it down there. I saw them down there later on.'

'Thank you,' said Müller. 'You have been a great help to us. You can go now.'

When the policeman had left the room Müller said to Eismann: 'You can send the rest of them back now too.'

'There should be another policeman there too, an older one,' Stirlitz reminded him. 'He'll bear me out as well.'

'Okay, okay, that'll do now,' said Müller with a frown. 'Why didn't you ask the policemen who organised the first cordon where my car was diverted?'

'We've checked that already,' said Müller. 'Scholz, they did confirm all the details that you gave them, didn't they?'

'Yes, Obergruppenführer. We already have Helwig's testimony to hand. It was he who organised the duty roster that day and contacted the traffic police,' Scholz explained.

'Thank you,' said Müller, 'you can all go now.'

Scholz and Eismann walked over to the door and Stirlitz started to follow them.

'Stirlitz, I'd like to keep you just a minute longer,' Müller remarked, stopping the Standartenführer in his tracks.

He waited till Eismann and Scholz had left, lit a cigarette and walked over to the desk. He sat down on the edge of it—a habit all the Gestapo staff had taken over from him—and asked: 'So far so good. All the details match up and I have great faith in details. But now just answer me one question: where is Pastor Schlag, my dear fellow?'

271

Stirlitz put on a show of amazement, turned round abruptly to face Müller and said: 'But you should have begun with that!'

'I think I am the person to know where I should have begun, Stirlitz. I understand that you have been getting worked up but there is no need to tell me my job . . .'

'Obergruppenführer, I shall take the liberty of being quite frank with you.'

'So you'll be taking liberties, will you? And who'll grant them?'

'Obergruppenführer, I am aware that the contents of all Bormann's telephone conversations find their way to the Reichsführer's desk after Schellenberg has looked through them. I realise you are not in a position to refuse to carry out the Reichsführer's orders, even if they are inspired by your friend and my chief. I should like to believe that Bormann's chauffeur was arrested by the Gestapo in accordance with direct instructions from above. I am quite sure that you were ordered to arrest that man.'

Müller gazed nonchalantly into Stirlitz's eyes as he felt himself go tense all over: he had been prepared for anything, but not that.

'Why do you consider . . .' he began, but Stirlitz went on undeterred.

'Obergruppenführer, you were instructed to compromise me by any means whatever, using anybody or any scheme, so as to prevent me from meeting Parteigenosse Bormann in future. I have observed how you planned today's proceedings; you went about everything in your usual manner, but you were lacking inspiration, because you were aware who stood to gain and who stood to lose if a stop was put to my meetings with Bormann. Why?—That I can tell you only after I return. Now I have no time, for Bormann is expecting me at five o'clock. I don't think it would be to your advantage to remove me from the scene.'

'Where are you to meet Bormann?'

'Near the Natural History Museum.'

'Who'll be driving the car? His second chauffeur?'

'No. We know that he was recruited by Schellenberg, through the Gestapo.'

272

'Who do you mean by "we"?'

'Patriots loyal to Germany and the Führer.'

'You shall go to the meeting place in my car,' said Müller, 'that will be in the interests of your own safety.'

'Thank you.'

'Take a tape-recorder with you, record the whole of your conversation with Bormann and bring up the fate of his chauffeur. You are right. I was made to arrest him and apply third degree. Then you'll come back here and we'll listen to a run-through of the recording together. The car will be waiting for you at the same place near the museum after your meeting with Bormann.'

'That's unwise,' replied Stirlitz, quickly running through in his mind the possible courses events might take in the immediate future. 'I live out in the woods. Here's the key to my house. You had better drive out there and wait for me. Bormann took me home last time: if his chauffeur had confessed to that, I hope you wouldn't have made my life such a misery these last seven hours.'

'You never know, I might have had to carry out my orders,' Müller commented, 'and your torments would have been over seven hours ago.'

'If that had happened, Obergruppenführer, you would have been left on your own to cope with a great many enemies, here in this building, and I am not sure that you would have emerged the winner.'

With his hand on the door knob Stirlitz inquired: 'Incidentally, in the scheme I had worked out I needed the Russian woman rather badly. Why didn't you bring her along? And what was that clumsy juggling with the coded message from Berne all about?'

'It wasn't quite as clumsy as you might imagine. We'll compare notes when we meet in Babelsberg after you've seen Bormann.'

'*Heil* Hitler!' said Stirlitz.

'Get on with you,' muttered Müller, 'my head's going round in circles as it is without that . . .'

'I don't understand . . .' Stirlitz stopped in his tracks as if he had tripped up against some kind of obstacle in his path, and did not let go of the massive brass knob on the ebony door.

'Come off it. You understand very well what I'm getting at. The Führer is incapable of taking decisions and the interests of Germany should not be confused with the figure of Adolf Hitler.'

'Do you realise what . . .'

'Yes, yes, yes! I do realise what I'm saying. This room isn't bugged and no one would believe you if you passed on what I'm saying; anyway, you would never dare pass it on. But if you're not playing a more subtle game than the one you're trying to fob me off with, you should accept the fact once and for all that Hitler has led Germany to disaster. And I see no way out of the present situation. You with me? No way out. Yes, sit down, go on. There are still twenty minutes to go, and it'll only take you five minutes to get there or at the most seven. So you think Bormann has his own emergency plans, do you? Different from those of the Reichsführer? Think about that for a moment. Himmler's men working abroad are being watched: he wanted too much action from his agents and did not take sufficient trouble to ensure their safety. And not a single person from the German–American, German–British and German–Brazilian institutes has been arrested. Himmler could not disappear in this world, however hard he tried. Bormann could. That's what you should concentrate on. Explain to him—but take good care to do it as tactfully as possible—that he'll have to make use of some professional helpers now that everything is going to go up in smoke at any minute. The majority of Himmler's funds have been deposited in foreign banks and the Allies know about them. Bormann's funds in foreign banks, on the other hand, are a hundred times larger, and no one knows anything about them. While helping him bring down his enemies now, make sure of some kind of guarantees for yourself in the future, Stirlitz. Himmler's gold is a mere trifle, child's play. It provides a cover for Bormann's gold. Hitler was well aware that Himmler's gold was not subject to control and that it was intended for immediate tactical objectives. When it comes to the party's gold, that is not meant for any lousy secret agents or ministerial chauffeurs trying to serve two masters and bringing their bosses' mistresses within the orbit of Schellenberg's all-seeing cameras, but for those who will eventually grasp that there is no other path in this world than National Socialism. The party's gold is a stepping-stone to the future that links up our present with our children, those who arc a month old, a year old, three years old. Those who have reached the age of ten have no need of us: they have no need of us or our ideas and they will not forgive us the hunger and the air raids that have brought them so much suffering. But those who are still incapable of reasoning will talk about us as about some legend, and the legend has to be fostered, it will require storytellers who will present our ideas in a new key, one that will appeal to people twenty years from now. As soon as someone somewhere starts to use the word *heil* together with some individual's name, instead of just "Good morning!", that's the moment for us to begin our great come-back. How old will you be in 1965? Pushing seventy? You're lucky, you'll live to see that day and be able to take part in the game: seventy is the prime of life for politicians. But I'll be getting on for eighty . . . and that's why I'm worried about the next ten years, and if you want to lay your stakes without fearing me, but rather relying on my support, then remember: Müller from the Gestapo is a tired old man. He didn't save anything up for a rainy day sitting here in this office. He just wants to live out his last few years on a little farm somewhere, complete with a swimming pool, and to that end I'm prepared to play the man of action now. Then again, but this is something you'd do better not tell Bormann, just bear it in mind yourself: haste is the one thing to be avoided if you want to get out of Berlin and get as far as that little farm in the quiet warm tropics. Lots of the Führer's hangers-on will get the hell out of here very soon, and that'll be their undoing. But when the Russian tanks start rolling in here and the soldiers will be fighting for every house, that'll be the time to make a quiet getaway. That will be the time to leave, taking along the secret of the party's gold which only Bormann and the Führer know about. When the Führer is no longer among us, that's when we'll have to make ourselves quite indispensable to Bormann, who will then become the Monte-Christo of the twentieth century. So it's all a question of staying-power now, Stirlitz, but the ultimate goal is one and the same. But now you'd better get

275

going. Scholz will give you a tape-recorder on your way to the car. Well? What's got into you? I won't believe you if you say you're convinced that Hitler will win. Don't bother, there's no need to answer. Simply think over what I've said on your way. Remember how I brought you round to my way of looking at things: five minutes flat and no monkey business. We'll talk about Schellenberg later on when there's more time. But you must tell Bormann that without my direct assistance none of your plans in Switzerland will work out.'

'In that case,' Stirlitz answered in a slow, deliberate tone, 'it will be you whom he will have need of, and I shall be superfluous.'

'Bormann knows very well that I can't do anything on my own, that is without you. I haven't got all that many of my men in your chief's employ.'

After Stirlitz had gone, Müller sat for a long time in Holthoff's office by himself. He sat there with his head slumped forward on his chest, his shoulders hunched and his arms hanging limply by his sides. Then at last he pulled himself to his feet and walked down to his own office. As he walked past Scholz, he asked: 'Well?'

'They've combed the whole area but didn't manage to find her . . .'

'What news from the men sent round to Stirlitz's place?'

'No one's telephoned or turned up.'

'Let them stay put for a bit. But when Bormann's car appears in Babelsberg tell them that they should move out then. There's to be no smoking in the house or ash dropped on the carpet. Inform all police stations that all young women carrying small babies are to be detained. All of them, without exception. Anyone carrying a small baby is to be taken in. Have photographs been circulated?'

'Yes.'

Müller gave a nod by way of reply, then went into his office, opened the safe and brought out a bottle of crude Bavarian vodka. He took two large swigs, without bothering about frills like glasses.

Käthe could feel her legs gradually growing numb. By this time the little girl had woken up as well and now the two children were both crying. She realised, however, that they could not be heard up in the cellar, after remembering that the noise of the flowing water had only reached her after she fell onto the metal hatch. But fear still prevented her from pushing up the man-hole cover and climbing back out. She pictured to herself in every detail how she would push up the hatch with her head, put down the children on the stones, stretch her cramped arms and give herself at least a minute's rest before she made her way out of the man-hole. She decided to put the manoeuvre off a little longer, forcing herself to count out the time second by second. When ever she caught herself hurrying and cheating as she went along, Käthe stopped and started all over again.

'How much time has passed now, I wonder?' she thought, 'an hour? No, more. Or perhaps not as much? I'm past judging it any more. I'd better go ahead and open the hatch, come what may. If they're still here or someone's lying in wait for me, I'll jump down the way I came and it'll all be over.'

She pressed up against the man-hole cover with her head but it did not give an inch. She tensed her legs and started pushing with her head again. 'They were standing on it,' she realised. 'That's why it's so hard to open now. I'll manage though. The iron is old and rusty, I'll loosen it a bit with my head and then, if it does not give after that, I'll free my left arm, give it a bit of time to unstiffen while I hold the children in my right, and then use it to open the hatch. Of course, I'll manage. It would probably be best to switch the girl to my right arm now. I won't drop her, of course I won't, how could I possibly do that. If nothing else works, I can always take hold of the blanket in my teeth. But that's just a last resort. Then I'll be able to rest my left arm.'

She carefully transferred the tearful little girl to her right side and was about to lift her left arm when she realised she could not do it: she had cramp in her arm and it would not obey her.

'Never mind,' Käthe reasured herself. 'That's nothing terrible. Soon I'll be getting pins and needles, then it'll start functioning again and I'll be able to use it properly. My right arm will support the children. They're light. If only the little girl doesn't wriggle too much, she's heavier than mine, older and heavier.'

Käthe at last managed to lift her left arm, which still did not really seem to belong to her, and with her half-numb fingers she fumbled for the hatch above her head. Soon the hatch started to give. Käthe then used her head to push and the hatch lifted a fraction. Without looking to see whether there was anyone in the cellar or not, Käthe put the babies down on the floor, climbed out herself and lay down next to them in a daze of complete exhaustion.

'Death only differs from life in two respects: volume and movement. A living being inhabits a close space considerably larger than a coffin and he is also able to vacate that closed space from time to time, whether it be a house, a clinic for mental patients, a brothel or parliament. Or alternatively, come back to it. Strictly speaking, that is the total extent of the difference.' A tall scraggy Italian was talking to the pastor; he was evidently very old, but nevertheless presented a defiantly youthful exterior to the world. 'I am not afraid of appearing cynical. I am calling on you to be frank and in the circumstances frankness cannot but be cynical. Frankness is the supreme, reasonable and purposeful substance of cynicism.'

'I find it bitter to listen to you,' the pastor commented, 'because nowadays each minute means that more hungry women in Germany are dying and more defenceless children are being killed in air raids. Making illogical deductions is all very well in peace-time but not while a terrible war is going on . . . then it's a very heartless preoccupation.'

'Again I cannot agree with you: every day of peace is fraught with war, and vice-versa: terrible hours of war herald the approaching days of peace. We are living in an enigmatic parabola and even diplomacy, that double-faced profession, appeals to me on the strength of its elegant mathematical combinations, when contemplated from a distance.'

'I find it difficult to talk business with you,' said the pastor, 'and there is no time for intellectual niceties at the moment. The gentlemen who were kind enough to promise me their help informed me that you are in a position to somehow put me in contact with those people, on whom depend the fate of millions back in Germany. If we could bring that longed-for peace even a day nearer, that would mean we'd be forgiven for a great deal in the future.'

'Please proceed. I am ready to answer all your questions.'

Not all of them, for that there is no need. I would cease to believe you if you agreed to answer all my questions.'

'Most sensible.'

'I am not a diplomat. I have been sent here on a mission . . .'

'Yes, yes, I know about that. I have already been told something about you. My first question is whom do you represent?'

'Forgive me, but first I must hear you tell me who you are. I shall be talking to you about people still working back in Germany. They are risking their lives and the lives of their relatives. You, on the other hand, are risking nothing, for you are in a neutral country.'

'So you don't think there are any Gestapo agents around in neutral countries? But that's a detail and has no direct bearing on what we're discussing. I am neither an American nor an Englishman.'

'I realised that from your English, you're most probably an Italian.'

'Yes, by birth, but I am a US citizen and therefore you can talk to me quite frankly, if you have faith in the people who helped you reach me.'

The pastor thought back to the copy of the conversation that Brüning had showed him and then he went on: 'My friends back in Germany hold—and I share their point of view whole-heartedly—that the earliest possible capitulation of all German armies and the disbanding of all SS units would save millions of lives. My friends would like to know which representatives of the Allies we should contact to discuss these matters?'

'You mean simultaneous capitulation of all the Reich's armies: in the West, East, South and North?'

'You suggest some other way?'

'This conversation is following a strange course: it is the

279

Germans, not us, who are above all interested in negotiations, so surely it is for us to put forward the conditions? For my friends to be able to have concrete discussions with you, we must know with whom we're dealing, and what backing they have? Otherwise we might well see you as an agent who has gone over to the Gestapo, or someone lacking sufficient authority for such negotiations or, again, merely a person being used for purposes of misinformation.'

'I am not a politician. Perhaps you are right. But I would ask you to have faith in my sincerity. I do not know all the people behind the group of men who sent me here, but I do know that the man who represents that group enjoys considerable influence.'

'This is mere playing at cat-and-mouse. In politics everything has to be specified from the outset. Only the people who read editorials in the newspapers think that politicians play crafty games against each other and conceal their real motives, don masks and lie. Politicians haggle, because for them there is no such thing as a secret. They weigh up different factors, each for what it is worth. When they are bad bargainers, they are overthrown by their associates in totalitarian states or toppled at the next elections in the parliamentary democracies. I would advise you to give your friends to understand that we are not going to start talking to them unless we know whom they represent, what their political platform is, particularly as far as ideology is concerned, and their plans concerning Germany, if they succeed in enlisting our support.'

'Their ideological platform is perfectly straightforward, it is based on anti-Nazism.'

'That is the first stage of an ideology. But how do your friends picture Germany's future? How will that future be orientated? What slogans do you envisage for the German people? If you are unable to answer those questions on behalf of your friends, I should be interested at least to hear your own personal opinion.'

'My own point of view is bound to be somewhat subjective,' replied the pastor. 'But if you are afraid that the orientation is a communist one, you may rest assured on that score. At the same time it seems just as monstrous to me to even contemplate the retention of any form of suppression in Germany, even if different from the present.'

'To counter that question: who is in a position to maintain order among the German people if Hitler goes? The Church leaders? Those now held in concentration camps? Or the men actually in charge of police units?'

'The police force in Germany is subordinated to SS Reichsführer Himmler . . .'

'I had heard that . . .'

'In other words, you intimate the SS should remain in power, since it alone is in a position to keep the people in order and avoid anarchy?'

'And who is putting forward such a proposal? As far as I know, the matter has not been raised anywhere yet,' replied the Italian, giving the pastor an inquiring look and for the first time without smiling.

Hearing these words the pastor took fright, for he realised that he had said more than he should: the crafty Italian would be bound to seize on that and then wheedle out of him all that he knew about the verbatim report of the negotiations between the Americans and the SS which Brüning had shown him. The pastor knew that he was incapable of lying: his face always gave him away.

After returning home the Italian, who was on Dulles's staff, thought over their conversation for a long time before sitting down to write a report. 'Either he's just a complete nobody,' he thought, 'who doesn't represent anyone back in Germany, or he's a subtle agent. He's proved a poor bargainer, but, on the other hand, he didn't give anything away. I should even say that he has a clearer idea of what we're after, than I do of their potential. But his last remark shows that they know something about our negotiations with Wolff.'

Käthe had no money for a ticket on the Underground and she had to find a place that was warm and where she could feed the babies and change their nappies. If she didn't manage to do that they would perish, because it was now several hours that they had been out in the cold.

'Otherwise it would have been better to put an end to all this in the morning,' thought Käthe, her ideas seeming to float in from somewhere far away, 'or simply drop down into the manhole.'

Her sense of danger was blunted from all she had been through and, without looking round, she walked out of the cellar and then over to the bus stop. She had no clear idea where she was going, how she'd get a ticket or where she could put down the children even for a minute. She told the conductor she had no money with her, because she had left all her belongings behind in the bombed flat. After muttering something under his breath the conductor suggested she should go to the refugee reception centre. Käthe sat down next to the window and felt herself gradually sinking into a haze of oblivion. It was warmer inside the bus and she immediately felt sleepy. 'I won't fall asleep,' she said sternly to herself, 'I have no right to sleep.'

And at that she promptly dozed off.

The next thing Käthe knew—she was being prodded and her shoulder shaken, but she could hardly open her eyes; she was warm and comfortable sitting down at last and the cries of the babies seemed to be coming from far, far away.

'*Meine Dame!*' Someone gave her a sharp push so that her forehead banged against the cold glass of the window. '*Meine Dame!*'

Käthe opened her eyes. The conductor and a policeman were standing over her in the dark bus.

'What is it?' she asked in a whisper, clutching the babies to her breast. 'What's happened?'

'An air raid's begun,' answered the conductor in a similar whisper. 'Come along.'

'Where to?'

'To the air raid shelter,' said the policeman. 'We'll help you carry the children.'

'No,' said Käthe clutching the children more tightly still. 'I'll hold them.'

The conductor shrugged his shoulders at that, but did not say a word. The policeman took Käthe by the elbow and led her over to the shelter. It was warm and dark inside and there were some crying babies to be heard. Käthe made her way over into a

282

corner where two boys got up from a bench to make room for her.

'Thank you,' she said to them and then put down the babies next to her and turned to the girl from the Hitlerjugend who was on duty: 'My house has been bombed and I haven't got any nappies, please help me! I simply don't know what to do.'

The girl gave a nod and then walked over into a dark corner where a group of women with small children were sitting. That must have been the safest corner. Soon the girl came back with some nappies.

'Here you are,' she said, 'I've brought you four, that ought to keep you going for the time being. Tomorrow I think you'd do best to go to the nearest "Aid for Bomb Victims" centre, but you must have a chit from your local police station and your identity card.'

'Yes, of course, thank you very much,' Käthe replied and began changing the children's nappies at once. 'Please, can you tell me is there any water in here? Water and a stove? I'd wash the nappies I've got here and then I'd have eight and that ought to see me through tomorrow then.'

'There's cold water down here and I think we'll be able to fix you up with some soap. Come over to me later on and I'll see to it.'

'Thank you so much.'

'It's all part of my work.'

When she had fed the children and they had fallen asleep, Käthe leant against the wall and decided she'd snatch some sleep, for half an hour at least. 'I can't think straight at the moment,' she said to herself, 'my head's burning. I probably caught cold while I was down the man-hole . . . . But the babies can't have done because they were properly wrapped up in blankets and their legs were warm when I changed them just now. I'll have a tiny doze and then work out what to do next.'

She slept for half an hour. When she opened her eyes she felt better, but her forehead was still on fire. 'Yes, I must have caught cold, I'm feverish and that must account for the strange nightmares I've had. But that's a mere trifle. Chills don't kill anyone.'

Suddenly, as if out of nowhere, the figure 42 75 41 sprang to her mind. 'I say,' she whispered to the youth sitting next to her and dozing away, 'can you tell me if there's a telephone anywhere around here?'

'What!' he asked in a scared voice, jumping to his feet.

'Quietly does it, quietly does it,' said Käthe, calming him down. 'I was asking where the nearest telephone was?'

The Hitlerjugend girl must have heard the noise, for she came over to Käthe and asked: 'Do you need any help?'

'No, no,' replied Käthe. 'No, thank you, everything's all right.'

At that moment the all-clear sounded.

'She was asking where the nearest telephone was,' the youth explained.

'At the underground station,' the girl told Käthe. 'It's right by here, just round the corner. Do you want to ring some friends or relations?'

'Yes.'

'I can wait here with your babies while you go and phone.'

'But I haven't even got twenty pfennings to put in the slot.'

'I'll see to that. Here you are.'

'Thank you . . . You're sure it's not far?'

'Two minutes, that's all.'

'But if they begin to cry . . .'

'I'll pick them up,' smiled the girl reassuringly, 'please don't worry, they'll be all right.'

Käthe climbed up the steps that led out into the street. The station was only a stone's throw away. The ice on the little puddles round the open telephone booth glistened in the light of the bright full moon. 'The telephones aren't working,' a nearby policeman told her. 'The blast put them out of action.'

'And where can I find a telephone that works?'

'At the next underground station. Do you need a phone very badly?'

'Urgently.'

'Come along then.'

The policeman took Käthe down into the deserted underground station and opened the door of the police room. Once inside, he turned on the light and gave a nod in the direction of a telephone standing on the table.

'Go ahead and phone, but please be quick about it.'

Käthe went round to the other side of the table, sat down in an armchair and dialled 42 75 41. It was Stirlitz's number. While she listened to the long ringing tones, she did not notice the large photograph of herself lying under the glass table-top near a typed list of telephone numbers. The policeman was standing behind her, taking long leisurely puffs at a cigarette.

After listening to the recording, one of the first questions Müller asked was 'Where's the bit about the chauffeur?'

'There was no room for it on the tape. I couldn't say to Bormann "Just a minute, while I rewind the reel, Parteigenosse Bormann!" now could I! I told him that I had managed to find out that you, precisely you, had done all you could to save the man's life.'

'What did he say to that?'

'He said that the chauffeur was most likely a broken man after being tortured in the Gestapo cellars and that he wouldn't be able to trust him any longer. He did not seem to show much interest in the subject. So you have nothing to worry about on that score, Obergruppenführer. But just in case keep the chauffeur in here for a bit longer and see that he gets properly fed. And then we'll see . . .'

'D'you think any more questions about the chauffeur are going to be asked?'

'By whom?'

'Bormann.'

'What for? The chauffeur is a closed chapter, he's fulfilled his function. But in your place I would keep him on here for a bit, just in case. And then there's the question of the Russian pianist. She could have been most useful to us here and now. How is she getting on? Has she been brought back from the hospital yet?'

'In what way could she have been any use to us? She'll do

what she's told to do when it comes to transmitting radio messages, but otherwise . . .'

'That's true,' agreed Stirlitz. 'There's no doubt about that, you're quite right. But just imagine, what it would mean if she is put into contact with Wolff in Switzerland?'

'That's mere utopia.'

'Perhaps. I'm simply letting my imagination run away with me.'

'Yes, and then, in general . . .'

'Well, what?'

'Oh, it was nothing,' Müller said, stopping himself from speaking his thoughts aloud. 'I was just analysing your proposal. As it happens, I've transferred her to another place. Let Rolff deal with her, I don't think she's the right kind of material for you now.'

'You mean he went too far, do you?'

'Yes, he did rather.'

'So that's why he was killed?' asked Stirlitz in a soft voice. He had heard about the murder in the corridors of the Gestapo headquarters when he was about to leave for his meeting with Bormann.

'That's my affair, Stirlitz. Let's have things quite cut and dried: what you need to know from me you shall learn from me. I don't like keyhole-peeping.'

'From which side?' asked Stirlitz in a harsh tone. 'I don't like being taken for a dummy in a game of whist. I'm a genuine player, not a dummy.'

'All right then. But for the moment let's have another run-through of that last little bit.' Müller released the stop button, which had cut off Bormann's words in the middle of a sentence, and asked: 'Wind back about two minutes.'

'Just as you please. Shall I make some fresh coffee?'

'Go ahead.'

'Will you have some cognac?'

'I can't stand the stuff. Once I did drink some in Kaltenbrunner's office which was not at all bad. But for the most part I stick to vodka. After all cognac contains tannic substances that play havoc with your circulation, but vodka, that is real peasant vodka, merely warms you up.'

286

'Do you want to note down the text?'

'There's no need. I'll remember what's important. There were some interesting twists there:'

Bormann. Does Dulles know that Wolff is representing Himmler? ✓

Stirlitz. I think he suspects as much.

Bormann. Thinking in this case is no answer. If I had at my disposal conclusive evidence to the effect that he saw Wolff as Himmler's representative then we could really start talking about the imminent collapse of the coalition. If they agree to have dealings with the Reichsführer then I must get hold of a recording of their talks. If it gets into Goebbels's hands and he uses it on the radio, then I have no clear idea how things will develop in Moscow, London and the White House.

Stirlitz. What about here? What about Berlin?

Bormann. That goes without saying. Yet that doesn't worry me for the moment. To be more precise, it is not the only thing that worries me. Could you put your hand on such a recording?

Stirlitz. First of all, we'll have to get assurances from Wolff to the effect that he is acting as Himmler's emissary.

Bormann. Why do you think he didn't give any statements of that kind to Dulles?

Stirlitz. I don't know. I'm simply putting forward a hypothesis. Enemy propaganda has always singled out the Reichsführer for special treatment. They see him as the devil incarnate .... It's more likely than not that they'll avoid the issue of whom Wolff actually represents. The main thing that will interest them is how powerful he is, whom he represents from a military point of view.

Bormann. It is vital for me that they should find out whom he represents from Wolff himself. Wolff and nobody else . . . or, in the last resort, from you . . .

Stirlitz. Why?

Bormann. For a very important reason, Stirlitz, believe me— for a very important reason.

Stirlitz. For me to carry out an operation I need to grasp the initial motive behind it. It wouldn't be so vital if I was working with a whole group of men, each member of which would deliver specific pieces of information to a chief, who, in his turn, would piece all the material together and thus gain an exact picture of the situation in question. Then it would not be important for me to know the over all scheme, I would simply carry out my mission, work on my link in the chain. Unfortunately, we are unable to set about this job in that way . . .

Bormann. What do you think, would Stalin be pleased if we let him know that the Western Allies are having talks with not just any Nazi, but none other than the leader of the SS, Heinrich Himmler, not with a group of generals who wish to capitulate, not with that wretch Ribbentrop who's gone to the dogs and is completely demoralised, but with a man who could make Germany into a steel barrier in the face of Bolshevism.

Stirlitz. I do not think Stalin would be glad to receive such news . . .

Bormann. Stalin would not believe it if he heard about all this from me. But what if he was to learn of it from an enemy of National Socialism?

Stirlitz. It would probably be best to pick a candidate for the job in conjunction with Müller. He could single out a suitable person and organise his escape.

Bormann. Müller seems to be trying to get on the right side of me the whole time.

Stirlitz. As far as I see it, his position is an extremely ticklish one: he cannot afford to stake his all like I can—he's too prominent a figure for that and, then again, he's directly responsible to Himmler. If one bears that in mind, I think you would agree that no one except him is really in a position to carry out this task, provided, of course, that he feels he has your support.

Bormann. Yes, yes . . . More of that later. That's a mere detail. But the most important thing is for you to promote those negotiations, not disrupt them in any way. Your task is to bring those contacts to light, not conceal them. Spotlight them sufficiently so as to compromise Himmler in the Führer's eyes, Dulles in Stalin's eyes and Wolff in Himmler's.

Stirlitz. If I find I need practical assistance of some kind, with whom should I maintain contact?

Bormann. Go on carrying out all Schellenberg's orders, that's your pledge of success. Don't ignore the Embassy either, for that would only irritate them: the advisor on party affairs there will know of your movements . . .

Stirlitz. I understand, but what if I need assistance against Schellenberg? There is only one person who could assure me of it and that's Müller. To what extent can I count on him?

Bormann. I haven't much faith in men who are too devoted in their allegiance . . . I prefer the silent types . . .

At that moment the telephone rang and Stirlitz noticed how Müller started at the unexpected sound.

'Excuse me, Obergruppenführer,' he said, 'perhaps it's . . .'

'Yes, yes . . . Go ahead.'

Stirlitz lifted the receiver and said: 'Stirlitz here . . .'

Then out of the blue came Käthe's voice . . . 'It's me . . . me.'

'Oh!' said Stirlitz. 'I'll be along right away, Parteigenosse. Where should I wait for you?'

'It's me,' Käthe repeated.

'How can I best get there?' asked Stirlitz again, prompting her and at the same time pointing a sign to Müller in the direction of the tape-recorder to convey that it was Bormann on the line.

'I'm in the Underground . . . using a police phone . . .'

'What?'

'I just came in to phone you . . .'

'Where exactly is it?'

Stirlitz listened to the address that Käthe gave him and then put down the receiver after repeating 'Yes, Parteigenosse' once more. There was no time to sit back and think things out now. If his telephone was still bugged then Müller would have the low-down on that conversation by the small hours. By then he would know how he should act in the circumstances. The main thing now was to rescue Käthe. He already knew a good deal about the situation and the rest he might well manage to guess. But now—Käthe.

Käthe carefully put down the receiver and picked up her beret which had covered her photograph under the glass table-top. The policeman was still not looking in her direction. She walked

289

over to the door, feeling more dead than alive, expecting every minute to hear him calling her back. True, the Gestapo had informed the police that they were to arrest a young woman of twenty-five and who would be carrying a baby, but Käthe was looking forty if a day, with grey hair and not carrying any baby.

'Perhaps you'll wait till I get back, Obergruppenführer?'

'What was that call about? You didn't tell me Bormann was going to ring.'

'You heard . . . he asked me to drive over at once . . .'

'As soon as you've seen him, come to my office. I shall be spending the night there.'

Half an hour later Stirlitz had picked up Käthe. Then he spent another half hour driving about the town to make sure they were not being followed and listening to Käthe who was telling him everything that had happened. While he listened to her, Stirlitz tried to work out whether her amazing rescue had been part of Müller's diabolical scheming or whether it was one of those spontaneous miracles that every agent knows about, but which only happen once in a lifetime.

After meandering about Berlin for some time, he headed out of the city. It was warm in the car, and Käthe was sitting next to him with the babies sleeping on her lap, as Stirlitz planned his next move. 'If I get caught out now, with Müller about to learn that it was a woman I was talking to on the phone and not Bormann, I'll have had it. Then I won't have a chance to spoil Himmler's game in Berne.'

Stirlitz braked near a signpost that told him it was five kilometres to Rubinen Kanal. From there he would be able to get to Babelsberg by way of Potsdam.

'No,' Stirlitz decided, 'judging by the way my cups have been moved around in the kitchen, Müller's men were at my house earlier in the day. Who knows, perhaps just in the interests of my "safety" Müller will have sent them back, especially after that phone call?'

'Käthe,' he said, braking suddenly, 'get into the back.'

'What's happened?'

'Nothing's happened. Everything's all right. All is under control now. You and I have come out on top. Well, haven't we? Just draw the blue curtains at the back there and go to sleep. I won't turn the heater off. I'll lock you in—nobody will touch you in my car.'

'Where are we going?'

'Not very far for the moment,' Stirlitz replied. 'Not far at all. You just get a nice sleep. Tomorrow there'll be a lot to do and a good deal of excitement.'

'What excitement?' asked Käthe, settling herself more comfortably on the back seat.

'The pleasant variety,' Stirlitz answered and thought to himself: 'It's going to be difficult coping with Käthe now. She's in a state of shock, but not through any fault of her own.'

He stopped the car three houses away from Walter Schellenberg's private residence. 'If only he's at home,' thought Stirlitz. 'If only he hasn't gone to see Himmler at Neuen or Hebhardt at Hohenlichen. He *must* be at home.'

He was.

'Brigadenführer,' Stirlitz began, without taking his coat off. He sat down on the edge of the chair opposite Schellenberg who was wearing a warm dressing-gown and had sandals on his bare feet. Stirlitz noticed how white his ankles were. 'Müller knows something about Wolff's mission in Switzerland.'

'You must be out of your mind,' said Schellenberg. 'That's impossible.'

'How could I have found out about it then?'

Schellenberg pulled his dressing-gown tighter about his chest and after pulling himself together, he asked: 'Incidentally, how did you find out?'

'Müller suggested I started working for him . . .'

'And why did Müller choose you in particular?'

'Probably his men got wise about the pastor. That'll be our salvation. Meanwhile I must go to Berne. I shall take charge of the pastor, and as soon as you get a signal from me, you must disown Wolff.'

Stirlitz always went straight to the point, and Schellenberg always caught on immediately.

'Yes, go to Berne without delay.'

'But what about papers? Or should I use the pastor's "window"?'

'That would be foolish. Swiss counter-intelligence would be on to you immediately, they want to get into the Americans' good books now that the fighting's almost over . . . No, go back to the office and get yourself some reliable papers. I'll ring them to say you're coming.'

'Don't bother. Just give me a note.'

'Have you got a pen?'

292

'It would be better if you used your own.'

Schellenberg rubbed his face and, forcing himself to laugh, said: 'I haven't woken up yet, that's the trouble.'

After Stirlitz had left, Schellenberg called a car to come round at once and instructed the chauffeur to take him to Doktor Hebhardt's sanatorium.

It was here that Himmler had his headquarters.

Stirlitz pushed his Horch to the utmost to get to the border as quickly as possible. Now he was armed with two passports—one for himself and the other for his wife, Frau Ingrid von Kirstein.

Once the German barrier at the border was behind them, Stirlitz turned to Käthe and said; 'There we are, my girl. You can reckon it's all over.'

Here in Switzerland the sky was dazzlingly clear. A dozen metres or so behind them the sky was equally fathomless and you could pick out the yellow disc of the moon blurred now by the early-morning light. There were also larks hovering in the bluish–yellowish sky, and the view was just as beautiful—only the sky was Germany's and any moment shimmering white planes belonging to the Allies might appear and bombs drop down on them.

Stirlitz made straight for Berne. On their way through a small town he braked at some traffic lights. He and Käthe watched children walking past, chewing sandwiches. Käthe burst into tears.

'What is it?' asked Stirlitz.

'It's nothing,' she replied, 'it's just that I've seen peace-time and he'll never see it now.'

'You must only think about the future now,' said Stirlitz, and before the words were out of his mouth he realised what a clumsy ill-timed thing he had said.

'Without a past there can't be any future,' Käthe replied, wiping her eyes as she spoke. 'Forgive me, I know how difficult it is to comfort women when they start crying.'

After he had seen Pastor Schlag and gone through his material on the negotiations between Dulles and General Wolff,

Stirlitz realised how sadly mistaken he had been when he told Käthe that everything was behind them. Nothing was over; on the contrary, it was now that things could really get started . . .

'JUSTAS' to 'CENTRE'

Together with enclosed material on the Dulles-Wolff talks I must inform you of the following:

1) It seems Dulles is not keeping his government completely in the picture with regard to his contacts with the SS. He seems to be informing them of contacts with Hitler's 'opponents'—a category to which Wolff does not belong.

2) Roosevelt has declared on several occasions that America's goal, like that of all other members of the anti-Nazi coalition, is Germany's unconditional surrender. However, Dulles has been talking of compromises, even of preserving intact certain Nazi institutions.

3) Every coalition presupposes the honesty of all participants with regard to each other. Supposing for a minute that Dulles has been testing the Germans by means of these talks then I shall be obliged to refute my own theory, in so far as it will be obvious to any secret agent that here the Germans stand to gain and Dulles to lose.

4) I have also considered the possibility that agent Dulles has embarked on a provocation directed against the Germans. However, in the Swiss press he is openly referred to as the President's personal representative. Is it possible for a man in the position of Roosevelt's personal representative to stage such provocation?

Conclusion: Either certain circles in the West have begun to play a double game, or Dulles is about to betray the interests of the United States—a member of the anti-Hitler coalition.

Recommendation: It is vital to let our Allies know that we are informed as to the negotiations now being conducted in Switzerland. I count on being able to send in all details of the talks being conducted by Wolff and Dulles in the near future via a newly arranged contact. By the way I would consider them as separate negotiations rather than talks in the accepted diplomatic sense of the word. I have gone against my principle of not making any kind of recommendation only because a critical situation has developed, and it is essential to take urgent measures to save the anti-Hitler coalition from provocations, possibly even from two sides.

'JUSTAS'

Stirlitz also went to the Virginia pension where the professor had taken a room. He had alluded to that in his postcard where he had written: 'the Virginia tobacco here is quite excellent.' They had agreed beforehand that everything connected with the professor's accommodation would be expressed through some reference to tobacco. If he had been staying in the Grand Hotel, he was to have written to Stirlitz: 'Even in the Grand Hotel I was unable to find what you wanted. All the cigarettes are imported.'

The Virginia pension, which Stirlitz had no difficulty in finding, was virtually empty: almost all the inmates had taken to the mountains. The skiing season was almost over and the tan you could acquire in those last few weeks had something special about it, a ruddy, bronzed glow that lasted particularly well, and so anyone who could possibly manage it had set off for the mountains where there was still ample snow.

'Can I deliver some books for the Swedish professor, I'm sorry I've forgotten his name?' Stirlitz asked at the reception desk.

'The Swedish professor sent everyone his best wishes for a long time. He hopped out of a window to his death.'

'When?'

'Two days ago in the morning. And, you know, he walked out so cheerfully that morning, and then never came back.'

'How sad . . . My friend working in the same field gave me some books to deliver to him and asked me to pick up those of his which the professor had been using.'

'You'd better ring the police then . . . They collected all his things. They're bound to let you take everything if you have some means of proving that they're your books.'

'Thank you,' replied Stirlitz. 'That's just what I'll do.'

He then made for the street where the cover address had been. The pot-plant was standing in the window to signal danger. Seeing that, Stirlitz realised what must have happened. 'And to think I took him for a coward,' he said to himself. 'Poor old Pleischner. Forgive me.'

All of a sudden he pictured the professor throwing himself to his death, the small frail figure hurtling earthwards. He thought of the horrors Pleischner must have gone through in his last few seconds, driven to commit suicide after getting out of Germany into free Switzerland. Obviously, the Gestapo must have been on his heels.

'To the centre, please,' Stirlitz directed the taxi-driver, 'anywhere in the centre and preferably somewhere where I could hire a car for a few days.'

As soon as Käthe and the children had fallen asleep in their hotel room, Stirlitz took two strong caffeine tablets—he had hardly been able to snatch any sleep for several days—and left to have a second talk with Pastor Schlag, whom he had warned of his arrival by telephone.

The pastor asked him: 'This morning I did not dare to bring up the question of my relatives, But now I can't keep silent any longer. Where's my sister?'

'Do you remember her writing?'

'Of course I do.'

Stirlitz handed the pastor an envelope. Schlag eagerly read the short note: 'Dear brother, thank you for your generosity in taking care of us. We are now living up in the mountains and are able to forget about the horrors of the air raids. We are staying in the house of a peasant family and the children are helping to look after the cows. We have adequate food and feel quite safe. We pray to God that the misfortunes which befell you will soon be over. Your loving sister, Anna.'

'What misfortunes?' asked the pastor. 'What's she talking about?'

'I had to tell her you had been arrested. I went to see her not as Stirlitz, but as one of your parishioners. Here's their address, when it's all over you can find them there. And here's a photograph to convince you beyond question that they're all right.'

Stirlitz handed the pastor a small proof: he had taken several photographs up there in the mountains, but it had been an overcast day and so the quality was rather poor. The pastor took a long look at the photograph and said: 'To be honest, I would have believed you even without the photograph. What's given you such hollow cheeks, though?'

'God knows . . . going a bit short on sleep, I suppose. Well? Any more news for me?'

'There is some news, but I am not in a position to judge how important it is. One either has to stop believing anyone or become a cynic. The Americans have started negotiating with the SS. They took Himmler at his word.'

'Facts?'

'What do you mean?'

'What facts have you got to go on? Where did you get your information from? What documents have you got? Otherwise, if you're only going by rumours, we may well find ourselves victims of a skilfully fabricated lie.'

'Alas,' replied the pastor, 'I would be only too happy to believe that the Americans were not conducting negotiations with Himmler's people. Well, you obviously haven't read what I gave you this morning . . . And now there's this.' With that he handed Stirlitz several sheets of fine paper packed tight with lines of small, round and slightly backhand writing.

Wolff. Good morning, gentlemen.

Voices. Good morning.

Dulles. My colleagues have come here to lead these talks.

Wolff. I am happy to see that our talks are to be conducted at such an authoritative level.

Dulles. I must say that it made a most favourable impression on me and my colleagues to note that when a top-ranking officer of the SS embarked on negotiations with the enemy he did not make any personal demands.

Wolff. My personal demands are confined to peace for the Germans.

An unidentified voice. Bravo! That is the answer of a true soldier!

Wolff. Kesselring has been summoned to the Führer's headquarters. This is a most unpleasant piece of news.

Dulles. So you assume . . .

Wolff. I expect nothing good to come of any urgent summons to the Führer's headquarters.

Dulles. But, according to our information, Kesselring has been recalled to Berlin so as to be given a new appointment, to be put in command of the Western Front.

297

Wolff. I heard about that, but these assumptions have not yet been confirmed.

Dulles. They will be any day now.

Wolff. In that case you would, perhaps, be so kind as to tell me who is to be Kesselring's successor.

Dulles. Yes, I can name him for you. It is to be Colonel-General Vietinghoff.

Wolff. I know him.

Dulles. What is your opinion of him?

Wolff. He is a conscientious war-horse.

Dulles. I would say one could apply that description to the vast majority of the Wehrmacht's generals.

Wolff. Even Beck and Rommel?

Dulles. They were true German Patriots.

Wolff. At any rate, I am not on close or confidential terms with General Vietinghoff.

Dulles. And what about Kesselring?

Wolff. Feldmarschall Kesselring, being Göring's deputy in the Luftwaffe, was in direct contact with all military leaders of Vietinghoff's rank in the Reich.

Dulles. How would you view our suggestion that you should go to Kesselring and ask him to capitulate on the Western Front, having previously secured Vietinghoff's agreement to a simultaneous capitulation in Italy?

Wolff. That is a risky step.

Dulles. Aren't we all taking risks as it is?

An unidentified voice. At any rate your contacting Kesselring at the Western Front would help us to form a clear idea as to whether he would be ready to capitulate or not . . .

Wolff. In view of the fact that he agreed to that when in Italy, it stands to reason that he will not change his mind when he is in Strasbourg.

Dulles. When could you visit him on the Western Front?

Wolff. Kaltenbrunner has summoned me to Berlin but I put the trip off, seeing we had agreed to meet . . .

Dulles. It follows then that you could fly to Berlin immediately you get back to Italy?

Wolff. Yes. In general that is possible. But . . .

Dulles. I understand. I must say you are really taking very big risks, much more than we all are, probably. However, I see no other way out of the present situation.

An unidentified voice. There is a way out.

Gävernitz. You are the initiator of these negotiations, but you probably have definite backing at home in Berlin. That should enable you to find a plausible motive for going to visit Kesselring.

Dulles. If you are concerned first and foremost for the fate of Germany, then in this case it rests—to a certain extent—in your hands.

Wolff. Of course, that argument of yours cannot leave me indifferent.

Dulles. Can we then assume that you will set off for the Western Front to meet Kesselring?

Wolff. Yes.

Dulles. And so you think it will be possible to bring Kesselring round to capitulation?

Wolff. I am sure of it.

Dulles. And hence General Vietinghoff will follow his example?

Wolff. I shall return to Italy afterwards.

Gävernitz. And if there is any hesitation on Vietinghoff's part, do you think you will be able to influence the course of events here?

Wolff. Yes. Naturally, if the need arises *you* will have to meet General Vietinghoff, either here or in Italy.

Dulles. If that seems expedient to you then we would be prepared to contact Vietinghoff in this connection. When can we expect you to come back from your meeting with Kesselring?

Wolff. If everything goes well I shall be back within a week, bringing you and Vietinghoff the exact date of capitulation for the Reich forces in the West. Our Army Group in Italy will time its capitulation to coincide with that date.

Gävernitz. Tell me, how many prisoners are languishing in your concentration camps at the moment?

Wolff. In the Reich's concentration camps in Italy there are several tens of thousands of prisoners.

Dulles. What is to happen to them in the immediate future?

Wolff. An order has been given for them to be exterminated.

Gävernitz. Can that order be implemented during your absence?

Wolff. Yes.

Dulles. Is it possible to take some steps to prevent that order being carried out?

Wolff. Colonel Donenni stays behind in my place. I trust him as I would trust myself. I give you my word of honour as a gentleman that the order will not be carried out.

Gävernitz. Gentlemen, let us go out on the terrace. I see that the table is ready. It will be more pleasant to continue our conversation out there than in this over-heated room . . .'

That night Käthe left with the children for Paris, taking with her a coded message from Stirlitz. The station was quiet and deserted. Käthe had said goodbye to Stirlitz in the hotel: it was impossible for him actually to see her on to the train: someone from the Gestapo might have caught sight of him. She looked out on to the deserted platform. The rain came steadily down. The engine started sleepily getting up steam. The light from the station lamps made blurred yellow ripples in the puddles on the wet platform, reminiscent of some fantastic Indian garlands. Uncontrollable tears were pouring down Käthe's face, because it was only now, when the terrible tension of the last few days was no more, that she could see Erwin before her. His image was with her constantly, relentlessly vivid. It was one particular memory of him that followed her now—Erwin standing in the corner with the radiograms that he had so enjoyed mending in those days when he had not had to send radio messages to Moscow.

Stirlitz could not help himself. He went to the station after all. He wanted to watch, if only at a distance, how Käthe's train pulled out of the station, carrying her away to France where she would be safe with her children, and from where he could expect his long-awaited contact any day.

300

Stirlitz sat down in a small station café by a large window from where he had a view of the whole train.

At last the train started slowly to move. Stirlitz looked at all the windows but could not see Käthe's face at any of them. She was probably crouching in a corner of the carriage like a little mouse, sitting there with the babies, hardly able to wait for the moment when she would see some of her own kind at last . . .

He watched the train pull out of the station and then left the café.

Molotov summoned the British Ambassador, Sir Archibald Clark Kerr, to the Kremlin at eight o'clock in the evening. He refrained from inviting US Ambassador Harriman to come and see him at the same time, knowing Clark Kerr to be an experienced intelligence expert with whom he could discuss matters in an atmosphere free of that superfluous emotional exuberance which was an inevitable part of any discussion with Harriman and which used to irritate the People's Commissar for Foreign Affairs.

After lighting his Kazbek, Molotov sat back in his chair to enjoy a quick smoke: he had a reputation for being a chain-smoker, although he, like Stalin, never used to inhale.

He was noticeably dry in his exchange with Clark Kerr, and the alert dark eyes behind his pince-nez had a sombre, cautious look about them.

The interview did not last long: Clark Kerr, after reading through the note handed him by Molotov's interpreter Pavlov, stated that he would acquaint His Majesty's Government with its contents without delay. It read as follows:

Acknowledging your letter with regard to the negotiations going on in Berne between the German General Wolff and officers of Field Marshal Alexander's staff, I must point out that in this instance the Soviet Government sees not a misunderstanding but something worse.

General Wolff and the persons accompanying him have come to Berne in order to conduct negotiations with representatives of the English and American command with regard to the capitulation of the German troops in

Northern Italy. When the Soviet Government declared that it was vital for representatives of the Soviet command to participate in these negotiations as well, this was turned down.

This means that in Berne for two weeks, behind the back of the Soviet Union, which is bearing the brunt of the war against Germany, negotiations have been going on between representatives of the German Military Command on the one hand and representatives of the English and American Commands on the other. The Soviet Government considers this action quite inadmissable.

V. Molotov

Bormann's reaction to Stirlitz's report on the negotiations between Wolff and Dulles was unexpected: he was pleased. In fact, he was even surprised at his own reaction: Berlin was being bombed by the British, Russian batteries were bombarding Frankfurt, the whole Reich was falling apart, and yet he felt a sense of malicious relish. Being of an analytical frame of mind, he realised that his joy was like that felt by envious aging women. 'It's best for me to have a clear picture of what I am really like, to know the whole cruel truth,' he thought, 'then it will be easier for me to both defend myself and attack, for I'll know where my own weak spots are.'

Bormann believed in psychotherapy. He hardly ever took any medicine. He would undress completely, work himself up into a tranced state and concentrate the full charge of his will on whatever part of his body might be causing him pain. He could cure himself of violent sore throats in a day, took chills completely in his stride. He also managed to overcome attacks of envy and depression—no one had ever found out that ever since his youth he had suffered from terrible bouts of hypochondria. In the same way he also managed to keep under control this sudden wave of joy.

Bormann stopped himself from picking up the receiver and telephoning Himmler. He could picture to himself all too clearly how the Reichsführer would start tearing his hair at the the news he had just received.

'In his frenzy he'd be bound to lose his bearings and run round to Schellenberg,' thought Bormann to himself, 'and

Heaven knows what that clever Dick would start scheming . . .'

'Bormann here,' the Reichsleiter announced down the receiver, 'Good morning, Kaltenbrunner. Please, will you come over to see me immediately.'

'Yes,' Bormann thought, 'I must tread carefully and act via Kaltenbrunner. Although I mustn't tell even him anything concrete. I'll just ask Kaltenbrunner to summon Wolff to Berlin again, and I'll tell him that Wolff, according to my sources of information, is betraying the Reichsführer's cause. I'll ask him not to say anything to my friend Himmler so as not to unnerve him unnecessarily. But I'll tell him to arrest Wolff as soon as he gets here and to drag the whole truth out of him. If they managed to do that with outsiders, let them now get used to doing the same thing with their own men. And then, after Wolff comes out with the evidence we need, his testimony taken down and Kaltenbrunner has laid it before me on my desk, I'll show it to the Führer, and that'll be the end of Himmler. Then I'll be the only man still close to Hitler; Goebbels is a hysterical maniac—he doesn't count—and, anyway, he doesn't know what I know. He has plenty of ideas but no money, whereas I'll hang on to all their ideas and the party funds. I shan't repeat their mistakes and I shall come out on top. When the actual moment of victory comes is not important: struggle is joy in itself, and victory is merely what crowns that struggle.'

Bormann had made only one mistake in his otherwise most accurate deductions: he considered that there was nothing he could not do, that nothing was beyond him and that he had a wider grasp of any situation than his rivals. Bormann saw himself as the ideological organiser of the National Socialist movement and this led him to regard with a certain disdain various small details, in a word, everything that came under the heading 'professionalism'.

Ribbentrop, Göring and Himmler all feared him and had to reckon with him all the way. Yet the minor officials in the Foreign Ministry, the Ministry of Aviation and the counter-intelligence organs used to smile amongst themselves at the instructions issued by the party leader. They, after all, knew like the backs of their hands all the inner workings of their outfits; it was they who prepared all major operations in diplomatic affairs, intelligence work and also in industry and the army. The dilettante approach of all-knowing figures like Bormann aroused in them a sense of resentment which would eventually find its outlet in contempt.

It was this dilettantism that was to prove Bormann's undoing. Kaltenbrunner naturally said nothing to Himmler—such were the instructions the Reischsleiter had given him. Once more he gave orders for Karl Wolff to be recalled from Italy immediately. Nothing ever occurred within the enormous apparatus of the Reich Security Office that eluded the eagle eyes of those two powerful rivals Müller and Schellenberg. A radio-operator on Kaltenbrunner's staff, whom Schellenberg's men had recruited, informed his unofficial chief of the top-secret telegram which had been dispatched to Italy: 'Keep track of Wolff's departure by plane for Berlin.'

Schellenberg realised the alarm signal had been given. From then on all was more or less plain sailing. It was no trouble at all for intelligence to find out the exact date of Wolff's arrival. Two cars were waiting for him when he flew into Tempelhof airport. One was a bullet-proof Black Maria containing three thugs with degenerate faces from the guards of the Gestapo's basement prison and in the other sat SS Brigadenführer Walter Schellenberg, head of political intelligence. The three professional gaolers dressed in black walked out to meet the plane and alongside them strode handsome, intelligent-looking Schellenberg dressed specially for the occasion in his impressive general's uniform. Steps were drawn up to the door of the plane and, instead of handcuffs, it was Schellenberg's strong fingers that took hold of Wolff's cold hands.

The prison guards did not dare arrest Wolff; they made do by following Schellenberg's car. The Brigadenführer took SS Obergruppenführer Wolff to the home of General Fegellein, Himmler's personal representative at the Führer's head-quarters. It was not Himmler's presence that prevented Bormann from taking any action, but something else. Fegelein was married to Eva Braun's sister and was thus indirectly related to Hitler. Indeed, the Führer once had referred to him at the tea-table as 'my dear brother-in-law'.

After turning the wireless on full blast, Himmler yelled at Wolff: 'You've messed up the whole operation and so now I've got to face the music! How did Bormann and Kaltenbrunner find out about your negotiations? How did Müller's wretched tracking dogs sniff out the whole business?!'

Schellenberg waited for Himmler to stop shouting and then in a quiet and extremely calm voice said: 'Reichsführer, you probably remember that it was I who was entrusted with the organisation of all the details of this operation? As far as the cover operation is concerned, everything is all right. I have also worked out Wolff's alibi in this situation! He penetrated the ranks of conspirators who were in actual fact seeking to negotiate a separate peace in Berne. We can discuss all the details at once, and here and now Wolff will write a report addressed to you about the negotiations being conducted with the Americans that have been brought to light by us, the SS intelligence service. I will dictate the report to Wolff now.'

It was within Schellenberg's power to organise an air crash to get rid of Wolff. But since he did not know how much Kaltenbrunner had found out—although it could not have been more than some very general outline of the situation, for otherwise he would have arrested Wolff in Italy—he reckoned that an air-crash would not be expedient at the present juncture, since it would mean that Bormann through Kaltenbrunner would be given a chance to flaunt the information that compromised Himmler, even if all that information was of a most general nature.

The reports Stirlitz had sent in from Berne about Schlag's talks with the Western Allies and the story he himself had concocted, adding a whole list of names of the parties supposed to be involved in the talks, enabled Schellenberg to scare the Führer with the mere prospect of a conspiracy.

Indeed, if Wolff, 'a loyal soldier of the Führer fostered by the SS and Himmler himself', had not, as instructed by his superiors, seized the initiative in the negotiations on which he now proceeded to report to the Reichsführer, there is no knowing what course events might have taken in the future.

305

Bormann realised he had lost when Himmler and Schellenberg came out of the Führer's office with Wolff. As he shook hands with Wolff and conveyed to him his 'sincere gratitude for his courage and loyalty', Bormann asked himself whether he should summon Stirlitz and bring him face to face with that white-faced scoundrel who had betrayed the Führer in Berne. He thought about it again after Himmler had led away his little gang, calm in the assurance that he had won out over him, Bormann.

He found it almost impossible to come to a firm decision, and then, all of a sudden, Müller's face appeared before him. 'Yes,' he decided, 'I must send for that man. Half measures are not enough. It's "either-or" now. I need someone else, not just a man like Stirlitz. I must have someone at the top working with me as well. Otherwise I'll never get the better of Himmler. I'll discuss all possible alternatives with Müller and I'll talk to him about Stirlitz as well. After all, I've still got one chance left—Stirlitz's evidence and that I could use at a party hearing of Wolff's case.'

'Bormann here,' he said in a flat voice to the telephone operator. 'Summon Müller to my office.'

PERSONAL AND MOST SECRET MESSAGE FROM MR CHURCHILL TO MARSHAL STALIN

1. The President has sent me his correspondence with you about the contacts made in Switzerland between a British and an American officer on Field Marshal Alexander's staff and a German general named Wolff, relating to the possible surrender of Kesselring's army in Northern Italy. I therefore deem it right to send you a precise summary of the action of His Majesty's Government. As soon as we learned of these contacts we immediately informed the Soviet Government on March 12th, and we and the United States Government have faithfully reported to you everything that has taken place. The sole and only business mentioned or referred to in any way in Switzerland was to test the credentials of the German emissary and try to arrange a meeting between a nominee of Kesselring's and Field Marshal Alexander at his headquarters or some convenient point in Northern Italy. There were no negotiations in Switzerland even for a military surrender of Kesselring's army. Still less did any political-military plot, as alleged in your telegram to the President, enter our thoughts, which are not as suggested of so dishonourable a character.

2. Your representatives were immediately invited to the meeting we attempted to arrange in Italy. Had it taken place, and had your representative come, they would have heard every word that passed.

3. We consider that Field Marshall Alexander has the full right to accept the surrender of the German army of 25 divisions on his front in Italy and to discuss such matters with German envoys who have the power to settle the terms of the capitulation. Nevertheless, we took special care to invite your representatives to this purely military discussion at his headquarters, should it take place. In fact, however, nothing resulted from any of the contacts in Switzerland. Our officers returned from Switzerland without having succeeded in fixing a rendezvous in Italy for Kesselring's emissaries. Of all this the Soviet Government have been fully informed step by step by Field Marshal Alexander or by Sir Archibald Clark Kerr, as well as through United States channels. I repeat that no negotiations of any kind were entered into or even touched upon, formally or informally, in Switzerland.

4. There is however a possibility that the whole of this request to parley by General Wolff was one of those attempts which are made by the enemy with the object of sowing distrust between the Allies. Field Marshal Alexander made this point in a telegram sent on March 11th, in which he remarked: 'Please note that the two leading figures are SS and Himmler men, which makes me very suspicious.' This telegram was repeated to the British Ambassador in Moscow on March 12th for communication to the Soviet Government. If to sow distrust between us was the German intention, it has certainly for the moment been successful.

5. Sir Archibald Clark Kerr was instructed by Mr Eden to explain the whole position to Mr Molotov . . . The reply . . . handed to him from Mr Molotov contained the following expression: 'In this instance the Soviet Government sees not a misunderstanding but something worse.' It also complained that 'in Berne for two weeks behind the back of the Soviet Union, which is bearing the brunt of the war against Germany, negotiations have been going on between representatives of the German Military Command on the one hand and representatives of the English and American Commands on the other.' In the interest of Anglo–Russian relations His Majesty's Government decided not to make any reply to this most wounding and unfounded charge but to ignore it. This is the reason for what you call in your message to the President 'the silence of the British'. We thought it better to keep silent than to respond to such a message as was sent

307

by Mr Molotov, but you may be sure that we were astonished by it and affronted that Mr Molotov should impute such conduct to us. This, however, in no way affected our instructions to Field Marshal Alexander to keep you fully informed.

6. Neither is it true that the initiative in this matter came, as you state to the President, wholly from the British. In fact the information given to Field Marshal Alexander that General Wolff wished to make a contact in Switzerland was brought to him by an American agency.

7. There is no connection whatever between any contacts at Berne or elsewhere with the total defeat of the German armies on the Western Front. They have in fact fought with great obstinacy and inflicted upon our and the American armies, since the opening of our February offensive, up to March 28th, upwards of 87,000 casualties. However, being outnumbered on the ground and literally overwhelmed in the air by the vastly superior Anglo-American air forces, which in the month of March alone dropped over 200,000 tons of bombs on Germany, the German armies in the West have been decisively broken. The fact that they were outnumbered on the ground in the West is due to the magnificent attacks and weight of the Soviet armies.

8. With regard to the charges which are made in your message to the President which also asperse His Majesty's Government, I associate myself and my colleagues with the last sentence of the President's reply.

PERSONAL AND SECRET FROM PREMIER J.V. STALIN TO THE PRESIDENT, MR F. ROOSEVELT

1. In the message the point was not about integrity or trustworthiness. I have never doubted your integrity or trustworthiness, just as I have never questioned the integrity or trustworthiness of Mr Churchill. My point is that in the course of our correspondence a difference of views has arisen over what an Ally may permit himself with regard to another and what he may not. We Russians believe that, in view of the present situation on the fronts, a situation in which the enemy is faced with inevitable surrender, whenever the representatives of one of the Allies meet the Germans to discuss surrender terms, the representatives of the other Ally should be enabled to take part in the meeting. That is participation in the meeting. The Americans and British, however, have a different opinion—they hold that the Russian point of view is wrong. For that reason they have denied the Russians the right to be present at the meeting with the Germans in

Switzerland. I have already written to you, and I see no harm in repeating that, given a similar situation, the Russians would never have denied the Americans and British the right to attend such a meeting. I still consider the Russian point of view to be the only correct one, because it precludes mutual suspicions and gives the enemy no chance to sow distrust between us.

2. It is hard to agree that the absence of German resistance on the Western Front is due solely to the fact that they have been beaten. The Germans have 147 divisions on the Eastern Front. They could safely withdraw from 15 to 20 divisions from the Eastern Front to aid their forces on the Western Front. Yet they have not done so, nor are they doing so. They are fighting desperately against the Russians for Zemlenice, an obscure station in Czechoslovakia, which they need just as much as a dead man needs a poultice, but they surrender without any resistance such important towns in the heart of Germany as Osnabrück, Mannheim and Kassel. You will admit that this behaviour on the part of the Germans is more than strange and unaccountable.

3. As regards those who supply my information, I can assure you that they are honest and unassuming people who carry out their duties conscientiously and who have no intention of affronting anybody. They have been tested in action on numerous occasions.

Stirlitz was ordered by Schellenberg to return to the Reich as it was essential that he make a personal report to the Führer on the work which he had been carrying out in order to disrupt the 'treacherous negotiations conducted by such traitors as Schlag' in Berne.

However, Stirlitz could not go back to Berlin immediately. He was expecting an agent from Centre any day now: he could not carry on with his work without a reliable contact. He bought various Soviet newspapers while in Berne and was amazed to see how people at home seemed to think that for Germany everything was already over, the Reich's days were numbered, and that there were no more surprises to come.

Yet Stirlitz felt that there might well be terrible surprises to come, knowing as he did the potential might of the German army and German industry and being closely acquainted with the secrets concerning the negotiations between the SS and the Western Allies. What he did not know was whether his coded messages dispatched with Käthe had got through to Centre and the State Defence Committee.

He realised that if Himmler learnt of his part in the wrecking of the talks or if Bormann learnt of his double game, and if they all discovered even a thousandth part of the truth about him, then his days would be numbered . . . Stirlitz also realised that if he went back to Berlin he would be sticking his neck out. To return to Berlin on his own simply to breathe his last would be senseless. Stirlitz had mastered the art of assessing the point of his existence in a detached manner, almost as an outside observer, treating it as some abstract category quite separate from himself. To return after being sent a reliable contact guaranteeing him an immediate link with Moscow when necessary—that immediate reliable link with Moscow was something quite indispensable at the moment— would not be senseless though. Otherwise it was time for him simply to step out of the game now that his part in it was over. His conscience was clear. He was desperately tired but, after all, that was only a minor detail. The main thing was that he had accomplished his mission.

They met in a bar as arranged. Some crazy girl, who had just been accepted at the maths faculty of the university, was trying to chat up Stirlitz and would not let him out of her sight. She was drunk and fat but had a certain blousy attraction about her. She kept whispering to him: 'They say that we mathematicians are as stiff as they come. It's all lies, we're just as inventive in bed! I'm an Einstein when it comes to love! I'm relative and irrelative! I fancy you, you grey-haired handsome!'

Stirlitz found it quite impossible to shake her off. He had already recognised the contact by his pipe, briefcase and wallet. He had to approach him now but did not know how to get rid of the mathematician. A scene was the last thing he wanted, in fact, quite out of the question.

'Look, go out to my car,' said Stirlitz. 'I'll be with you in just a minute, Einstein . . .'

'Is that for real?'

'Yes, yes . . .'

'Swear?'

'I swear,' laughed Stirlitz. 'I'll be out in a jiffy. Honest. Off you go and write me out a few formulae while you're waiting.'

The contact informed him that Centre could not insist that he went back to Germany, realising the problems involved in the given situation and the risk it might mean for him. However, if Justas felt up to it, the Centre would, of course, want him to return to Germany. Yet Centre left the final decision to the discretion of Comrade Justas, informing him at the same time that it had made an application to the SDC and the Presidium of the Supreme Soviet for the title Hero of the Soviet Union to be conferred on Justas for 'Operation Crossword'. If Justas considered his return to Germany possible, he would be supplied with the necessary contacts, namely two radio-operators—one in Potsdam and one in the Berlin district of Wedding.

The Horch sped along with a powerful even purr. The blue and white sign on the Autobahn showed 240 kilometres to Berlin. Patches of dark blue sky were to be seen in the gaps between the low clouds. The snow had melted and here and there the ground was carpeted with rust-coloured oak leaves. The woods had a blue shimmer about them, and the air was filled with a scent of mould and a sense of awe-inspiring quiet.

'Seventeen moments of spring,' sang out the young star Marika Rökk, 'will be captive in your heart . . .'

Stirlitz braked abruptly. There was no traffic about and he got out of his car without driving it off the road. He walked into the pine wood and sat on the ground. The first green leaves of spring were unfolding. Stirlitz touched the earth beside him. He sat there for a long time relishing the feel of the earth. He knew what he was walking into now that he had agreed to go back to Berlin. He had every right to linger there sitting on that cold earth soon to be adorned by a resplendent spring.